Just when Stephen thought things couldn't get worse...

Lights flashed, bright and constant.

It might have been the blast of noise; it might have been the glaring lights; it might have been the freak show; maybe the simple, quick instinct to survive—something made Stephen fall backwards and down.

Alien tongues, with curved needles protruding from the ends, groped over his head.

Stephen rolled around the side of the bed and out of reach.

With a roar of fury, the tentacles wrapped around the bed, ripped it away from the floor—there was a horrible tearing sound of metal bolts pulling from the concrete—and the bed was yanked. It spun in the air. It slapped flat into the bars. Then it was cast aside.

Stephen heard his own voice now, shrieking. Quick as lightning, the snakes reached for him.

*THE NEW ADVENTURES OF *STEPHEN CROWN

**James
Steimle**

 **TDF Books**

Technical Data Freeway, Inc.

THE NEW ADVENTURES OF STEPHEN CROWN

Copyright© 2014 by James Michael Steimle

TDF Books
Technical Data Freeway, Inc.
P.O. Box 308, Poway, CA 92074

Visit www.tdfbooks.com

For information about special discounts for bulk purchases, please contact TDF Books Special Sales at wholesale@tdfbooks.com.

The Technical Data Freeway Speaker's Bureau can bring authors to your live event. For more information or to book an event, contact the Technical Data Freeway Speaker's Bureau at speaker@tdfbooks.com.

Cover art by Elartwyne V. Estole

This book is set in 10-point Goudy

ISBN-13: 978-0-9841600-8-2

ISBN-10: 0-9841600-8-6

Printed in the United States of America

*This new adventure is dedicated to my friends and fellow
students of things intellectual, magical, and fantastic:
Alexis McIff, Brandon LeFevre, Chayden Troy Christensen,
Ellie Smith, Garrett L., Hunter K. Schaub, Jaden Sedgwick,
James A. Adams, Josie H., Kaden M. Finlinson,
Kadenza S. Hansen, Kassidy Peterson, Makayla H.,
Matthew Cowley, Nico C. Aguilar, Robyn R.,
Sophie Murdock, Tanner Turnbow, and Tyler Berdell Barton.*

✶CONTENTS✶

Contents

A LOVELY SATURDAY

Without any reason to think that anything monumentally shocking might happen at all on this first day of September, Mr. Allyn made himself a thick ham and cheese sandwich for breakfast. He never fixed breakfast for the boy. The boy had to take care of himself.

Especially on a fine morning for fishing, golf, or a run on the beach. It was Saturday, as I said, and that meant *fun*!

When Mr. Allyn was a child, he had watched cartoons on Saturday mornings. Now that he was a grownup, he played outside in the garden, invented grand schemes for getting rich, and demanded that everyone leave him alone.

Obligingly, Mrs. Allyn stayed in bed.

Mrs. Allyn was absolutely fine with this lovely idea of sighing under the warm covers of her rose-scented bedroom until well after ten o'clock. Mrs. Allyn also remembered her youth. It had been an ugly time when her parents had made her get up early to work, work, work. Who wanted to work on Saturday mornings when *the cartoons* were on? The idea seemed cruel and crazy.

Until *the boy* came to live with the Allyn family.

Before the boy arrived, Mrs. Allyn used to roll her super-sized body away from the comfort of her blankets, sit on the edge of the bed and wonder if she was a good mother. Her own mammy had taught her words like "discipline" and phrases like "the early bird gets the worm." To this day, Mrs. Allyn didn't quite get the point. Who wanted a worm? And why learn strange words that no one else used in the course of daily gossip?

Mrs. Allyn had felt guilty though, before the boy came into their lives. She would lounge there alone in her room and wonder if she was failing to teach an important principle to her daughter. After all, Mrs. Allyn's mother would never have allowed Mrs. Allyn to stay up so late and then sleep in so long.

Then came the boy.

Mrs. Allyn had promptly put the child to work.

And the boy worked hard, fully aware that the rest of the people in the house were busily relaxing and enjoying this fine Saturday morning.

Like Valendra Allyn. Val knew she was a special girl—far more special than *the boy*, whom, for the record, she hated with a particularly special form of glee. On this particular Saturday morning, she cracked one eye open at the sound of the garage door humming to life. She heard her father pull his red beetle onto the road. And the garage door shut again. Contented, she dropped her eyelid, as if given permission by daddy.

Val had been out all night with her friends—she was the only girl in Harmon her age with high school chums who let her tag along. The seniors and juniors had no idea that she still attended Montreal Middle School. Valendra Allyn walked the walk, knew the lingo and had all the right moves.

She had also taken up smoking—her father would strangle himself if he knew that, the hypocrite. (Mr. Allyn wore a spare tire of fat around his waist but imagined himself to be one step away from becoming a muscle man worthy of the Mr. Universe contest. His mantra was, Healthy is as healthy does.)

She had also taken up boyfriends, as many as she could get, in fact—which would drive her mother insane, if Mrs. Allyn ever learned about Val's adventures around town. Mrs. Allyn said that marriage was sacred. Val's mom had nabbed only one boyfriend in her life. He was the one she had forced into a wedding. And Mrs. Allyn was so proud of her purity that it made Valendra ill.

Val had a fake California driver's license. A lot of friends and the strangers that she met owned impressive IDs. They weren't easy to come by, not with the fancy holograms worked into the face of the cards, but they were worth the price she paid. Valendra Allyn had three of them, actually.

The counterfeit IDs might get her thrown in jail one day, but wouldn't that be a grand adventure? Life would go on! Who cares about a bad rap? Like her friends said, "You can always move to a new city if you have to."

With the fake identification cards, Val could get into clubs at night with grownups. She could buy beer—which was gross, but at least she *could*. And no one at home would be the wiser.

Except the *boy*.

Everything had been fine before *he* joined the family. One day a few months back, the boy had pretended to be nice. But Valendra Allyn knew what he was really doing: poking though her purse!

Okay, the purse had fallen off the arm of her father's reading chair. (Mr. Allyn didn't actually read in the over-stuffed purple monster. He sat there and watched T.V. and ate his triple-sized sandwiches. But Mr. Allyn called it his reading chair.) The contents of the purse had spilled over the carpet. The boy had scooped them up, put them back inside, and that was when he handed her the driver's license with her picture on the front.

Val had just turned fourteen.

"You have a driver's license?" the boy had said.

Valendra Allyn had snatched the card from his hand and leaned close to his face. *"No I don't! You will forget that you ever saw it. If you fail, you will wish you'd gone to some other family! Because you'll be dead!"*

The boy got the message. He wasn't a fool after all. And lucky for Valendra Allyn, the boy didn't have enough brains to realize that he might have easily blackmailed her for anything he wanted.

Val liked to party. She intended to keep it that way.

So she woke on this happy Saturday, like her mother, and like her father, completely unaware that the unimaginable was about to occur.

THE BOY THAT
NOBODY WANTED

Life with the Allyns was a blessing and a curse. It was a blessing because when you are unwanted by everybody, it's better to live somewhere with someone rather than nowhere with no one. It was a curse, because *sometimes* Stephen Cowen thought it might be easier to live nowhere with no one.

But running away was out of the question.

Stephen wasn't an idiot. Valendra liked to call him Idiot. Val also enjoyed calling him Numb Skull, Block Head, and Steve, even though Stephen told her—albeit politely—that if his parents had wanted him to be called Numb Skull, Block Head, or even *Steve* they wouldn't have named him Stephen.

Val called him other names. Stephen Cowen brought her such happiness: he was always available to mock and harass for a laugh.

If Stephen never saw Valendra Allyn again, he thought he might weep tears of joy. After all, it wasn't like they were really *family*.

Val enjoyed glowering at Stephen. Her conniving eyes made Stephen's skin crawl.

Mr. Allyn never looked at Stephen Cowen, not even when he spoke—unless he was angry. It did not take Stephen long in the Allyn home before he realized that to Mr. Allyn he was little more than a useful family pet.

Like a cat who caught mice, Stephen served a purpose.

Foremost, Stephen Cowen was yet another in a long line of Mr. Allyn's attempts to make more money. "Multiple streams of income!" Stephen had heard Mr. Allyn teach his daughter on the day after *the boy* had arrived.

The boy. That's what the Allyns called him. Stephen didn't mind. Sometimes he wished that he could become invisible. They didn't make him do the laundry or invent new chores for him when they pretended not to see him.

"The more little rivers of money that flow in your direction, the more money you make in the long run!" Mr. Allyn told his daughter.

"Huh?"

Stephen was not meant to hear *that* conversation. "Do you really think that men and women across the country take foster children into their homes out of the kindness of their hearts?" said Mr. Allyn.

Val said, "Huh?"

"People take in foster kids because it's a job."

"Huh?"

"I *explained* all this to you! It's why you are getting the raise in your allowance! *The boy* is a new stream of cash, even for you."

"Huh." Valendra didn't see Stephen at the top of the stairs. She was too busy picking the black polish off her nails. "So he has to stay?"

"The longer he stays, the longer the government pays."

So that's why Stephen Cowen was living with Mr. and Mrs. Allyn and their hideous daughter who thought she was a hottie.

What saddened Stephen was the knowledge that a lot of what Mr. Allyn had told his daughter was spot on, correct, no matter how bad it sounded.

Stephen had lived with a nice family once. The Greenbergs were ministers with eleven children. Seven of them had been foster kids. Most of those had been special education students at school.

They had been so nice. When the Greenbergs died in a car accident, the four kids with Greenberg as a last name went to Greenbergs living in Ohio. The foster children, including those who had no idea what was happening, were returned to the government to be placed elsewhere.

After the Greenbergs, Stephen was shoved into the home of a man and woman who smiled beautifully whenever Stephen's caseworker visited. They frowned the rest of the time and fought like archenemies after work. Stephen was happy when they decided they couldn't be a family anymore and sent Stephen back into federal custody.

After them, Stephen lived with a sweet old woman who had cared for many foster kids in her lifetime. Mrs. Bellnap died early of old age. No one could explain to Stephen how *that* could happen.

The last family Stephen lived with before the Allyns took him in wasn't much different from the Allyns. The wife, Jury Dziemianowicz, was as skinny as a twig and equally coarse. Her husband, Robert Dziemianowicz, got angry at Stephen constantly for failing to pronounce their last name correctly. He was the one who spilled the beans about how lots of people, including the Dziemianowiczes, welcomed foster kids into their homes because they came with fat monthly checks that paid the bills.

In other words, Robert Dziemianowicz clarified over a bottled of cloudy Jack Daniels, no one *really* wanted foster kids. Except for saints who went to heaven early.

No one wanted Stephen Cowen.

Stephen lived for a year and a half with the family-with-the-impossibly-difficult-name. Then they traded him in for a girl. They had told the caseworker that they were sick and tired of Stephen's sleepwalking and beeping in the middle of the night.

In response to a mention of this, the Allyns had told the caseworker that they didn't mind having a boy who walked in his sleep. Or beeped. Mr. Allyn had even joked it off. "I often made strange sounds as a boy!" He laughed. The caseworker didn't.

Nevertheless, Mr. Allyn's sad attempt at humor wasn't enough to save Stephen from living in their house. And when asked about the sleepwalking and the "beeping," Stephen told Mr. Allyn that he didn't know what Mr. Dizzymanokithseses was talking about.

THE CHANCE TO MAKE
EVERYTHING WORSE

It really was a beautiful morning.

Stephen watched the sunrise from his bedroom window. With his binoculars, he examined the craters of the full moon—as well as he could. Then he did a little detective work, spying on joggers with pony tails swinging behind them, two old men taking noble walks with canes in their hands, loose dogs hunting both the runners and the walkers.

He laughed quietly before leaving the window and going downstairs.

Saturday meant more chores for Stephen Cowen. It also meant that Mr. Allyn was not going to work, so he would be in a good mood. The man would also go away and play. It also meant that the ladies of the house would run to the mall.

It was September. School had not yet started in the Bromiando Unified School District. His first day at Montreal Middle School would begin on Monday. Stephen wasn't about to start worrying about that can of worms now!

Maybe—after the laundry was in the dryer, and the bathrooms were sanitized, and the flowerbeds were watered and weeded—maybe Stephen would give Hank a call.

Hank Doolin was the closest thing Stephen Cowen had to a best friend. Stephen and Hank had walked many cold spring mornings to Howard Phillips Elementary together. Last year, they'd had the same teacher, Mrs. Martin, who smelled like tuna every day after lunch but wasn't that bad to look at—Hank called her Tuna Breath, while

Stephen secretly thought she was pretty. It didn't matter, though: Mrs. Martin was in their past now. Chalk up another memory.

As far as they knew, Mrs. Martin was the only fifth-grade teacher at Howard Phillips who took foster kids. Being an unwanted child was the primary thing Stephen and Hank had in common. Being a "ward of the state," hopping from one family to another all his life, was also the reason that Hank frowned everywhere he went. Hank said that someday he would go into a terrible life of crime, probably get shot at, then die early.

Hank didn't frown so much when Stephen made things disappear. *Abracadabra.*

With the colors in the wash, Stephen ran to his bedroom and pulled a book off his shelf. *Sleight of Hand: Magic from the Masters.*

Stephen tucked the beaten paperback under his arm before Mr. Allyn passed him in the hallway and asked when he would be cleaning up the mess with the trash.

"What mess?" Stephen said.

"You can't see that line of garbage on the side of the house? Dogs, I imagine."

"Someone left the top off the trashcan again?" Stephen felt his hidden anger rise.

"Well if *someone* made sure the top was on each night before going to bed, then *someone* wouldn't have to clean it up this morning."

Mr. Allyn had said all this without getting angry—because it was Saturday and this was when he was busy getting out the condiments for his super sandwich breakfast, which he would leave on the counter for Stephen to put away. ("A man's got to earn his keep! So . . . earn yours.") He also had said this without looking once at Stephen Cowen. Seeing Stephen always seemed to upset Mr. Allyn; he didn't like to see a stranger in his house, even a stranger who was providing another stream of income, a stranger who had been living here for nearly half a year.

Magic book? What magic book? Stephen made it vanish before Mr. Allyn noticed it, said he'd get to the garbage right away, and then made himself go poof!

The Chance to Make Everything Worse

Keeping the peace, Stephen had decided, was important for any boy who wasn't wanted.

Hank disagreed. He enjoyed causing trouble. He even stole gum, coins, and dollar bills from the purses and wallets and dresser drawers of his foster parents. Stephen had told him, "You are the kind of person who gives foster kids like me a bad name."

Hank gave him a donut. Purchased with money of questionable origin.

They were friends. At least they had each other. They understood each other.

 ★ ★ ✦ ✝

Valendra came down the stairs long after her father had finished his sandwich and driven away. She didn't find Stephen anywhere, and she *loved* to catch him red-handed whenever she could.

"Ah, ha!" Val said, spotting him at last in the laundry room beside the rumbling washer. "What are you reading?"

She snatched the book from his hand.

"Give it back."

Val turned away, flipped through the pages of *Sleight of Hand*, and read a line in bold writing. "Prometheus Fire."

"Valendra." Stephen barked her name. But it came out an unimpressive puppy growl, because he didn't want Mrs. Allyn to hear him.

Val cleared her throat. "Objective: Steal a flame from a volunteer's hand."

Stephen made a grab for the paperback.

Expecting the move, Valendra did her own sleight of hand. Stephen snatched the air. Val laughed. "Does my mother know you are playing with fire?"

Stephen knew that look on her face. Blackmail time!

He tried to steal her steam. "I'm not playing with fire. If you keep reading, you'll see that. The whole book is about illusions, Val. Now please. Give it back."

Deflated, she tossed it at him, watched it bounce off his stomach and hit the floor. He dove, expecting her to jab her toe forward and kick the book into the dark gunk beneath the washer or dryer.

"I thought you wanted to be Indiana Jones or Allan Quarterhead."

"Quatermain."

"Whatever. Finally figure out that you're not the brave adventurer type? You hoping to become a magician now? Go work in Las Vegas on a stage and do TV specials with a line of pretty assistants?" She laughed with venom in her voice. "What a moron."

That was all she was going to get? Val wandered back into the kitchen.

But her mother must have heard her laughing, because the floorboards above Stephen's head began to creak and moan beneath Mrs. Allyn's prodigious weight.

Stephen checked the time on the washer, the time on the dryer, and then rushed out the back door to take care of the garbage.

"Get back in here!" Mrs. Allyn said from an upstairs window after finding out that the boy was no longer inside the house. "Have you seen this downstairs bathroom? There is toilet paper everywhere."

"Who do I look like, Cinderella?" Stephen said to the trashcan.

"What was that?"

"I said I'm on my way."

"Ah, huh. I need to take a shower soon so hurry up!" Mrs. Allyn never took showers in the master bathroom upstairs. She said she just couldn't get herself to bathe where her husband had washed himself. Stephen understood why: Mr. Allyn was a bear, and Stephen had to clean up all the disgusting hair in the shower every week. Just another chore.

So Stephen finished the trash. He rushed into the downstairs bathroom and swept the toilet-paper bits, while Mrs. Allyn talked on the phone with one of her neighborhood girlfriends about *the latest*. When he finished, he slipped into the kitchen to put Valendra's breakfast dishes into the dishwasher and eat something for himself.

His stomach was growling like a beast. The Allyns were like the nightmare bosses that many foster parents described at work: impossible to please, irate whenever you took a break, furious if you asked about Christmas bonuses. (At least that's how Hank described adult life.) If Mrs. Allyn caught Stephen at ease at the kitchen table on a Saturday morning, it wouldn't matter if he needed breakfast as much as everyone else in the house. She would ask him if he'd finished his chores. She would get specific listing them.

Even Valendra tried to act like his employer. The fact that Val was fourteen and he was only two years younger did not stop her. She had attended Montreal Middle School for *four* years: sixth grade, sixth grade again (because she hadn't mastered elementary mathematics and spelling well enough before leaving Howard Phillips and moving on with her friends), seventh and eighth grade.

Stephen *could* get away with eating a bowl of cold cereal if he was busy cleaning in the kitchen. He just had to eat on his feet and pretend that the bowl of Wheat Chex belonged to someone who had eaten before him. And, of course, he couldn't get caught scooping the breakfast into his mouth. Someone would likely get disgusted, possibly throw up, and then who do you think would have to mop up that mess?

When Mrs. Allyn got off the phone, the first impossible event of the day took place.

Mr. Allyn walked in the door.

Mrs. Allyn gasped. She wrapped arms around her tent-sized nightgown, ashamed that her husband saw her in such disarray. And then she ran for the stairs.

Valendra pushed mute on the television and raised her eyebrows. Looking at her dad, Val put on a face of worry: *no shopping today? But it's Saturday!*

"Everybody freeze!"

Stephen let his spoon slip back into his bowl.

Val stood up.

Mrs. Allyn spun around on the first and second step of the staircase and grinned as if only now realizing that her husband was home.

"I have just returned from a meeting with Myron Bluntwasp—"

"A meeting on a Saturday?" Mrs. Allyn gasped again and fanned herself. Her world was falling apart.

Val wondered if they would ever go shopping again!

Stephen rolled his eyes.

"—and Myron has offered our family a monumental proposition."

Another stream of income is what he means, Stephen realized.

"Proposition?" said Mrs. Allyn obligingly.

"Indeed!" He looked briefly at Stephen from the corner of his eye. "Why don't you go upstairs."

"I haven't finished eating in the kitchen."

"You can eat in the kitchen later."

"I haven't finished cleaning the kitchen."

"Don't make me tell you twice, boy."

It took just a little more sleight of hand. Stephen had picked up his bowl and glass of apple juice—he was never allowed the orange juice ("Your check doesn't cover that kind of expense, boy!")—when he had mentioned cleaning the kitchen. With these items in hand, he turned away and said, "Okay. I'm going. Time for a *family* meeting, is it?"

"Indeed!" said Mr. Allyn, jovial again.

Stephen passed Mrs. Allyn as she slowly stepped off the stairs. She saw the bowl of half-eaten cereal. She scowled from the break-fast to his face.

Caught, Stephen thought quickly. He offered her the half-empty dirty dishes.

She sneered and waddled past him.

Stephen grinned as he went up the stairs.

And . . . that was as far as he went.

Mr. Allyn surely expected him to go into his bedroom. He had an important "proposition" for the Allyn family to consider, after all. But Mr. Allyn had not told Stephen to go into his room. Not really.

Silently, Stephen hid himself just out of sight, ate his breakfast, and listened.

Downstairs, Mr. Allyn said, "Myron needs someone to work for his geriatric father. Take care of the house. Clean the toilets. That sort of thing. He didn't specify the details, but the short answer is clear. Old Mr. Bluntwasp requires a volunteer."

"Count me out," Val said right away.

"Oh!" said Mrs. Allyn. "But I'm so busy!"

Stephen laughed hard enough to shoot milk out of his nose. Luckily, he kept quiet and didn't die.

"Naturally," said Mr. Allyn, "I told Myron that his arthritic daddy wasn't likely going to get a volunteer very easily. He would have to hire out, if he wanted good help. Then, I came upon an idea!"

"What idea."

"Well, I told him that he ought to file for a foster brat—I told him that you can get a good worker sometimes, like our boy, and that you get *paid* to keep them in the house!"

"How is that a proposition for us?"

"Well, now this is for Myron's father, remember. The man's too old and decrepit to qualify. And Myron Bluntwasp has an extensive criminal record."

"So he can't do the foster thing," Mrs. Allyn said, amazingly able to follow along.

Stephen almost choked again.

Mr. Allyn continued, "I said that he and I might be able to come to . . . an arrangement. If he offered us enough, depending upon the amount of work needed at the place, I might be able to send *our* boy after school for a little bit. No more than three hours, I told him! Maybe four. If the price was right."

"You mean," Val said with a tone of jealousy, "you'd let Stephen get a job? Make *money?*"

"No, no, no. Don't you see? Stephen will go to work as a volunteer—one family helping another. That's it!"

Stephen felt his skin itch beneath his clothes.

But the ladies downstairs didn't seem to understand.

Val said, "Huh?"

Mrs. Allyn said, "I don't think the boy will volunteer."

"The deal is done," said Mr. Allyn. "Starting Monday, right after the boy's first day at Montreal Middle School, he will go to the address I give him, and he will . . . help out with the chores."

Stephen shook his head. He wondered if he should telephone his caseworker about this. Then he thought about what that would mean: roll the dice. He would get pulled from the Allyns and go . . . to another set of foster parents. Stephen's situtation could be much, much worse.

Mr. Allyn seemed to be reading Stephen's mind. "Trust me. The boy knows he's got it good here. He will do what he is told."

Mrs. Allyn must have started to think a little bit. She said, "But we need him here!" There was enough panic in her voice that Stephen could almost see the images going through her mind: images of Mrs. Allyn bent over on her knees scrubbing the floor, cleaning up the trash, doing the—gulp!—the laundry. She would lose her happy Saturdays. She would labor all day at the chores around the house.

"Oh, the boy will still be here. He will finish his chores. Meanwhile, the decaying, old Mr. Bluntwasp will pay to our family . . . one more beautifully steady stream of dollar bills . . . each . . . and every . . . week . . . of the year."

THE APPROACH OF
SOMETHING NEW

Stephen decided that it might be a good idea to barricade himself in his room after all. He really didn't want to hear anymore. He still wasn't sure which was worse, living here or moving to a new foster home.

What he really wanted was to get away from his life altogether. Impossible!

At the window, he sat down and rested his chin on his arms, his forehead against the cool glass.

There went another grandpa. Instead of a cane, this one had a grandchild by the hand. The old man was small. The little blonde kid didn't come up to his belt.

Yet the small boy stared into the eyes of the elderly fellow and glowed with a happiness that Stephen had only felt in his dreams.

Oh, how Stephen ached to be loved like that. How he longed to have a grandfather.

Most kids, it sure seemed to Stephen, had even more. A mom who made them cookies and gave hugs. A dad who could teach them things and carry them to exciting places. They had aunts and uncles, grandmas too. Cousins. Real sisters. Brothers.

A tear ran down his cheek.

It was an old sadness. He had known it for as long as he could remember. Like Hank and other pass-along orphans, Stephen always wished that the next family could be . . . real. So he could have what that little blonde kid going around the corner had.

What a fairytale. What an impossible dream.

But this was a day of impossibilities.

Stephen floated away from the glass and wiped his face with the back of his hand. He sniffed and turned around to find two dark eyes, hinting at blue, staring at him from the mirror.

They were Stephen's eyes, of course. His mother's eyes? His father's? He might never know.

And who was to blame for that hair color? Stephen's mop was neither dark nor light. When a worksheet on the first day of school asked him to describe himself, Stephen didn't want to say gray. Only ancient people had gray hair. It wasn't really gray anyway! He always answered brown. But his hair didn't look brown at all. Maybe because it lacked that slight tint of red that so many people with brown hair had. It just looked . . . uncolored and boring.

He stopped staring.

Footsteps approached outside his door.

Stephen listened. He listened until he realized what he was listening to.

Someone else was listening to him.

The footsteps went away.

Swiftly, he finished his breakfast. He thought about Hank. Having not heard the garage door lift, Stephen figured that Mr. Allyn was still down there, his presence so unnatural on a Saturday. He thought he heard the water running through the pipes: Mrs. Allyn taking her shower at last. That might have been Val at the door. Nevertheless he had imagined Mr. Allyn grinning voraciously at the prospect of making even more money off the boy that nobody wanted.

Stephen considered opening the window and running away, just for today. He could be home in time for harsh reprimands and the dinner dishes. Would the Allyns really care?

Hank would have ideas about where to go. Heck, Hank would say they should hitchhike to LA and become gangsters! That was the problem with Hank.

He was a friend. But he was likely to run off a cliff and figure out that it had been a bad idea one second before hitting the ground.

Instead of throwing away his pitiful life, Stephen reclined with his book of magic. He read for a while, practiced a few tricks in front of the mirror, and then got restless.

Easing down the stairs, he heard the telephone play a tune from the other side of the wall.

"Hello," said Valendra.

Valendra was in the kitchen. Mrs. Allyn was showering downstairs. Stephen lifted an ear to find Mr. Allyn but could not hear him anywhere.

"Who?" she said a few seconds later.

After twice as long, Stephen heard Val say, "He's not here right now. No, I don't know. Sorry." Then she hung up without a polite goodbye.

The sliding door to the backyard opened. "Dad?" she said.

"Yes, sweet cheeks?" Mr. Allyn said from the garden.

"Don't call me that."

"What is it, honey?" Mr. Allyn rarely sounded so happy.

Valendra growled. The door started to slide shut. But Stephen heard the beginning of her message. "You wanted us to tell you if—"

The door clicked shut.

Stephen climbed the stairs and rushed into Valendra's bathroom, so called because no one used it but Valendra. Her mother didn't shower in there, because of the overpowering scent of flowers—mostly jasmine oil. Stephen didn't shower in there because he'd been forbidden to enter.

Stephen opened the shower door and climbed onto the lip of the tub. He lifted himself to the narrow window, nudged away bottles of conditioner, body wash, and shampoo, and peered outside.

Val stood with one hand on her hip, the other pointing this way and that, into the house, outside again.

Mr. Allyn frowned with terrible confusion.

The floor squealed outside the open bathroom door.

"What in the world are you doing, boy?"

Stephen hadn't heard Mrs. Allyn on the stairs. *Think fast!*

"What do I do *every* Saturday? I'm cleaning!" He looked at the ledge. "I never knew it could get so filthy up here!"

"Well," said Mrs. Allyn. "If you cleaned a little better, maybe it wouldn't build up like that."

"I'm sure you're right."

Mrs. Allyn thumped into her bedroom.

Stephen lowered himself, then got out before anyone else sneaked up on him.

The phone rang again before he reached the living room.

"Yello," said Mr. Allyn, shutting the glass door as he entered the kitchen. He saw Stephen and turned away. "No, I said *hello*. Who is this? I see. Nope. No, he is—he is out with friends at the moment."

A moment later, Stephen heard the beep of the phone line being disconnected.

He couldn't see Mr. Allyn's face. But Valendra saw it when she returned from outside. "Dad? You look like you've seen a ghost, Dad. What's wrong?"

At last, he turned his face to Stephen. "There's a . . ."

Mrs. Allyn came down the stairs and sighed with fabulous contentment. "Ah! Was that for me, darling?"

"There's a what?" Stephen read Mr. Allyn's drowning expression. "Was that call about me?"

"You?" said Mr. Allyn. His eyes went to his wife and turned red. He rubbed them and chuckled into his hand. "Why would the call be about you?"

"Well," said Stephen. "School's starting on Monday. Maybe—"

Mr. Allyn slapped the table and stood. "It was about you. Seems you will be starting your work for Mr. Bluntwasp almost immediately." All at once, he was wearing his workday face, and everyone noticed.

Val backed up, stepping through the sliding door and onto the deck behind the house.

"Was that Hank?" Stephen said.

Mrs. Allyn fell back a step. Just as quickly, she touched Stephen's shoulder. "Don't speak to Mr. Allyn in that tone!"

"Was it my caseworker, Mrs. Ryan?"

Mr. Allyn was trembling. He wasn't pale anymore. Now his skin went deep red, blushing the way he had on the day his wife caught him munching in the garage through an enormous bag of Reese's Peanut Butter Cups.

"Of course it wasn't your caseworker. Did you want to call your caseworker? Is that why we are speaking about your caseworker? I already said that that was Mr. Bluntwasp. He expects you at his father's house right away!"

I know you're lying. Stephen didn't say the words. He still hadn't decided if leaving was one of the safest moves for him right now. He let the expression on his face say the words for him.

"So that's it, then," said Mr. Allyn, whose Saturday smile seemed to have permanently evaporated. "Go upstairs and change into some work clothes."

Stephen spread his arms. "I'm *in* my work clothes.It's Saturday!"

Valendra was getting an inkling that something else was going on. "Daddy?"

"Not now, Pretty," he said. Then he snapped his fingers. "I forgot to ask for Old Bluntwasp's address!" He grinned his misery. "You run along and wash up. I won't have you going over there smelling of— of garbage! Yes, no one from our house is going over there smelling like they've been picking up garbage that's spent half of the night on the ground after the dogs have been picking through it. You can't smell yourself, can you, boy?"

"No."

"Wash."

Stephen headed for the sink.

"The bathroom!" Mr. Allyn pointed with the phone.

Spinning on his heel, Stephen crossed the kitchen and followed the hall to the downstairs bathroom.

Everyone watched him until he rounded the corner and turned on the sink.

He stayed in the bathroom but leaned close to the hall.

"*What*," said Valendra, "is going on!"

"Honey?" said Mrs. Allyn.

Stephen held his breath to hear better.

Mr. Allyn punched buttons on the phone.

With the sink running, Stephen couldn't understand the first part of his answer. But he heard the last part. "On the brink of our second residual stream of income, we may be losing our cash cow!"

THE STALKERS IN SILHOUETTE

Mr. Allyn smashed a piece of paper into Stephen's hand. Stephen opened the little wad and saw the address:

MR. BLUNTWASP
13604 RAMONA ROAD
HARMON, CA

Then Mr. Allyn nudged Stephen out the front door.

Harmon, California.

Was that helpful bit of information written down just in case Stephen walked until he left the city? Or the state?

Stephen loitered on the doorstep and chuckled. What a joke!

Then the peep hole shouted in Mr. Allyn's voice. "Get going! You're expected. Mr. Bluntwasp will give you an envelope for me. Bring it back!"

"You couldn't have told me that before pushing me outside?"

Stephen waited for the door to swing open and the *real* yelling to begin.

The telephone rang. Stephen barely heard it.

The dead bolt slid from the door into the doorframe with a harsh metal *THUNK!* Then Stephen heard the patter of feet and a muffled burst of conversation.

He cupped his ear to the wood.

Mr. Allyn answered again. "Yello? No, I'm sorry, but the boy will be away for the day. Possibly the weekend. Oh, yes! Some kind of school excursion. Well, that's true: school doesn't start until Monday. This is a preschool activity of some sort. No. I'm not saying he's in preschool—I'm sorry. The boy just doesn't tell me very much. Bit of a communication problem, if you get my meaning. Raging hormones. Diarrhea. I don't know. Must dash. *Ciao*!"

Stephen laughed so hard, he hoped they heard him inside the house. He launched himself off the stoop and toward the road.

This was, after all, what he wanted. Sort of. To get away!

And off he went.

Mr. Allyn didn't exactly say *when* to arrive at the address. Would it be a problem if he arrived late? Stephen didn't think so.

Which made him think about Hank, because that was the sort of trick that Hank would pull. Stephen had prided himself on being the kind of boy a good family would want to adopt.

Maybe it *was* time to call his caseworker.

Mrs. Ryan had made him memorize a phone number. In case of emergencies. Like abuse. Did slave labor count as abuse? Stephen wasn't sure.

He followed Midland for a bit, distracted so much that when the a dog came suddenly to life in Mrs. Herkamer's front yard, Stephen nearly jumped out of his skin. Or rather, he nearly leapt off the sidewalk and into the path of a beat-up Trans Am that was doing its best to break the speed limit.

The dog on the other side of the fence barked with more hate than Stephen had ever felt from foster parents. The monster tried to eat its way through the fence, just to kill him.

Normally prepared for this beast, Stephen's heart banged against his ribs as if this were the first time he had encountered the menace. "Someone ought to put you out of your misery!" he said to the fence.

Infuriated, the malamute/pinscher threw its head over the top of the fence. It bit at the gate, and fought to hang on, to climb over using nothing more than the great muscles in its dark brown neck if it had to. Its black eyes rolled. It chomped and chomped.

"Ah," said Stephen, "you're not worth it." Then he ran away, just for a stretch, in case the werewolf got out.

Distracted by the dog, he tripped on the shattered chunks of a stretch of sidewalk that Hank had told him an earthquake had long ago twisted into pieces. Stephen went all the way down.

Grumbling, he arose, then laughed at his own fear of the dog—which he examined over his shoulder. He checked his skinned palms, and wiped away the stinging sensation on his pants.

Soon thereafter, he came to Harmon Road, what had been called Main Street before some politician or city board decided that every avenue in town had to have a proper name.

A gas station sat on the corner, with what Mr. Allyn called a Ma-and-Pa shop.

Stephen only had a quarter and two pennies wedged into his coin pocket, as he hadn't been planning on any "excursions" this morning. He only had a few dollars socked away in his bedroom. But he thought a rope of red licorice might make his trek a touch more pleasant.

Mrs. Farley waved hello as he slipped down the candy aisle. She finished with a customer while Stephen daydreamed.

He liked to stand here. *Imagine if I could buy as much of whatever I wanted! Enormous chocolate Charleston Chews. Hefty bags of M&Ms. One pound of Lemon Heads.*

"Where are the Allyns off to today?" said Mrs. Farley. "Road trip? That a new car?"

The old lady was as nice as they come. She wore a grandma bun on the back of her head, just like Peter Parker's Aunt May in *The Amazing Spider Man*. And Stephen could easily see her serving cookies to good twelve-year-old boys like himself, when they visited. But she had been working in this Ma-and-Pa for a bit too long, according to Hank. And he said that she never left.

Stephen liked her. But something she *did* made her seem a little touched in the head.

He had no idea where she got the idea that the Allyn family would take him on a road trip. "Did you say *new car?*"

"The blue one out there?" She squinted at the window.

Stephen walked a long Red Rope to the counter.

He thought she was squinting because her eyes weren't too good. That would explain her misunderstanding of the situation.

But when he looked outside, sunlight from across the street reflected off the windows of Nate's Upholstery and blinded him.

He blinked away.

And then he saw what she had seen, only Stephen saw the image like a photograph in his mind.

Two people stood on either side of what might have been a short, four-door sedan. The car was blue.

He looked out the window again, squinting hard against the sunlight.

Two people. Two figures like shadows blocking the sunbeams for the few seconds in which Stephen tried to look at them. He saw no faces.

"Those aren't the Allyns."

"Oh?" Mrs. Farley didn't bother to look anymore. Through her own blinded eyes, she tried to see the licorice. Tapping her glasses up her nose, she talked to herself for a moment. "Okay. Let's see now. What do we have here." When her vision registered the candy on the counter, she typed in the price and took Stephen's quarter.

"Two cents is your change," she said. "Beautiful day, is it not?"

"Sure is," he said, smiling as if this were the best day of his life.

"Have a wonderful adventure, dearie!"

"You too," he said, and felt silly only after saying it. The door sang a couple of tones as he exited the building.

He tried not to think about the two people beside the blue car. He kept his eyes on Harmon Road and crossed the short parking lot and gas pumps at a gallop.

He cut between a Nissan and an old Geo Metro. He ran across the traffic coming and going. (They had to stop for lights anyway, didn't they?) And he thought that if an officer of the law spotted him and decided to deal out punishment, he could say he was being chased by strangers and ride back to the Allyns' driveway in a police cruiser with flashing red and blue lights. Oh, the story he could tell Hank on Monday!

Chewing away the plastic and then gnawing at the red rope of cherry flavored candy, Stephen decided to jog.

He wanted to get away from the feeling that he was being followed.

He crossed Harmon a few more times. He landed his feet on an island between the four lanes of Saturday traffic and sprinted along the line of bright purple Jacaranda trees. Blood raced through his veins. *Is this what Hank feels like all the time?*

He paused at their favorite haunt.

The electronics store had a long series of windows. Behind the glass sat toys for children of all ages: remote control cars and helicopters, antennae for listening into space, telescopes for spying on neighbors, and robots, kits for making robots, whether dogs, cats, or even humans (though they were really just glorified dolls with enormous price tags).

Stephen pressed his hands to the glass.

Rockets! Radios that could hear stations around the world, even if the power blew up and down the street! High definition screens as large as walls! And all the James Bond and *Mission Impossible* techno-gear that grownup kids could invent!

Oh, how Stephen wanted to *live* inside that store.

He sighed until the glass fogged before his face.

Then he shuffled along Harmon Road until it was time to make a right through the deliciously oily food joint that rested under a big sign bearing the words Aliberto's Mexican Cuisine.

A crowd of scary teenagers loitered in front of the restaurant. Wearing gang colors and flashing hand signs at one another, they sat on concrete tables with smoothly tiled tops, their worn-out shoes on the benches. Hank had once called them the self-proclaimed neighborhood watch.

Stephen kept his head down and his hands in his pockets as he crossed the little corner of asphalt. He tried not to make eye contact. But when he did, a kid with a toothpick in his mouth jerked his chin in Stephen's direction to say hello.

Stephen jerked his chin back at the guys.

And somehow, like magic, he felt safe.

A ditch ran along the road for a little while. Stephen followed its rotten scent until he came to a sign and another parking lot. The sign said, LION'S PARK. Behind it, an old sandbox filled with woodchips held an old pirate boat made for little kids.

Stephen made a right. He ran straight up the slide to the top deck of the pirate ship, spun the wheel, yelled, "Land ho!" and then dove into a tube that spun him to the ground, face first.

For as far as the eye could see, beyond the ship stretched a great ocean of green grass that no city gardener had touched for the last couple of weeks. The wind blew. The grass moved in waves visible to the naked eye.

"More magic!" Stephen said. Then he bolted into the fields of green and ran in great figure eights until he was too tired to keep going—and that took a little while.

He had to go on, though. Mr. Bluntwasp of Harmon, California—ha, ha—was waiting for him. Blah!

Stephen returned to the street, and he followed the ditch a little more.

Catching his breath, he examined a front yard with a lawnmower busily pulling a grumpy teenager talking to himself.

Stephen paused next before a house completely surrounded by hidden gnomes. Well, not all of them were hiding.

The nearest grinning imp wore a red hat, blue pants, and a white shirt. The dwarf, which was made of painted clay, stood in the middle of the front yard where Stephen needed to turn left on his trek to Ramona Road. This little guy looked so much like Santa Claus, Stephen smiled at him. "Ho, ho, ho!"

The happy little Santa, of course, did not answer.

Another one waved from the shadow of an oleander bush. A third leaned forward and examined something in the grass. A fourth sat on the front step. A fifth stood on the porch—Stephen counted a dozen, and stopped counting when he saw more.

The gnomes froze all over the yard, as if they had taken a break from their duties to wish him a good day as he passed.

Stephen kept going.

He glanced back a few times.

He glimpsed the blue car.

He tried to ignore it.

After all, the haunted house came next.

He and Hank had visited the haunted mansion before—they called it the haunted mansion after Hank's trip to Disneyland with his newspaper-slinging buddies (the adventure was some kind of reward for selling subscriptions).

The Allyns had refused to let Stephen become a paperboy—Mrs. Allyn needed his help too much around the house.

Everyone said the big place was haunted. No one lived there. No one alive, anyway. Stories abounded: people had died in the place. Hank said that was why no one bought the fixer-upper and improved it.

The windows were boarded shut. There was a bulky lock around the doorknob. The lawn had gone to seed and then dried up entirely, leaving a fractured driveway as the main attraction in the front yard.

Stephen decided not to look at the house. He thought about the shadow men in the blue car and imagined them pulling up along side him and grabbing him and throwing him in the backseat while his eyes and thoughts were distracted by the house of horror. Nuh-uh.

He turned right at the street on the other side of the haunted mansion, crossed the road, and turned left at a bungalow crawling with cats.

After a while, he began to hear the steady *thump, thump, thump* of a basketball. A tall boy with brown hair hanging straggly over his ears shot for the basket without a net that had been set up over his driveway.

He missed.

After fetching the ball, the tall boy noticed Stephen as he turned right onto Ramona Road. "What are *you* looking at?" the boy yelled.

Stephen gazed at the road, at the blue in the sky, and the trees blowing in the wind, at a crow picking at something in the gutter a block a way.

For a long time, the basketball made no sound.

Stephen kept walking.

And then, finally, the hollow *thump-thump-thump*ing started again as the poor high school nobody practiced his hoops.

Stephen felt bad for the tall boy. He thought he understood the older kid somehow, that they might even be friends, if only they could get past the pent-up anger in the basketball player's eyes.

These distractions helped Stephen avoid thinking about the men in the blue car. He didn't peer around to see if the men without faces were still back there, parked. Watching him.

When Stephen reached a brown-painted home bearing Mr. Bluntwasp's address, he changed his mind and searched for his pursuers. He saw them nowhere.

Panting a little with his hands on his knees, Stephen waited a moment to catch his breath. He wiped sweat out of his eyelashes and turned to knock on the door.

The door was already open.

A skeleton wearing flesh stared at Stephen Cowen from the shadows.

6

NEW FRIENDS IN STRANGE PLACES

With arthritic fingers bent painfully away from his thumbs, Blunt-wasp clung to a silver walker. He wheezed in an attempt to gather the necessary strength for speaking. "My goodness," he said with a voice that sounded like a dry stick scraping the concrete at the boy's feet. "You look like..."

Stephen wanted to help when the old man did not continue. "Like..."

"Never you mind," said the old man.

"Like I ran the whole way? I didn't."

"Can I help you, young man?"

They stared at each other. The old man was almost as short as Stephen, possibly a hundred years old. Most of the teeth had escaped Mr. Bluntwasp's bumpy gums. Long white hairs grew from his giant nostrils like plants from misshapen pots.

"I'm," Stephen said, then thought a moment. "I'm the *help* Mr. Allyn sent over."

"The help? Ah . . . I got the call nearly an hour ago."

"Sorry about the delay."

"You're Mr. Allyn's son?" His voice was changing: a little friendlier, a little more business.

"Mr. Allyn only has a daughter. I'm his foster child." Stephen didn't like saying those words. They always made him feel like he was saying, *I'm the leftovers in the back of the refrigerator.*

The old man perked. "Ah! You were transferred into the Allyn home?" He looked Stephen up and down. "My goodness!" he whispered, this time sharing a secret with himself.

Stephen felt like a slave again. Like an animal for sale. He considered saying, *Do you want me to turn around? You'll get a better look that way.*

"May I ask you a . . . personal . . . question."

"Well, I don't know," Stephen said.

"Where do you go to school, my lad?" The old man stretched his grin as wide as it would go.

"Oh. I'll be going to Montreal Middle next week."

The old man frowned. "Where is that?"

"Few blocks down Harmon Road, up Midland. Why?"

The old man's head jerked. He winced like it hurt to change the direction of his thinking. Then he smiled again. "You look *so much* like someone I have long missed. Do you like books?" Mr. Bluntwasp turned and went into the entryway.

"Sure, especially if—" Stephen said, then he saw a box of heavy hardbound books on the floor. The box, with U-Haul printed on the side in fat letters, was open. The books that had been taken out of the box were on a tall bookcase that was mostly empty. Next to the open box on the floor rested five more unopened cases of the same size. "Uh, oh."

"I love books. This is where I need your help, see? I just don't have the muscle to move these heavy volumes. Would you do that for an old man?"

"Well, I guess I could."

"I would be most indebted to you, Stephen." He turned around with an excited grin on his face. "Your name is Stephen, is it not? Stephen . . . Crown?" Mr. Bluntwasp's eyes lit up with eager hope.

The pronunciation of Stephen's last name was close enough, especially for this grandfatherly type. "You thought I was Mr. Allyn's son."

Now Mr. Bluntwasp looked like he was about to jump right out of his old skin and bounce off the walls. "Incredible!" he whispered. Then he wiped the expression off his face. "Will you take care of the books for me? The rest are right in here."

Mr. Bluntwasp turned and moved into the next room, lifting and pushing his walker ahead of him.

Stephen didn't have much of a choice, did he? Could he say no?

But he was derailed by the way the old man had been staring at him. "How do you know my name?"

"Not to worry. You have a friend here. Would you like some cookies and milk as you get started?"

"Sure." The house smelled of dry desert and green pine. Stephen followed Mr. Bluntwasp into a room painted blood red. "So . . . you just want me to put the books in the bookcase."

"Oh, no. It's much easier than that. I'm moving! I need you to carefully load the boxes."

Stephen smiled. Taking the books down sounded a whole lot easier than putting the books up.

He came around a bend in the wall of the red room and gaped.

The red room was a library. Bookcases filled every wall, except the far one that he had been looking at when he entered. Flattened boxes covered the floor.

There was also a musty smell in here, like old cheese that had been lost somewhere in the room and doubled in size with green mold. Stephen wondered if finding the cheese would be the grand prize of this horrible day.

Mr. Bluntwasp continued sliding and stepping forward until he crossed the room. There stood a doorway. Beside the doorway hung a large painting of a beast that could not have existed in this world, not even in mythology.

There were stars in the background of the painting, two moons, and three planets listing in the distance. Purple bushes covered the ground.

In the center of the artwork was a huge, snarling animal with two heads. It might have been a two-headed dog, if not for the long single-point antlers racing away from the animal's evil eyebrows like horns.

"*What is that?*"

"Oh," said Mr. Bluntwasp, "you like him?"

With fangs bared, both heads snarled in frozen silence. The artist had even captured the drool falling from the creature's black gums in wonderfully grotesque detail. This was not a monster that Stephen ever wanted to see in his nightmares. He hoped he would forget its existence before bedtime.

"It's frightening."

Moving down the hallway to a kitchen a short reach from the library, Mr. Bluntwasp laughed with a friendly voice. "The boobalander? Ah! Like me, he's the best friend you could ever have."

Mr. Bluntwasp turned and waved Stephen into a room of glass cabinets. Scented with a refreshing air of lemon water and strawberries, it was a pretty kitchen, the sort Mrs. Allyn would have gone gaga over. Maybe there had been a Mrs. Bluntwasp at one time. But the other smells in the house made Stephen think that she couldn't possibly be around anymore.

"Glasses are there. Milk's in the fridge. And cookies are—argh!"

Stephen was already going for the glass and the milk when Mr. Bluntwasp collapsed. He turned to see the old man falling through the metal pipes of his walker.

"I'm all right. I'm all right." Bluntwasp kept saying the phrase as Stephen took one arm and helped him again into a standing position. "All right. Will you help me back into the library?"

They left the walker in the kitchen.

Stephen fit himself under the little man's elbow and served as a human crutch. By the time they reached the room filled with books, Stephen was ready to collapse—the thin grandpa was crushing him.

They both sighed when Stephen settled Mr. Bluntwasp into a red leather chair.

"Go on," Bluntwasp said with barely enough breath to speak. "Start your snack."

"I can stay with you, Mr. Bluntwasp."

"I insist. Get going. I'll be here when you get back, Stephen."

Stephen wasn't so sure about that. He didn't know what it looked like when somebody had a heart attack, but he guessed this was pretty close.

Mr. Bluntwasp opened his eyes and caught the hesitation on Stephen's face. "Get moving."

Stephen shook his head. But when Bluntwasp pointed at the kitchen hall with a finger made of old skin, bones, and knots for knuckles, Stephen turned and marched.

I'm going to pour the milk, spill it, have to clean it up, and then I'll find the old man DEAD when I get back in there, Stephen thought to himself. *Then what will I do? Call 911? Run home and tell Mr. Allyn that I killed one of his paychecks?*

Stephen wondered if the day could get any worse. Especially after he'd met such a nice guy.

Deep inside, Stephen felt a quiver of familiarity: Something about Mr. Bluntwasp reminded Stephen about the best of his foster parents. That stirred a powerful emotion in his heart, the desire to stay.

When Stephen returned, he found Mr. Bluntwasp alive (thank goodness) and staring at the painting with love in his eyes. He looked like a man reliving memories too precious to forget.

"Apus."

"What was that, Mr. Bluntwasp?"

"Best boobalander a boy could ever have." Mr. Bluntwasp was talking to the wall. Then he slid his gaze to Stephen. "If you have a companion like that, you'd never worry about getting bullied, I tell you."

Stephen's face turned red. Had Mr. Allyn said something about him getting bothered by thugs at school? (Hank had called them 'prison inmates in training.') Valendra used stories of fights with frightening middle-school students to scare Stephen whenever she wanted to push his buttons—especially whenever he spoke positively about going to Montreal Middle.

(Hank had said on more than one occasion, *Why would ANYONE want to go to middle school? There's no recess!* But Stephen refused to believe that there was no recess. The horrible notion seemed inhumane at the very least.)

The slobbering, two-headed monster with spikes growing out of its head grinned from the painting. A smile reshaped Stephen's mouth as he thought about going to school with *that* on a leash. "Yeah."

Then he realized that Mr. Bluntwasp was talking like the boobal-ander was *real*. And that Stephen just couldn't believe. He found it more likely that there really might not be any recess in middle school.

The idea that the nice old guy might be a friend only because he was also crazy made the smile fade.

His ate his cookies and milk quickly.

Then he said, "I should get to work."

Mr. Bluntwasp said nothing, but sat quietly in the chair until he fell asleep.

Stephen looked over the books and the boxes. The job was going to take him the entire day.

He hoped Mr. Bluntwasp wouldn't die before he finished.

Mr. Bluntwasp said only one thing in his sleep. With his chin tucked in between his collar bones, he mumbled gibberish that sounded faintly like someone speaking on one side of a telephone conversation.

"Yes ... m'sure ... n'know, every attempt failed ... found him ... b'accident ... m'positive ... v'located Stephen Crown ...."

THE GIFT

After Mr. Bluntwasp's heart attack, or whatever it was, the old man didn't say much. All day, he sat in the chair, dropping in and out of sleep. More than once, he looked dead.

But his chest continued to rise and fall with each shallow breath. Stephen left him alone.

The eyes of a few dozen statuettes the size of his forearm watched him from perches along the bookshelves around the room. Made of wood stained almost black, they each stood at attention, arms at their sides, on little legs, and they grimaced with wide mouths. Stephen watched them for a while. He thought they might have been from Africa or the Polynesian islands. He had never seen the like.

Stephen did his work, packing boxes with one book after another—they had the strangest titles.

Ancient Waterways for the Ulites had been resting beside *Hanover Jovian Picnics, Kale on Offwater Worlds,* and *Wormholes.* Why anyone would collect books about worms, water, and picnics, Stephen would never understand.

Then there were the books with titles that he couldn't read at all.

At least half of the library was made up of volumes of foreign origin. Some of the books were clearly Spanish: *Los Relojes de Espania, Lazarillo de Tormes, Egmont y Horne,* etc.

Other tomes contained strange letters that curved and bounced and then hung lazily.

The peculiar alphabet intrigued Stephen the most. The print appeared both ancient and futuristic at the same time. Stephen decided that the script must have been a modern form of something really old, the sort of thing that people in the US generally didn't know much about. Like Sanskrit. Or Laotian. (Two of Hank's discoveries in the library).

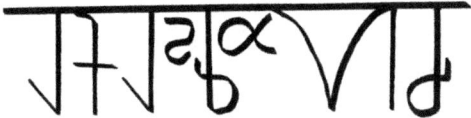

Didn't matter anyway.

Stephen did his job.

Sometimes he caught Mr. Bluntwasp awake, watching Stephen from the side of his eye as if he had no memory of inviting the silver-haired boy into the house. Other times, Stephen found the old man staring at the picture of the "boobalander."

And then the day came to an end.

The sun went down through the windows, spreading the library with light filtered through giant bushes beyond the glass.

"Mr. Bluntwasp?"

The old guy was asleep once more. Or maybe he'd finally passed on.

The thought made Stephen ache—it had happened to Mrs. Bellnap; it could happen again, couldn't it? And even though they hadn't spoken since he arrived before lunch time, the man's statement replayed again and again in Stephen's ears: *Not to worry. You have a friend here.*

Stephen didn't like the idea of walking home. Or even running. In the dark.

Seeing the job nearly complete, his stomach growled fiercely enough to remind him that it was dinnertime and his "lunch" had consisted of cookies and milk.

Stephen's head filled with images of the silhouette people in the blue car that had followed him from the Ma & Pa shop.

Stephen told himself that the pursuit had just been his imagination. It didn't work; he didn't believe himself.

Not to worry. You have a friend here.

If only he could . . . stay.

With the sun long gone, and Mr. Bluntwasp looking dead again, unblinking, Stephen finally forced himself to touch the man's shoulder. "Mr. Bluntwasp?"

"Uh? Ah. Stephen Crown!" In his quaking voice, the old man said the name like he was speaking to the President of the country.

"I ran out of boxes."

The old man looked at him, not at the books that remained on the shelves in the library. At first, Stephen thought he was thinking about asking when he planned on coming back to finish the job. Then he saw that the old man was grinning, so pleased to have Stephen there in the room with him.

Bluntwasp reached out and grabbed Stephen's arm with one frail hand. "Thank you, Stephen Crown. Thank you for coming to *my* house today."

The old guy really had Stephen's last name *wrong*, but Stephen liked Bluntwasp too much to correct him. Grandpas should be cut a little slack, he told himself. "Sure, Mr. Bluntwasp."

Blinking, Bluntwasp came out of his drunken glee. With wet eyes, he gave the room the once over. "Well. Adventures await! You'll be wanting to get home, I expect. School starting so soon, and all. The envelope there by the door is for your—for Mr. Allyn."

"Right," said Stephen politely. He waited for the old man to tell him that he needed to return the following day. He frankly hoped that Mr. Bluntwasp wanted him back.

"Wait!" The old man felt into his pockets, then he looked around the room. Light returned to his face when his attention locked onto one of the strange figurines. "Will you fetch me that treasure?"

Without a word, Stephen weaved his way through the towers of boxes that he had filled. He lifted the polished wooden shape and was surprised to find that it wasn't made of wood at all.

The gaping monster standing on a coil of tentacles felt like baked clay, light, delicate, and hollow.

"Thank you." Mr. Bluntwasp took the idol with trembling fingers bent the wrong way with age.

The old man immediately dropped it. The treasure shattered.

The Gift

Stephen's blood went cold.

Bluntwasp smiled.

"Now, would you hand *that* to me?"

Among the dark potsherds rested a golden disk.

Stephen brushed the sharp pieces of clay out of his way.

The ornately designed circle was the size and shape of a pocket watch. There was no chain, however, and there wasn't a knob on one side to wind or open it. Nor could he discover the face of any clock. Instead, there was an elaborately fashioned picture in the metal: three stars around a moon or a planet. On the other side, rings ran around rings in expanding concentric circles.

Stephen handed the heavy little disk to Bluntwasp.

The old man did not lift a hand to retrieve it. "Stephen Crown, will you let me give that to you?"

"What is it?"

"A gift of infinite value."

It didn't seem right to receive this present. For one thing, it had the radiant shine of *real* gold wherever the light touched its curves and etchings.

"Please. I have no one else."

"What about your son?"

"Myron is . . . an orphan child that I adopted after his mother's death. He is . . . more like that poor woman than myself. It would be inappropriate for me to ever show him such an item."

Stephen turned it over in his hand. He was flattered. But it still felt wrong to take some ancient golden thing from a man he just met. He handed it to Bluntwasp again. "I couldn't."

"You hold an absconder, Stephen," he said with the wide eyes of a man who had just bequeathed to a boy a free rocket ticket to the International Space Station. "It is a singular treasure that might be especially appreciated by boys your age in school, I imagine! Do me this favor? Please accept this gift. And please do me one other thing?"

Stephen liked the old man. But he didn't like where this was heading.

"Tell no one about the absconder. Until you understand it? And then . . . pick your friends with care!"

Stephen opened his mouth to say no. *Never take gifts from strangers.* The warnings of good foster parents insisted that he not take this . . . this absconder thing.

But there was such longing in the old man's waiting eyes.

Stephen gave a nod and put the absconder into the pocket of his jeans.

Mr. Bluntwasp raised a crooked hand, like a tired but pleasant elderly businessman.

Still unsure of what to do, Stephen gingerly took the old man's hand and shook it.

Mr. Bluntwasp gave Stephen's hand a faint squeeze. Once again, Bluntwasp lit up like a Christmas tree. He smiled with such kindness that Stephen felt the sudden urge to beg the old man to let him stay.

But that was silly. That was the stuff of dreams. If there was one thing that foster children were *great* at, it was dreaming of happily-ever-after homes. They so rarely happened.

"Nice to meet you, Mr. Bluntwasp."

The handshaking continued.

Stephen let go at the sight of tears in the old man's sparkling eyes. "I should go."

"Unquestionably," Bluntwasp managed to say. "I'll see you around the galaxy, Stephen Crown?"

Cowen, Stephen almost said. "You bet." Stephen backed toward the front door. "I'll let myself out."

The old man simply could not speak. He tried. He nodded. He lifted one frail hand, and he waved goodbye before lowering that hand to the armrest of the leather chair.

Then . . . Stephen was standing outside.

Adrift once more, he sniffed at a darkening sky. White flowers decorating a star jasmine bush wrapped him in a magical fragrance. He looked at the moon and guessed that it must be past eight.

He was very sad.

So as he started walking away from the house, he concentrated on the hunger twisting his stomach into sounds of horrible emptiness.

8

A DARK ROAD HOME

Shadows lurked everywhere.

Or rather, Stephen's imaginative mind painted human shapes beyond the reach of yellow streetlights, around the corners from porch illumination, creeping with every passing vehicle.

He considered running the whole way home. "I'll only panic myself if I do that," he whispered, just to hear a friendly voice. "Dogs only chase you when you run. If I start running from ghosts that aren't there, I'll think every nightmare on the planet is after me!"

With hands stuffed into the pockets of his jeans, he walked briskly as he cut through the back streets toward Harmon Road.

He squeezed the absconder. Something told him that the little gold disk could help him, a lot.

More silly thoughts!

He shook his head.

It seemed that he walked forever, at first. No one followed him.

(Of course, he didn't actually turn around to confirm that.)

Cars drove right on past him. Stephen appreciated their headlights casting out the darkness. But just as those helpful drivers appeared, they left him again. Each was a bittersweet blessing.

At last he reached the terrible basketball player on the corner. The guy was still dribbling—he couldn't possibly have been practicing hoops all day, could he?

"What are you looking at?"

"Nothing. Sorry," Stephen said, averting his eyes to the road.

But still, he felt safer while the basketball player was near.

He turned left at the corner and felt the safety diminish with every step. The dribbling sound grew quieter the farther Stephen walked. *THUMP*, *thump*, thump.

He turned right at the house of cats.

The felines no longer looked like little friends, happy to see the boy that nobody wanted. From fence tops, porch railings, window-sills, and the sides of bushes, the cats froze and peered at him with suspicion and distrust.

The hungry pride lowered to the ground, hindquarters tensing in the air, legs tightened like powerful springs. Eyes glowed yellow and reflected the light from houses across the street.

The predators held perfectly still.

Finally, Stephen looked away because their attention was giving him the willies.

He approached the haunted mansion at the end of the block.

Staying across the street, Stephen hoofed it a little more cautiously, just to stay away from the crumbling, empty building. The last thing he wanted to do was trip on a curb and land on his face right where the poltergeists would grab him.

To his astonishment, in some illogical twist of the night, the house looked less haunted and simply locked: boards over the windows; a heavy padlock thing over the doorknob; bushes and weeds choking the walkway and the falling porch.

The unused building didn't appear haunted at all. The place just looked like a piece of forgotten trash the size of a—well, a house.

Stephen traveled left around the mansion, keeping his eye on the place, mostly because he didn't want to search the path in front or behind him for scary shapes.

A Dark Road Home

His heart didn't slow down and relax one bit as he reached the house of gnomes. In fact, it was quite the opposite.

The cute little Santas in red hats and blue pants seemed to be scrutinizing him. Their smiles had turned into evil grins.

Stephen had liked the gnomes, but he did not like them now. So he averted his eyes to the road.

But he had *really liked* those happy little elf guys!

So he looked at them again, hoping that their appearance had changed the way the haunted house had lost its haunts.

The gnomes had changed all right.

They had *moved*.

Stephen looked away.

He eyed them again. And he determined that he could not blink away anymore.

It was like a game of red light green light. When Stephen had gazed off, the gnomes with the evil grins had all raced forward on their little legs and then petrified themselves when he peered at them.

They were still grinning. And they looked worse.

But ....

"It's all in my head," Stephen told himself. And as soon as he said the words, he knew that it *had to be* in his head. Of course it was!

Nevertheless, Stephen did not move his attention from the gnomes until he was as far away as he could get.

And then?

He sprinted toward the next corner.

If I look back ... I will see an army of gnomes standing on the sidewalk!

Stephen's fears mounted when he reached Lion's Park.

Towering light poles stood at intervals over a little parking lot. But they did not brighten his situation. In fact, they did not turn on at all with the arrival of the night.

The grass fields were black.

Stephen refused to see the shadows cast there by the yellow streetlights far behind him.

He ran, instead, as fast as he could.

✳ ✳● ✝

He began to smell the deep-fried air of Alibertos before he reached Harmon Road. Then he saw the cars passing left and right.

The sounds of normal city life refreshed him.

Brave, now, he looked into the gloomy neighborhoods behind him.

And he plowed through a pack of dark gang members twice his age, apologized, and slowed to a jog.

They let him live. Probably thought him too small to kill.

Stephen kept going. His stomach churned with terrible hunger. The hot and greasy smell of the fast-food restaurant might have stopped him on the spot had he any money left to purchase an entrée.

"There is food at home."

✳ ✳● ✝

He ran across the street, stopping beneath a jacaranda tree on the island as he waited for traffic to clear enough for him to cross to the electronics store window. He touched the glass covetously.

At the Ma & Pa gas station, Stephen began walking again. His lungs burned. He spotted no blue cars, no gnomes, no ghosts, no shadow men.

But the hairs on the back of his neck rose as if he were being watched by someone hidden somewhere at the intersection.

From here on out, Midland Road grew darker the farther Stephen stumbled from Harmon Road.

Thoroughly exhausted and starving out of his mind, Stephen tripped on a crack halfway along the earthquake-shattered sidewalk. He fell. He rammed his knee into the concrete. He stood and rubbed the pain away, because he was almost home.

He just had to pass by Mrs. Herkamer's beast.

Then, with the Allyns, he would be safe. *With the Allyns*—the thought made him laugh. Life, no matter how bad he might have thought it to be, would at least return to something close to normal in a minute.

Or so he thought.

STRANGERS AND ODD FACES

When Mr. Allyn unlocked the front door to see who was there, he was chuckling.

"You locked me out," Stephen said. He was dripping with sweat. He wanted to get inside, use the bathroom, and eat something—not necessarily in that order.

Mr. Allyn's twisted grin and peculiar choking laugh stopped him cold.

Hanging onto the wall and the doorknob, Mr. Allyn blocked the entrance anyway. "Envelope?"

It took Stephen a moment to remember his mission: Work at Bluntwasp's, receive an envelope, deliver said envelope to Mr. Allyn.

Stephen pulled the folded envelope from his back pocket and put it into Mr. Allyn's hand.

Amazingly, Mr. Allyn did not rip it open right then and there to gloat over the amount of extra income indicated on Mr. Bluntwasp's check. He shoved it into his own pocket, almost secretively. And he still did not open the door farther and get out of the way.

He was grinding his teeth together, even as he continued to chuckle and speak. "How was your trip home, Stephen?"

"Mrs. Herkamer's werewolf nearly chewed through the fence when he saw me coming. Other than that? Peachy."

Stephen might not have acted so rudely—his dinner, after all, hung in the balance—but other than chatting with a nice couple of elderly people, he had not had a particularly good day.

And Mr. Allyn was acting very oddly.

"Did you call me *Stephen?*"

"We have company, my good lad!" Mr. Allyn said, holding the door ajar. His eyes flashed red and wide, communicating clearly, *If you screw this up, I'll have your head on a platter for Thanksgiving dinner!* Then Mr. Allyn became a ball of glowing joviality, the perfect foster dad again.

He let Stephen into the front room and shut the door, saying, "I locked the poor son outside when I let you in. How terrible of me!"

A matronly woman in a red blouse and a white floral skirt rose slowly from the couch. She held a cup of hot chocolate in one hand and a peanut butter cookie on a saucer in the other.

As she rose her eyes grew wider and her mouth fell loose. A tiny sound, like a moan, slid from the back of her throat.

The cookie began to slide off the edge of the plate. The cocoa wavered, leaned, threatened to spill a layer of mini marshmallows onto the carpet.

"Stephen . . . ?"

On the couch beside her, Mrs. Allyn's round face colored like a purple beet.

Stephen looked down at himself, suddenly shamed by what might be causing such a reaction.

Not only was he sweating, but having fallen on the trip home his clothes were matted with dark splotches of whatever filth he had landed in without being aware. The knee of his nearly threadbare blue jeans had torn. And, now that he was examining himself, he noticed a trickle of moisture escaping his left nostril.

He wiped his nose on his shoulder.

The old woman looked him up and down. Then she simply stared as Mr. Allyn began to ramble at no one in particular.

Mrs. Allyn grinned so hard, she looked like a woman sitting on a cactus, struggling to hide the pain, and failing. She pinched her eyes into thin slits.

Mr. Allyn jabbed Stephen in the ribs with an elbow. "Had a day, it looks like, Stephen, did you? I'll bet! Serving the elderly; running about as boys do! Ha, ha, ha! Bravo. I remember those wonderful years. Kiddo—" (Mr. Allyn only called Valendra Kiddo, and

Valendra was nowhere to be seen) "—I'm proud of you. Like I always say: a child shouldn't let his youth slip away too quickly!"

Mr. Allyn laughed once more. It was such a mechanical, fake sound that no human on Earth would have mistaken it for a real expression of happiness.

The old woman's face magically changed. She lit up. The cup leveled itself, just before the first marshmallow was about to leave the chocolate. The cookie balanced on the rim of the plate, snowing a few crumbs toward the carpet. No one but Stephen seemed to notice.

It had been a full day. Stephen's arms were growing sore. Tomorrow he might not be able to move them at all, let alone straighten his back. For now, all he wanted was food. After that he wanted to go to bed.

"Stephen," said Mrs. Allyn, sounding like she had never actually said the name before, "do you have any idea who this is?"

"I'm sure young Stephen does not," said the wrinkled woman as she put down her cup and plate on the coffee table. She had an accent. Like she was from England or somewhere else far away overseas. She smoothed her skirt.

Young Stephen? Weird.

"I am your . . . aunt."

"My . . . aunt?"

"Once removed."

"Aunt," Stephen said again, bewildered and uncertain that he was understanding at all what she had said.

"Gretel!" she added, as if she were making it up. Or as if she just didn't know how to talk to *young* Stephen. (Super weird.)

Nevertheless, a tingling sensation rushed through Stephen's shoulders at the impossible thought. (Really?)

He still needed to go to the bathroom. His stomach turned over in desperation for food. And his muscles were already beginning to knot up.

This is what every foster kid I've ever known has always wanted!

A single word tumbled out of his mouth. "Family?" Tears threatened to rush from his eyes.

It was too good to be true.

Certainly. *Too* good.

Because there was no reason for the Allyns to be smiling and issuing false laughter, was there? Not if they were losing both slave and "cash cow" all in one terrible blow.

And . . . and an aunt once removed? Stephen had never heard of such a thing.

Mr. Allyn's fabricated chuckle vibrated the air near Stephen's ear. "Our sad little buddy is in shock! Come, boy—Stephen! ha, ha—sit down before you fall over." He bumped Stephen until the "boy" reached the loveseat opposite the couch.

Mrs. Allyn reached out with soft hands across the coffee table and waved Stephen gently with all ten fingers toward the cushions. "Sit, child, sit, sit."

Still no Valendra. Stephen gazed at the stairs.

Mr. Allyn read his mind. To the bedrooms on the second floor, he called with the nicest voice, "Dear? Darling, sweet, Valendra? Won't you come? Twiddle on down now, won't you?"

Never was there such a sickeningly loving father.

(Never had Mr. Allyn tried so hard to *sound* so tender.)

Valendra appeared on the landing. She alone would not smile. But something passed between her and her father, communication hidden from those in the living room.

She leaned against the white banister and stood there with her arms folded. She looked angry.

"Oh," said Mrs. Allyn, "I think our humble girl is sad that Stephen will be leaving us."

"Leaving?" Stephen said. Again the chills washed over him. He thought he might faint with glee (or the need to visit the bathroom).

Mr. Allyn laughed again.

And that was just *not* right.

He sat beside Stephen and explained. "Your aunt will be taking you, until next summer."

"Really?" Stephen still couldn't believe it. Nor did he understand the last part of Mr. Allyn's statement.

Probably because there were too many tiny clues warning him that nothing was as it seemed.

For instance, Val should be the one elated at the thought of Stephen's departure. Mr. Allyn should be frantic at the loss of his little moneymaker. Mrs. Allyn should be panicking about all the domestic jobs that would become her responsibility again. And Stephen's Aunt Gretel . . . well, she looked old enough to be Stephen's great grandmother! Even as she stood there, Stephen noticed her swaying slightly, like she might lose her balance, fall over, and—

Die. That's what they do, the really good people. They die. And then I'm back with the horrible foster parents. That's what ALWAYS happens.

"You're my aunt?" Hope pushed disbelief away.

"Once or twice removed. Sort of. I *am* family," she said, sitting across the coffee table from him and beaming.

"The resemblance is uncanny!" said Mr. Allyn. "You share the same hair color!"

"Well," Gretel said, touching her wild, gray curls. "Almost. But you won't get these white streaks until you are *much* older." She giggled. "Isn't this wonderful?"

"Yes." Stephen smelled something strong, like a new kitchen-cleaning agent. He used Val, thumping down the carpeted stairs, as an excuse to turn his head and take a breath in the hopes of fresher air.

Valendra wouldn't look at him at all. She turned Stephen into a hole in the living room and peered at the floor, the ceiling, the dark window, the lamps, her black fingernails, the polish chipping away as she scratched on them.

"I've made all the arrangements," Aunt Gretel said. "Your foster parents have been gracious enough to agree with the, um, *arrangement*."

Mr. Allyn chuckled. *This* time there was real feeling in the short laugh. A glimmer of sick intelligence shone in his eyes. "That's right, boy—Stephen."

"Arrangement." It seemed the most peculiar word to use. "I'm leaving?"

"Right," said Mrs. Allyn.

"The Allyn's have been so good," said Gretel, "to keep you through the summer. I would have contacted you earlier. But, you know: circumstances." She giggled.

Stephen felt totally lost, not to mention extremely uncomfortable so close to Mr. Allyn, who wouldn't leave his side. "What do you mean?"

Mrs. Allyn was kind enough to answer with words that he would understand. "Mrs. Lackluv is taking you to school."

"To—huh?"

"Yes, yes, yes. But we'll see you again, never fear. That's how this works! You'll return for a little while next summer." Honesty radiated from Mrs. Allyn's eyes. Stephen spotted a hint of sadness there also, though he suspected that had more to do with her chores again.

"I've never heard of that before."

"Heard of what before? School?" said Mrs. Allyn.

"Of—foster children leaving a family and then . . . coming back."

"Oh, you would come back for the holidays too," said Aunt Gretel, "normally. I hope you'll forgive me! I just can't afford to get you there and back again in the middle of the school year. Transportation costs being what they are. But as your foster mother said, you'll return to your happy home here in June!"

"Oh," said Stephen in the background of Mr. Allyn's rumbling glee. "Goodie."

He caught Val watching him from the corner of her eye. She swiveled her eyes away.

This still didn't make sense to Stephen. *But then, a lot of things that grownups do don't make much sense,* Stephen thought, *do they?*

He was *leaving.*

That was the point.

He was coming back in June?

"Mr. Allyn?" Stephen said. "May I ask something?"

"Of course, *son!*" Mr. Allyn put an arm around him.

Stephen cringed at the conspicuously unfamiliar sensation. "What do you get . . . I mean . . . you are okay with this?"

"Oh yes!" he said, and understanding shone from his face. "You see, everything has been taken care of with your social worker, Mrs. Ryan, if that is what you are worried about."

It wasn't. Stephen had expected everything was fine with the government, until Mr. Allyn had said this.

Stephen frowned. He wondered if he was about to be flown to a foreign country to work nineteen-hour days in some kind of horrible, manufacturing sweatshop that only employed orphans, who died early.

Mr. Allyn winked at Aunt Gretel. "Mrs. Lackluv has initiated a rare opportunity. We will continue to be your foster parents of record. We will receive," he couldn't hold back the chuckle, "a continuation of logical compensation. With the understanding that we say nothing about the school you will be attending."

"Huh?"

Mrs. Allyn said, "It's top secret government stuff!"

Valendra coughed and gagged in clear disgust.

Slowly Stephen studied their faces.

"Secret? Like, experimental? The government is experimenting on foster children?"

No one's expression changed.

"And you'll continue to get the check in the mail. While I'm gone. And all you have to do is keep quiet?"

"Oh!" said Aunt Gretel, "Never fear! You are going to a *famous* school! SA-6. It's private, if you are wondering. Quite fabulous!"

The tears threatened to rise again in Stephen's eyes. He looked at the woman who said that she was his aunt. "I'll be living with you?"

"You're going to school."

"It's a *boarding* school," Valendra said with a stinger in her voice. She grinned a little, just to make sure the words hurt.

Stephen swallowed loud enough for the sound to be heard by everyone in the room. "Why can't I live with you?"

"Just not possible at this time, dear. I'm . . . between addresses, at present. You will love SA-6, though!"

"It's famous!" Mrs. Allyn said, as if this were good news. She still sounded sad at the thought of her chores.

"Have I heard of it?"

"Probably not." Mr. Allyn squeezed him with the arm around his shoulders, then removed it. "You are young!"

Val coughed again. She looked ready to vomit a long list of complaints, no longer pleased with her attempt to wound her foster brother.

"And *you* are keeping this government secret as well?" Stephen asked Valendra.

"Oh," said Mr. Allyn, "our little doll definitely will.*" If she knows what's good for her!* Mr. Allyn added without using his mouth. Everyone in the room heard that last unspoken part, except the strange woman with Stephen's hair color.

"I'm so very sorry," Aunt Gretel said to the Allyns. "Young Stephen and I are running terribly late as it is—my fault, my fault—but ..."

"Of course!" Mr. Allyn said, jumping to his feet.

"Yes, yes, yes!" said Mrs. Allyn doing her best to rise with her husband and the old woman. "Stephen, son, you good boy. Run up stairs now. It's time for your departure!"

"What—now?" His stomach growled.

"Ah!" said Gretel. She touched Mrs. Allyn's forearm and whispered, "He can eat on the way."

"Valendra, little flower?" said Mr. Allyn.

"What."

"Help your good bro-bro?"

She marched up the stairs and straight into Stephen's room.

Stephen slipped into the bathroom.

10

THE BITTER TRUTH

Stephen was still starving when he finished taking care of more pressing emergencies. The adults chatted at the bottom of the stairs, following him up with their eyes, so he went directly into his room.

He expected Valendra to hit him with books, old toys, or at least a few mean statements.

She was staring into his underwear drawer. Just to humiliate him, no doubt. But Stephen felt numb.

Val said nothing until he asked a question. "You want to tell me what's really going on?"

"Oh," she said, kicking the door so that it swung most of the way shut, "you wouldn't believe the day you missed!"

"You didn't go to the mall?"

Her face flamed red. "Thanks to you. And on the Saturday before school starts? EVERYONE'S at the mall. Thanks a lot."

"I was gone."

"And the phone rang off the hook."

"My aunt?"

Val squinted at him and laced her tone with poison. "You don't really think that *thing* downstairs is your aunt, do you?" She imitated the woman's squeaky voice. "'I'm between addresses!' Give me a break."

Stephen opened the closet but couldn't reach the gray suitcase that had followed him his whole life. Val sighed with a volcano in her throat and got it down.

While Stephen opened his other drawers and began packing, Val turned away and folded her arms. "Anyway, it wasn't *Gretel Lackluv* on the phone."

"My social worker?"

"Someone else from the office, I guess. Yolanda Zang. She said that she's been sent by family services to offer you a special and rare experimental option for qualified foster children."

"Huh?"

"Her words. She said you qualified—whatever that meant. My parents spoke for you, of course."

She meant that last part as an insult.

Stephen didn't know how to take it. He didn't know how he should feel about any of this. Family? Leaving the Allyns? But . . . boarding school? *Coming back* to the Allyns?

"She said you will be going to a private school far away. No questions asked—you know how the government can be."

"And I come back for the summer," he said with a pang of confusion and unhappiness.

"For which," Val said, "Mom and Dad will continue to receive their check, plus a secrecy stipend. You can imagine how Dad likes the *plus*."

"Of course."

"And," she said with a little spice in her expression, "if at any point we break our contract, Dad loses all future money and future possibilities of getting paid by the government for '*services for which they currently are qualified*'."

"They can't be foster parents anymore," Stephen concluded, sneaking his underwear into the suitcase.

Val spun around as if to catch him with his hands on the Fruit-of-the-Loom. "Wrong, dork! You come back. You stay, I betcha! And you can never go off like this again! Do you know what that means?"

He held his breath.

"*I have full power over you now!*"

"I don't understand."

"I'll make it clear to you. If I squeal, you come straight home! If I tell people the truth, Dad will be furious—he'll blame you! So you will do *exactly* what I tell you, or I get to pull the plug."

Stephen held very still and watched her gloat. Then he said, "But . . . I have real family now. Why would I come back here?"

"Oh," Val said, nearly bursting with laughter, "you haven't seen the car your *aunt* came in? Come here!"

Valendra opened the door as quietly as she could. She put a finger of silence to her lips. Then she flattened herself against the wall outside the room and guided him into her room.

Like an uninvited vampire, he stopped automatically at the threshold.

Val rounded a bed covered with a lifetime collection of pink-and-black teddy bears. She pulled the lattice blinds to the top of the window. "Take a look!"

First of all, this room had been completely off limits since his arrival in the house. Val had threatened him with his life. She had done that often; but in the case of her room, she meant it. Stephen felt like he couldn't touch the carpet with a single step.

She waved him over, waved like her fingers were on fire.

At last, he crossed and brought his eyes to the glass.

The backyard was dark. The porch light that Mr. Allyn kept lit to repel burglars, as if they enjoyed prowling backyards, was extinguished.

But there *was* something in the center of the giant square of grass he had cut a hundred times.

Stephen concentrated.

It looked like an impossibly large trampoline. But it wasn't.

"I can't see it."

Valendra sighed her contempt again and crossed to the light switch.

The room lights went out.

And then Stephen *saw*.

Perfectly circular, the metallic object was larger than a backyard swimming pool. Circles filled circles, much like the absconder in his pocket. In fact the machine was so large, Mr. and Mrs. Allyn might have parked all of their cars beneath it.

He stammered. "Is that—is that—?"

"Your aunt's *car*. Or what she landed in, anyway."

TAKE-OFF

Stephen ogled through the window for a long time. Val started to laugh. He thought she was mocking him, that it was all a big joke and he was the butt of what they would be talking about for the next year and telling everybody.

You should have seen his face, Daddy! Oh did we FOOL YOU, boy!!!

Then Stephen noticed the faintest squeak in Valendra's laughter. Like *she* was the one going crazy.

He crept to the top of the stairs.

The grownups looked up at him. Mr. Allyn, Mrs. Allyn, and Gretel Lackluv each froze like kids caught playing in the principal's office.

"Aunt Gretel?" said Stephen.

The old woman swallowed. "Yes, Stephen?"

"Who are you really?"

"Me?" She turned red in her red shirt. "Why, I am . . . a distant relative."

She sounded honest.

"Mr. Allyn?" said Stephen, amazed at his own audacity. But, folks, what was he to think about all this?

Val's dad wrung his hands together, smiled, but had that look in his eyes. "Yes, bo—Stephen?"

"What is that thing in the backyard?"

Mr. Allyn sighed through a guffaw that came out almost a cry, conveying one message: *Mr. Allyn* didn't quite know what to make of this situation either!

"Well, son, I—I can't begin to tell you. We were all outside when your auntie arrived. Took us by surprise, I will have to admit. It was hard to believe the, ah, the caseworker who was here earlier."

Valendra spoke behind Stephen's left ear. "I already told him about Yolanda Zang. The one who paid us a call." Val seemed to like the name: each time she said Yolanda Zang, the words rolled off her tongue like music. Or like a girl who didn't really believe that this other woman in question actually possessed the name Yolanda Zang.

"Already told you? Oh!" said Mr. Allyn. "Very good then!"

"Mr. Allyn," said Gretel Lackluv. "We really are running terribly late. If we don't leave now, I'm afraid I might not be able to get him . . . where we are going . . . on time."

He wrinkled his face in bewilderment—his smile looked stretched and exhausted from lack of practice.

"No one goes to school late, Mr. Allyn," she said, pausing until it was obvious that Mr. Allyn still did not get it. *"The bus* is leaving." She cleared her throat and spoke with a different voice entirely: grandma replaced by a gruff director of military troops. "The deal would be off."

Mr. Allyn clapped his fingers. "Hurry along now, boy! Hup! Hup! Val, help him!"

Valendra ran into Stephen's rooms, zipped his suitcase shut, burst out, and tossed the case over the railing.

Before the gray bag hit the middle step and rolled to the living room, Mr. Allyn and Mrs. Allyn had each taken one of Gretel Lackluv's arms and began steering her toward the sliding glass doors and the backyard.

"It has been *so nice* to meet you, Mrs. Lackluv," said Mr. Allyn.

"You really must stop by," Mrs. Allyn said, before hearing her own false sincerity. She added quickly, "In June! When the boy—"

"Stephen," interjected Mr. Allyn.

"—returns from school. Yes, yes!"

"Well, I don't know if that will be possible," said Gretel Lackluv, casting her eyes at Stephen.

She caught him on the stairs.

Valendra was prodding him down with both hands. She released the claw-like grips that had been digging into the back of Stephen's arm. And she smiled.

Take-off

Mrs. Lackluv returned the happy expression.

"I haven't finished packing," said Stephen on the bottom step. He lifted his overly light suitcase.

Mrs. Allyn opened the sliding glass door.

"There really isn't any time, dear," said the silver-haired woman, her voice sweet once again.

Mr. Allyn ushered Gretel into the backyard.

At her presence, tiny lights—red, yellow, green, blue, purple, and white—danced to life around the giant disk. A gentle humming sound welcomed them all.

Val jostled Stephen across the living room. Then she caught him in her claws and pulled him close to her mouth. In whispers, she said, "Your aunt says we'll be able to write you. *Prepare to receive my demands!*"

She prodded him into the backyard.

The flying saucer held perfectly still. But the *lights* around the craft went crazy. They spun faster and faster around the circumference of the ship.

Within seconds, the lights blurred together. The glow became one color that Stephen could not exactly identify.

And then his mouth fell open. He *knew* the color, though he had never exactly thought of it as a color: Stephen could see Gretel's "car", but he could also see what was behind it. In fact, the saucer had become so colored by invisibility, if he hadn't known it was there he thought he probably would not have been able to see the ship at all.

"That's your car?"

Mr. Allyn laughed, just to air his amazement. "Call it that!"

Gretel Lackluv lifted her hand to take Stephen's bag, though she didn't look strong enough to actually lift it—were it packed. "We *must* go now."

* * ◖ ✝

So this was it.

Stephen Cowen was about to leave the Allyn Family at last. He would be returning. But he was *leaving*.

At the same time, Stephen just couldn't believe that he was going anywhere at all.

There is an invisible flying saucer in the backyard. A woman who says she's my aunt but then admits that she really isn't more than a distant relation is going to—what?—take me to school. And I haven't packed my favorite sleight of hand book, let alone said goodbye to the only friend I have in Harmon, California.

Stephen saw no ramp leading into the base of the flying saucer. In the movies, flying saucers always had ramps beneath them. The ship didn't have any kind of landing gear either. And it wasn't flattening the grass. It simply floated, just behind that blurry color of invisibility, about three feet off the ground.

To his credit, it occurred to Stephen Cowen that leaving the Allyns might actually be the *worst* thing that he could do right now.

Gretel Lackluv took the suitcase. She grasped his hand. Then she said, "Now . . . touch it!"

Against his better judgment, Stephen reached up for the spinning lights that he could no longer see.

There was a brief tingling in his fingers.

And then the backyard vanished.

HOME SWEET HOME

Gretel Lackluv maneuvered the gray suitcase beside a tall leather chair. The walls were painted white, but the coat had chipped away in places revealing the previous teal color. Roses sat in a vase on a stand beside the chair. The room smelled faintly of other blooming flowers and spring pollen.

"Please," she said, "sit. I'll get you some tea."

Tea? I'm STARVING. The words passed somewhere in the back of Stephen's mind. They didn't come anywhere near his voice box.

The ceiling was white, though a darker hue than the walls. A dome light brightened the room from one side of the lamp; Stephen noticed that one bulb had burned out.

Gretel Lackluv flicked the switch of a desk light standing on a square end table beside the second of four chairs. The chairs faced a tiny black and white cathode-tube television mounted over the heater pressed against one wall.

The second light had been unnecessary, though it put a smile on her face. There was a window. Sheer drapes were pulled to each side. Through the glass, Stephen saw morning sunbeams spilling across a golden field of grain offset by ancient maple trees. Spring leaves were budding from the branches.

Stephen couldn't sit.

Gretel Lackluv had no problem. She took to a thin chair that seemed just perfect for her oddly narrow and loosely flabby shape. Stephen thought she might have lost a couple of hundred pounds recently, and might be busy trying to lose another seventy-five more—hence the tea instead of solid grub.

She lifted a bit of cross-stitch needlework. In the cloth, Stephen saw a red robin carrying an earthworm in its beak. The worm bent over backward in terror. Of being eaten, Stephen thought.

In fact, that's about how Stephen felt.

"Oh!" said the old woman, seeing him there, as if he only now arrived in her home. Certainly, he felt that way.

Stephen wondered if he was dreaming. He wanted it to be a dream. He never really understood how people on television always thought that they might be dreaming. Stephen knew he wasn't dreaming.

But he also wasn't entirely frightened either.

After all, he had been moving from one strange place to another all his life, from one good set of parents to one twisted set, back and forth, over and over, endlessly. He was only twelve years old. But Stephen felt hardened against radical change. He had never known anything in life to be consistent.

Except, maybe, reality.

And none of this seemed real anymore.

Gretel Lackluv jumped to her feet. Stephen had the impression that she would morph again into the harsher voice that he had seen hiding inside of her, that she might actually rush forth and shove him out of the—out of what, exactly? The room? The . . . ship?

"Tea!" she said. And she left.

In careful stages, Stephen followed her into the kitchen.

The kitchen smelled of cookies and generally matched the living room. Yellow flower patterns decorated a tablecloth, the drapery, and even a hand towel hanging from a knob below the sink.

Stephen saw what looked like a paper plate glued high to one wall and painted over with white that went with the walls. He recognized the ornament instantly: the Greenbergs had had the same strange decoration over their stove. They had explained that, once upon a time, there had been a black cast-iron oven where the stove sat. A stovepipe had run from the back of the oven, up, and into the wall where that "plate" was. The plate wasn't paper at all, but metal, and it capped an old hole that led into a chimney.

"I'm really hungry," he managed to say.

"Would you like some biscuits?" she said as she filled a smiling golden teapot with water at a nicked porcelain sink.

"Yes, please." Biscuits would do. At this point, cardboard was starting to sound palatable.

She waved a hand to one counter. "Right over there, love. Help yourself?"

Stephen wasn't sure if that was an invitation or a question. He was too lost to continue the conversation anyway.

Weren't they in a hurry?

He crossed the kitchen and lifted the lid on a cookie jar. Oatmeal chocolate chip rose in heaps before his eyes. "How many may I have?"

She put the water on the stove, turned a knob, and waited for the tick-tick-tick-tick sound of a gas burner lighting. After the flame appeared with a quick, little burst, she turned and smoothed down her floral skirt. "As many as you would like."

Stephen politely took three. When she turned back to the small living room, he grabbed as many as his other hand could hold without dropping. He put all these into a scooped curl of his t-shirt and began swallowing them as fast as possible.

They were delicious. And filling. He took another—smaller— handful and hid them in his shirt. Then he tried to pretend he wasn't hording any at all.

Before he reached the living room, Stephen had devoured three more and was busy munching a fourth without even chewing it all the way.

"May I . . . may I ask you a question?"

"Certainly," said the old woman.

He was going to say, *Weren't we getting onto your ship?* As strange as it sounds, the answer seemed obvious already. So he chose a better question. "Where are we?"

"Oh, I know it is a little confusing. But you *know.* Don't you, Stephen Crown?"

"Inside . . . your ship." It only occurred to Stephen after he had answered that Mrs. Lackluv had called him Stephen Crown, the exact error that Mr. Bluntwasp made.

"Precisely." She returned to her needlework.

"It doesn't look like a flying saucer anymore."

"Flying saucer!" she said. "How quaint." When she looked up a minute later, she said, "You think my transport should look different? I rather get pleasure from this. It is *mine* after all. You might decorate your own differently."

"Have we left the Allyn's backyard?"

"Of course."

"So we are *going*. Who is driving?"

"I am."

"How did we get inside?"

She sighed. "Do I look like a teacher to you? So many questions! You'll learn everything you need in school." She waggled a finger at him. "Just don't become a dropout!"

Over the next few silent minutes, he stood at the window and finished his hoard of cookies. Thankfully, he found that he had room for more. But now he was thirsty.

The hot water whistled on the stove as if it had heard his thoughts.

"Ah!" she said. "Ready for tea?"

He followed her and sat at the kitchen table. "If you're not really my aunt, what should I call you then?"

She smiled at him for a moment, then scooped dry herbs into two little teacups. While pouring water that looked too hot to drink into each cup, she said, "Mrs. Lackluv, if you like."

Eyes circular, Stephen jumped to the cookies. "May I have some more?"

"Have as many as you wish, dearie."

Stephen opened the jar again, telling himself that he would take only one and maybe count how many there were left so that he could brace himself for the inevitable scolding.

Rich peanut butter cookies rose in a mountain all the way to the top.

He gawked at them. Then he put the top back on the cookie jar.

"I thought . . . you were rushing me to a bus stop."

"Won't you have tea?"

"Oh. I'm waiting for it to cool. Unless, I mean, we're in a hurry."

"You wouldn't want to drink this too quickly. There are glasses in the cupboard above the sink, if you need water. We almost missed the transport from Earth. Ship has told me that they are waiting. But only because I had filed a flight plan. *Me thinks* the administration won't be happy."

Mrs. Lackluv sipped her tea and shut her eyes.

Stephen fetched a glass and tasted the cold water from the sink. Like the cookies, it was perfect—almost better than perfect. It was as if "ship", as Mrs. Lackluv called it, was striving diligently to please him.

"The administration?" he said.

"If we are late reaching the transport, then we are *all* likely to miss the school bus over Proxima Centauri. You don't want to miss the school bus, do you? Ah! We're on final approach. Get your suitcase!"

"We are?" Stephen looked at the young branches swaying in the breeze outside the kitchen window.

"Do you want to see?"

"Yes, please."

"You *are* a polite boy, Stephen."

"I've learned it pays to have manners."

"Go the window. And hang onto something. Your first time, it can be a little shocking."

There was nothing but a chest freezer near the window. Stephen grasped the polished steel handle of the freezer door and rested the other on the windowsill.

The view through the glass faded into darkness.

If the sight of fields and trees had seemed real, the view of the blue planet covered with the faintest hint of swirling clouds seemed twice as real.

He recognized the planet from photographs and computer animation. What he did not recognize was how the planet with faint rings was listing slowly from the bottom of his view like the arm of an enormous time piece, up the side to 9:00, overhead—noon, or midnight—and then back around towards 3:00, 4:00, 5:00.

His gut figured it out first. He grabbed his tummy. "We're spinning."

"That we are."

"Neptune?"

"Uranus," said Gretel Lackluv.

"Of course. I think I'm getting seasick."

The field brilliantly reappeared. At first, the splash of sunlight over grass and trees didn't look real at all, no matter the illusion's perfection. Then it did. And then—at the thought of *illusions*—Stephen smiled and felt steady. "It's like magic."

"What is magic but a strange thing not yet explained to the one who finds it magical?"

"Like the way your ship became invisible *using* lights? And the way we got into your—how we got into Ship from the Allyn's backyard."

"Well done!"

"So . . . I know I will learn it in school, but how did we do it? I must know. All I did was touch the side."

"Have you learned about the Commutative Property of Multiplication in your elementary school?"

Stephen warmed red in the face. He didn't quite remember the lesson, but he said, "Sure. Mrs. Martin taught us that."

Intelligently and patiently, Mrs. Lackluv nodded. "A x B = B x A. The A can move, but the answer remains the same: 2 x 3 = 3 x 2. Correct?"

"Yeah."

"Well. *You* are just a variable, a number, or more accurately a combination of numbers."

"Oh, you mean like Beam me up, Scotty! *Star Trek*. Transporting. Stuff like that."

The old woman cringed, showing off, to his surprise, a perfect set of white teeth. "Barbaric, but something like that, yes."

"You have a spaceship and you don't like science fiction?"

"Well . . . *Star Trek* transporters supposedly work by disassembling a person, molecule by molecule, atom by atom, and then reassembling atoms and molecules in a different location so that they match the exact mathematical combination that the person had been in prior to being disassembled."

"Huh?"

"There are only two problems with this idea of transportation. One problem is that if we really did that to you, you would be taken apart—you would cease to exist. Then, a duplicate of you would be fashioned elsewhere that would go about living your life, with your memories—it would be you, in nearly every respect. It would be you to everyone else. Just not to you. In short, the process would begin with your death."

"Gulp," Stephen said, just to be funny, because he didn't really comprehend what she was going on about. And it didn't sound good anyway. "So what's the second problem?"

"No one's been able to get it to work. So . . . it's just science fiction." Suddenly she stood up. "Your bag! Run! It's time."

Almost as soon as Stephen reached his suitcase, the walls around him changed and Stephen experienced the Commutative Property of Real Magic for the second time that day.

STEPHEN GETS AN EARFUL

This time, Stephen felt the movement of his body as it traveled from Mrs. Lackluv's ship into what she called the Earth Transport. The commute was quick. The transfer from the first location to the second was so fast, in fact, that he could only feel the experience in hindsight.

It was like getting sucked through a straw. Only his body hadn't gotten any smaller. He was only aware of countless tiny things passing through him as he passed through the walls of both ships. Or maybe even that was his imagination.

The light changed around him. Instead of a happy little kitchen and a bright living room with four chairs and a beautiful view, Stephen saw the dim lobby of something like an inn.

Only, there wasn't a main desk, concierge, or even a porter to take his bags. There were, along the walls, candlesticks holding up flames without candles. The hall was made of dark gray stone cut it rough patterns. Giant rugs covered the floor with quadrilateral patterns in faded colors. And plants grew along the walls, straight out of ringed holes filled with soil in the floor.

"This way, Stephen," mumbled Mrs. Lackluv, almost reverently. She swept past him, smoothing down her skirt once more, and making for steps on the far side of the entryway.

Stephen's stomach quivered, maybe from staring too long out her kitchen window at the rotating shape of Uranus, more likely from passing for the second time in less than twenty minutes through solid spaceship walls. The thought alone upset his insides.

He wondered what the transport looked like from outside. Another saucer? A rocket, this time? Something more exotic, like one of George Lucas's creations or one of the latest *Star Trek* vessels?

They went up the steps and moved along corridors that seemed to slant upward or downward. When he asked Mrs. Lackluv about this she said, "Actually, we are not going up or down at all—apart from the steps. Your brain is trying to process the sensations of artificial gravity.

"Shouldn't we be floating away from the floor if we are really in space? Why are there no elevators or staircases? Why is everything here so flat?"

"Did I say I was a school teacher, Stephen?"

The corridors smelled of candle smoke and wet dog hair. Only Mrs. Lackluv smelled of sterile chemicals, a familiar scent that Stephen couldn't quite place. Better than dog hair. But she was also strong and repellent.

They walked for five minutes before seeing anyone. Stephen dragged his bag, which wasn't hard because he and Val probably filled it with nothing but socks. He tried to remember what he'd thrown in before the entire universe had turned upside down.

A dark-haired kid about five years older than Stephen exited a room on the left of their passage. His mouth was stained red with the strawberry sucker that he busily worked between his teeth.

He spoke a couple of words at Stephen. The language had to be Chinese or something from another planet. To Stephen it didn't make any difference.

Mrs. Lackluv leaned forward as if to catch the teenager's arm. She stopped an inch from his blue Adidas sweatshirt. "Pardon us, my dear. Shouldn't linguistics be around here?"

Stephen lifted his eyebrows. "You're lost?"

She ignored him.

But the kid didn't. With intelligent eyes, he looked at Stephen and said . . . something. Must have been funny. The guy chuckled. Stephen still didn't understand.

The boy told Stephen one other thing, and apparently found the subject even more amusing. His face smiled until his eyes squinted so much, Stephen doubted he could even see anymore.

Stephen hoped the kid couldn't, because he could feel his face warm with blush.

Then the boy looked at Mrs. Lackluv and rattled off a few more ticking and whistling lines, pointing behind him.

"Thank you, dearly," she said. "Let's go."

They made a left at the next corridor.

"This is the Earth Transport?"

"Yes, Stephen."

"It looks like a castle."

"Really?" she said, amused. "Have you been inside many castles?"

That seemed a callous thing to say. Stephen lowered his brow and pinched his mouth shut. He decided to avoid speaking altogether, if his inquiries were only going to continue to embarrass him.

They stopped in a room filled with plants, where a sign on the wall displayed characters that were both vaguely familiar (where they the same as some of those books at Mr. Bluntwasp's house?) and totally alien.

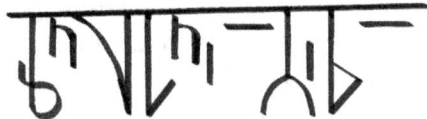

Bushes grew from pots this time along every wall. Some rose all the way to where they pressed against the ceiling, spreading their leaves and their green aroma in a canopy.

In the center of the room, an old woman with spectacles on the edge of her nose sat at a wide desk covered with papers.

She looked up, smiled, and then proceeded to make bird sounds. Or rather, she was clearly *talking*, making fine, natural expressions with her face, but the language she spoke came out in squawks that made Stephen think for a second that she was making fun of Mrs. Lackluv.

Until she looked Stephen in the eye.

Only then did he spot and understand her sincerity and loving warmth. It was like looking into the eyes of the mother he always dreamed to have one day. He also saw her youth. She wasn't old at all—though her hair shined with beautiful silver.

Stephen's guide leaned over the papers on the desk and said, "Brian Bumhandel."

The nice woman scanned one sheet with letters moving up the page like credits at the end of a movie.

Only, the letters looked like they had been handwritten—Stephen even saw smudges.

If the paper was some kind of computer screen, it was the best imitation of paper he had ever seen.

The lady behind the desk dropped her finger on a line of cursive that Stephen could not read, even though he had seen that script before—his brain refused to tell him where.

"Information overload," he said, without realizing that he had spoken out loud.

The nice woman looked at him, perfect understanding in her face. She said something briefly. Then she raised a hand to Stephen, then to a chair set beside one of the plants.

Mrs. Lackluv did not need to translate, but she did so anyway. "Have a seat."

"All right."

"Try to relax."

As soon as Stephen put himself into the chair, he became aware of a breeze that he did not feel. His brain told him it was a breeze because the leaves on either side of his head were moving, rustling together.

"The plants will do everything. You will understand in a moment."

"The *plants?*"

That's when he knew there wasn't a wind at all. Why would there be?

(Why would there be stone walls inside of a spaceship?)

Leaves gently settled, one by one, around his head. They encircled the back of his skull, covered his hair on all sides, and then lowered themselves over his forehead.

Stephen's breath quickened. He knew he was panicking, afraid that the leaves would continue to drop over his face until he couldn't breathe.

"Just relax," Mrs. Lackluv said again, her voice a little more demanding.

"And . . . that," said another voice, "should . . . do it. Brian?"

Stephen didn't say anything. He had shut his eyes in anticipation of the leaves and branches smothering him. He opened one eye just a crack.

Both women were patiently staring at him, Mrs. Lackluv a little more anxious than the woman at the desk.

"Do you understand her now?"

"What's happened?"

The woman at the desk gleefully said, "We've mapped the linguistic center and lingua-perceptual cortex. You understand me?"

"Not at all."

"But," said Mrs. Lackluv, taking his bag from the floor and pulling Stephen to his feet, "it *does* sound like Mrs. Hearty is speaking to you in English now, doesn't it?"

"Well—yes."

"I need to get the poor boy some food in a hurry," she said to Mrs. Hearty. "We barely made it to the transport in time."

"It was nice to meet you, Brian," said Mrs. Hearty as Mrs. Lackluv forced him to the door.

"Brian?" said Stephen.

But Mrs. Lackluv was already speaking over him. "I will be *right back*, Mrs. Hearty. To finish paperwork and get directions."

"That will be fine," said Mrs. Hearty.

"I think it is about time you met the other children from Earth!"

"Why did she call me Brian?"

Mrs. Lackluv stopped him against the stone of the corridor and looked both ways. "Stephen Crown, you are going to have to trust me about this, all right? I won't lie to you. But you *must* do as I tell you, for the time being. All right?"

"And why do you keep saying *Stephen Crown* instead of—?"

"Until the time is right, you *cannot* tell anyone your real name. Do you understand?"

"No."

"But you will! Until I tell you, your name is Brian Bumhandel."

"Bumhandel? You've got to be kidding me."

THE KIDS FROM EARTH

"I'll complete the formalities. Then we'll see you to your sleeping quarters. While you are waiting, why don't you get to know your classmates. Make some friends."

"Will I understand Chinese now?"

Mrs. Lackluv laughed. "Ah, here we are."

They entered a hall with a high ceiling and a grand fireplace that was so large, a small boy Stephen's size might easily explore the inside of it without bending at the waist. Pillowed couches held bags, suitcases, and bodies.

"The kids from Earth?" said Stephen as he loitered at the entrance. For another minute, they watched boys and girls Stephen's age and older talking, laughing, ignoring one another, sitting on the loveseats, wandering around the couches, lying on the lounge chairs, pretending to be asleep.

The floor dropped six steps below the wide doorway where Stephen and Mrs. Lackluv stood. There was another arched entrance directly across the hall, matching this one, and three along the left wall mirroring three more on the right.

"What is this place?"

"Call it a waiting room." She squeezed his shoulder. "Wait for me here."

It was like a first day of school all over again. The place didn't look anything like an academy of learning, but then it also did not resemble a transport of any kind that he could imagine.

People looked up at Stephen. In some cases, their gazes passed him by as if he didn't exist. Others fixed their eyes on him and spoke to their friends, before their curiosity waned.

Stephen found it hard to look into anyone's eyes. He dragged his suitcase down the six steps to the floor and followed the rugs to the nearest unoccupied couch.

His muscles were really beginning to ache, everywhere: his legs from running across Harmon, California, his back and arms from packing hardbound books all day.

He collapsed into the pillows. A sigh escaped him. He shut his eyes and contemplated ignoring all other surprises by giving in to sleep.

"Comfortable, are you?"

Stephen lifted his heavy eyelids.

A boy with raven-black eyes sneered over him. Behind him stood four other boys, a private army.

"Sorry?" said Stephen.

"Obviously." Raven Eyes snickered at his friends. When he turned back to Stephen, his smile melted away. "I claimed that couch before the transport reached Earth, you know. If you had come up with the other spikes and barbarians, you'd know that. So I take it that *you're* the reason we are only now leaving orbit."

"I—I'm ... new."

Raven Eyes leaned threateningly over the couch. "*Obviously.* Get off."

Stephen held his breath. Then he grabbed his gray suitcase and rolled away before the threats in their eyes turned into something worse.

Finding no other free places to sit, Stephen made one of his own. He parked beside the fireplace, slid down the wall, and snuggled beside the hearth with his luggage.

He hurt inside.

He no longer wanted to get away from the Allyns. He longed for Mr. Bluntwasp again.

You have a friend here, the old man had said.

And that made Stephen think of the golden gift.

In his grief, Stephen wondered if he had packed the little disk while hurrying out of the house. Then he remembered. He touched the circle bulging through the heavy cloth of his jeans.

As he reached for the absconder in his pocket, Stephen felt someone watching him. Or maybe he just noticed the boy with the blond hair examining him from the nearest couch facing the fireplace.

Immediately, the boy looked away. He started whistling nonsense. Then he peeked in Stephen's direction again.

"Hello," said Stephen.

The boy's pursed lips froze and went silent, like he'd been caught kissing the air. He looked over his shoulder to see if there was someone standing behind him. He gazed back at Stephen.

Stephen waved.

"Me?" the boy said. "Oh. Hello." He sank into the cushions as if they could surround him and protect him from being seen.

At least the kid had a sofa. He shared this with an enormous carpetbag the color of orange and brown leaves gone to rot.

He summoned some courage. "This is my first time on a transport." He scanned the room. "If you ask me, it's all kind of freaky. I mean," he pointed, "*fireplaces?* On a spaceship? And you should have seen the thing that brought me here!"

Stephen grinned. "Let me guess: living room and a kitchen?"

The boy furrowed his brow. "Why wouldn't it have a living room and a kitchen? No. It had *three* fireplaces! Like the driver had a thing for fire. Did you notice all the candles?"

"Candlesticks without candles, you mean?"

The kid leaned forward from the edge of the sofa to keep from being overheard. "If you ask me, I think these space jockeys have a thing for *fire*. Must be the newest fad off-world."

Stephen nodded, only mildly confused. Still . . . it was nice to see a friendly face.

"I'm Brian Boar, by the way."

"Ste—Brian," Stephen answered, not sure why he said the false name at all. Seemed more than strange. "Brian Bumhandel."

In his gut, Stephen didn't trust Mrs. Lackluv, no matter how kind and old she seemed to be.

"Ah! Brian and Brian. Two BBs. I guess that makes us something like blood brothers."

"What are blood brothers?"

"Friends who used to cut their hands, then slap them together."

"That sounds both painful and disgusting."

"I only meant it figuratively. Where are you from?"

"California."

"Really? I'm from South Dakota. Ever been to Disneyland?"

"Sure."

"Lucky mutt. I'll go to Disneyland someday. I know it's not as good as Wildworld, but they say that it *is* the happiest place on Earth. That's got to count for something. You'll see. I'll go there someday."

"I'm sure you will."

"Well, come have a seat. Unless you wanted to crash on the floor against a cold wall."

Stephen gladly moved to the softer choice. He looked around for food but didn't see any. "So we're the kids from Earth?"

"Oh, about half of us. Anyone from Alpha Prime gets dropped off at the Earth Transport. Those rich snobs won't even send their kids to school in their own transports—my sister says they're *very* efficient."

Stephen craned his neck to peer at the four boys leaning on the couch claimed by that raven-eyed bully.

"Oh, I see you already know some of them!" said Brian Boar. "We should feel sorry for them, I guess. But when you look into the eyes of Cutter Hertmor and his cuddly crew, I find it a bit difficult to have charity."

"They don't exactly go out of their way to build alliances, do they?"

A girl engaged in conversation with others tripped over Stephen's outstretched legs. She fell straight onto Brian's lap.

The other girls snickered and continued walking and talking.

"Thanks a lot," she said, scrambling to her feet. She stood and fixed her navy-blue blouse, which had come untucked from her white skirt.

Stephen smiled at her when she didn't dart away. "I'm sorry."

"No big deal," she said quickly, still fixing some flaw around her belt that Stephen couldn't see.

"Your friends are leaving," Stephen said, trying to be helpful—and make her go away.

She wasn't ugly—silver haired, much like the rest of the kids in the room, though hers was darker and matched her gray eyes in a way that made them look like cold metal. She had a darkness in her expression that warned him of trouble. He guessed she was from—what was that planet Brian mentioned?—Alpha Prime.

"Them? I don't know them. That's why they are busy laughing at me."

They shot quick looks over their shoulders. And they *were* laughing at her.

Brian mustered his courage. "Y-you were walking with them."

"I was just listening to all the hub-bub. Trying to ask questions."

When she looked up at last, she didn't look so cold. But she also looked intrigued by their obvious lack of information.

"Haven't you heard? Someone's hacked the data matrix. There's an *imposter* on board."

STANDING CENTER STAGE

Brian looked at the girl, at Stephen, and back at the girl. "What's an imposter?"

"Someone who isn't who they say they are."

"Oh." He looked at Stephen.

Stephen couldn't breathe. He forced himself to sit as still as possible, petrified by the idea that he might not be acting normal. But he had no clue what "normal" should look like in a place like this.

He *wanted* this to be a dream. He wanted to wake up and say, *Whew! That was weird.*

The girl went on. "They are saying that when he's found, they will dump him on the first hospitable planet that we pass."

"You mean he doesn't have to go to school?" Brian said, eyes wide. He raised his hand and lifted his voice. "It's me! I'm the imposter! Drop me at Wildworld and leave me there until summer."

A few of the kids in the giant room chuckled. A couple more told him to shove various articles of clothing into his mouth. *Which* articles, however, became a matter of debate.

Stephen sank even more deeply into the couch as he felt eyes swiveling, checking him out, then swiveling away, searching for the real imposter.

The girl lifted her pretty eyebrows in high arches. "That's not very funny you know. On Earth you can be arrested for *joking* that there is a threat in an airport or a bomb on a plane. Did you know that?"

"Did I know that?" said Brian. "You're not from Earth, I take it?"

Stephen tried to change the subject, again while attempting to appear "normal." He opened his mouth, but the girl responded to Brian too quickly.

"Actually, I am from Earth. Tokyo, Japan."

"Oh. You don't look Japanese," Brian said.

"And you've dyed your silver hair blond, I see." She turned to Stephen. "You have not—an obvious sign that you originate off-world."

Stephen had opened his mouth again, but her words threw him.

"You're from Alpha Prime then?" Brian said.

The strangest thing happened to her face: she relaxed her eyes with pride, then darted them around in shame. Also, with one hand she swept her hair over her shoulder, and she started blushing. "I was moved to Alpha Prime last year."

Stephen finally joined the conversation, speaking quickly. "I don't like moving. I've moved around a lot in my life. Sometimes it's cool to tell people where you are from. Other times it's embarrassing. Depends on where you're from."

The girl's face continued to change colors as she tried to hide her tension. "Well, as I said, I'm from Alpha Prime. And I'm from Earth. So I know a thing or two—and *you* shouldn't joke about being the one they are looking for. You'll likely end up in a white room where they will question you for the rest of the trip, trying to ascertain the truth."

"*Ascertain* what?" Brian said with confusion. Then he nodded and grinned at Stephen when he suddenly understood what the girl had been saying. "Oh! You're like the poor girl from the wrong side of the tracks who's moved to the rich side of town, right? Bet you don't have many friends."

The girl made two fists. She clamped her teeth together, then covered them with her lips in a tight little ball that promptly turned white, and stormed away.

"Oh . . . well," Brian said. He looked sad. He nudged Stephen, "To be honest, I've never been very good at making friends myself. Especially girlfriends." Then he smiled. "But I am very good at making enemies!"

"Not exactly something to be proud about."

"I know. At least she isn't thinking that one of us is the imposter."

"Would it matter?" Stephen said with a shiver.

"Are you kidding? Last year Mr. Jerund, my teacher, taught us about World War II—said that during Nazi Germany times, if a neighbor pointed you out to the cops for any reason, you just disappeared in the night. They just took you away." Brian frowned. "Or maybe that was a book he was talking about. Mr. Jerund was a babbler. Anyway, if that girl thought you were the imposter, or me, the transport authorities would probably take you without a ruckus and make you disappear. *Ascertain* stuff, you know."

Stephen was trembling. He tried to stop. "What's a ruckus?"

An older girl in black leggings, a long white shirt that might have come from some frilly bygone era, and the most dazzling eye makeup that Stephen had ever seen, walked into the center of an arched entrance close to their right. With a large, black microphone in one hand, she called for everyone's attention with the words, "Why's everyone so glum?"

Brian covered his face like a man afraid to be seen. "*That* is a ruckus."

Stephen sat up. The beat of electronic drums began to pulse through unseen speakers overhead. The sofa vibrated with each throb. An acoustic guitar picked up the rhythm and added life. A keyboard gave the music color, as the girl continued.

She laughed into her mike. "It's school, guys, not your private execution. Who wants to add a little commotion to this motion?"

Hands went into the air. A few people clapped. A couple of girls and boys whistled. A lot more just looked in her direction and looked away.

For Stephen, electricity charged the air.

The girl was beautiful. Seventeen years old, maybe sixteen. Instead of silvery hair, long brown curls rolled over her shoulders and down the small of her back. The brown was highlighted with what appeared to be natural red tints offset by a hint of blonde that made her hair sparkle like gold in the light of so many flames.

Standing Center Stage

A smile drew her face into an image from which Stephen could not look away: high cheekbones, gorgeous lips, touches of hot gold at each earlobe, around her neck, over her fingers.

She started clapping. Hypnotized, the crowd followed, led by Stephen.

"That's right!" she said, catching the beat. "Here we go!"

She started to sing.

Though he didn't quite understand the lyrics, Stephen fell instantly in love.

Tip me out and splash me down,
You're gonna make me run around,
I know the game,
I know the lies,
It's just the way
Young hearts'll fly.

You chase me here,
You chase me there,
I'm running but I want you near,
The game's afoot,
I'm aching now,
Won't you please stop faking—

I run for you,
I run for you,
I run all night,
I know the truth,

I want you fast,
You know I do
Please make it last,
I'm dying too.

Her feet slipped back, forth, and around as she spun and danced to the pop song that came from her perfect throat. Stage lights from nowhere played over the curves of her face, her shoulders, and her wavy hair.

She continued.

At the side of Brian's head, Stephen's issued a breathless, "Who IS she?"

"I know. Disgusting!" Brian sat with arms folded tightly. "She waits all summer for this moment. Says it's the only time she can really 'shine.' And the words? Do you hear? They mean NOTHING. Erk! Just kill me now, please."

Stephen found no more energy for speaking. He simply stared at the girl. His heart leaped.

Then the impossible happened.

The girl lifted her long lashes and her attention landed *right on Stephen*. And she came to life even more, if that was possible, beaming with utmost appreciation and love.

At the end of the song, applause bounced off the walls. Even if Brian wasn't clapping along with them.

Stephen clapped loud enough for them both.

"Nice of you," Brian said in his ear.

"Do you know who she is?" With a steadily sinking heart, Stephen watched the girl signal at the crowd and turn. The embroidered hem of her shirt lifted and fell like a mini dress. She spun around again, kissed her fingers, and then waved that kiss at the crowd, radiantly, departing as powerfully as she had arrived.

"That is Mimi."

Out of the blue, the idea of going to this faraway private school, with all of the weirdness around him, didn't seem so bad. Not if Mimi was going to be there. "Mimi?"

"Yes," Brian said. "Mimi. My sister."

16

THE NEAR-DEATH EXPERIENCE OF BRIAN BOAR

A hand landed on the back of Stephen's neck. Fingernails bit into his skin. "Let's go."

Stephen jumped.

He was, after all, the imposter. He knew it.

They *weren't* taking him back to the Allyns. They were going to dump him off on some rock, the likes of which he probably hadn't even seen in science fiction movies. He would be homeless in a cold universe—no more bad foster parents, no more good ones.

He would not make it to school with Brian and (gasp!) *Mimi*.

His heart stopped. He leaned forward, away from the claw.

Then he saw Gretel Lackluv's grin. "Oh! Poor child, did I startle you?"

"Yes."

"Please forgive me." She ran her hands over an opened booklet of loose papers approximately the size of a paperback novel. The letters, that foreign Sanskrit stuff, moved on the page. Even with the translator plant thing working for him, he couldn't read them.

"What's that?"

"Your accommodations on the transport. May I?" She pointed to the spot on the couch occupied by Brian's carpetbag.

Brian nodded. "Sure." He moved the bag onto his feet and held it against his legs.

To Brian, Mrs. Lackluv said, "Thank you, young man. Might you be an Alpha, like *Brian*, here?"

"Yeah," the real Brian said, lighting up again at the idea of a friend sharing his first name.

Stephen shrank, expecting transportation marshals to burst from the crowd and arrest him at any moment. Gretel Lackluv had put him into this position, after all. She was at least as guilty as he was.

His fake aunt squeezed her hips between Brian and the armrest.

Brian cringed while Mrs. Lackluv messed up the words, like an explosion of scurrying black ants, on the fold of sheets in her hand and started mumbling to herself.

Brian took this moment to rotate his head toward Stephen and speak from the side of his mouth. "Is it just me, or does her hair smell like nail polish?"

Stephen widened his eyes and nodded quickly.

"Ah!" said the old woman. "Are you familiar with memory paper?" she asked Brian.

He shook his head, trying not to inhale.

"Splendid," Mrs. Lackluv said to both boys. "I'll be your first off-world teacher!" She leaned closer, placing the sheets of strange writing over Brian's knees.

He held his breath. His face began to redden, then shadow into purple blotches as she talked, mostly to Stephen.

"This figure that looks like a compass controls one's movement through the data loaded onto this page of the paper. Consider a word processing program back home. Ever use one?"

"I've seen some," said Stephen, heartily ashamed that he had never been allowed to touch a computer outside of school—and every school he went to had all sorts of helpful reading, writing, and testing programs that they used. Nothing like the word processing and spreadsheet programs that he had seen grownups use. But he wasn't dumb.

Mrs. Lackluv indicated the four arrows pointing away from the center of the circle. "Press the right arrow, and one—um—turns the page. The left arrow brings you back to the previous page."

She paused and examined both boys to confirm understanding.

Stephen nodded on cue. "Forward and back. Got it."

Brian still wasn't breathing. Stephen thought that the poor kid might die.

"The *down* arrow, now that brings one to the next piece of writing altogether. The up arrow carries the reader to the previous document." She paused again, checking the boys.

Brian, whose eyes had rolled back in his head, straightened them, grinning politely, and nodded like Stephen.

She continued. "Press the center of the circle, and a list of other functions appear here. Can you both see?"

"Yes, but . . . but I can't read this."

"Of course you can't. You won't study Uniscript until your classes begin." Mrs. Lackluv giggled briefly. "Press the circle and hold your finger on it for two seconds, and the contents of the paper are displayed. From here, one might navigate to each of the documents at one's leisure."

"So this paper is really a kind of computer."

"Yes."

A logical idea struck him. He tried to be quick, as Brian's skin was turning blue now. "Is there is a function that translates the—the Uniscript into English? I've seen that kind of thing on the Internet. For Earth languages, I mean."

Mrs. Lackluv pulled her chin into her neck. "Well, that would be a feature on beginner-grade memory paper. This is the grownup kind. Unnecessary, if you've gone to school. You see, English is one of the most complicated languages in the Universe: a mixture of Latin, German, Greek, Dutch, Spanish, and a dozen other Earth languages. Uniscript is far more mathematical, logical, simple to—is your friend going to sleep?"

Brian's eyelids had dropped. His chest wasn't rising and falling. Stephen thought that he might have died.

"Maybe he's just getting too squished on the couch."

She stood. "Pardon!" She fanned herself.

Brian's eyes opened, his chest moved, and a healthy color returned to his skin. "I'm sorry," he said. "It's just been such a big . . . day. You know."

"Of course, dear!"

Stephen rose from the couch. "You were going to say something else."

"Right. Your accommodations." She played a finger over the little compass on the paper until she was ready to show him some completely unhelpful chicken scratch. "There. You will be staying in . . . New York, this evening."

"Huh?"

"Oh!" said Brian. "That's where I'm bunking for the trip too!"

"Splendid." She tapped again on the dial. A map appeared. "Shall I guide you to your apartments?"

Stephen looked at Brian and thought he might faint if he had to wander through the halls of the Earth Transport in a cloud of Gretel Lackluv's alcoholic perfume.

"Actually, could I borrow that paper? I'd like to see if I can use the map myself."

A spark seemed to flash behind the old woman's eyes. One corner of her mouth rose. It was an expression that an evil trickster might use if everything was going according to plan.

She handed him the paper. "You will get your own paper soon enough—Alpha grade, as I said. But you may use this until we reach Proxima Centauri."

"The school bus?"

She stared at him. "Yes . . . Brian," she said to Stephen. "You are so very bright, aren't you!"

"Thank you," he said, looking at the paper to avoid the awkward gratification on her face.

"Well. If anyone asks you, a copy of your credentials can be found on the paper. Tickets. Admission certificates."

Brian suddenly straightened himself. "Um, shall we get going?" He was peering through the room as another girl was weaving her way straight at them, like a torpedo.

"Yeah," said Stephen.

They hurried to the nearest exit.

BUNKING WITH BULLIES

The map led Stephen and Brian directly to their accommodations, distracting them along the way from those who might have caused them trouble. The few catcalls and slurs—"Hey, look at the newbies!"—were easily ignored by the two boys.

The rooms were nothing special. Nothing at all. Brian said, "This is it? You'd think there would be something nicer to look at."

Beds filled the narrow hall. Bunks rose to the ceiling, five high, thin ladders running up the sides. They circled the walls, filled the floor, so that aisles ran between the sleeping towers. Each bed had a little curtain that could be closed wherever there was an open side.

"Here's mine," Stephen said, matching a number on the memory paper with a bunk three beds from the floor and standing in the middle of the room. He couldn't imagine getting any shuteye there: it just seemed too exposed.

"Great," said Brian, wandering. "Guess I need to find mine." He pulled a scrap of paper from his carpetbag—his luggage looked something like a punching bag made out of an old rug.

They weren't alone. Other boys mumbled, loitering at the sides of bunk beds. Some had crawled inside and were busy taping up pictures of family or girls, which made Stephen feel oddly queasy, or things that looked like sleds flying over moons and stars.

Stephen tossed his suitcase onto his bed and pulled the tan curtain shut. Then he rushed after Brian. "So these beds are like our private rooms?"

Brian was examining his splotchy blue ink and terrible handwriting. He scanned the posted numbers and letters, then the room like it was a maze instead of a collection of resting places. "Yeah. Home sweet home."

"But for how long. Some of these guys look like they're moving in."

"I don't know. How far away is Proxima Centauri?"

"Far enough that we need a bed, I guess. Hey, if I knew how far away the school bus was, would you know how long it would take us to get there?" Stephen felt a like a dummy having to ask such a question, but then he felt like the only kid onboard who was new to all this flying in space stuff.

"Cripes, are you kidding me?" Brian flopped his carpetbag on the lowest bunk before him.

Stephen grinned. "You don't have to climb? Lucky man!"

"No he isn't," said a familiar voice behind them. "I realize that you are unfamiliar to off-world rules, spike, but that lower bunk is mine."

Brian turned around and clammed up. He even turned as white as the shell of a clam.

Cutter Hertmor and his four thugs stood in a curved dam, trapping the two boys from Earth against the bunks. He sneered at Stephen. "Do you have a comprehension problem?"

"I was only wondering how off-world rules give you a bed that isn't yours. It *isn't* yours, is it?"

Cutter stepped forward enough to allow Stephen to smell his bitter-coffee breath. He wasn't any taller than Stephen, but he had his own private army. "Look at the brave little fish out of water."

Brian opened his mouth to say something helpful. All he managed was a breathy "Uuuh."

"And you must be Mimi's pip-squeak brother. You know," Cutter smiled wickedly, "I'll wager she and I have a future, once we are all happily nestled in SA-6. You sleep there, against the ceiling."

Brian said, "Errr."

A tall brute leaned over Cutter's right shoulder. He spoke with the deep voice of an older kid, with cotton tucked into his mouth. "What's wrong? Boobalander bite off your tongue?"

Stephen grabbed Brian's carpetbag. He gave it a tug to lift it from the bed, but didn't move the baggage very far. If he'd had time, he might have given Brian a stare that said, *What are you packing in there, blocks of metal?* But there was no time.

Stephen leaned down, wrapped the sling over his shoulder, and swung the luggage over his back.

Before anyone, including Brian, thought to say another word, Stephen started climbing the narrow ladder.

The bed didn't seem so high, not from the floor. Stephen heard someone slapping the rungs beneath him. He looked down, to see Brian—he evidently didn't want to be left alone in the half-circle of bullies. And *then* the floor looked very far away.

Reaching the top, Stephen shoved himself and the monstrously heavy bag onto the bed and fell beside it to rest.

Brian found a spot to roost near Stephen's feet. Frowning, he pulled the thin curtain shut. "This was *his* bed. Bet it has the number on his ticket."

"I'm sure you're right. You could go complain."

"No."

"Then I suggest you escape, to fight again another day."

A deep gong pounded and echoed into the distance. The gong banged a second time, like an old clock taking its time announcing the hour. After the third BONG, Brian frowned, shifting his eyes right and left.

"Great."

"What's wrong?"

"When the bell rang twice, it was lunch time. My guess? Dinner."

"Is the food that bad?"

"The food's not the problem." He pushed his face to the thin curtain and tried to look down five bunks to the floor. "It's the wolves circling the bottom of the tree that concern me."

"They still there?"

"I see people moving. Shadows." Brian wouldn't actually peek around the curtain.

Stephen steeled himself. Then he stuck his head between the curtain and the post attaching the bunk bed to the ceiling.

Kids their age and older traveled in a continuous flow heading in one direction. It looked like a sea of silver and blond hair, with sometimes obviously dyed hair swimming along like logs through the rippling surface.

"They've gone."

"Are you sure?" said Brian.

"I don't see anyone sticking around." Stephen clutched at his stomach. "Now, do a guy a favor?"

"Sure."

"Take me to the food? I'm starving!"

Brian cringed as they pulled the curtain open all the way. "You think we'll run into Cutter again?"

"How do you know those guys if they're from Alpha Prime and you're from Earth?"

"They were here when I arrived; their reputation precedes them."

Stephen shrugged. "Forget about them. They won't see us!"

"You sure?" Brian followed Stephen down the ladder.

"Of course," Stephen said, hitting the floor. "Because we are spies! We sneak in, get the grub, and slip out of there! What do you say?"

Brian didn't say anything. He thought about the adventurous images in his head. And he smiled, the happiest Stephen had ever seen him.

THE BIG SECRET

The cafeteria was fashioned much like the place that Gretel Lack-luv had called the waiting room. Instead of couches and fireplaces, this room had long lines of students moving swiftly. Above each line hung a sign that magically projected three-dimensional meals that would shock the people who made television commercials back home.

At least, that's how Stephen saw them.

Hamburgers shined in such perfect color, that even at a distance they looked delicious; French fries glowed with golden color; baked potatoes made room for chicken strips on the side; fish sticks waited beside pota-to wedges; soups; chili; salads—there were more options than Stephen could handle.

At the moment, he wanted them all.

"Uh, you choose," he said to Brian.

"What! Do you *see* them?"

It took a few beats for Stephen to figure out the subject of Brian's blurt.

It had been fun slinking through the hallways, ignoring the stares of older teens (who no doubt wondered what the pups were up to, while writing it off because Brian and Stephen *were* pups), stopping at corners, peering around them and then jerking their heads away as if they might be shot if they didn't.

The smell of gravy, chips, and cheese had distracted Stephen from the game. Reality had derailed Brian.

"Great." Stephen saw Cutter and his barbarian horde in line be-neath a bowl of what looked like steak and raw eggs. "We'll steer clear."

"I'm all for that," Brian said.

Stephen studied the signs positioned far from the Alpha Prime bullies, illuminating other choices: blobs of meat and vegetables heaped over rice; spaghetti; something like a lumpy onion soup.

"Spaghetti?"

Brian saw the sign, checked the attendants in line, and grinned. "Perfect!"

Amazed at the quick efficiency of the cafeteria workers, Stephen and Brian were handed heaping plates of spaghetti, buttered French bread, and a salad of unidentifiable leaves.

"Thank you," Stephen said to a lady with a third eyeball evenly spaced between the two *normal* eyes on her face.

To Brian, he whispered, "Did you *see* that woman?" She hadn't been ugly, only shocking.

"Yeah. Scary, huh? But don't talk now. She has eyes in the back of her head. Really."

They followed the current of people bearing food. The crowds led Stephen and Brian into yet another matching room, this one filled with unremarkably normal cafeteria tables.

"Brian, how did you keep from swallowing your tongue when you saw her?"

"The Selurian? Oh, my sister's had them over for dinner." He looked at walls covered with blazing torches, rafters that seemed to be made of wood carved into a network of interlocking dragons, the likes of which no artist had imagined on Earth. "This is all new for me too, you know. I take it you don't have any older siblings."

"You and your sister, you're not . . . not orphans?"

They had found a table, but Brian paused to stare at Stephen with sincere commiseration in his face. "I am *so* sorry." Then he shrugged and plopped himself on the bench hard enough to warrant a dark growl from the girl nearest him. "Didn't know you were a tranc."

"Tank?"

"Tranc. With an R. It's what most people call a Transfer Case." Brian continued with his mouth full of spaghetti. "A lot of people on Earth are trancs. Maybe most of them. I don't really know, though. You know. Just what my sisters tell me. Not Mimi, mind you. She's too busy pouting and writing music."

At the sound of the singer's name, Stephen lit up. "Why would *she* pout?" He started eating, despite the sensation of butterflies in his stomach.

Brian gave him The Stare. "Oh, please, no. *Please* don't tell me you're another fan."

Stephen stuffed his mouth full, shook his head, and spoke around the food. "Are you kidding? I've never seen her before. I'm a—a tranc, remember?"

Brian accepted the answer with a shrug. "Well you see, Mimi wants to be this big famous pop singer, right? And she's really getting there, as I am sure you noticed. She has albums."

Stephen hummed at his plate, like it was the most delicious plate of noodles and spicy tomato sauce that he had ever eaten, which wasn't far from the truth: he was so hungry for real food, he found himself splattering dinner all over the table—and his shirt.

"But Mimi has to choose, you know? If she sings at all on Earth, eats up the attention, gets noticed, she could end up in the spotlight. She could become the new teenage superstar."

"And that's bad?"

"Well you get the reporters stalking her every hour of the day and night—"

"Happens when you're going for fame and—and all that."

"Right. But if she wants to reach the top of the charts *in the universe*, then she'd have to leave the planet permanently. My parents aren't too keen on the idea of her maturing so fast."

Stephen nodded, swinging noodles until they slapped him under the chin. He looked around for a napkin.

"Lots of people who leave the planet for school learn things, skills and stuff, that would make them hotshots on Earth. But there's that *rule*."

"Yeah?"

"Enter the spotlight on a country heap like Earth, and you *can't* ever leave again. You get blacklisted. Illegal to make any contact with off-world travelers, let alone get near a spaceship of any kind."

Stephen chewed slowly. "Why?"

Brian leaned in close. "It's a big secret, that's why. Ever watch the Discovery Channel? Most scientists on Earth believe that there's life out here in the universe. Those same scientists tend to shake their heads at talk of UFOs. They listen with radio telescopes—"

"Huh?"

"Radio telescopes. They're like giant satellite dishes that listen for messages from *beyond—they're mostly used to spot new stars and stuff, since they never* pick up what is really going on."

"Why's it a secret?"

"Buddy, can you imagine what would happen if people knew there was an Earth Transport that picked up and dropped off travelers multiple times a year? NASA spends billions of dollars sending basic satellites into orbit; think of what people would *want!*"

Stephen could only think of one thing anyone would want if they knew they could leave the planet. "To get—to get off-world?"

"Precisely. So." Brian slapped the table, bouncing a fork. It didn't matter, there was so much noise in the hall, the only person who responded was the girl beside him. This time it was the Stare of Death.

Stephen smiled at her. "Sorry. He *likes* his spaghetti."

The girl rolled her eyes and looked away.

"Mimi has to choose. She can become a star on Earth, maybe— you know how *everyone* on Earth wants to be a star—or she can become the most famous singer/song writer from one side of the Milky Way galaxy to the other."

"So she pouts?"

"Right. Mimi doesn't want to limit herself to Earth. So she *can't* sing at all in public. She's afraid she'll get spotted, like a baseball player or something."

"Living the dream," Stephen said when there was nothing left to say. He finished his bread. It was delicious. He filled his guts, gleefully.

"Whining all through summer is more like it."

The Big Secret

★ ★● +

They finished and decided to wander around the parts of the ship permitted by the staff.

The grownups were polite but almost robotic, like school bus drivers that never got angry or excited. Stephen watched them, standing along the hallways, meandering, watching students, but never engaging in conversation unless it was to listen to someone who had to talk. They kept their answers short, as in *Your question will be answered later.*

If the adults were searching for an imposter, Stephen couldn't see how they were going about it. Then imagining cameras, he searched the walls and ceilings, and almost asked Brian if he saw any. But Stephen didn't want to give himself away.

Stephen *knew* he was the imposter. He didn't want to be dropped off in the middle of nowhere or be sent home.

There probably were hidden cameras, Stephen decided, before exhaustion drove him toward the bunkrooms.

Brian talked about his favorite movies. They hung out around Stephen's bunk for a little while. Stephen nodded, but wasn't really listening.

He thought about the clandestine police onboard lurking out of everyone's sight.

Then he realized how silly the whole idea was: the adults weren't talking to anyone about anything. So how could the Alpha Prime girl, who had fallen onto Brian's legs and said all that stuff about "imposters", know what the grownups were doing?

Only one thing continued to bother him.

There *was* an imposter aboard. That was true. Stephen's name was not Brian Bumhandel (thank goodness).

He hadn't seen his "aunt" anywhere during their wanderings, and the thought struck him with the chills.

"She must have her own bunk."

"What?" Brian said.

"Um, nothing."

"I know. I should be getting back over there. Before *they* do." Brian stared in fear in the direction of his bed, or the bed that had been stolen from him before his exile to a top bunk. He frowned at Stephen, his eyes pleading.

"Sorry, guy," Stephen said.

"Yeah. So am I." Brian rose from the bed. "Well. See you tomorrow? If I'm alive in the morning?"

"Breakfast?"

Brian nodded, walked a few steps away, then turned back with a nervous grin. "Can't be any worse than today."

Stephen waved.

Alone, he pulled the curtain shut and wondered how he could possibly sleep with all the noise beyond the cloth.

What a day!

"I'll wake up tomorrow," he said to the shadows. "And this will all be . . . a dream come true?"

He had asked himself the question, but his eyelids dropped.

And Stephen was completely unaware of falling into a deep sleep four minutes later.

HORROR BEFORE THE END

Stephen searched all the next day for Gretel Lackluv. Brian caught on, sometime after breakfast. He thought Stephen was watching out for the creeps. Stephen corrected him. Brian shuddered, then tried to be polite about it: "So, has her hair always smelled like she has nail polish?"

Stephen shrugged, nearly laughing.

Brian caught him by the shirt. "Wait. I thought you were a tranc. But you have an aunt?"

Stephen shrugged again.

"Hmm," Brian said. "I have *plenty* to learn."

Two bangs of a gong in the hallways sent them to lunch. Afterwards, Stephen began to feel sleepy. "I think I'm getting jetlag."

He had never been on a plane before, but also didn't know how else to describe this sensation. He started talking to himself: "Let's see. Dinner last night must have happened somewhere around midnight, Harmon, California time. I lost—started dreaming about two hours later. I have no idea what time the lights came on this morning, or what time breakfast started—I didn't get a chance to get my watch before racing off of the planet Earth."

"It's all different anyway, Ship Time. So you haven't seen the museum?"

"No!" said Stephen.

"Let's go!"

There were plenty of amazing things to see on the transport, the museum was only one of them.

They played all day. No one stopped them!

And Stephen thought more and more that the grownups weren't human—the ones that *looked* human, that is. The thought that they were robots or silent watchers made him stay far away.

Then he thought about Mrs. Hearty in Linguistics. She had been so nice, so human, she seemed more than human.

Stephen tried to think up excuses to visit her. Never found one. Finally, he just blasted it out. "Hey, let's go visit that nice lady in Linguistics."

Brian said, "Nah," and continued whatever it was that he had been saying. Brian had plenty to talk about. At least it was nice to have a friend.

That night after dinner, Stephen said, "Why do we need to take a transport to the—the, ah—*school bus*." He imagined a standard yellow bus, with a long line of windows running from front to back, floating in space.

"Jackie says SA-6 is too far to go for the Earth Transport."

"Who's Jackie?"

Brian turned red and withdrew into himself a bit. "My sister." He changed the conversation to *Batman* movies.

Later in the bunkroom, Brian craned his neck to see through the maze of beds and knots of kids. "Hey, I'm going to bed early."

"Huh?"

"See ya."

Stephen watched him zigzag through the towers of beds.

After a good night's sleep, the lights came on. Stephen woke at the noise of a small pack of boys running past.

He rubbed his eyes.

Inches from Stephen's nose, Brian called through curtain. "Hey! You still in there?"

"I'm in here. Already time for breakfast?"

"No breakfast today, my friend."

Stephen didn't know how it was possible—he'd been eating plenty since boarding the Earth Transport—but he was starving again.

Brian's voice whispered, "Showers!"

"What?"

"I know. Horrible! Come on. We don't want to get naked anywhere near Cutter's kind."

Stephen sat up. He didn't open the curtain. This had to be some kind of sick joke.

At the same time, he was well aware that he had not bathed in days. By now, Mrs. Lackluv probably smelled better than he did.

Stephen had never taken a shower on a field trip. He'd never washed anything more than his hands at school. The deplorable idea of bathing within sight of fellow students had been rumored throughout the fifth grade. But Stephen had simply not been able to believe that such a thing could be legal, let alone allowed by the grownups.

So he decided that he would rather die.

"Come on." Brian sounded equally horrified. "They stamp the back of your hand after you're through. Then they start *checking* the students with an ultraviolet light. Jackie says if they don't find the stamp, they run you through the water like cattle."

Stephen pulled the curtain aside. He felt like he might be sick. "Then *this* is the worst day of my life!"

A SCHOOL BUS UNLIKE
ANY OTHER

Stephen tried not to think. He put on the robot faces of the adults around him.

Ten minutes later, they had finished with the showers, dressed, and were running from the embarrassing experience. They followed the flow of guys returning to the bunkrooms without any word of bathing. A moment later, it was as if the event never happened.

"What are we doing here?" Stephen said.

Brian looked dumbfounded.

They watched as people removed photographs, gathered their belongings, and zipped up luggage.

A polite female voice spoke from the ceiling. "Attention students. Please make your way to the observation deck for departure." The recording played again, then repeated a third time.

Stephen said, "There's an observation deck?"

Brian didn't answer. He stopped and stared in the direction of his bed.

Cutter was busy packing his gear . . . alone.

"Look!" said Stephen. "No army? We outnumber him two to one."

"I'm not much of a fighter." Brian tried to snag Stephen's arm, but his fingers slipped from the hem of Stephen's shirt.

Stephen marched right to the ladder.

Brian followed.

"Oh, they didn't throw either of you off the ship for being an imposter?" Cutter said as soon as Stephen passed him and started up the ladder.

Brian forced an answer. "Uuuuh." He followed Stephen.

Cutter pointed a finger and shouted to the room. "There he is! There's the imposter right there!"

Stephen climbed faster. He made himself slow down, to avoid looking guilty. He considered turning and spitting onto Cutter's head.

"Dump him!" the guy with black eyes continued to shout. "Feed him to the gravity of a red dwarf! Imposter! Right *here*!"

Stephen crawled onto the top bunk. It was a mess with blankets, unfolded clothes, candy, Little Debbie snack wrappers, pictures, and electronic toys.

Cutter traded shouting for mocking laughter.

Brian grimaced at the mess on his bed and then at Stephen.

Stephen said, "You been living here for a month?"

"Just say it: I'm a slob." He glanced at Cutter, who wasn't paying them any more attention. "I haven't received enough abuse today."

"Attention students," said the voice from overhead, which then repeated the previous message.

"We must have reached Proxima Centauri." Brian grabbed handfuls of his belongings and rammed them into his carpetbag. He saw the question on Stephen's face and said, "It's the star closest to our sun."

"How long will it take us to get to school?"

"I don't know."

Stephen smiled. "Could be fun! Unless we get bored. Is the school bus like this transport?"

"*Nothing like*, according to—to my sister." He pulled the ties snug at the top of his bag. "Once on the bus, try to find me, okay? I'll try to find you."

"Is it going to be that hard?"

Brian shrugged. "From what I've heard, the bus carries all the kids from all the worlds with transports to Proxima Centauri. That's a lot of people."

"The ship must be huge!"

Brian shook his head and looked over the side of his sheets. "He's gone. Let's get your stuff."

Soon they were lugging their gear onto the observation deck. Grownups at the doors were scanning the backs of everyone's hands with purple glowing lights that made the shower stamp appear in magical yellow letters. Only after the stamp was read were students allowed through the doors.

Stephen gasped. Even Brian fell away from the enormous windows (or view screens in disguise) when he saw them.

Twenty feet high, from floor to ceiling, and at least fifty feet wide, the windows made Stephen feel once again that he *really was* in outer space.

A red sun burned brightly far away. A dusty planet, or a moon (Stephen thought), studded with enormous buildings made of rounded cylinders rolled slowly beneath them, but quickly enough for Stephen to notice. Stars twinkled in the vast backdrop of space.

They weren't spinning wildly like Gretel Lackluv's ship had spun.

Waiting as the room filled with other people dragging baggage, Stephen became aware of the subtle movement of Earth Transport.

The populated moon seemed to swell as they approached. Within minutes, it filled the window.

"You ready for this?" said the voice of a pretty girl with spiral curls of blonde. She stood beside Brian.

Brian grunted.

If it wasn't for the girl's baby-blue duffle bag, Stephen might have mistaken her for a grownup. She had a sparkle in her eyes and a wide grin. "Who's your friend?"

"Uh?" said Brian. "Oh. This is Brian Bumhandel."

"Brian, huh?" She stuck out a hand to shake his. "Nice to meet you. First time heading for school off-world?"

"Yeah," Stephen said, holding her soft fingers until she let go.

"I'm Brian's sister, Tabby. I apologize for having to introduce myself. He's not exactly enthusiastic about hailing from a family of all girls." She bumped Brian with her hip. "I don't blame him."

After a moment, Stephen said, "So . . . where's the school bus."

"Oh. It's right there. A T-90. Pretty sweet, don't you think?"

Stephen and Brian stared at the city over which they hovered. Stephen felt a bit of vertigo: it was weird to look *down* on a city, especially one so futuristic.

He couldn't tell the buildings from the ships.

The Earth Transport drew closer to a bulbous craft. It looked bigger than an aircraft carrier.

"*That's* the school bus?" He looked at Brian.

Brian sighed.

Tabby laughed. "Well . . . it's a *lot* smaller on the inside than it is on the outside."

"How—how's that possible? It looks like a torpedo the size of a mountain!"

"You'll see soon enough. Oh, hang onto your stuff!"

A voice started over the speakers as soon as the ship stopped. "Please grasp onto all of your belongings and prepare for transfer to the school bus."

Seconds later, Stephen opened his eyes. He was lying in a bed. His suitcase was gone. White sheets covered what he could not see: his arms and feet were tied down to the bed.

He smelled a faint odor of plastic. A twitch of a nose, and he felt tubes as thin as wires running across his face to a mask gently fixed over his mouth and nostrils.

A wall of pebbled glass hung inches from his face. It was white, so he couldn't see through it very well. But he did sense people moving on the other side.

Stephen panicked.

The same soft, kind, female voice spoke to him.

His breath quickened. His heart raced. He fought to lift his hands, kick his feet from the mattress, even lift his head—*even his head* was somehow fixed to the bed.

The recording said something about relaxing, something about his first time on a school bus. The woman even called him Brian. But Stephen wasn't listening.

He was trapped.

A DREAM WITHIN A DREAM

Stephen had been laughing so hard, he had to grab his stomach. His throat hurt. Big tears rolled out of his eyes—he would have been so ashamed, if he weren't so happy.

Ocean waves rose out of the distance, grew taller, sharper, and then fell toward the beach. The impact was an explosion of pleasant thunder, churning peace.

Sand pipers ran their little, fast feet across wet sand. Tiny sand crabs swam through the whitewash and burrowed beneath the earth to hide from the hungry birds.

Sea gulls sang overhead.

Dad—no *not Dad*, there was no Dad for Stephen Cowen, but— Mr. Greenberg chuckled, then fell back on the beach towel and stared into the receding breeze. The Pacific wind brushed the graying hair out of his face.

On the side of a nearly complete sandcastle, Mrs. Greenberg waved for him to come.

Stephen leapt to his feet and ran as fast as he could.

A moment later, panting, Stephen bent and examined the sea damage done to the walls, towers, and detailed battlements.

Hank appeared over the wet side of the toppling construction. "Quick! The tide is coming in!"

"I think it's helpless, boys."

"We need a bigger moat!" Stephen dropped and dug a trench to funnel the water back out to sea.

"That's it!" Hank worked beside him for a full minute before it occurred to Stephen that his friend hadn't been on the beach with his parents—*foster* parents—until now.

Suddenly, he couldn't hold back the news. He grabbed Hank by the shoulders. "Hank. Oh, Hank!"

Boggled, and desperate to return to the castle rescue efforts, Hank laughed in Stephen's face, "What is it, you crazy man!"

"They're going ..." Stephen choked up, the words catching in his throat. "The Greenbergs . . . "

"The Greenbergs are going and this makes you happy? I thought you loved the Greenbergs?"

"I do!"

"So?"

"They're going . . . to keep me!"

Hank stared in shock. It was every foster child's dream-come-true. Then he punched Stephen in the chest. He gave him a high five. He clapped and—and accidentally jumped, lost his balance, and fell into the castle.

This time, Mrs. Greenberg chuckled. She turned back toward her husband, who was picking up the beach towels, coolers, and body boards.

"Oops," said Hank from the ruins. A wave of rising tide splashed through the fortifications and soaked him with salt and sand and cool water. "Gaaugh!"

"When you boys are ready, head on back up to the house. We'll get some dinner fixed."

Stephen waited as Hank ran into the surf to rinse off all the grit. Then they raced each other to the beach house.

They dragged chairs to the edge of a white balcony that overlooked the coastline and the ocean. Gulls watched them and sang in a sky splashed with clouds that looked like whipped cream.

As the sun fell towards the horizon, the view overhead glowed with incredible lights in slow motion. The blue became deep. Portions of clouds brightened, as if banks and drifts of white reflecting snow. Others turned into vast stretches of yellow, brilliant oranges, even red.

Mr. Greenberg lit the Outback barbeque. Mrs. Greenberg brought out the wide hamburger patties. Mr. Greenberg slapped the meat onto the grill—it sizzled, sweetening the air with the delicious promise of dinner. Mrs. Greenberg kissed Mr. Greenberg on the cheek and returned to the kitchen.

"Isn't this the life?" Hank said. "And this is going to be yours? All this? Wow! You have to invite me over *every day.*"

"Of course I will!"

"Like I always said," Hank chuckled, "sometimes stories have good endings."

"*You* always say that," Stephen said, laughing with him at the sarcastic lie.

"Well, I do now." Hank stared into Stephen's eyes, and it was wonderful.

To have a friend like this.

To have a *family.*

To live in such a fine place.

"Do you—" said Hank, "do you see that?"

Stephen leaned forward. "What is it?"

There was a blob on the beach. Tentacles grew out of black smoke and . . . wings.

The boys squinted. Hank bit his fingernails. "It looks *alien.*"

But that wasn't right. "Maybe it's nothing."

"How can you say that?"

Stephen shrugged and lowered his brow. "I can't really see any-thing. Must be some kind of optical illusion."

"You're just pretending that there isn't a ghost over there."

"Dad?" Stephen said, without even thinking of what he had called Mr. Greenberg.

Closing the barbecue, the man turned with a paisley mitt over one hand and an oily spatula in the other. "What are you guys look-ing at?" He stood at the railing.

The shadow floated closer and closer along the beach. Shifting, it seemed to pause in the salty breeze, changing shape.

One octopus tentacle reached toward them, pressed into the sand, and was followed by another. Surging forward, the smoky amoeba began to take on the colors of the sunset.

"It's *walking*," said Mr. Greenberg.

Hank raised his eyebrows. "Should we be *running?* I think that is the question."

Mrs. Greenberg shut the sliding door behind her and placed a cookie sheet, decorated with sliced tomatoes, onions, cheese, peeled lettuce, and other hamburger condiments, onto the short table beside the cooker. "What are you staring at, boys?" she said, wiping her hands, "a mermaid?"

"Not exactly," said Stephen.

A moment later, she stood beside them, equally transfixed by the warping image that was now crossing the little bumpy sand dunes between the water and the house.

When the thing reached the steps, no one moved.

The sun appeared beneath a line of purple-red clouds. Yellow rays blasted in long lines from the horizon, splashing gold over every surface and everyone's face.

The light illuminated the walking mirage as well. Tentacles became hands, arms, legs. A head. A smile that Stephen recognized.

"Cripes, this is marvelous!" said Brian Boar. He nodded to Mr. and Mrs. Greenberg, to Hank. "Hello there." To Stephen he said, "Is he real?"

"Who?" Stephen frowned.

Brian pointed at Hank.

Mrs. Greenberg pinched Stephen's arm. "Aren't you going to introduce us?"

"Yeah," Stephen said, wondering when he and Hank had stood up. "This is Brian . . . Boar."

"Nice to meet you," Brian said, checking out the sky. "Hey, we gotta—"

Stephen didn't let him say more. "Brian, this is my friend, Hank. And these are . . . the Greenbergs. They're adopting me."

Brian's jaw dropped. He stared at Mrs. Greenberg. He stared at Mr. Greenberg. He stared at Stephen, speechless.

Stephen's almost-new parents shook Brian's hand, elated to meet him.

Finally, Brian—who looked as if Stephen had punched him in the gut—turned away and leaned on the railing. He watched white birds balancing on the wind.

"Well!" said Mrs. Greenberg, spinning around to the food.

Mr. Greenberg followed her lead, returning to the barbecue. "Hey, Brian. You are more than welcome to join us. We have enough— don't we, honey?"

"Oh, definitely!" she said.

Hank, suddenly clearing his throat like a third wheel, watched Brian with suspicious eyes. He raised his eyebrows at Stephen.

Stephen shrugged. He had no idea what to think. Suddenly his social ties were all quite confusing.

Something pulled him to Brian's side. They leaned against the railing.

A magical orange color now, the sun disappeared halfway into the ocean and was sinking fast enough that they could watch it vanish.

"This is," Brian said, "so nice." He appeared to be only seconds away from leaking tears.

"It is," Stephen said, still unable to wrap his brain around the facts before him.

After all, wasn't Brian Boar just some kid from a strange dream that Stephen once had about spaceships with fireplaces?

"It took me forever to find you. Now I can see why."

"Brian—"

"They seem like really wonderful people." Brian lowered his head after the sun dove out of sight.

"The Greenbergs? Ah, they're the best! This has *got* to be the happiest day of my life!"

"I sincerely hope not," Brian said, barely loud enough for Stephen to hear.

"Why do you . . . why would you say that?"

"Yeah," said Hank protectively, standing at Stephen's elbow. "How can you be so insensitive? You're supposed to be a friend of his? Some friend! Come on, Stephen." Hank grabbed Stephen's arm and started dragging him into the whitewashed beach house.

Brian cocked his head. "*Stephen?*"

"Let's go." Hank tugged him toward the kitchen.

"Brian," Brian whispered to Stephen. "It's time to get up. We've already docked. We're here!"

Stephen shook his head. But he didn't let Hank pull him hard enough to dislodge his feet.

"No, Brian," Stephen said. "We are *here!*"

Brian shut his eyes. "The ship sent me in after you. To come and get you out. Thought it would be best this way. Since you're new. And a tranc and all." He brightened. "Quite an honor, really!"

Tears welled up in Stephen's eyes and mixed with a rising anger. "No, Brian—you're a dream."

Brian shook his head. "*This* is the dream. You know it is, don't you?" He glanced at Hank dismissively, then at the Greenbergs both working over hamburgers that were nearly finished and smelled so good Stephen's stomach growled. "Please tell me that you know that you are dreaming."

Stephen shoved Brian away. "Get out of here!"

Shocked, Mrs. Greenberg said, "Stephen!"

Brian nearly toppled down the steps. He caught himself, then braced as Hank approached. "Why is everybody calling you *Stephen?*"

It only took another two seconds.

Brian's eyes blew wide. He gawked at Stephen as understanding flashed on his face.

"*You* are the imposter!"

Hank blushed.

And Stephen began to cry.

The bruised orange light in the sky painted the Greenbergs in a beautiful sadness as they held each other. They looked apologetically at Stephen. "Oh," Mr. Greenberg said, as if they had known that this was nothing more than a carefully constructed dream all along, "I am so sorry."

Hank took a step backwards.

"You're not real," Brian said to Hank, "are you?" It wasn't a question.

Stephen sank into the nearest plastic chair.

Brian sighed and crouched before him. "Brian—Stephen, who—whoever you are . . . look." He didn't know what else to say. He sighed again, painfully.

Stephen had stopped himself from blubbering any further. But he also kept himself from seeing the Greenbergs. He let his attention slip out to sea, as if the ocean could carry him into a happy dream within a happy dream.

"All right," said Brian. "You got your reasons. I can respect that." He looked around him. "I can respect *this*! And I can respect them. You're a foster child. That means, I guess, you've had it harder than I've ever known. I can see what you are feeling."

Stephen tried *hard* to carry himself away without getting up and sprinting—he doubted that running would really work. But he wouldn't meet Brian's eyes either.

"So I figure . . . I can keep your secret. You can tell me," Brian looked at the Greenbergs again, "what you want to tell me, *when* you want to tell me."

Stephen sniffed and wiped his face.

"But for now, my friend, we got to go. The ship wanted me to come get you, since you've hidden yourself away so well inside this fantasy."

"Why doesn't everybody know?"

"Your secret?"

"If I'm dreaming, if I'm asleep in some hospital-bed-thing, and all this is some kind of castle-in-the-sky that the ship can get *you* to enter . . . I mean, this does not feel like a dream to me!"

"No, the ship is tied to your brain. I don't know why they don't know. Maybe it's a privacy thing—you know: lawyer stuff. All my sister said was that these things are like the Internet, like Facebook, *a social networking forum*, is how she put it; you know, where you can live a life while we travel, where time doesn't matter, where you can hang out with friends or be by yourself—the idea scares me to death, to tell you the truth: what if you got stuck in a nightmare? That's what I wanted to know. But my dream was rather cool—you don't bump into people you don't want to bump into. No Cutter Hertmor and gang, you know?"

Stephen wasn't listening. He was processing. "Maybe they *know* about me."

Brian coughed. "So . . . are you going to assassinate somebody famous at the school?"

"No."

"Are you a thief?"

"No."

"Then you're just insane: someone stowing away to *go to school*."

"No."

"Well . . . if you're not going to hurt anybody or anything, then we need to *git!*"

"Wake me up then."

"Wake yourself up. I'll see you when I see you!" Brian smiled. Then he shut his eyes and said the words, "Ready to wake up now." And he vanished.

Barely keeping the tears from showering down his face again, Stephen turned in the cool sea breeze.

The Greenbergs had gone into the house. The sliding glass door was shut.

Hank stood with hands in his pockets.

Stephen stared for a long time. "Are you just a ghost of my imagination?"

Still peeved, Hank shrugged. "Who knows?"

"I guess . . . I should."

"Just tell me, Stephen. Do you think you can trust that guy? Brian Boar?"

Stephen didn't answer. He walked off the porch and ran toward the splashing ocean waves.

LINE OF CHANGE

Stephen awoke and almost fell over his suitcase. He had been standing, for one thing. He had never returned to reality in the standing position before. Blinking rapidly, he focused on balance. He yawned. He stretched. And he punched a girl in the side of the head.

"Watch it!"

"Sorry. I just—woke up."

"Clearly." The gray-eyed girl rubbed a hand into her loose curls. "Do you normally assault people when you get out of bed? Ah, it's you."

Stephen held his breath.

He recognized her then: the jabbering young lady who had fallen into Brian Boar's lap and told them there was an imposter onboard the Earth Transport.

"It's me. Um, Brian."

She softened, as if she understood more than she was letting on. "Well, come along then, *you*. We're nearly the last. You slept in?"

Stephen grabbed his suitcase and followed her into the line streaming through a doorway ornamented with crystal garlands. "Good dream."

"Me too. I went to a week of prelims, but still feel hardly prepared for all this."

"Prelims?"

"Earth, right?" She blinked at him. "Are you a transfer case?"

He felt ashamed, as if she had just found out that he was a foster child, that he did not really belong to anyone. What kid wanted to be called a *case* anyway. "So I'm told."

She smiled with kind understanding. "I'm Lorenza Westing."

Line of Change

They fell into a procession of bewildered students who passed skinny adults with welcoming faces. Soon they began to wind through narrow passages and rooms where everything happened so quickly, Stephen could hardly keep up.

In one room, desks ran along both sides of the line. Workers in white uniforms with blue badges pulled student luggage onto the countertops, labeled them, took eye scans with small handheld devices, and kept the students moving.

Lorenza stood one step ahead of Stephen, so he copied everything they had her do. When they called for her twin bags decorated with yellow lilies, she placed them on the counter. Stephen set his weightless suitcase beside Lorenza's, and the worker in uniform grinned with thankfulness beneath a nose as large and knotted as a kindergartener's fist.

The worker scanned Lorenza's eyes, then made her luggage disappear.

Stephen leaned forward and let the same grownup scan his eyes too. Then his luggage was swept around, placed on a silver scale of some kind, where it dematerialized in a way so slow and magical, Stephen couldn't help but whisper, "Whoa!"

The worker looked pleased. "Welcome, Brian Bumhandel."

"Let's go." Lorenza gave him a polite yank.

The next room looked as if the walls had spread apart to accommodate the vast number of teenagers. While the line itself continued along one wall where workers in the same white uniforms (this time with pink badges) were touching some other kind of handheld device to the left side of every new student's head, the other side of the room was teaming with shouting protesters.

From the crowd of older students banged the chant, around and around, "We won't lie, so don't you spy!"

They lifted signs made of glittering lights without visible edges to hold. Banners were made of bright silver material with flashing, moving, or spinning letters. Some messages had simply been drawn onto poster board, or even paper.

Signs read:

SAFETY YOU SAY?
WE SAY _FREEDOM!_

And

NO MORE!

And

END TRACING NOW!

And

YOU KNOW IT'S WRONG!

Stephen recognized one slew of words from fifth grade:

GIVE ME LIBERTY,
OR GIVE ME DEATH!

As he came to the first free worker, a man with huge buck teeth, Stephen said, "What are _they_ all about?"

The worker blinked at him as if Stephen had asked _Why don't I have permission to drink poison like other people?_ The man didn't answer at all, but ran his little machine along the side of Stephen's left temple.

Afterwards Buck Teeth grumbled two short words with disdain: "Student logic." Then he was blinking rapidly past Stephen at another distracted kid. "Next!"

✳ ✳ ✝

As Lorenza passed into the next room, Stephen leaned toward her to ask about the riot behind them. But immediately, the line broke in two.

A nice woman, rotund in the extreme, stood like a highway divider in front of them. "Girls," she said, lifting a hand to one side.

Lorenza split off the main line into a new one running along yet another extended wall of counters, workers, and a vast display of labeled cubbyholes.

"Boys," said the big woman, who looked somewhat like a kind Mrs. Allyn. She was gazing right at Stephen and had lifted her left hand to indicate a matching fork, counter, and battery of workers.

Stephen followed the guys ahead of him, who were busily chatting in words that Stephen couldn't understand even with his head translating the words. Instantly, he felt lost and looked across a line of white tape that separated the boys from the girls.

Lorenza was leaning against a counter and speaking with a woman with a long streak of white hair running through the gray like a pretend mohawk.

Stephen heard a grownup behind him call, "Young man?"

He turned and swallowed at the sight of a fellow who might have been old enough to be Stephen's great, great, great grandfather. The man blinked long white lashes and said through a gentle smile without lips, "Hold still."

He waved a flashing wand near Stephen's head, then examined the side of the device. "208-B," he said, gleefully, as if he had guessed the numerical code and was happy to have measured him correctly.

He reached into a cubby—marked 208-B—and withdrew what looked like two white pillows, one squarely atop the other. As soon as he took these away from the shelf, another matching set materialized in its place. From beneath the counter, the man withdrew a set of black shoes.

Putting the little pillows on top of the shoes, he set them in front of Stephen. "Change in the next room. Your home clothes will be washed and sent to your domus."

"My what?"

"Your domicile."

"My what?"

"Your home—away from home." He winked. Stephen wasn't quite sure why.

* * 🌑 ✝

The line continued into a large room with benches and what looked like lockers without doors. Stephen investigated the pillows a little more closely and found that they were really a set of sharply folded clothes: white underwear and undershirt, a white outer shirt with a black stripe running down one side, matching pants (with a matching stripe), and black socks to go with the shoes. The shoes were more like short boots that would cover his ankles.

Without "watching" he saw other boys change out of all their clothes and put on the new stuff. They shoved their old clothes into the doorless lockers, and the dirty clothes disappeared.

Stephen wanted to faint.

A MALL OF WONDERS

There was simply no way he was going to undress in front of these other guys. He watched them talk, laugh, and joke, but also skillfully avert their eyes, as if pretending that nothing out of the ordinary were happening.

Talk was about gravity and suns and baskets and skiff racers and the oldest teacher at the school. Stephen even thought he heard someone say his name, but the animated discussion had something to do with a bomb and a "babe" and the end of a world—it sounded like the latest in a string of exciting movies.

A short stranger, with a similar look of pale horror, passed at Stephen's right. He didn't say a word, but held dirty clothes in front of his new attire as he approached the nearest locker.

Stephen kept his eyes on the frightened boy's dusty red hair and the gap between his front teeth.

He looked at Stephen. Then he looked to one side of the room where young students, who all wore that same yellow mask of sickness on their faces, slipped into little booths and disappeared behind curtains that pulled themselves shut. Others exited those booths, dressed in white and carrying their home clothes.

A wave of gratitude shook him: some grownup somewhere had figured out that new boys would be shy and need some alone time right about now.

Stephen nodded at the boy, a silent thank you. Then he made his way to one of the empty booths and slipped inside where he could change privately.

He changed in a matter of seconds.

A moment later, the curtain pulled aside and he walked out, bearing his clothes like the quiet boy who had helped him without a word. Stephen placed his old shoes and the wad of Earth clothes on a counter. They were taken. Then he realized that he might have placed his belongings into one of those lockers of disintegration by himself.

A worker scanned him again. "All set." He removed the clothes. "You'll get this back in a jiffy."

A line on the far end of the changing room had formed and was exiting slowly, almost too slowly. Stephen soon saw why.

No one was walking.

The *floor moved*, carrying a bottleneck of chattering guys down a sloping hallway. The path continued, turning until Stephen entered a large theater bustling with students.

As the noise increased, one young kid near Stephen said, "This is more like it!"

✴ ✴ ✢

The center buzzed with student life. Nearly everyone wore white uniforms with black stripes. The hall echoed in an endless roar with chatter, music, and colored lights that reminded Stephen of a circus.

The moving floor dumped the line of students into this three-story hall with shops on every side. Streamers with messages (*Vote No on 22! Killian's Sandwiches are to die for! 3188 Solar Races—GO SA-6!*) hung from a vaulted ceiling that Stephen couldn't actually see: instead, he noticed dark space, violent purple, orange, and yellow clouds, and stars everywhere—a stationary window looking outside.

Above him, a circle of students and shops much like the mall back home ran around the second level. Above that, Stephen saw a third floor packed with thrills and animated kids from twelve to twenty.

"You are supposed to follow the lights on the ground." Lorenza stood in a school uniform that matched Stephen's—she looked different in pants. "I mean, we are, I guess. From the direction everyone else is heading, it seems that if you are a *returning* student, you can do what you want."

Stephen felt his head spinning. There were simply too many signs, too many lights, too many sounds, too many people.

"Look." She pointed at the floor.

Colored green lights drew arrows and spelled out the words, *New Students!* And *This Way!*

It only occurred faintly to Stephen that the letters were somehow *wrong*, that they had been wrong in the previous rooms as well. They seemed to flicker when he stared straight at them. They were nothing like letters from Earth, but then they were. It wasn't as if the letters were changing. It was more like Stephen's brain blurred the shapes until they spelled out something in English that he would recognize.

"Are those—do you see English on the floor?"

"I see Japanese." Lorenza passed him.

"Must have something to do with linguistics," he muttered.

"Come along!" Lorenza said.

He obediently followed.

But a constant barrage of distractions assaulted them along the way. Young men and pretty older girls pushed fantastic devices in front of their faces and spoke quickly: "You new? Then you'll really need this barometric pressure gauge! How else will you know if air is leaking from the hull? You might explode!"

"Tear drops! Saddest candy in the world! Makes you cry, just when you need the best excuse—makes angry teachers *soften on the spot!*"

"Eveready Pencils—write on anything, anywhere, anytime, even memory paper—they don't run out of lead!" To Stephen, the Eveready Pencil looked just like normal sharpened pencils.

Of course, the trinket sellers blurted specific prices.

The idea of alien money made Stephen very nervous.

"We're in a shopping mall."

"Obviously," said Lorenza.

"I don't have a dime in my pockets. In fact, I'm not sure that I have pockets."

Lorenza laughed, and it made her sound light and pretty. "You have pockets."

Lifted by the friendly sound of her voice, Stephen searched his new pants anyway, because he didn't believe her. He thought he would *know* if he had pockets.

Carefully hidden along the seams at his hips, he found pockets.

And then his face turned white.

Stephen had forgotten to clear out the pockets of his blue jeans when he changed. Mr. Bluntwasp's absconder . . . it would be destroyed in the wash!

Still ... easy come, easy go.

He felt sad.

And he still didn't have a penny.

Lorenza led him into another thick column of young students. He recognized some of the faces from the changing room, mugs that he wanted to forget. Except for the quiet boy: the little red-headed kid who had wordlessly pointed out a place where Stephen could change in silence.

The red-headed boy had freckles.

And *red* hair.

The boy stood out, despite his lack of height. He wasn't speaking with anyone, but he was also too far ahead of Stephen to engage in conversation.

Red hair. Like he didn't belong here.

Stephen examined the other kids.

Many had different colors of hair, but none had the speckled face of this little kid or the same red color dusted with gray.

The boy slipped out of view.

✳ ✳ ✝

"What are we doing?" Stephen said, leaning forward.

Lorenza actually looked kind of cute, in a goofy way, without her dark blouse and white skirt. Dazzling lights of the mall reflected off her shirt and brightened her face, as did her smile. She looked like a glowing kid visiting Disneyland for the first time.

"According to what I learned in prelims, this is where we buy our school supplies: you know, books and things."

A Mall of Wonders

Stephen hesitated a moment, and then just blurted out the truth that had previously haunted him. "I don't have any money."

"No one does, silly. Not yet anyway. Well, no one who is new, I think. I hear there is a teller machine sort of thing where you can get money if you want to carry it around. That's what *they* are after."

With her chin, Lorenza pointed at the teenagers pushing their exotic wares in front of the faces of kids in the line that had formed behind them.

The line ahead of them soon separated from the rest of the mall by a thick blue rope. The rope steered Lorenza and Stephen directly into one of the stores along the side.

"Um. How do I—" Stephen suddenly decided that to continue speaking would make him look more like an idiotic imbecile than before; Lorenza wouldn't want to be caught in public with him. So he shut his jaw and sealed his lips together.

She blinked at him, stared for a moment.

Stephen gazed away.

"Don't worry, Brian. They told me they make it easy on Alphas."

"I take it we are Alphas."

She nodded. "You're American."

"So are you."

She shook her head, then leaned it to one side. "I was an American ex-patriot in Japan. Then I moved, remember?"

"To the planet of the snobs."

She colored.

Stephen raised a hand. "I wasn't trying to be insulting. From what I remember you saying, they weren't very accepting of you."

She shrugged. "They say I'm from Earth. They're right of course. Anyway, I was saying, you are American. So you would have gone on to the sixth grade. Elementary or Middle School?"

"Middle school."

"Exactly. Three grades, followed by four more in high school. That's a twelve-tier system. Well, SA-6 begins approximately where you left off after the fifth grade. Your new school, here, is an eight-tier system."

"*Eight* grades?"

"Essentially, though students only go as far as they need to. Depends on what you are studying, what you want to become. Also, age has little to do with your advancement through the tiers."

"Sounds . . ." (Stephen was going to say *confusing*, but he didn't want sound dumb) ". . . interesting." The line continued forward past glass counters and beautiful displays, but it was also starting to surge and stop, surge and stop.

"You only have to go to school for four years, if you want: Alpha, Beta, Gamma, Delta."

"Isn't that Greek?"

Lorenza shrugged. "Language isn't what you think. Contrary to what most people on Earth suppose, languages are not evolving, they are *devolving*. Some linguists have noticed. Most haven't a clue. But they don't really know foreign languages either."

"Um—"

"Exactly! The older the language, the more complicated and complete it is—on Earth. The more recent, the more it has become a twist of bits from other languages, slang, torn up versions of its previous self."

Stephen raised his hand again, this time for a different reason. "You learned all this on Alpha Prime?"

"I like history and mystery. To me, every mystery can be understood if you figure out its history."

"Okay." Stephen waited for her to use the word *ascertain* again, stifling a laugh intended to hide his feelings from his ignorance. Instead, he knew he just wasn't as smart as he wanted to be sometimes.

"The further back in Earth history you go, the more you find proof that all languages originate from a small handful of very complicated and more complete languages."

"You said that."

She reddened again. "Well, you asked!"

"Did I? I was just wondering why you called us *Alphas*."

"We can't call everyone our age sixth-graders, can we? The people here at SA-6 have come from one of a dozen or more solar systems! School is different on every planet. The one thing we all have in common is that this is the *beginning* of our time at SA-6."

"I get you. So we're Alphas, and we only need to go as high as a Delta—four years. Ninth grade."

"Yep."

"Then what?"

"You go to work."

"*What?*"

She blinked at him as if identifying Stephen for the moron that he really was.

He gazed away.

"That's why we go to school, isn't it? So we can find our place in society and become a member of this interstellar civilization?"

"Is it?"

Lorenza rolled her eyes.

Stephen was saved by the first grownup they reached.

Or he wasn't.

GEARING UP

Stephen watched patiently.

A man in a thick silver beard said, "Young lady?"

Placing her hands on the counter, Lorenza smiled at the man in uniform. Stephen thought he detected a flicker of uncertainty in her face. Nevertheless, she played it cool.

The old man waved a little blinking box past her nose, then grinned at it. Next, he plugged the box onto a square of black plastic on the counter. A drawer opened. The guy in uniform pulled out a little booklet of memory paper.

"There you go," he said, setting it into Lorenza's quivering hands. "Good luck!"

"What's that?" Stephen asked her.

With wide eyes, she stared at the first page of the memory paper and turned away.

"Face forward," said the gentle man, though it took an extra heartbeat or two for Stephen to realize that the man was addressing him.

"Oh? Sorry."

"Hold still," the man said, again as kind as could be.

Stephen froze.

A light flashed from the blinking box. The man stuck the box into the little dock on the counter. The drawer produced another pad of memory paper.

"There you go! Take care, now."

"Thank you." Stephen took the memory paper.

Before he could slide along the counter to where Lorenza had stopped to chat with a woman with white hair that ran so long it touched her beltline, the man with the beard caught Stephen's sleeve.

He leaned across the counter and whispered generously, "You don't have much money, young man. Don't buy anything unnecessary." He patted Stephen's forearm, gave a little wink, then looked at the student behind him. "All right! Hold still please."

With a sinking feeling, Stephen lifted the paper.

At least he saw English—and he was very sure that the letters and language hailed from his home planet.

On the first page, he read

Stage One: *Morning Block*
Stage Two: *Advanced Mathematics*

And he said, "Advanced? Oh no."
The list continued.

Stage Three: *Social Studies–Ancient Earth*
Stage Four: *A) Educational Technology B) Gym*
Stage Five: *Uniscript 1*
Stage Six: *Reading - Earth Scripts*
Stage Seven: *A) Music B) Basic Science*
Stage Eight: *Study Hall*
Stage Nine: *A) Health B) General Mechanics*
Stage Ten: *Night Block*

Then the woman who had been speaking with Lorenza reached across the counter with an open hand. "May I?"

Stephen handed her the memory paper.

She blinked the prettiest silver lashes, offset by dark mascara drawn along the underside of her eyelashes, smiling at the first page. She turned the first sheet and smiled at the second page, nodding, and saying, "Okay!" When she turned to the third page, her smile disappeared.

When she looked up at Stephen, she was grinning again. It was a softer smile, one he recognized, the sort of affection he received from school secretaries when they found out that he was a new kid with no parents to call his own—no real parents. (Of course, some of the secretaries looked at him with worry, distrust, or disdain, but he preferred to remember the loving ones, the kind who seemed like they might make nice mothers themselves.)

"Mr. Bumhandel. We're going to get you all squared away, all right?"

"All right," Stephen said, though it didn't feel very right to him. He also didn't like the idea that everyone was going to call him Bumhandel or Brian, or both, during his first school year on another world.

Hey, he thought, at least I'm not going to Montreal Middle!

She handed him a bag that matched his clothes. But she kept the memory paper, which she shared with one of a number of busy grownups and older kids who passed it along and busied themselves like a bunch of bees behind the counter and the shelves that lined the walls. Some disappeared behind the shelves while others reappeared with all sorts of things: ancient books with flaking covers; technological devices in various shapes; cans of what looked like metal pick-up-sticks or thin knitting needles.

Confused, Stephen examined the bag. It was pretty simple, also not very large. There were moveable and removable straps on the back, so that it might become a purse, a backpack, with two straps or one, a large fanny pack . . . .

"Why are you laughing?" said Lorenza.

"No reason. I was just thinking, about all this white and black. And here I am in this space-age, futuristic place. I just thought that people—or aliens—*this* advanced would know that kids can't keep these colors clean! Alphas and Betas must look filthy."

Lorenza shook her head. She held up her bag, which held paper and utensils now. "The cloth is made with repellent fibers. Pour red punch on this, it doesn't soak in—just rolls right off, like rain off a house with a metal roof."

"I was talking about dirt, dust—you know."

"If red punch couldn't get this dirty, do you think a little dust will?"

He chuckled again. "Sounds like a challenge."

She sighed.

"Here you go." Lorenza was handed a black box. There were no lights on it, and Stephen didn't see an obvious way to open it. About the size of a shoe box for a younger kid's footwear, the shiny plastic or metal object fit neatly into her bag.

The young guy who had given it to her now handed over her memory paper.

"May I have some licorice too?"

Stephen perked up. "You have licorice?"

"Nope." On the guy's chest, a pin flashed with neon-colors: STOP INHUMANE RACES! "No food here. But," he leaned on the counter, "the best candy's on the second level. At Zellion's!"

A supervisor behind him said, "Orrin!"

"Sorry sir!" Orrin spun around, took some memory paper from his boss, and sped behind the shelves and out of sight.

"Brian?"

An older teenager, about Orrin's age, searched the Alpha faces in line.

Stephen raised a hand.

She lifted her eyebrows. "Over here, please."

Lorenza said, "I'll wait for you."

Stephen almost said, *You don't have to do that*, but he liked the idea that somebody who knew something might be waiting for him.

Besides, the throng of students seemed to be thinning; students collected their things, filled bags, and wandered out the backside of the shop, which had curved their path into the bustling mall again.

The girl was tall, a whole lot older than a Delta, but not yet eighteen. Her hair was the color of a sunset: bright, blonde, with touches of colors leaning in the direction of red.

"Okay, here is your Math book."

Stephen was totally blown away. And not by the book.

The longer he stared at her, as she led him to an empty space of counter beyond some of the others, he noticed that the girl's hair was *changing* like a sunset. It grew darker, redder, and threatening a little purple and nighttime as she spoke.

The girl set a pink rod, one of those thin knitting needles that was no longer than a pencil, on the countertop.

She saw his expression and lit up, just as her hair shifted from night to morning, hinting at a blue-white sunrise on a distant horizon. "When you get your memory paper back," she said with a tone more conversational than professional, "you just take the book—and the stick—like this, holding the end with your fingertips, and slide it over whatever page you want to use. The paper will do the rest. Adult memory paper has navigation glyphs. Students use separate pages for separate books. It's easier. Okay?"

"Okay," he said, and then he asked her to marry him.

Well, not exactly. He looked away instead.

"This is your Language book."

"Pink, Math. Blue, Language."

She dimpled.

He nearly fell over.

"And this is your Social Studies book," she said when an older fellow appeared at her side with the massive volume.

She placed the tome on the counter. It landed with a thump. Dust exploded from the cover and fell in little clouds.

Stephen nearly fell over, again.

The girl laughed, her voice musical. "Yeah. Don't rub this across your memory paper. Won't do anything."

Orrin's supervisor snapped at her now. "Debbie! Time! Time!"

Without turning, she sneered at the older guy.

And Stephen knew he had seen that sneer somewhere before. He just couldn't say exactly where.

"Give me your bag," she said.

"My hand?"

"Your bag."

Stephen put the bag on the counter.

She put a few more items inside its pockets. "Don't worry. Someone will tell you about the rest of these things. Just don't lose your memory paper. Stay here."

Debbie swept away her bright sunrise hair following her now, and she returned a moment later with a few more supplies, including a black box just like the one Lorenza had received.

Debbie glanced at the old boss, then whispered. "Gotta forgive the guy. He just wants to finish the rush and take a break before the next ship arrives. Can't blame him."

"What's that?"

The black box was the last thing to go into his bag. "Science. You'll see!" Debbie looked excited by the idea.

"You like science, I take it?"

"Oh, you will too!" She put Stephen's memory paper inside last. "You're all set. Don't have much money, but that's all the stuff you need to begin with. Just don't buy junk food—you need your cash to last." She seemed instantly ashamed at her words. "I mean, a lot of Alphas waste their money on the first day and then run out before they get more. I wouldn't want you to make the same mistake."

"Debbie!" said the boss.

"Gotta go. Take care, now."

"Thank you." Stephen took hold of the bag, dragged it off the counter, and leaned from its weight after Debbie waved and walked away. It was packed. He had no idea how she could have fit everything into the narrow bag and wondered if there were some magical principle of scientific technology that explained it all.

Lorenza paced outside the shop. She watched others eating ice cream cones.

"They have ice cream and licorice here," Stephen said. "It's not all bad."

"Who said it would be bad?" she asked.

Stephen looked for Brian Boar. "There must be thousands of people in here!"

"Possibly."

Stephen wondered if he would ever see Brian again. Maybe not seeing him would be for the best. After all, Brian had heard Stephen's real name in that dream of the Greenbergs and Hank at the beach.

They went for licorice. Stephen didn't know how to pay for any-thing—Sunrise/Sunset Debbie had said that he didn't have much to spread around, but that meant that he *had money*.

Licorice couldn't cost too much. Stephen fully intended to get some.

But they were continually distracted by amazing sights, sounds, smells, and free tastes—for a poor boy, that was just about the best thing of all!—in the form of samples where vendors hoped to push more of the same for "low, low prices!"

A half hour passed, then an hour, and Stephen decided that they must not be in any kind of hurry. His bag weighed a ton, but he was dazzled in a World of New. And while Lorenza didn't have many an-swers, she shared in his enthusiasm for all the fun stuff around them.

In fact, Lorenza seemed to need Stephen as a friend as much as he needed her. Without each other, they would each likely be wander-ing around the mall by themselves, alone.

"There it is!" Lorenza pointed at a brilliant sign that seemed to come in and out of existence: *ZELLION'S TOTALLY ILLEGAL CANDY!*

She zipped through the crowd.

Stephen started after her. A heavy hand pressed down on his shoulder.

Two buff guys, in black uniforms with stripes of white running up the sides, stood over him like prison guards. "Brian Bumhandel?"

Stephen swallowed.

"Come with us, please?"

By the look in their eyes, he knew they weren't giving him a choice.

BRIDGE TO NOWHERE

Stephen knew from the beginning that it couldn't last. The fact that he had seen so much should be enough! But no matter what, he did not belong. He had never belonged, not anywhere, not to anyone. And that was all that mattered.

Without speaking, the two men led Stephen to an elevator hidden between a shoe store and a clock shop. He wanted to make a joke, to ask one of the men why people in space needed grandfather clocks or windup watches, like the ones in the windows they passed, but he didn't think that either of them would crack a smile.

Inside the elevator, he watched the doors shut. The silence almost hurt his ears. Had it been so very loud in the mall?

He felt the tears starting to rise.

They wouldn't really drop him off somewhere between here and Earth, would they?

As the elevator car began to move (it went down first, then began to travel sideways, Stephen thought), memories of that wonderful dream on the beach returned. Wouldn't it be nice if they sent him back to Earth through one of those dreams? It would. At least for a time. And if they gave him another chance, he wouldn't wake up at all. Stephen decided that he would live with the Greenbergs on the beach until his body got old and died. That would be *just fine*.

Of course, he suspected that the happy dream home wouldn't be an option.

Horrible realities flashed through his mind as the elevator ride continued into eternity.

Might they dump him back on Earth? Probably. And no one would ever believe his stories of flying saucers, an Earth Transport with giant fireplaces, and a shopping mall selling impossible and unpredictable items *at* a school in space. Stephen wouldn't be able to tell anyone.

He wiped his eyes.

This was worse than not having real parents.

The doors opened.

Stephen took one step forward, then two steps back, slamming into both men.

"Come on, kid. Don't make us carry you."

It took a moment for Stephen to see that there was more than a black pit waiting for him. There was also rock, a metal path, sparse railings, dim lights.

"Go," said the other voice behind him.

Stephen started forward slowly. One of the men put a hand on his shoulder to speed up his shorter legs. Stephen was actually *glad* to feel that firm grip on him.

Because right outside of the elevator, they crossed a dark bridge that loomed over a rocky cliff side framing a canyon of bottomless darkness.

It had to be more than a hundred feet to the rocky ridge on the far side of the ravine. On the other side, four yellow lights sparkled around a perfectly square door.

Stephen's heart sped up with his breathing. The tears dried against the imminent threat of accidental death.

"Don't worry, kid. We won't let you fall. Just do as we tell you."

Across the bridge, they paused on a landing before the door. One of the men stepped forward, reached into a pocket, withdrew a square coin, and dropped it.

"Ho!"

The coin banged on the edge of the metal bridge and fell flat. If it had been round, it might have rolled right off and down the abyss.

"That was too close," said the guy holding Stephen by the shoulder. "I would have *loved* to watch you explain *that* to the Board."

"Oh, you don't know?" said the man in front. He bent and picked up the golden square. "You *can't* drop these off the bridge. Watch." As if Stephen weren't there anymore, he flicked the coin into the air.

Glimmering yellow against the four lights, the square went end over end in a mighty arch over the railing. Before it could fall beneath the bridge, Stephen heard a tiny humming sound. The coin moved like a ray of light and slapped itself to the side of the metallic walkway.

"Whoa!"

"Magnetized. Safety protocol, I guess." The guard retrieved his coin for the second time, then tapped it twice against the door.

There weren't any knobs, latches, or windows. But the door must have understood something. It slid straight up into the ceiling.

They passed beneath it. Stephen watched the man spin his coin-key across dry knuckles like a wanna-be magician. The door shut behind them. Before doing so, Stephen noticed that the barrier was thicker than his shoulders were wide.

As they approached a second door, the guard lost control of his knuckle-sliding coin, and the square fell to the ground again.

"Here." The man behind Stephen released his grip, laughed, and put a hand into his own pocket. "Let me." He produced a matching coin-key and tapped this door three times.

The door slid into the left wall. At the same time a matching door immediately behind it slid into the right wall.

They led Stephen into a room with a desk and a rust-colored robot in the shape of a man. The android quivered on grating motors and looked up from the desk, leveling cold blue lights on the newcomers.

"Is this the boy?" The voice from the slit in the robot's expressionless face sounded tired and stressed.

"Yes sir."

The robotic head cocked to one side, jerking, then stopping in such a frozen position, Stephen thought the moving puppet might not be able to straighten out again afterwards. "Are you sure?"

One of the men pulled a black baton from the black side of his pant leg. He pointed it at Stephen and brought it up. Stephen watched alien letters made of light hover in the air at the side of the stick. "Confirmed."

The android straightened its head, then froze again. "I thought it had to be a mistake. He can't be older than an Alpha. I tell you, this is getting sick!"

"Yes sir." The guard put his baton away.

"No. I don't believe it. What are you?"

No one answered.

"I said, what are you."

"Me?" Stephen's voice was a squirrel's squeak.

"Where are you from?"

"I—I'm . . . California." The tears were rising again, threatening to do an imitation of Niagara Falls from his eyes any second.

"This has got to be a mistake, sir," said the man who had balanced Stephen safely across the bridge. He had a hard face, and black hair like his uniform, but there was a sparkle of human understanding in his eyes that was lacking in the man-shaped robot across the desk.

The robot shifted at every joint. "That is not for you to judge!"

"If this infiltration is as strategic as you think it might be, then this boy's just the scapegoat." He bent his knees to bring himself down to Stephen's eye-level. "Kid, if you're innocent, you don't have nothing to worry about. You hear me? Just wait for the Board."

The other man didn't look so trusting. He might have been a coin-dropping joker, but he kept a hand on his belt as if ready to draw a weapon that Stephen couldn't see.

The robot grumbled meaningless words, then sighed. "Stick him in the can. Jake."

The nicer man stood up. "Yes, sir?"

The other guy waved Stephen toward another doorway, pulled his coin-key, and tapped the door once.

"You come see me right now, Jake. You and I need to have a little chat about your current professional opportunities."

Jake snapped to attention. "Yes, sir." He turned to the outer doors, which scissored open when he tapped them. Then he was gone.

"Let's go, you."

Before the man could lead him through the inner portal, the android swiveled its head and torso at Stephen. "What's your name, Alpha?"

Say 'Stephen', and you're out of here, said Hank in Stephen's head. *Say 'Brian', and you're out-out-out. This is what I call a "no win situation." Sorry, pal.*

Stephen didn't answer in time.

"Get him out of here."

"All right, kid," said the coin flipper.

Within a minute, Stephen was in a jail cell with transparent bars. The room was dark except where the bars came out of the floor and ceiling. They seemed to be made of nothing more than beams of light.

"See those?" said the guard, pointing at the bars. "Wouldn't touch those if I were you."

Mercifully, he left.

So that Stephen could cry without being heard.

CELLMATE

About an hour later, food arrived through the wall. Stephen was no longer surprised to see matter transfer through solid objects like this. But he was very sad that he wasn't able to see another person during the delivery.

Though he would never admit it, he had cried a lot before the meal arrived.

Dinner was a combination of meat under gravy over something that tasted like potatoes mashed with radishes. On the side waited a crop of peas and a red fruit that otherwise looked and felt like chunks of peaches—and he cried some more.

On a bunk in the center of the cell, Stephen quietly cried himself to sleep.

When he woke, he sniffled for a while.

"Hey."

Stephen held his breath.

"You get all that out of you?"

Stephen didn't move. He scanned the darkness outside of his cell.

Beyond the faintly illuminated bars, Stephen could only see other prison cells. He had thought them all empty. Each was as poorly lit by the light bars as his own.

The cells were organized along two walls with a walkway between them. Directly across the walkway from his cell, an older kid folded his legs on a bed in the center of another cell. He swept long hair out of his eyes. "No shame in crying the stress away. Not every day you go to jail, am I right?" He laughed a little. "Unless you're like me. I have rich parents, so the Board won't deport me. I rather like it down here. Most students don't even know this place exists! Lucky us, huh?"

Cellmate

Stephen didn't say anything. His face glowed hot with embarrassment.

"Name's Freddy. You?"

"Brian."

"So. You must really hate school to get yourself stashed down here on your first day, Brian."

"How . . . how did you know it's my first day?"

"Well you're tiny. Alpha, right?"

"Not for long."

"Don't be so hard on yourself. First offense. They'll slap you once really hard across the face, then let you go. What did you do? Try to steal something in the mall? Ah." Freddy swatted at the air to say that was nothing. "Problem is, you're a puppy. You want to walk out of a store without paying, you got to do what I call Advanced Sleight of Hand."

While Stephen had no desire at all to become a thief, his attention was piqued at the wizarding words *sleight of hand*.

"Oh! You like the sound of this practical skill, do you? I could teach you. I think after we get out of here, Brian, you and I are going to become close friends. Just don't tell your parents: I'm the kind of joe they probably warn you about."

"Don't have any parents."

Freddy paused. "No?" He sounded sincere, in spite of the words that followed. "No loss. Who needs a dad always telling you how to live your life or a mom constantly telling you to eat your vegetables? I'm an Eta. Know what that means?"

"No."

"Last year! You don't get any older here at SA-6 unless you become one of those stooges who get a local job and never bother to leave—like there ain't no life outside of school! Poor suckers. Any-whooo, once they let me go and get back to classes—which I despise—I can finish what my pops wants me to finish, and then I can rocket and never do anything that they want me to do again."

Stephen didn't say anything.

"Aw, you don't understand. You're wishing you had parents, right? You a tranc then?"

"Yeah."

"Don't take my fits personally. Not everyone with parents is happy, is all. Not all *parents* are happy. Guess that's the real problem. Not every story is a happy one. So . . . know what I do?"

"What's that?"

"Rewrite the story!" Freddy bounced from the mattress and sheets and approached the bars. "Look at this." He lifted empty hands. Then he reached into the air and produced a coin like a pro.

Stephen grinned.

Then he recognized the square shape and the yellow color. "Hey, isn't that a key?"

"Sure is. Here!" Freddy tossed it. It crossed through the narrow pillars of light, spun over the breach between their cells, and sang against the concrete floor just after passing between the bars on Stephen's side.

Stephen dropped a foot on it.

Freddy shrugged. "I've had my fun. It's useless against these bars anyway. Tuck it away."

Stephen held up the coin to examine it a little closer. There was a head on one side, the head of a lion. On the other was a symbol he had never seen before. Writing covered the object, but it was that upside-down Sanskrit alphabet he had failed to decipher earlier.

He made the coin-key walk over the top of his knuckles without letting it fall.

"Whoof!" said Freddy. "Seems you have some skills yourself." He sat on the floor and rested his arms on his knees. "I've never heard of an Alpha in prison before. I didn't even get in trouble like this until I was a Beta. I was—hee, hee—ahead of my class!"

Stephen put the coin-key into his pocket.

"You're missing Orientation, you know."

"Is that important?"

"Nah. It's the big meeting for Alphas, when the Board members explain all the new stuff you need to know. About the school and whatnot. Rules and procedures."

Cellmate

So, Stephen thought, *even if they do slap me on the wrist and, by some miracle, let me stay at SA-6, I won't know the regulations; I'll end up in this dark detention again and again. Great!*

Realizing that Freddy was his only hope, Stephen said, "Um."

"Yeah?"

"Will you tell me?"

"Tell you what?"

"What they are saying in the Orientation? What I'm missing?"

"Hey, pup, I got your back." Freddy looked at the ceiling and searched for information long gone—he looked a little too much like he was making things up. "First, they're talking about the different stages, then the levels. SA-6 is—well, where are you from, Earth?"

"Yes."

Freddy slapped his hands together. "I pegged you as a kid from Earth from the start. Well, SA-6 is freaking huge! I mean, it is bigger than any school you have ever been to. There are kids from all over the galaxy here—well, our part of the galaxy."

"Easy to get lost," Stephen concluded.

"Oh, not really. There is plenty of help. No dilly about that. But what they'll tell you in the Orientation is—I mean, what they're telling the other Alphas is that *Alphas* are restricted from every level off the mid-range."

"What—what does that mean?"

Freddy laughed and brushed the hair out of his eyes. "It means that Alphas don't ever go this deep, or anywhere where SA-6 actually touches the planet. Alphas never see the pit and the prison!" He barked laughter at the shadows behind him.

Stephen laughed in spite of his worried thoughts.

"Can't go up, either." Freddy held his hand out, palm down, and drew an invisible line horizontally in the air. "Alphas stay here: mid-range. Anyway, you couldn't go very high or very low even if you tried. Even if you found a way, they'd know it and—zzzzip—in come the black uniforms to haul you away."

"How would they know?"

Freddy snapped his fingers. "When you came off the bus, did you see a bunch of protesters with signs about 'freedom' and stuff like that?"

Stephen remembered easily. *Give me liberty or give me death!* "Yes."

"In that same room, you were tagged by a worker with a fancy doodad. *The Powers that Be* can find you, now, in a second!"

Not that it mattered. If Stephen were thrown out as an imposter. At least the "Board" knew who Freddy, the rich kid, was. Stephen wanted to hear all about this alien place before they came for him. It certainly beat worrying about what would happen next. (If he made it back to Earth and the Allyns, Mr. Allyn would be furious at losing whatever the government was paying for his silence.)

"So what else?"

"Oh, the regular stuff. Punctuality. 'Tardiness is not tolerated,' though you'll see it everyday. The teachers can kick you out of class any time they want, for *anything!* There are sentinels everywhere, left over from the FF days, of course."

Strange terms were buzzing past Stephen at high speed. He managed to say, "Sentinels?"

"Guards. Like the one in black who dragged you in here?"

"Sentinels."

"Trust me, I've tested the limits of this place. A rebel with any cause I can claim! The truth is, most of the teachers are pretty good to you. You gotta really jab them in the ribs to get on their bad side." He swallowed. "Well, most of them. A few . . . you start on their bad side and have to climb out of it."

Freddy said that last bit while staring intently at some recent memory. Then he hefted his shoulders.

"Course, I never bothered. What do I care, anyway? What does anyone care." He darkened into loneliness.

No matter their differences, Stephen felt the guy's pain. "I care."

For the first time since his appearance, Freddy's hard face of cool indifference dropped like a mask. He was years older than Stephen, but with his eyes softened he looked about the same age. He even gave Stephen the impression of being frightened.

The fear warmed into an expression of real friendship.

"Aw, don't you worry, Bri. You're not missing much. It's all, if you break the rules, blah-blah-blah; if you follow the rules, blah-blah, blah. Uniforms are mandatory outside of your domus. Planet colors are allowed when the sports start up. All you need to know is this: act like good student, you get all the good stuff."

"Thanks."

"You probably knew that already. School is school, no matter what planet you're on."

Freddy drifted in his thoughts and scratched at his fingernails for over a minute.

Stephen walked around the bed in the center of his cell. When he came around to Freddy's side again, he saw the teenager smiling once more.

"Of course, you'll *love* the cafeterias. For one thing, the eateries are open all day long."

"All day?"

"Yeah, and that's nothing. The food selections change constantly, and there are like a hundred different dishes!"

"No way!" On cue, Stephen's stomach growled.

"In a place like this, I wouldn't joke around, Brian."

At the sound of the fake name that had been the center of all his problems, Stephen's grin slipped.

"Don't look so sad," said Freddy, wandering to his bars again. "You'll go free. Trust me."

"You don't know what I know."

"Wait until you see the gym. Think about it—a gym *in space?* They play games out here that you will not believe! If you like that kind of stuff."

"I'd like it."

"Then there's the mall."

"I saw that."

"Doubt it. Alphas always think the first cylinder is the mall. *That's the foyer.*"

Stephen's eyes widened.

"But you really think you're stuck, huh? What are you in for?"

Stephen didn't answer, though he also didn't quite see any reason to keep any secrets from this guy.

"Hey, if you tell me, I might know how to get you out of whatever hole you've fallen into. I have a motto: There's always a back door, always an easy way out of your problem, if you can just find it."

Oh, Stephen felt the temptation to say it all—he also felt the tears perilously close to coming again—but he held back.

"And every grownup in SA-6 knows *glitches happen*. Trust me, you'll be out of here in no time." Freddy coughed and wiped his nose on his sleeve. "It's just that there's been a few scares lately."

Stephen lifted his eyes. "Like what?"

"Terrorists. Nothing to be worried about. Obviously." Freddy barked one of his little laughs again. "They're arresting little kids now! Making things *too* safe for their own good. If you had parents, they'd complain and heads would roll!" Freddy shook his own head. "People need to read more history, learn how to avoid fascism and such. So who are you really, little man?"

"No one."

"Not true."

"Is true," said Stephen. "That's the problem. I don't really belong. I've never—" he stopped himself on the verge of crying, toughed his voice to sound more like Freddy. "I just came back to my horrible home one day, and this lady was in my living room, pretending to be a relative. She flew me to the Earth Transport, changed my name to Brian, and then disappeared."

"Changed your name?" Freddy said, close to his bars. He was seriously amazed. "Whoa, freak-meister! You don't know why you're really here? Is that what you're saying?"

"No idea at all. But it's—" Stephen's voice caught. "—it's been so much better than my life back home."

Barely a whisper, Freddy said, "So what's your name? If it's not Brian?"

"Stephen."

What happened next was a high-speed nightmare.

Cellmate

Freddy's entire body slammed into the bars of his cell.

His eyes rolled in different directions.

His head exploded into parts.

So did the rest of him.

It was as if someone had taken a bucket of water and thrown it into the hallway, except that Freddy *was* the water.

Yet he wasn't water. More like runny dough falling sideways.

One leg, both arms, his head, his shoulder, his chest, all elongated, twisted super-quick into long, stretching tentacles. The whips reached across the space between the cells and straight through Stephen's bars the instant everything went crazy.

Also, as soon as Freddy stopped being a teenage boy and smashed himself against his illuminated bars, a shrill alarm pulsed.

Lights flashed, bright and constant.

It might have been the blast of noise; it might have been the glaring lights; it might have been the freak show; maybe the simple, quick instinct to survive—*something* made Stephen fall backwards and down.

Alien tongues, with curved needles protruding from the ends, groped over his head.

Stephen rolled around the side of the bed and out of reach.

With a roar of fury, the tentacles wrapped around the bed, ripped it away from the floor—there was a horrible tearing sound of metal bolts pulling from the concrete—and the bed was yanked. It spun in the air. It slapped flat into the bars. Then it was cast aside.

Stephen heard his own voice now, shrieking.

Quick as lightning, the snakes reached for him.

A REASON FOR FREDDY'S EXPLOSION

Stephen ducked against the back bars.

The tentacles lashed at the air. They could not reach him.

The entire attack might have lasted thirty seconds, no more.

Rough men and women in black uniforms with white stripes filled the room. Each sentinel held some kind of T-shaped gun with the long barrel protruding from their knuckles like a ring that had grown into a weapon.

Before they could fire a shot, Freddy pulled himself together and then splashed all over the floor and his bed. There weren't even any clothes anymore, just a sticky wheat cereal all over the place.

And the smell! Sour, milky, acidic.

Stephen covered his mouth and nose to escape what certainly must have come out of something's stomach.

He dropped his hand when he saw the guns aimed at *him*.

At the back of his cell, he heaved. "Don't shoot!"

"Don't move!" said one of the women. She was a gruff creature with a jaw as hard—and hairy—as a man's. "Just don't move."

Nearly ten minutes passed. Authorities swept into the crowded hallway. In the meantime, someone had shut off the howling alarm and turned up the lights—no more pulsing, just a painfully bright white shine from the ceiling.

One of the newest arrivals surveyed the situation quickly. With a countenance of stone, he glowered for a moment at Stephen, then studied the filthy slop left in Freddy's cell.

The splatter did not flinch again.

Addressing the buff woman, Stone Face said, "Find out what that is."

Then he waved at Stephen. "Come on out of there."

Stephen had not realized that the bars in front of his cell had either receded into the floor or been shut off.

On quivering legs, Stephen skirted one side of his cell, keeping far away from the bed that leaned against the bars on the other side.

"This way."

Encircled by multiple guards, Stephen followed Stone Face out of the prison, across the bridge, and into the elevator. They left the elevators and arrived in a dark room that lit with pillars of light cutting through the darkness at the moment of their entrance. Somehow the walls and much of the room remained in shadow.

The room was round. The air smelled of ozone and electricity. Chairs rose from empty floors. One lifted into a cone of light.

Stone Face lifted his hand to this chair positioned beneath the central light. "Sit."

Stephen placed himself in the center of this oddly shaded horror chamber.

The room cleared, and they left him alone for a quarter of an hour. It felt like an entire night.

Stephen didn't move.

He wondered if he could get out of the chair if he tried, or if the oppression he felt around him like a magnetic pull might squeeze him into the seat.

Then the authorities returned. Unlike the sentinels dressed in black shirts and pants with white stripes, these men and women wore long coats that hung about their knees and displayed no white at all. With chins lifted and eyes squinting, they each claimed one of the chairs circled around Stephen.

As soon as they were positioned, he felt the chair begin to rotate. Moving him slowly around and around, each authority figure was able to peer into his eyes and examining Stephen more closely.

"What happened down there?"

Stephen wasn't even sure that he could explain it clearly to himself. It was like an illogical, impossible dream reviewed after waking. His heart refused to slow.

The possibility of being sent home didn't matter at this point. In Harmon, California, people didn't explode into giant fingers tipped with thorns and then collapse into a lake of tan-colored soup!

A man with a softer face and large eyebrows said, "Marcus, the boy's in shock."

A third authority figure with snow-white hair asked the question again. "What happened?"

Stephen wrung his sweaty hands. "With—with Freddy?"

Now a woman was facing him, her nose pointed to one side while she pondered him with one eye. "Yes."

"What—what was he?"

The next man in the circle stared at him down a large hawk-beak of a nose. "For now, please answer our questions."

Struggling to believe what he had experienced to begin with, Stephen told them everything. When he came to the part about the coin-key, Stephen dug Freddy's present from his pocket and held it out.

Frowning, Marcus took the key by one corner, as if it might be tainted with the Black Plague or something worse. He handed it to a guard, who locked the item into a yellow box.

Stephen finished his memory of events. He stumbled over the last part, almost thinking that *they* wouldn't even believe what had happened.

But someone behind him said to one side, "Exactly what we saw."

The woman said, "But what was he?"

Stephen had no way to answer.

Yet the question had not been directed at him. The nice man with the bushy eyebrows tapped his chin. "We'll know more in an hour. Possibly identify a signature."

"You don't know that," said Marcus, still grimacing. Still looking at Stephen. He leaned forward as Stephen came around. "You were wise to give me the key. *Why* did Freddy attack you?"

Stephen only blinked at him.

The man with white hair said, "Ask him about the absconder."

Marcus drilled Stephen with his eyes. "Well?"

"Huh?"

The woman spoke up again. "This is absolutely the worst time for you to hide the truth, young man."

"I didn't—I didn't understand—um—can you ask me again, please?"

"The absconder," said Marcus. "It was found among your home clothes. Do you deny it?"

"My clothes?" Stephen said. He had been thinking so much about his cellmate, about nearly dying, about how he had only escaped death on accident that it took him another couple of seconds to understand the altered direction of their questioning. His voice cracked mid-way through his statement. "Old Mr. Bluntwasp gave it to me. What is it?"

No one responded.

Stephen began to tremble again at the painful memory of loss. "He was nice to me."

⋆ ⋆ ◗ †

A door slid open where there had not been a door.

Brightened by a white light behind her, a mature woman in red robes stood with her head high.

The adults in black stood.

"Be seated," she said. "I have heard enough of this! You poor child."

Everyone returned to their chairs but Marcus. "With all due respect, Magistra, you should not be here. This is a formal inquisition."

With her feet hidden beneath her dress, she seemed to float into the room. "*I can be wherever I want.* And *you* know this especially, Marcus! Sit down."

He did not. "We are determining the severity of this situation."

"This situation is a *boy*, from Earth, obviously. A tranc, I dare say. Mistakes happen—are you holding him because of his possession of contraband?"

"High-end military grade—" said the man with white hair, but he stopped when she silenced him with a single hand.

"Which the boy said that he received as a gift from an old man. A nice old man. And it is old high-end military grade, Shapiro. And then he was nearly assassinated by a plant so deeply placed, we never noticed the danger in spite of the fact that Freddy, himself, had been arrested numerous times!"

"An assassination attempt does not exonerate this child!" said Marcus.

But Stephen noticed that some of the other grownups were looking at each other with uncertain glances.

"Magistra, consider for a moment how one might dig a plant even deeper? Why not first get him arrested with questionable documentation and nail him into his lowly position by adding a device perfect for spies? Then, fake an assassination attempt! You will notice that Freddy—or whatever he was—self-destructed before we could question him. If we let this child go, now he will be *trusted,* when in fact he may very well be a new plant, firmly established, and likely to remain at SA-6 for the next seven years!"

The woman drew closer, but did not look angry. She said a single word, "Noted." Then added, "Please sit. If I am killed, I can be replaced. But if I am correct—and I have learned to trust my intuition—then this young man needs a friend. Certainly an advocate!"

She turned to Stephen and bent to his level. Tears sparkled in the corners of her eyes when she came into the light. She put a hand on his knee, another on his shoulder. Her presence repelled the electrical smell in the air and replaced it with something delicious and warm, as if she had until recently been baking cookies in a kitchen. "So, young man. Do you know me?"

Stephen sniffed back his own tears. He couldn't talk. So he shook his bowed head. But she held him with her eyes, and he didn't want the woman to let go.

"They call me Mother Miriam. If I worked on your planet, in your country, you would know me . . . as your principal." She looked over his shoulder. "These good people are charged with the safety of the school. Order. Discipline. We call them The Board."

The woman with the distrusting eye said, "Ask him if his name is really *Brian Bumhandel*."

Kindly, Mother Miriam lifted her curved eyebrows. "Is that your name?"

Stephen bit his lip. After a pause, he shook his head.

"Then what is your name, my good man?"

"Stephen. Stephen . . . Cowen."

The room gasped.

"Look at him!" whispered one of the Board.

Another said, "It's Stephen Crown!"

Even Mother Miriam's eyes grew wide.

NO MORE SECRETS

He didn't want to play any more games. More than anything, he suffered with the need to feel safe. "No. Stephen *Cowen*."

But the man who had spoken last said, "Are you sure? Tell us about your parents."

"I—I'm a foster child. I've never had—"

"Exactly."

Everyone had floated into a standing position, including Mother Miriam. With a gentle touch, she helped Stephen to rise from the chair. "Lights!" The roof obeyed and the room grew warm, the walls shining with a soft green glow. "Seal the room."

"Too late," said Marcus. To the sentinels, he said, "Outside. Say *nothing*." To the ceiling he added, "Freeze recording."

"No!" said the man with bushy eyebrows. "This is *history*! EVERYTHING must be recorded with perfect accuracy."

"He's right," said the woman. She continued to stare at Stephen with one eye, but now her face pointed to the left. "Stephen Crown?"

Stephen shook his head.

Marcus had snapped new orders, some kind of code to the room, but Stephen had stopped paying him attention.

Stephen was looking into Mother Miriam's eyes, which softened on him again. "I'm ... sorry," he said.

She grinned and glowed. "Don't be! *We're* sorry. You deserve greater respect."

"Don't be absurd," Marcus said, his voice lowered. "We do not know for certain that this is Stephen Crown. This is a *dangerous* conclusion to reach in haste."

Running a hand through his long, wispy, snow-white hair, Shapiro said, "It would explain the attack."

One eye said, "It might explain the absconder."

Mother Miriam was hugging Stephen to her side. "Dangerous for whom, Marcus? For us? For Stephen?"

"Certainly for Stephen," said one of the Board members.

"We can protect him. Especially when word circulates of his presence. He will be safe in the public eye."

"You *know* what will happen, Shapiro!"

"Of course, Reinault!" said Marcus. "But Stephen *doesn't*. He doesn't have the first clue. Nor has he had a single choice. Stephen ... how did you get here."

Again, Stephen told them everything, with perfect honesty.

"Faction?" Shapiro asked the Board.

Reinault shook her head. "Wizening Apartheid, Kendall?"

"It has to be the Order," answered the man with the bushy eyebrows.

Marcus shut his eyes. "*Assuming* that the Order knew about Stephen, they wouldn't have been able to find him any better than Black Nebulae or—we don't need to discuss this in front of him."

"I agree, Marcus," said Mother Miriam. "Stephen," she said, crouching beside him again. Her dress billowed around her. "All you need to know right now is that these good men and women of the board are charged with keeping you absolutely safe. They *will* be your greatest protectors. You are safe here in SA-6—as safe as you can be. I want you to go to class now. You will be a little late, but I will clear that with your teacher."

Marcus went to the door, which opened at his presence. "Fetch the boy's belongings."

"Are you hungry?"

He was starving. It seemed that he was always starving now. But he didn't think he could eat if he tried: his stomach had tied itself into a hard knot. "No."

"From now on," she glanced at the Board, "use your real name. Stephen Crown. I'm confident."

Marcus sighed his frustration. "I really do not think this is the best move for us to make."

"Kendall?"

"Yes, Magistra?"

"Will you escort Stephen to his Alpha Class please? Get him there before it ends. Introduce him."

Mother Miriam stood as Kendall approached.

"Shapiro, please fix his registration data."

"Right away, Ma'am." The old man left the room.

Marcus stood with his mouth *still* in a grim line. "Magistra Mother."

"*Tell me* which rule is being broken, Marcus."

"No law. No rule. Nevertheless…let us at least keep from making a public announcement. For *his* sake. Don't turn the school into a circus with Stephen as the main attraction. This will be hard enough as it is."

"I quite agree. Which is why I am placing you in charge of Stephen's care and comfort. Can you follow this order?"

Marcus snapped to attention. "You know that I can and that I will."

"Wonderful." She crouched one last time. "Stephen?"

"Yes?"

"I am so *glad* that you are here. You are very special!"

Stephen had begun to think that they had him mistaken for somebody else. After she said that he was special, he was sure of it. Stephen had never been special in his life.

Mother Miriam continued. "You were placed on Earth with a new name so that no one would find you. But you *matter*, Stephen. In time, you will understand just how important you are." She stroked his hair. "Stephen Crown!"

He didn't speak. It felt so good to be held, to be touched with so much love. Happiness wrapped him in a warm blanket.

"This is the *first day* of the rest of your fabulous new life!"

Kendall stood beside the door. Stephen's heavy bag hung from one hand. Stephen's brand new memory paper dangled from the other. "Okay, Stephen. Shall we?"

No More Secrets

Once more, Stephen was guided into an elevator, which carried him quickly to his location.

This time the elevator doors opened into a long hallway made of brick and mortar. Gas lamps hissed all along the side of one wall, casting a yellow color against the windows on the opposite. Through the glass, Stephen could see that night had fallen. A shooting star streaked across a brushstroke of Milky Way beauty.

"This is the Linguistics building," said Kendall with a proud grin on his face. "Every language in the galaxy is taught here! Well, almost every language. Once upon a time, I taught Uniscript on this very floor!"

The ceiling was vaulted, dark ribs lifting what looked very much like a wooden belfry. Wooden planks crossed under his feet. His shoes even scuffed the side of one beam and tore away a finger-length sliver—it was real wood, or a perfect fabrication. Most of the floor seemed to be polished by years of student abuse. All those hurrying kids running to class.

The corridor was empty now.

"Ah!" said Kendall, who had slowed to consult Stephen's memory paper. "Here we are."

He turned and helped Stephen with his bag. He placed the memory paper into his hands. Then he pulled open a door that seemed ancient but moved on absolutely silent hinges.

The class was lit by bright lamps hanging from a white ceiling. The lamps seemed to burn like the gas flames in the hallway, but there were no flames. No filaments inside of bulbs, either. Stephen couldn't quite make them out.

Along the walls were posters covered in an alien script that, while unreadable, was becoming more and more familiar to Stephen's eyes. While there were clowns, or strange animals drawn in cartoon caricatures on the posters, the writing dominated, surrounding and smothering them.

The class fell silent as soon as Stephen entered. Not that Stephen had heard any speaking prior to the door opening, but all eyes turned to him now.

There must have been twenty students, but no more. They looked bewildered and somehow grateful for the distraction.

An instructor in a long white smock held her hands clamped together. Before Kendall could meet her at the front of the room, the woman said, "Brian Bumhandel?"

Some of the kids snickered at that horrible last name.

The woman said something else. The words that came from her round mouth sounded eloquent but entirely foreign. Stephen didn't understand a bit of it.

Kendall answered with the same lip and tongue flapping. With one hand, he indicated the papers on the teacher's podium.

The woman crossed to the materials—the roll, presumably—and grinned at the name. Froze. And looked at the little boy standing beside the Board member with bushy eyebrows.

She waved him over to her side. She spoke again, but it still sounded like more cheek and jowl talk. She said something more, pressing her fingers against her chest.

Then she turned him to face the class. She said something to the room of young children and ended it with "Stephen Crown."

Throughout the class, there was a flash of wide eyes.

THE ALPHA CLASS

Brian Boar was gawking at him from the back row. Beside him sat the only empty seat. The teacher waved Stephen in that direction, clicking and slapping her gums with her tongue, the whole time.

Stephen sat at the desk.

Kendall made a hang loose sign by extending his thumb and pinky finger. He waggled both, grinning with pride, then left the room.

The staring continued.

It took more than a minute for the instructor to get everyone's attention, though she had not ceased her peculiar speech.

Brian didn't say anything, just ogled Stephen like the others.

Stephen melted into his chair.

He felt he should do *something*. His hand floated upward.

Brian shook his head. Then he whispered, "Don't bother. She's been going on like that since before she called attendance! *Stephen Crown*, huh?"

Stephen dropped his hand. He shrugged.

"The secret's out."

"Guess so."

The teacher started talking to them specifically. Distracted, they hadn't a clue until she positioned herself between the desks. Her face was soft. Her eyebrows lifted.

She spoke to Stephen, calling him by his first name.

The sounds meant nothing. But Stephen felt guilty all the same. He flushed.

She addressed Brian the same way.

Brian lifted his chin, cleared his throat and said something like, "*Oni Brian Boar*." He cleared his throat a second time, turned to

Stephen, touched his chest as the instructor once had, and repeated the words. "*Oni* Brian Boar."

The room went silent.

Brian's eyes grew wide. He waited. Then he pointed at Stephen.

Again, Brian tapped himself, this time near the collarbone. "*Oni* Brian Boar."

"Oh," said Stephen. He looked at the teacher.

She stood patiently, her big eyes shining with intelligent expectation.

Stephen took a deep breath, then answered with the voice of a mouse. "*Oni* Stephen Crown."

She said something different, followed by his name, and though he could not have repeated the words, he was sure the message was complimentary. Putting her fingers under her chin, she said, "*Oni* Lampia Seni."

"Lampia Seni," said Stephen.

She beamed. Then she turned to a girl with blonde hair, spoke quickly, moving her fingers and her eyes from the girl to Stephen.

Stumbling, the girl said to Stephen, "*Oni* Tania Reech."

"Tania," said Stephen, because he didn't know how else to acknowledge her.

Lampia Seni then nodded to a girl in front of Tania, who introduced herself as Justeen Foreye. She wore green glasses.

And so it went around the room, until all nineteen of Stephen's fellow students had reviewed a process they had already practiced once prior to his arrival. Stephen counted them: nineteen; and it was obvious that even the most courageous among them was experiencing this language for the first time.

Chatting gibberish, Lampia Seni touched a boy on the head and lifted his memory paper. She did the same at the next desk that she passed, then from each desk until everyone who did not have their collections of memory paper ready fetched it.

The class continued without a word that Stephen could understand. Actually, the few times someone spoke in a *different* language, like English (Brian Boar slipped twice into his South Dakota dialect), Lampia Seni politely bit their heads off.

Stephen began to decipher most of what she meant in the quiet room from hand gestures and other context cues: *Welcome; my name is Lampia Seni; I'll be your teacher; you will need to bring your memory paper every day; you will need your black knitting needle thingy every day; you will need to pay attention, watch my lips, listen, THINK.*

Stephen gulped. He imagined sitting in this class all year long and not understanding a word: easy F!

He saw the same fear in Brian's eyes, which gave him strength. Maybe they could learn together. Or at least suffer together. If Brian would still talk to him.

(Imposter or not, Stephen was *still* at SA-6, walked into class by a Board member, and those points had to count a little.)

Many of the students continued to steal glances at Stephen.

Finally a gentle chime sounded on the air, a sound that Stephen wasn't entirely sure that he had even heard.

No one moved.

Lampia Seni smiled at each of her students, then signaled for them all to rise and depart.

The halls filled with the noise of students eager to share their excitement, complain, or talk about whatever they had not been able to say in class. The corridor also filled with kids Stephen's age, Alphas. Their exuberance was electric. They surged in one of two directions.

Stephen felt himself being swept along, though he had no idea where he was headed. His stomach growled. He hardly noticed.

Some of the kids were pointing at Stephen and saying his name. Or rather, the name *Stephen Crown*. Others shook their heads in obvious disbelief. The gossip spread like spring pollen in a high wind.

To escape, Stephen parked himself against a wall.

All of a sudden at his elbow, Brian Boar said, "If Lampia Seni's going to talk like that for the rest of the year, my head is going to explode!"

"Yours won't be the only one." Stephen felt so thankful that Brian was speaking to him, and that he wasn't treating him like a monkey in a cage. He wanted to ask about the pointing fingers and the whispers, but he figured it had to do with him being identified as "the imposter."

"So where have you been?" Brian led them toward an elevator. They stopped before a wall of them, four lifts in all, but there were lines, while a stream of Alphas were roaring up and down staircases on either side of the sealed doors.

"You would *never* believe me."

Brian lifted his shoulders. "Oh, you don't know that. Remember, my sisters have been going here for years. I have inside knowledge."

Stephen told him.

Brian said, "Okay. You were right. I *don't* believe you."

"That's all right. I don't believe it myself. Tomorrow I'll wake up in the Allyn's house on Midland Road and have to go to Montreal Middle School with Valendra."

"Who's that? Your ex-girlfriend?"

Stephen shook his head. "The demon of the north."

"Well, no worries about that. But *Freddy*? Sounds like something from those old adventure stories!"

"Not the kind I used to read. Allan Quatermain! He would have handled this differently. And he was old when his real adventures began!"

They entered an elevator. "Who's that?"

The elevator car was a chatterbox so loud, Stephen actually had to increase his volume to be heard. "Indiana Jones?"

"Yeah?"

"Indy's kind of a late copy of Allan Quatermain."

"Cool! Good old Dr. Jones would have whipped Freddy in the face," Brian said. "Literally!"

With a grin, Stephen corrected him. "Indy would have shot the monster in the chest. If he still had his gun. I didn't have anything! Anyway, it's over now."

"True!" Brian pulled out his memory paper and flipped it open to a map that moved as their elevator car lifted in what felt like a diagonal direction.

"Do these elevators carry us everywhere?"

"I wish. Maybe someday they'll invent an elevator that carries you right to the door of your classrooms."

Stephen fumbled with his own memory paper, dropped it, retrieved it, and started flipping through the few pages that were filled with writing (thankfully, *English*). "Um, what's next, by the way. Do you know?"

"Sure. Domus!"

"But what's that?"

"Our home away from home. Don't worry. Unlike the school bus, there are no assigned bunks. Not unless you get in trouble." As soon as Brian finished the words, his face colored. "Sorry."

Stephen frowned. "I'm not *in* trouble now."

"Right! Let me see your paper."

Stephen handed it over.

Brian turned to a page entitled *DORMITORY AND MEALS.* They read the words together.

GEB STRUCTURE—ALPHA LEVEL: BOYS

BREAKFAST TOMORROW: 030
LUNCH TOMORROW: 050
DINNER TOMORROW: 075

NOTE FOR ALPHA STUDENTS
MEALS UNAVAILABLE DURING SCHEDULED CLASS TIME
WITHOUT WRITTEN PERMISSION

CHECK YOUR MEMORY PAPER OFTEN
FOR UNPLANNED CHANGES!

"There you go. Just as I thought. You're coming with me! With any luck, we can get a room together."

"You mean, like college?"

"Huh? You ever been to college?" Brian started to shut Stephen's booklet of memory paper when he stopped on another page. "Holy Bank Account, Stephen! You're rich!"

Stephen took the paper. "I am?"

"Well, compared to me!"

"In the mall, they said I didn't have much money. You must be reading this wrong."

"Sorry, pal. You got cash! Look right there." He touched a number with a symbol beside it that looked something like a triangle with a snake eye in the center.

The elevator opened and let out half of the crowd. Two others entered. They stated their destinations to the lights above the door, while Brian and others spoke. Brian said, "Geb Structure."

Stephen was amazed that any computer could decipher all the voices at once and carry passengers to correct destinations.

"We'll be roomies!" Brian said. "I'm glad. You don't know how worried I was that I'd get trapped in a prison of bullies!"

"I have money?" Stephen said to himself. His stomach churned with hunger.

"We're here! Just pray all the good bunks aren't taken."

The doors opened. Kids streamed around Shapiro. With hands dangling and dignity in his eyes, the old man with snow-white hair grinned at Stephen. He stepped forward.

"If you will come with me, my good man . . ."

Stephen shook his head. "This is Brian Boar. He's my friend. I want to room with him."

"You will make many friends."

"I'm bunking with Brian."

"Stephen ... I am charged with your safety and—"

"I got that. I also realize that the Board decided that I was innocent. I don't understand the details, but I got that much."

"This is true, Stephen, but now—"

"So if I am innocent, then why didn't I get an apology from any one of you?"

Brian choked on his own spit.

Stephen felt himself shaking. He wasn't really angry. Yet he had no desire to get pushed around anymore today. He looked at Brian, maybe for a little support (Hank would have jumped right in and given the grownup a piece of his mind).

Brian had taken a step to the side, his jaw hanging open.

And he wasn't the only one stunned by the argument between young boy and old Board member. There were other Alphas, staring at him again.

"My good young man," Shapiro said, growing taller before the pressure of the crowd. "I can speak for the Board ... when I say how terribly sorry we are for what, you must admit, was a logical misunderstanding."

"If I had parents—real parents—I suspect the Board would be much more apologetic."

Shapiro's kind face darkened. He drew closer and bent forward, aware of the quieting conversations in the wide corridor behind him. "Young man, you may be special. But there are rules—"

"Then I want to see Mother Miriam."

The man's mouth locked, half open.

"Right now."

He shut his mouth. He grinned. And then his eyes brightened. "You really are Stephen Crown, aren't you! Well then ... I suppose there is no reason why *you* cannot sleep with your friends." Tall again, the gentleman with snowy hair said, "Lads, I bid you good night!"

After the elevator doors shut, Brian Boar said, "I can't believe you talked to him that way!"

"You're lucky you didn't get thrown into the clinker!" said a kid with straight hair and an Irish accent.

"I've already been there."

"Honestly?" The kid was a head taller than Stephen, and his eyes were on fire with awe. "Well, nobody else talks to Board members that way. Except you, it appears. I'm Davey Finton, your Gamma Guide."

Stephen noticed some twenty others smiling at him. One kid waved and shook a fist of triumph in the air.

"Welcome to your home away from home!"

GRAVITY BALL

In the morning, Stephen awoke from a sad dream about the Allyns leaving him at Oceanside Harbor and forcing him to walk all the way home. Yet it felt like waking *into* a dream rather than out of one.

He still couldn't believe the room he was staying in. There were six beds in all—not too crowded. Each of the rooms was themed. The Geb Structure was patterned entirely from Earth culture and history—all the Alphas from Earth resided here.

This room was filled with African artifacts. Giant ceremonial masks cut out of ebony wood hung beside the heads of buffalo. The floor was covered with exotic furs. The blankets were fashioned in exotic tribal patterns. Before retiring to bed, Brian had pointed at the giant elephant tusks curving up and over the sides of the door and asked, "Aren't those illegal?" To which Stephen had answered with interest, "Not during the days of Allan Quatermain." They had gone to bed discussing stories of the great hunter.

Now, dawn poured sunlight into their room from windows set high on walls that appeared to be made of wooden thatch.

The colors from outside pulled Stephen from his warm covers. What awaited Stephen beyond the glass astonished him all the more.

In the East, a tiny sun shot yellow beams from the horizon. Notwithstanding this beauty, a few stars twinkled in the sky—it seemed impossible, but there they were. In the end, they were still not as shocking as the *other* source of light.

The glow of the distant sun reflected off a giant planet that filled the western sky from the horizon to, well, higher than Stephen could see, even with his face pressed against the glass.

Gravity Ball

The planet streamed with clouds and warm colors. The heavenly object looked similar to Jupiter, tilted partway to the right, though the patterns differed. Oranges, pinks, and yellows dominated, but Stephen also saw soft ocean blues, magical purples, and nimbus whites.

It seemed that most of the radiance in the sky reflected off this giant orb. And it was so beautiful and impossible, Stephen couldn't remove the smile from his face. He almost wept with joy.

Yawning, Brian appeared at his shoulder. "Simon's grabbed his clothes and left. You showering?"

Stephen thought about it, remembering his previous experience. "No. You?"

"Not until the sentinels pull out the cattle prods."

"You think that will happen?"

"Guaranteed," Brian said with a sinking sound in his miserable voice. "I've got Gym this afternoon." Then Brian saw the planet outside. "Jumpin' Jackrabbits! Is that for real?"

"I think so."

"Must be Supermira 5—I heard about it, but seeing is—"

There were two knocks. Davey Finton poked his head into the room. He had explained the night before that he was their Gamma Guide because this was his third year. It was a task assigned by his counselor, but one that he clearly expected to enjoy.

"Morning block, gentlemen. A few choices. If you've reviewed your memory papers, you know that breakfast is available, though Alphas aren't expected until 030." He said *Oh-thirty*, which reminded Stephen of military time back on Earth, though with Davey's Irish accent, the words came out more musical than stringent. "You're free to shower, study, or . . . join us for a game of gravity ball on the courts. My advice? Play first, eat later!" He grinned, then disappeared.

"You know, Stephen, I was thinking."

"Thanks for the warning."

"No, I'm serious. If you see one of the Board members, it might be best to speak politely and not, you know, *push* it. If my sisters taught me one thing about school that I agree with, it's this: Don't make enemies."

"Thanks for the advice."

Stephen and Brian dressed in twenty seconds, then raced after Davey.

✳ ✳ ● ✝

Gravity Ball was a blast!

It didn't take Stephen long to learn the rules.

It was the *court* that took him by surprise. For one thing, the game took place in a room that was perfectly spherical—not just circular, but spherical: there was no floor, per se. Stephen felt like a flea about to play a sport inside a giant ball.

The game was banging away when Stephen got there. Brian was so shocked he said, "Batman in pantyhose!" before he could stop himself.

Stephen burst out laughing.

Gravity ball was a lot like soccer.

An energy shield stopped the ball from reaching the walls; the ball could *never* pass out of bounds, because it always bounced right back into play.

Only the size of the older teens playing in the court scared Stephen.

The court was at least as large as a football field, but again *perfectly spherical*. In the center glowed a light, like a sun, but it must have been a projection of some kind, because kids were forever sliding through it.

Everyone was floating.

Upon entering the court, Stephen cried out. They called it *gravity* ball for a reason.

Davey Finton laughed and held the other twelve kids near the door. "Watch your step, gentleman." He grabbed Stephen by the collar and dragged him from where he had started to float away from the wall. "Are you ready now?"

Braced again, and shocked that he wasn't falling down the slope to the far bottom of the court, Stephen said, "Um . . ."

Laughing again, Davey stepped right off the bottom part of the doorframe and swam a little to the left.

Gravity Ball

The others followed. Brian held onto Stephen. Until someone looked back. Then they let go of each other and tried to act like they had floated in empty space lots of times. (Brian even started whistling.)

Stephen heard himself laugh. He found the experience very similar to moving in a pool of water, he just couldn't *feel* anything like water pressing against him.

"Pretty simple," said Davey, swerving around to face them. "No hands! You are allowed to push the ball in any other way with your own momentum. Do you see the goals?"

"Yep." Goals floated all over the place! Or so seemed. There were six in total.

Stephen watched the ball zing through one goal positioned straight up, at the top of the court, directly above the central glowing light. A bell sounded, followed by a round of cheers from the winning team.

Another goal waited straight down, below the sun. The other four had been placed around the court: one very close, one exactly opposite this one, on the far side of the sun mirage, then one way to the left, and one way off to the right. Goalies hovered near each goal, which was colored by some kind of projected glow, green or red, depending on which side owned it.

Every player glowed faintly with one of those two colors: a green team, a red team.

"Don't bang heads with anyone," Davey added. He crossed the energy barrier, which lit yellow around him as he passed. "You'll end up in the infirmary with a major headache."

Brian gulped.

Players chasing after the ball were slamming into one another and bouncing off, spinning away and *whapping* other players with pin-wheeling arms and legs all the time.

Instantly after crossing the boundary, Davey's clothes tinted green. "Don't worry, guys. The court protects the players, generally speaking: energy buffers. Collisions don't hurt as much as you might think."

"So that's it?" said Stephen.

"Well," Davey chuckled, "flying will take some getting used to. And another of the complications that you will figure out on the court: the closer you get to that light in the center, the faster everything moves. There's a gravitational pull, you see. It's easy to combat, unless you aren't paying attention or can't control your own momentum, like the ball. And if the ball passes into the sun, your team loses one point."

He glanced at one of the scoreboards.

Everyone followed his gaze.

GREEN: −3
RED: −1

"Green's got *negative* three points. You see, it is almost harder to keep control of the ball enough to stop it from falling into the sun than it is to get points. Good luck!"

And off he went, in the direction of a scrimmage in progress.

As quickly as Stephen, Brian, and the others (who wanted to play; plenty cowered against the wall) joined a team and went at it (mostly wasting all their time avoiding the ball and flying—which in itself was an extreme pleasure), it seemed that Davey was calling them all back.

An older boy shouted, "Time to hit the showers!"

Another responded, "Wash and wear, or the girls won't stare!"

THE FIRST FULL DAY
OF SCHOOL

The game broke up. The only ones left soaring across the court looked like the hard-core athlete types who *lived* for sports, as well as the kids who seemed like they didn't care if they were tardy—even on the first full day of school.

Stephen and Brian went straight to their rooms and changed into fresh white student uniforms.

Davey led them to the Geb Eatery.

Brian stuffed himself with sausages—"Can you *believe* this? All you can eat!"—and Stephen ate eggs, toast, hot oatmeal, and bacon. He sighed with gusto. How long had it been since he'd had a hot breakfast? Stephen didn't know. Breakfast at school, he decided, was heaven.

Then Brian and Stephen parted for separate classes. "Health!" Brian had said at breakfast, pointing at his memory paper. He scowled. "I bet they weigh me and say, 'No more sausage!'"

Stephen didn't think he would locate his first class very easily, but there were plenty of adults in the halls ready to help Alphas and others in the right direction.

His first class was Math, taught by a blind man with thick glasses. Stephen heard someone say, "Do people in space really need glasses that thick?" That summed up Stephen's thoughts exactly. The class was far duller than he expected. Most of time ate away slowly. Haggith Seni told his students to bring their plume sticks next time.

Everyone in the room was an Alpha, and most seemed to have no idea what "plume stick" meant.

"*This* is a plume stick. It is a black rod that everyone should have picked up in the mall. You write on your memory paper with it. Like this!" Haggith Seni drew a frowning face on the paper belonging to a girl, who also happened to be wearing glasses. He held it up. The girl shrank in the seat beside Stephen.

Stephen found his plume and dragged it across a blank piece of memory paper. It made a line. More experimentation showed that the memory paper turned letters, numbers, and drawings instantly into beautifully printed copies, as if they had been stamped onto the paper by a professional press.

Stephen's next class was led by one Bigtuth Seni, a bumbling woman with hair hanging all around her face. In fact, Stephen couldn't ever tell which student Bigtuth was questioning, because he rarely saw her eyes—her hair was like a mask, covering not only her shoulders and her back, but her forehead, her cheekbones, and sometimes even her smile.

Bigtuth Seni taught Social Studies. After introductions, she had them pull out their massive, dusty, textbooks and open to the title page. "You will notice that our current focus is not only Ancient History, but the ancient history of Earth in particular. That is because you are all Alphas, and Alphas study the ancient history of their own home worlds. You are from Earth, so—despite your cultural differences—you have many things in common."

Brian was there, and they were able to sit together. So Stephen asked him, "Why are the last names of every teacher Seni?"

Brian took a writing stick from his mouth. "Seni means *teacher* or something."

Bigtuth Seni said, "Thank you, Mr. Boar."

"What?"

"Didn't you hear me ask who would read the first page for us?" she said through her curtain of hair. "Do pay attention! How about *you*, young man."

No one replied.

"Stephen Crown?"

The eyes turned.

"Oh, me! Sure. Um, where are we?"

✳ ✱ ● ✝

After Social Studies, Brian left for Math with Haggith Seni while Stephen went looking for Educational Technology (ET).

Stephen *loved* the class. Gemgemi Seni (a friendly lady with a false smile) spent the entire period talking about all sorts of fabulous alien doodads, then gave everyone a chance to play with their memory paper. Stephen asked questions and ignored staring students.

Lorenza shared the class. She looked embarrassed and raised her hand often to make inquiries that finally caused one girl to whisper, "Are you *really* from Alpha Prime?"

She and Stephen exchanged glances.

They did not sit beside each other, but were close enough to communicate when allowed. Yet she lowered her eyebrows at him whenever the name "Stephen Crown" was mentioned.

People seemed to enjoy saying his whole name. One boy shook his hand at the end of class and said, "Nice to meet you, Stephen Crown. I'm Scion."

✳ ✱ ● ✝

Lorenza caught him on the way to lunch. "Are you really Stephen Crown?"

Stephen only shrugged.

"So you were the imposter?"

Timidly, he nodded.

Then she surprised him by saying, "I understand." And she changed the subject! She discussed memory paper, some of the shops that supposedly existed in the mall (but just couldn't possibly, their names were too incredible), and their favorite teachers so far.

Brian bumped into them coming into the lunch lines. He joined their conversation by saying, "Oh, no."

"You remember Lorenza?" Stephen said.

"First girl to ever sit on my lap."

"Stephen tripped me, remember."

"Did I?" said Stephen

"I believe so," said Lorenza.

"Okay," said Brian.

"Sorry about that," said Stephen. "This is my friend, Brian Boar."

"Nice to meet you, Brian."

They spent lunch enjoying Earth food and listening to Lorenza talk about her classes. Amazingly, she and Brian had shared Health and had not even known it.

After lunch, Brian and Stephen left Lorenza for Lampia Seni's Language class. The whole way, Brian worried. "She's going to speak in gobbeldy-gook the whole hour—I just know it! My brain is going to melt. I am *never* going to learn a bit of it."

"You saved my neck last night," Stephen reminded him. "You're already ahead of me."

"Yeah, but I've already forgotten what we learned!"

They sat in the back. Lampia Seni explained, in easily understood words, that she had blocked their translators the previous evening just to give them a little flavor of the real universe. Lampia was very sweet. Brian fell in love with her eyes before the end of class.

After Lampia Seni's discussions and smartboard displays of Uniscript and the Unitongue language, Reading: Earth Scripts was a real letdown. The teacher, Smyther Seni, seemed an old and mean woman. But the library of available texts was exciting.

The library itself towered in the core of the Reading Structure, with Reading levels branching off of it like flower petals from a stem. Every book was available at all times. If a physical volume was checked out, students could have the book placed for a limited time on their memory paper (which was often lighter, anyway). So while Smyther Seni was the sort that students wanted to run from,

The First Full Day of School

Stephen realized that he was completely free to run *into* books. It was what Hank, back home, would have called a bittersweet joy.

∗ ∗ +

Music came after Reading. Peni Seni held up a vast number of instruments. But after Stephen's name was spoken (it felt like someone throwing a spotlight onto him and letting it stay there), Cutter Hertmor's bitter grimace appeared through the crowd.

Cutter sneered at him on and off through the entire hour. "He calls himself *Stephen Crown*. He's from Earth!"

Judgmental eyes squinted in Stephen's direction: girls, boys, everyone.

Peni Seni, a little teacher forever whistling through a gap in her teeth, continued, oblivious.

Stephen missed most of the instructions.

Before Music class finished, he checked his schedule and found that he would next be heading for Study Hall.

To a shorthaired girl with a round nose, he whispered, "Psst."

She frowned at him with a square mouth and beady eyes.

"Do you know what we do in Study Hall?"

"You study, dummy!"

He didn't ask the girl anymore questions. One of the hall monitors or Board members would point him in the right direction. (Every time he left a class and started toward another destination, someone from the Board appeared; he got the distinct impression that they were positioning themselves strategically in his path so that they could watch him.)

Cutter Hertmor roped Stephen immediately after departing the class. "Do you think anyone really believes that you're Stephen Crown?"

Stephen didn't answer. A glance told him that Cutter had at least two people standing at his sides, maybe more.

"Think you're too high and mighty to turn and face me, do you? There you go, people! It's just a *name*. Don't be fooled. The Earth brat is nothing more than that. A lying brat."

Stephen kept walking. *Choose your battles*, he told himself. Mostly because he had no idea why everyone thought the name so special. It had to be a mistake.

✳ ✳ ● ✝

Study Hall consisted of nothing more than what the girl in Music had said: you study, dummy.

Stephen had never had a Study Hall class in elementary school. An explanation was given by a tall man in a blazer and blue jeans. His name was Underlaan Wedell (no Seni), and he seemed like a great guy. Maybe because he didn't pressure anyone. "No roll will be taken. This is essentially your free time. Smart kids study. You can do that anywhere, even in your dormitories. It's up to you." And with that, he left them.

Brian showed up, with Lorenza jabbering about classes behind him.

Brian whispered out of earshot, "Note in the boy book: When a lonely girl trips over your legs and falls on top of you, she will either be your enemy for life or one of your new friends. Could be useful, if I ever spot the girl of my dreams!"

"Didn't Lorenza trip over my legs?"

Lorenza led their "study session" before they could get away. Luckily, there wasn't much to review. But as she said, "It is only the first day of school." Lorenza, due to her limited time on Alpha Prime, knew some things way beyond their earthly learning. Stephen and Brian spent the whole time playing with their memory paper and asking her questions.

By then, Stephen felt that he had had *more than enough* school for one day. He nearly fell apart when Brian pointed out that they still had the evening block to contend with: one more class!

Stephen just couldn't believe it.

✳ ✳ ● ✝

A bald man made entirely of muscle attached to bone and covered by perfect skin met him outside of Health class. With a wide grin of perfect teeth, he shook the hand of each student. "I'm Brantid Seni, and I will be your Health instructor! What's *your* name?" He seemed genuinely interested in everyone.

Until Stephen shook his hand.

Someone whispered Stephen's full name.

Brantid Seni gaped. "Stephen Crown? Stephen Crown! In *my* class!" He shouted it to the entire hall.

Everyone stretched their necks to see him.

Stephen shrank. "Nice to meet you, sir."

Mr. Muscles continued to stand there, speechless, as if he had just shaken hands with the real Santa Claus. Stephen used the opportunity to duck into the classroom.

After that, Brantid Seni stumbled through his opening lesson.

Stephen only saw one friendly face. Actually, it was a timid face: the dusty redheaded quiet boy from the showers.

Stephen said, "Hi."

* * ● +

When the class came to an end, Stephen rushed out.

Brantid Seni failed to intercept him.

Stephen stopped down the hall to properly pack his bag, after his memory paper had fallen from the side pocket.

The quiet boy paused near him. "Are you really Stephen Crown?"

Exhausted, Stephen answered, "No. But everyone keeps calling me that."

"Why do they call you Stephen Crown?"

"My name is Stephen *Cowen*. That other name is close, I suppose. I think people want me to be Stephen Crown."

"So you're not Stephen Crown?"

"I'm just me. Sorry to be such a disappointment."

"No big deal," said the kid. "I'm Shad Tork. People call me Dork. At least you don't get that."

Stephen said, "Crown is getting to be bad enough. I feel like a freak on parade." Then Stephen thought about it and felt bad for Shad. Dork was pretty horrible, to anyone who spoke English.

"Stephen Crown *would* be bad," Shad agreed in his frail, little voice.

"I just don't understand why, I guess," Stephen mumbled.

"Are you kidding?"

Stephen stared, awaiting clarification.

Shad gave it to him. "You *really* don't know? Being Stephen Crown could get you killed."

✳ ✳ ◗ ✢

"I know what they are trying to do to us!" Brian said when Stephen returned to Geb. "Death by school!"

"Isn't that always the case?"

"This is worse! School all day long?" Brian squeaked the last word. "I'd rather go back to Earth! Middle school couldn't be *this* rough."

Stephen laughed. He unpacked his book bag, as he might have done living at the Allyns. Then he just stared at his gear. Something was wrong.

"I'm dead, I tell you!" Brian continued. He flopped onto his bed. "I thought the *night block meant party time—I've heard stories*, I tell you! What—what's wrong with you? Someone steal your writing stick?"

"No." Stephen spotted the problem.

"It happens you know." Brian shut his eyes, interlocked his fingers over his chest, and yawned big enough to swallow the bunk above him.

Stephen stared but couldn't believe it.

No one had stolen anything. It was quite the opposite, actually.

The golden absconder peeked at him from beneath his ancient Social Studies book. He snatched Bluntwasp's gift and turned to the window. It still looked like a strange pocket watch. Someone on the Board had said that it was some kind of "military grade" device.

They had taken it. "Contraband," they had called it. Expressly illegal to possess.

"I'm liable to fall asleep before I can change into my pajamas!" Brian said without opening his eyes. "You probably haven't heard yet, but school at SA-6 runs six days a week. I'm not joking! So you see? They *are* trying to kill us. I have a foot growing out of my head. That can happen to Earthlings in space. You're not listening to me. What are you looking at?"

Stephen jammed the absconder into his pocket. "Nothing."

Someone had slipped it *back* into his bag. But why? And who?

"You didn't even hear the horror I just revealed."

"Too tired I guess."

After a long pause, in which Stephen changed and moved the absconder into the pocket of his PJs, Brian said, "So…are you *really* Stephen Cr—"

"I'm beat," Stephen said. Escaping into bed, he quickly slipped into dream. All through the night, he felt the weight of eyes staring at him.

THE STUDY HALL DEBACLE

Morning came with sunlight and a run to the Gravity Ball court. Brian and Stephen howled as they flew about, generally trying to avoid the ball and, of course, the sun pulling them endlessly toward the center of the giant sphere.

Afterwards, Stephen and Brian discovered semiprivate stalls in which to shower—a relief for quick-bathing Alphas.

Stephen's second day of school in outer space (or on an alien moon, to be exact), consisted of a simple repeat of the first day, with some minor alterations.

Today instead of Educational Technology with Gemgemi Seni, Stephen had Gym with Scion and Lorenza.

Gym consisted of multiple coaches pushing students to sweat until they dried out and turned to dust, according to Scion. He ran beside Stephen and flushed like a man choking to death. Scion was taller, and he acted years older than Stephen.

Before the end of Gym class, Scion taught Stephen something very important and frightening about SA-6.

First of all, Scion was older. He was a Gamma student, like Davey, but he was in Alpha Gym class because he had yet to pass! "It's a blessing and a curse," Scion said. "If you finish classes early, you get promoted to the next level early. If you don't finish the work for promotion, you don't move up until you've completed what needs to be done. I'm just—well, how do I say this without totally humiliating myself in front of Stephen Crown?—I'm pitifully bad at pull-ups. Can't even do one. And what is worse, I don't even care! I'm more the cerebral type, if you get my meaning."

"So if I do bad in class," Stephen asked, "I take the class over?"

The Study Hall Debacle

"Actually, you never leave. This is my third year in Alpha Gym!"

Briefly, Stephen saw Lorenza there in shorts, running and chatting beside Justeen Foreye, the girl with green glasses in Stephen's Uniscript class and all the answers in Math. But neither of the girls noticed him.

★ ★ ● ✝

Instead of Music, Stephen was directed to the Science Structure. Lorenza was there.

Stephen sat next to her, just in case her training and experience on Alpha Prime made her specifically adept in Science.

With poofy white Einstein hair standing up in all directions, Illitileth Seni moved in front of floating images, much like the sun in Gravity Ball. The woman said, "We will be covering General Science in this class. The word *general* will have different meanings, depending upon your world of origin.

"You will have opportunities to study each specific area of science in separate classes in future years at SA-6." The holographic images in the air changed: planets and solar systems became molecules, atoms, and quarks.

Stephen loved the floating graphics: they zoomed directly overhead, stopped above them, spun around, blew up, and shrank—Illitileth Seni in control the whole time. It was like the images did their best to match her every word.

Seeing the galaxy was simply fascinating—Stephen even thought he saw Earth specified as a small blue dot.

Seeing the inside of the human body was disgusting. The class shrieked and choked.

Illitileth Seni chuckled.

★ ★ ● ✝

The last change to Stephen's schedule came after dinner. Health was replaced by General Mechanics.

Torrant Seni, a giant woman with black skin and red hair, had the students play with building blocks with tiny motors. Before GM ended, Stephen built something like an ant that would fall onto its back and kick at the ceiling.

"I'm going to love doing this!"

✳ ✳ ● ✝

That night, Stephen and Brian had plenty of stories to share. Neither of them referred to the name "Stephen Crown."

For the rest of the week, Stephen couldn't get Shad Tork's warning out of his head. *Being Stephen Crown could get you killed.*

✳ ✳ ● ✝

On the evening of the third day of the following week, he finally grew weak and asked Brian, "So what's all the hubbub about my name anyway?"

Brian, who had discretely set the subject until now, stared at him with a dumbfounded look on his face.

Stephen waved a slow hand before Brian's blank face. "Hello?"

"Are you telling me you don't . . . you don't know who *Stephen Crown* was?"

"*Was?*"

Sitting on the edge of his bed with his memory paper (for they actually had homework now—and no time to do it), Brian burped the smell of his dinner. "Well, if I tell you, I'll probably get it all wrong and backwards. I only know the stories. You should ask Lorenza; she's from Alpha Prime."

"I can't stand the way teachers look at me like I'm *a prize* they've just won."

"You are! I've already written home: I'm friends with Stephen Crown."

"But you're not. You know the truth. My name is Stephen Cowen."

"Well then you're missing the boat."

"I don't see how." Stephen thought about Shad's warning.

An idea struck Brian like a beam in the forehead. He glimmered. "What if I told you that your name was Indiana Jones—or that other adventurer you like, Allan Quarter—"

"Quatermain." Stephen felt goose bumps rise on his neck. "Wait a minute. Is *that* what you're saying?"

Brian nodded, then curled himself into the bed. "Indiana Jones in space. You're famous!"

"I have a famous name, you mean."

"No. *You* are famous."

"I don't understand."

Brian giggled. "Make Lorenza tell you tomorrow."

"Why wait for her?"

"Because you'll *believe* her."

Indiana Jones?

That night, for some reason, felt a whole lot like Christmas Eve. Stephen wondered what kind of present he would get in the morning.

Lorenza didn't technically have Study Hall during the morning block before breakfast, but she called it that. She had also said that if Stephen and Brian knew what was good for them, they would join her. So they knew exactly where she would be.

When the boys showed up, Lorenza beamed. They were dressed for school and ready to go, long before they needed to be. "You've taken my advice!"

"Absolutely!" said Brian. "Our friend here wants to know all about *Stephen Crown*."

Lorenza's smile gave way to a look of surprise. Then her face seemed to snap, as if she were only now waking up to find herself standing in the library in front of a couple of boys. "You're a tranc!" she said.

"You have me figured out," Stephen said, sarcastically.

"But *you* haven't figured yourself out."

Brian cut in. "He thinks it's only a *name*."

"Well, he would," said Lorenza, leading them down a long aisle of old books, "if he didn't know *why* he might have it."

"Could you slow down, please?" Stephen said.

She took them to a desk.

A librarian looked through glasses without lenses. "I love seeing young students so early in the morning!" She leaned forward secretively. "Only the bright ones come in before breakfast."

Brian and Stephen smiled at each other.

"Mrs. Ylla, might you have a general biography of Stephen Crown?"

"Your memory papers please?"

Stephen and Lorenza placed theirs on the counter.

Brian searched his bag. "Jumpin jelly beans. I've lost mine!" He snapped his fingers. "No. It's under my pillow."

Stephen frowned. "Why would you put it there?"

"Letter from Mom."

"You keep it in your bed?" Lorenza asked with confusion on her face. "Do you mind? That's kind of crossing the personal line, okay?"

Stephen said, "At least you *get* letters."

Mrs. Ylla took the papers and wandered behind a wall covered with posters of alien monsters, political personalities, and what looked very much like teachers or administrators. Each grownup held a book or a display on memory paper and smiled (the aliens just opened their mouths like they planned on swallowing you whole). Uniscript letters hung in fancy fonts over their heads.

She returned, handed back the memory papers, and said, "There you go! Now, I've put a short and sweet biography on there. Come back if you need higher-level material. Of course, you know, most is speculative. Take care, now!"

They found a table, and Stephen said, "Can't you just tell me who Stephen Crown was?"

Lorenza sighed and dropped her eyebrows.

Brian said, "See what I have to deal with?"

"Stephen Crown is credited with single-handedly ending the Machine Wars."

"What's that, like—"

"Machines getting too smart for their own good? Fighting for survival? Self-creating? Essentially, but not in the way you think. But that's beside the point."

Brian cut in. "Stephen Crown is like the hero of the universe!"

"Not exactly," Lorenza said. "But he has the reputation. Mostly because of the movies."

"So why do grownups think I'm Stephen Crown? Why did you say I was a tranc?"

"Oh! I didn't mean to offend you. Tranc stands for Transfer Case."

"I know that. I've been a Transfer Case my whole life, a foster child."

"Well, it could be a mistake. Do you remember your parents?"

"No. I'm an orphan."

"Hmm. Well, Stephen, the question I am going to ask you might sound very strange, but I want you to think about it." Lorenza's eyes kept darting at Brian, as if they both knew the truth. "Have you ever considered that, just maybe, you never had any parents?"

Stephen laughed. He stopped. He laughed again.

Brian wasn't laughing.

Lorenza waited patiently for an answer.

Finally, Stephen stood from the table. He put his memory paper away. "You know, after all I've been through, I actually wondered if I might be going crazy. Now I think it's *you* who might be crazy."

He walked away.

More than one person that day shook Stephen's hand and told him how wonderful it was to meet him. Stephen answered, "It's not Stephen Crown, actually, it's Stephen Cowen." But one of his fans, a Gamma student or someone even older, pointed out that the class rosters said it *was* Crown.

By Study Hall, Stephen's interest was piqued again. He found a quiet corner and pulled out his memory paper. Thankfully, no one could see what he was reading—memory paper was memory paper: a kid could be reading anything!

Before he could turn to the page with the Stephen Crown biography, he was approached by a mob. At the head stood none other than Cutter Hertmor.

"Well, well. If it isn't Stephen Crown."

Stephen's quiet corner had suddenly become a trap. He tucked his memory paper into the pocket on one side of his bag. "Hello, Cutter."

"From Earth, no less," said Cutter with a slur of obvious disdain.

A few in the gang behind him snickered. Others were ogling with strong curiosity. There were girls, boys, older kids, but mostly Alphas. All looked wonderingly at Stephen, who felt once again like he was a meerkat on display.

"What a joke! As if *Stephen Crown* would ever set foot on that boring heap."

Whispering opinions grew like a wind behind Cutter.

Stephen pulled out his memory paper again as if intent on *studying* in Study Hall. "I don't want any trouble."

"How long do you think you can keep up this act, little man?" As Stephen looked away, Cutter drew forward, the mob with him. He shoved Stephen in the shoulder. "I'm *talking* to you, imposter!"

Stephen was sick of being treated differently. He'd had enough of being "Stephen Crown."

He attacked in a single, fluid motion.

Accidentally, his left foot landed on Cutter's right foot, just as he pushed Cutter toward the crowd behind him.

With his foot pinned to the floor, Cutter didn't fall *into* the crowd. He lost his balance. He spun his arms in the air. He dropped and landed right on his backside.

Before the boy from Alpha Prime could rise, Stephen was standing over him with both hands locked into fists.

Study Hall echoed with, "Fight! Fight!" Students surged in a flood toward the corner of the room.

Stephen, who was more surprised than anyone at what he had done, followed the momentum of the moment. "Get up!"

Cutter grabbed the pants of a fat guy behind him and pulled himself upward.

In the process the other boy felt his pants slipping. He shrieked, twisting away. "Gaaaa!"

Then Cutter's fellow bullies moved in.

Stephen was going to get killed.

Thinking quickly, he shouted, "Oh, Cutter can't take me by himself?" Then he pointed a hard finger at the nearest thug. "You're next."

The brute gagged and fell back a step.

Now people in the Study Hall were shouting not only "Fight! Fight" but also "Stephen Crown!"

More than fifty people crowded around Stephen—again, *no chance in the world* that he was going to get away.

Cutter scurried to his feet in a way that gave himself a little distance from Stephen. A half circle fighting ring formed. Puffing like a bull about to charge, Cutter squared his shoulders.

Stephen kept his face hard, but knew he would crack any second now. A minute later, he'd be curled under the table, bleeding.

Instead of making the image come true, he jumped onto the top of the table, grabbing the higher ground and inadvertently placing himself where everyone in the room could see him.

That was when Stephen saw Brantid Seni. The bald teacher was standing near the entrance. With his arms folded.

Stephen looked at him, eyes pleading.

Brantid Seni didn't move. He was *watching*.

Stephen almost called for help.

But he wouldn't have been heard. Students poured into the room.

"Fight!"

"Stephen Crown!"

"Fight! Fight!"

"Stephen Crown! It's Stephen Crown! There he is! *Stephen Crown!*"

The chatter of *Stephen Crown!* dominated the room.

Cutter's eyebrows rose in a hint of weakness.

And Stephen noticed.

"You want to get famous, Cutter Hertmor?" he shouted for all to hear. He imagined Allan Quatermain, the mighty elephant hunter, doing the talking (though Stephen really didn't know how long he could keep up this act). "You want to be the first brute beaten by Stephen Crown? I'll make sure EVERYONE knows your name by the end of the day!"

Just then, Marcus forced himself through the mob of children. "Out of my way!"

Cutter didn't hear the Board member behind him. His eyes glazed over, as if he knew that he had punched a lion in the face and was about to get his head bitten off.

Marcus drew a weapon and fired right into the crowd.

The kids cried out. Some were forced to the left, others to right— an aisle through human flesh; Moses parting the Red Sea.

Cutter saw that he was not alone, nor as weak as he had momentarily thought. His brow dropped into a hard line. His face said, *Oh, I'll get YOU, little boy!*

Marcus was at his side. He snapped his fingers at Stephen and pointed at the floor. "Get down this instant!"

"He pushed me!" Cutter yelled. "He thinks he's Stephen Crown and can *push everyone around!*"

Stephen dropped to the chair, then to the floor.

"Come with me," Marcus said in his icy voice. When he turned and Stephen didn't immediately follow, the man grabbed Stephen by the back of his shirt and led him straight out of the study hall.

STEPHEN CROWN, DECEASED

The office suited Marcus perfectly. Darkness and shadows swam around a desk lit by a single light. Gloom ruled.

"Sit down." Marcus *put* Stephen in the chair. If he had shoved him any harder, he might have left a bruise on Stephen's shoulder.

Marcus rounded a faintly glowing desk, sat, and leaned forward. "Let us get a few things established, shall we?"

Stephen heard his throat *gulp* in the silence of the room.

"First: Being Stephen Crown does not give you license to push other kids around."

"I wasn't—"

"SECOND: Making a spectacle of yourself will not keep you safe at SA-6."

"Doesn't matter," Stephen said. "I'm a *spectacle* wherever I go. People are always talking about me. That boy, Cutter—"

Marcus stood, leaning hard on the desk. "I HAVEN'T FINISHED!"

Stephen rose and moved to the side of the chair. "If you're trying to protect me, you're doing a rotten job."

"I don't like your tone."

"Ah, haven't you heard? I'm Stephen Crown! Oops. That was your first point, wasn't it? Only one problem. *I have no idea WHY being Stephen Crown would give me LICENSE to do anything!*"

Marcus lowered himself into his seat. "You don't?"

"I told you the truth when you arrested me, and then surrounded me and *attacked* me in a dark room. I DIDN'T ASK TO COME TO SA-6!"

"You didn't?" Marcus stroked his chin. "No. Of course you didn't. What was I thinking? Stephen, please, sit."

"Why don't you just expel me? For the first time in my life, I think I might like the idea!"

Marcus shook his head. The man didn't seem capable of smiling, but his face softened. "Please," he said, raising his hand to the chair again. "Stephen. *How* did you get to the school?"

Stephen told him about Mrs. Lackluv and the Allyns. He felt like he'd said all this already, but couldn't remember *what* he had told the Board. By the time he finished, Marcus was stroking his chin again.

Then Stephen talked about his new friends, Lorenza and Brian, and their interrupted discussions regarding *Stephen Crown*.

Marcus covered his mouth with three fingers.

"You said it yourself my first day here: I might not be Stephen Crown at all. What I don't understand is why so many people would get hung up over the *name* of a famous guy. Aren't there any more people named Stephen Crown out there in the universe?"

"Plenty," Marcus said without moving. He reached into the air and a screen of dim blue light appeared. He moved the images, then turned the entire floating screen so that it faced Stephen. "*This* is why everyone thinks you are Stephen Crown."

A picture of Stephen smiled back at him.

"I can't read Uniscript yet. I'm still an Alpha."

"The twelve-year-old boy that you see here...is *not you*, Stephen."

"But..."

"He looks like your mirror image, doesn't he."

"Well, yes, but the hair is a little different. Are you saying that I *look* just like another kid named Stephen Crown?"

Marcus made the screen vanish. He clasped his hands together. "We can't expel you, send you back to Earth as an imposter, because you *might really be* Stephen Crown."

"How can I be someone else?"

"Stephen Crown . . . reborn."

"What?"

Marcus pursed his lips in thought. Then he said, "Stephen, you have seen many new things since your mysterious 'aunt' revealed that she was taking you off of your home planet."

"Boy, have I!"

"So you know that limited Earth technology . . . and medical science . . . do not apply to us."

Stephen didn't quite get that, but thought he might have understood that science was way advanced at SA-6. "Sure."

"Then see if you can comprehend what I am about to say." He struggled to simplify his words. "While we cannot keep people from dying, entirely, the technology exists to let you *live* after death."

The room grew quiet.

Stephen cleared his throat. "I . . . lived before, you're saying."

"In a manner of speaking." Marcus paused before taking on the know-it-all demeanor of a schoolteacher. "Stephen Crown . . . *died* over twenty years ago. Since then, he has become the sort of thing that legends are made of."

"Legends?"

"Movies. Songs. Novels. Comic books."

"You mean I'm a super hero?"

Marcus's cheeks darkened with anger. "No! You are nothing more than a small boy, an Alpha student at one of many schools across the galaxy, a child who might have died in a cell if you had been any closer to an assassin hunting for STEPHEN CROWN!" He took a breath. "But . . . a boy created from Stephen Crown and, possibly, *by* Stephen Crown."

"Why was I on Earth?"

"Stephen Crown had many enemies."

"I thought he was a good guy, a hero."

"Folklore."

"But . . . I *am* some kind of new Stephen Crown?"

"Possibly."

"Can't you run a test?"

"Tests can be faked. And genetic record-keeping is expressly illegal."

"I don't . . . "

"You will understand . . . in time. For now, you need to see your precarious position for what it is."

Stephen waited for more explanation. But a hushed sound vibrated on the air. Marcus lifted his head and studied an empty spot at eye level beside his desk. "Yes? What's that? I'll be there right away."

They stood up simultaneously.

"Stephen, I must go. And you must return to your studies." Marcus walked Stephen into the corridor, which was lit by more somber, blue lights in the ceiling. "I have some matters to which I must attend. Ah! Kendall."

"Marcus," acknowledged the Board member with bushy eyebrows. "Stephen!"

"Might you be in a position to escort Stephen to the lift?"

"Certainly!" He leaned close to his associate and said, conspiratorially, "I got the call."

"Yes, yes. Farewell, Stephen Crown."

Kendall looked overjoyed to see Stephen again. "Shall we, then?"

"So . . . I'm special," Stephen said to himself. He did not realize that he had said the words out loud until Kendall replied.

"Yes. You are! And, frankly, I am very glad that you are here!"

The elevator doors opened.

Kendall remained in the shady corridor, but poked his head into the car before the doors could close. "You got my gift, didn't you?"

Stephen didn't blink.

Kendall dropped to a whisper. "The absconder? You should keep it. Tell no one. I am confident that you are going to need it!"

"But I don't know how it works."

"Just . . . play with it. You'll see!" Kendall's wide smile reflected the white elevator lights.

THE BLACK HOLE OF SCHOOL

"What are you doing?"

Brian set up his giant Social Studies book like a wall on the library desk. He peered around it. "That man over there. He's staring at us."

Stephen gazed around.

Lorenza said, "Poor Brian. He's been studying so hard, he's seeing things."

The man with white scraggly hair followed Mrs. Ylla, who was carrying on in a way that only a true librarian could: Mrs. Ylla's face was red, and she was shouting, clearly, without making a peep. She faced him, spoke rapidly, jerked herself away, let her hands fly, then fall. And then she disappeared into the back. The man in the long black uniform followed her.

"Well," Brian said, "he *was* staring at us."

"Now you sound like Stephen," said Lorenza. "*Everybody's staring at me!* Wooo."

"That's Shapiro," Stephen said. "I wonder why he's bothering the librarian."

Lorenza sat up tall. "Should we go and save her?"

The two boys returned to their studies.

"Wimps."

Then came the worst day that Stephen could imagine.

First of all, Gravity Ball in the larger Open Courts did not go particularly well. While he and Brian had been floating around the periphery of the game with other Alphas, who were more than content to just *fly*, one of the players shouted, "Hey, Stephen Crown!"

The ball hit Stephen right in the face.

There were moans throughout the court, a few catcalls—"Oh, that had to hurt!"—and, most humiliating of all, the impact of the ball spun Stephen upside down. His feet kicked over his head until Brian caught him.

But that was nothing—an accident, a little Alpha Prime cruelty perhaps, but nothing lasting.

Later, in his room Stephen went through his things, went through them again, and then finally exclaimed, "I've lost my memory paper!"

"What?" said Brian.

They searched together.

Patting his pockets, Stephen took the elevator to a lost-and-found office called Discoveries, which was closed for another hour.

At breakfast, Brian told Lorenza about the disaster. "Stephen won't be able to study!" He slapped his forehead. "Jimminey Chiminey! Why didn't I think to lose *my* paper?"

Stephen said, "This is serious."

"Let's see, you had it yesterday, last night at dinner—did you use your paper in General Mechanics?"

"I . . . I don't—"

"Please don't tell me you don't remember. You were in class! You *use* your paper in class don't you?"

"I don't remember *not* having it." Stephen thumped his elbows onto the table and covered his face with both hands.

"Oh, you'll get by," Brian said. A blob of scrambled eggs flew from his mouth and onto Lorenza's plate. Brian didn't notice. "Once in the fifth grade, I lost my lunch card. I thought I was going to die. They sent me to the office, and everything worked out fine!"

Lorenza glared at him.

✳ ✳ ● ✝

Of course, the teachers weren't very sympathetic.

Certain cutting students made snide remarks: "Behold, the Amazing Stephen Crown can't find his memory paper."

Haggith Seni asked Stephen if he had been to Discoveries. Stephen told him the story. Then he lectured Stephen on the need to come prepared to class: "You can't very well do math without a math book and paper, now can you?"

"No sir."

Lampia Seni was kind enough to send him to Discoveries during class. Stephen's memory paper had not been turned in. A totally bewildered lady, who didn't seem capable of focusing on anything around her, said, "If it turns up, we'll let you know."

Stephen had to look on Brian's paper through the rest of Uniscript. Even then his efforts were rather pointless: he couldn't concentrate on anything but an early lesson wherein Lampia Seni explained the absolute and dire need of bringing one's memory paper every single day ("You can't read and write without the paper," she had said.)—Stephen felt that he was somehow insulting one of the sweetest teachers he had ever had.

And so it went through the day.

* * ● +

By the end, Lorenza said, "Brian tells me you have money."

"I think it's Stephen Crown's money."

"Doesn't matter who gave it to you. You need memory paper and all your books. If we can't find your old one, then we have to go to the mall before everything closes."

Brian pointed out that it was probably already too late. "But it would be *great* to have an excuse to go to the mall on a school day!"

They told every sentinel and adult on the way, "Stephen lost his memory paper; we're going to buy him new paper and books."

Stephen groaned. "Please stop saying that. This is embarrassing enough without you two making announcements whenever—"

Just outside the mall, another guard stepped forward to ask where they were headed during the night block. It was Jake, one of the two men who had first arrested Stephen and escorted him across the bridge to the jail cells beyond—in fact, it was the man who had gotten in trouble for telling his robotic superior that Stephen was probably nothing more than an innocent boy and ought to be treated better than a common thug. "You watching the time? It's nearly curfew." He smiled at Stephen and said, "You three should be heading back to your domiciles."

"Hello, Jake."

Jake brightened even more at the sound of his name. "Good to see you again. I hear you're the real deal: Stephen Crown!"

"Well . . ."

Lorenza piped right up. "Stephen Crown has lost his memory paper and his books! We're trying to get to the mall to buy more before everything closes."

"Then you had better hurry," Jake said, his grin faltering. "Here. Come with me."

Even Brian smiled while they hurried into the mall. Everyone else was pointed in the opposite direction. But at the head of Stephen's little entourage, a big man in a black uniform swept older kids out of their way with words of, "Make room! Coming through here! Step out of the way, please!"

Once inside the tower, Stephen thanked Jake.

Lorenza asked the man, "Any idea which shop might be best for memory paper?"

"Try Fenton Moss."

She gave him a nod, then said to Stephen, "We better hurry."

They ran.

Expecting a return to the horseshoe-shaped store that he had passed through with Lorenza on his first day, Stephen was surprised when she followed a map on her memory paper to a store front crowded with amazing computer parts, plants, and a scent of fresh hospital plastic.

The spindly woman behind the desk apologized, said they were closing, but Lorenza spoke fast.

"I'm sorry," the woman said, shutting down what Stephen thought of as a cash register.

Brian leapt to the counter. "Haven't you heard? Stephen Crown is back!" Then he simply looked at Stephen.

The woman's eyes didn't flicker from their cold state at first. And then, slowly, they grew as wide as golf balls. "You're Stephen Crown?"

Meekly, Stephen said, "Yes."

"I heard. I thought it was just a rumor. You know, just talk!" She reopened the register, gave Stephen a scan with one of her handheld devices, read a screen, and said, "I don't believe it!" Her eyes got so round, she looked like a frog.

Brian and Stephen had a good laugh about that after she sold Stephen the paper. But Lorenza kept them sprinting.

Next came the largest bookstore Stephen had ever seen. In a tower all its own, the bookstore rose three levels, a thin hollow center vaulting to a grand chandelier of sparkling lights *without* the rest of the chandelier.

Although many of the volumes (leather-bound books, hardbacks, paperbacks, and accordion kinds that Stephen had never seen before) displayed covers written in Uniscript, most used alphabets or symbols completely alien. He saw Earth languages too, but Lorenza sped into the center of the store.

At a rotunda with many stations, only one person continued to work. He raised his eyebrows at the sight of the three Alphas racing towards him.

Before he could open his round mouth and part his enormous lips, Lorenza said, "Emergency business! Stephen? Memory paper!"

He handed it to her.

She slapped it on the counter. "Replacement," she said. "We need all of Stephen Crown's school books."

The young man chuckled. "Stephen Crown?" Then he examined the new memory paper. "This is blank."

"But you can wand him, can't you?"

"And I can tell you my classes, and my teachers," Stephen said, trying to be helpful.

Brian joined in. "Someone *stole* his old paper!"

Lorenza scowled at him.

But the man behind the desk was obliging. It was a lot more work for a standard bookstore employee to replace Stephen's missing texts (he wasn't, after all, a school employee with easy access to school records). But he was able to determine that Stephen *was* Stephen Crown, that he had money for all these purchases, and he was even able to get Stephen's schedule printed on the paper.

"Thank you!" Lorenza said.

✳ ✳ ● ✝

Stephen worried about all that was *missing* from his memory paper. All of his notes were gone, of course. Every addition, worksheet, and library book that he had received in class or elsewhere, gone for good.

On the way out of the mall, Lorenza asked Brian, "Why did you say that someone had taken Stephen's paper?"

Brian lifted his shoulders. "Seemed like a helpful lie at the time." Then his shoulders sank. "Please don't act like my mother—I can hear her talking in my head enough already: *By telling a lie, I could have ruined the whole deal, unless I quickly concocted another lie, which might require another, and probably another to cover the first.* Trust me, I've heard those lessons enough, Lorenza."

Stephen nudged him. "Obviously not *enough*." But Stephen was joking—any happy excuse to avoid the stress that had only escalated through the day.

Brian frowned in shame.

Nevertheless, Lorenza stopped both of them before they reached the elevators. "Stephen, maybe your paper *was* stolen."

"Why would anyone take my paper?"

Lorenza's face grew dark with thought.

Brian ran fingers into his blond hair then snapped his fingers. (His hair stood up like a bush in need of a good pruning.) "I know! If you had a chance to actually *feel* Indiana Jones's whip in your hands, wouldn't you be tempted to run away with it?"

"What are you saying?"

"You're famous, man! In a school this size, there have got to be some people who will want a piece of you. Trust me," Brian said, shivering before finishing his point, "Mimi has told me a bunch of stories about people taking her," gulp, "stuff, just because she's getting to be a popular singer."

Lorenza didn't look convinced by Brian's argument. Yet the wheels behind her eyes spun as she tried to figure out what might really be going on.

Whatever it was that she was thinking, she did not tell them before the elevator doors opened.

* * ● +

School got worse.

Homework assignments piled up enough to make Brian Boar scream for real. "I don't understand these square roots at all! The square of 31? How can there be a square of 31? Aaaaa!" A lot of the other boys at Geb gave him strange looks that night.

Lorenza knuckled down and stopped hinting that the other boys needed to do the same because both were certainly putting forth enough effort, and enough whining.

Stephen felt like he was choking on the workload.

One day, Stephen told Brian, "You know the only good thing about all this work?"

"My friend, there is *nothing* good about having so much work! I'm ready to surrender and go hang out at the mall with the losers. Are you with me?"

"As I was saying, the only good thing about having so much work is that people seem to be leaving me alone."

"Or you just don't see them on their tiptoes trying to get a glimpse of you."

"Either way, I win."

"Homework makes you win? Good gargling gargoyle! You are sadly deluded! Wait, I got an idea. Why don't you take mine?"

"No way."

"But think about how wonderful it would be to be *alone!*"

"No means no."

"They leave you alone in the loony farm too."

✳ ✳ ◍ ✝

The school buzzed with talk about the holidays.

In the library during Study Hall, Stephen found the alien decorations distracting. A flock of pretty girls hung streamers and sparkling lights. Lorenza glowered and seemed excessively disturbed. "Ignore them."

Brian was looking at the girls more than the decorations. "Easy for you to say."

Stephen, of course, did not recognize the holiday the girls celebrated.

Lorenza jumped. "Justeen!" She grabbed the passing student by the shoulders. "Won't you study with us? My table stinks of boys."

Justeen Foreye brightened behind her glasses. She sat next to Lorenza and said, "Are you ready to disappear for the holidays? I can't wait!"

Stephen blinked around the table. He chuckled. He waited. He held his breath. Then he felt a chill of fear.

"Most people are looking forward to leaving for the Holiday Break." Lorenza explained.

Stephen looked at Brian. "Leaving? You're going home for the holidays?" He thought of his mysterious aunt and then of the wide selfish grins of the Allyns.

"Don't look at me," Brian said. "My parents can hardly afford to get us into SA-6. They can't pay for extra holiday adventures."

Lorenza kept her eyes in her book. "I'm not going either. Anyway, I've heard that more than half the school clears out of here during the break. It could be nice."

"Yeah." Stephen nodded at Lorenza.

Brian caught on. "Of course it will! Don't look sad. After all, you'll have me!"

"Joy of joys."

Stephen waited a minute, to be polite, then asked, "So ... when will I know if I'm going anywhere."

Brian and Lorenza blinked at him. Then Lorenza patted his arm. "It's like Brian said. You'll have—you'll have us."

DISTRACTION

Brian slammed his nose into the library door.

Lorenza touched the enormous barrier with both hands.

Stephen gawked. He had not known that there *was* a door.

The old paper-scented library had become their hang out. Every day for weeks and weeks, they had occupied the third table on the south side, a place that was both black in decor and brilliantly lit by a small window that was ignored by other students who favored larger windows or no windows at all.

There was normally an energy shield that blocked what Lorenza had called "sound waves" from outside the library. Passing from the corridor into the library had been a little jarring until Stephen had grown used to it: noise...*silence*!

But there had *never* been a literal door.

It was more like a wall of ornamental woodwork. Lorenza kept touching it, disbelief in her eyes.

"There isn't a doorbell, if that's what you're looking for," Stephen said.

"The library *can't* be closed!"

Four taller students came around the corner, talking like boys practicing for the debate team. "See?" one of them said.

They stared at the door, then stared into their memory papers.

Stephen looked at Lorenza. Then they dug out their own papers and found an Official Notice:

THE LIBRARY

WILL BE CLOSED

UNTIL FURTHER NOTICE

Brian had gravitated toward the older students.

"Read it out loud!" a whip of a tall girl said.

Lorenza looked confused at first. Then she slapped her forehead. "It's *The Daily Orbit*, the school newspaper!" she whispered.

Stephen flipped through his own memory paper again.

"Only available by subscription," she said.

Other kids were filling the space before the library door. One of the newcomers shouted, "What?" then heard the person reading and said, "Start over, Xander! Louder!"

The guy who had been reading looked up and grinned at having an audience. He had rich brown hair (no silver showing at all), swept back with gel on the sides, but long and hanging in one big shark's fin over his eyes.

"Art?" he said.

Another boy, this one with a similar lick of hair falling over his left cheekbone, knocked over a potted plant, flipped the pot, and turned it into a short stage.

Crunching the spilled dirt and the tossed bush-tree beneath his boots, Xander took the spotlight and started reading.

LIBRARY CLOSES WITHOUT EXPLANATION!
Check your Official Notice Page:
the Library is "closed until further notice."

Investigative reporter Opil Wriggler caught up with Librarian Kay Ylla to find out why.

"I am not pleased with the situation," said Mrs. Ylla, "but I recognize that the safety of each and every child at SA-6 is one of my primary responsibilities, even as a librarian."

The teenagers snickered at the word "child."

Brian laughed with them. Until one noticed him laughing and lowered eyebrows. Then Brian looked around and returned to Stephen and Lorenza.

Xander finished the article.

Mrs. Ylla also stated that it is a crime for students not to have adequate library facilities when they need them most."

Oddly, the Official Notice fails to explain the specific danger requiring the library to be closed. Nor could Mrs. Ylla give further answers.

Bugsey Wright, Director of Physical Operations for SA-6, said, "We're looking into the reasons for the closure. The library will be opened again as soon as we can get it open."

Students agree that Mr. Wright was evasive. He has been unavailable for further comment, as have Board members, and even Mother Miriam.

So what is really happening inside the library?

We promise to discover the facts. YOU will be the first to know!

Xander shrugged.

"Come on," said Lorenza. "We'll have to find somewhere else to study."

It wasn't exactly what Stephen wanted, but he was busily trying to catch up with his notes, which was a complicated venture. After the loss of his memory paper, his only hope was copying from other papers. Justeen had promised to provide her notes, and hers were, in Stephen's opinion, by far the best. She had likely come and gone already.

Even though the study halls reminded Stephen of his one horrible experience trapped in a corner and forced to fight, they found one such room and parked at a secluded table.

Brian rather enjoyed watching Stephen copy notes from his memory paper. It kept Brian from studying his own schoolwork, giving him the noble excuse that he used each time Lorenza asked him what he was doing. "Self sacrifice. I am sacrificing—for my friend!" He grinned across the table, his arms folded, his eyes free to wander after every passing girl.

The only problem for Stephen was the chatter. Brian muttered endlessly. Brian apologized when Lorenza glared at him. Then another thought would pop into his head, like, "You think they'll give us a few days off to watch the races?" Then Stephen would growl at him.

Stephen dropped his plum and rubbed the sore muscles in his hand. "With all this technology, I don't understand why I have to *rewrite* these notes. Why can't I just move them directly onto my paper."

Face in a report that she was writing for Alpha Prime Social Studies, Lorenza answered. "I *told* you, Stephen. You can transfer all the words directly from Brian's book to yours. But that will erase all of Brian's notes. Nevertheless, I am quite sure that he would be willing to sacrifice for a friend."

"You kidding? That would be horrible!" Leaning back in his chair, Brian stretched his grin. "I'd be miserable!" He imitated Lorenza's voice: "Whatever would I study?"

"Besides, Stephen," Lorenza said, firing a shockingly jealous glance at Brian, "notes in your own handwriting will be far more valuable than *those* chicken scratches."

"Yeah, by the way," Stephen said, pushing the paper at Brian. "What in the world does *this* say anyway?"

Brian put his hands up. "Hey, don't shoot the self-sacrificing messenger. I'm a camper, remember? It took me years to write legibly with a pencil on Earth; I am sorry to say that it will take me awhile to master the plume stick, trust me."

Stephen understood the complaint. "But what does it *say?*"

"What, you can always read *your* handwriting?" Brian said to both of them.

Stephen looked at Lorenza, and they answered simultaneously, "Yes!"

The next day, they found themselves in the same place doing the same thing. School tended to be that way, and Stephen couldn't figure out why he liked it so much.

Frankly, he felt a little embarrassed. He didn't want Brian or Lorenza to know that, compared to living on Earth and not being wanted, SA-6 was an adventurer's paradise!

Distraction

He was in outer space!

Now and then, he saw women with eyes all around their heads (freaky, but cool at the same time)!

And even strangers here seemed to think that *Stephen Crown* was important.

He still hadn't looked very deeply into the mystery of Stephen Crown yet.

At first he'd been excited.

After Marcus's exclamation that Stephen was *not* Stephen Crown, even if he somehow was, and all the talk that Stephen Crown was some kind of comic book hero, Stephen knew that he just couldn't fill those shoes: he was nervous to read about that historical figure who would, no doubt, be nothing like Stephen.

He awoke from his daydreaming and looked across the table.

Lorenza and Brian were staring into the same memory paper, mumbling to one another (both complaining for different reasons) about Health. Lorenza found the subject of circulation fascinating. Brian sat confused and disgusted by the pictures. He whined, while she wanted to move on to the next page.

A smile returned to Stephen's face. He had been copying out of Lorenza's paper. Now he sat back, taking a little break, and fiddled with the little golden thing that Mr. Bluntwasp had given him as a gift.

He gazed down, found himself practicing sleight of hand without having been aware of it.

Here it is. Swish—poof! Now it's gone.

Where did it go? Why, it's in *this hand—look at that!*

Stephen stopped the show and examined the thing. So much like a pocket watch, but not a time-telling device. No face with dials. Only a lot of fancy circles and lines and artwork on both sides.

He thought about his interrogation. Someone had called the absconder "military-grade" and someone else had said it was illegal. Later, Kendall had quietly given it back to Stephen.

What had Kendall said about it?

Stephen tried to remember.

Then he heard the Board member's words in his head. *You should keep it. Tell no one. You're going to need it! Just . . . play with it. You'll see!*

He turned the absconder in his hands. He turned it again. He *had been* playing with it. But this "illegal, military-grade device" had never served as anything more than an oversized magic coin—that he had to hide from everyone.

It *had to* do more.

Stephen gripped it tightly, gave it a squeeze.

Nothing.

Between finger and thumb, he clamped it tightly and started fiddling with the lines and the circles.

Pressing down upon one ring of metal, Stephen felt it sink and slide. He twisted it counterclockwise.

Brian jerked.

Lorenza gazed away from her work with unblinking eyes.

"Where are you going?"

"Stephen?"

They weren't looking at him at all.

Both leapt to their feet.

Lorenza said, "Stephen, what is it?"

Brian grabbed his things and raced out of the study hall.

Lorenza grabbed her memory paper from across the table, Stephen's paper right along with it.

Stephen stood up, right in front of her. The feet of his chair scraped on the floor.

Running around to Stephen's chair, she scooped up his bag.

Then she too ran out of the study hall after Brian.

Stephen blinked at the absconder.

Stunned, he waited a few minutes for his friends, nearly running after them more than once.

Instead, he got a good hold on the device again and twisted the same circular piece of metal, this time *clockwise*.

Nothing happened.

Of course *nothing* had happened before Lorenza and Brian started talking to the air and rushing away. Nothing that Stephen could see.

Scion passed with his nose close to his memory paper. (Scion liked to pace while he studied, often circling the library—but the library was closed, wasn't it.) He glanced up as he passed. "Hey, Stephen."

Stephen gave the guy a nod. "Scion."

And Scion moseyed away, brow furrowed over his Uniscript.

So what exactly *had* happened? Stephen had not become invisible. In fact, his friends had acted like Stephen had gotten up and rushed out of the study hall without them. That would explain Brian's reaction and the reason that Lorenza grabbed all their gear, as if no one were coming back anytime soon.

Sitting, Stephen decided to "play" with the golden absconder a little more.

Almost immediately, he regretted it.

Pressing and twisting a smaller, more central circle, the absconder vanished in his hands.

His heart sank.

Real magic!

Or science in disguise.

He had been staring right at it, sitting there like a metal sun in his hand. Then—zaam!—it was gone. He could not see it. He no longer felt its weight or the cool temperature of the bronze or gold or whatever it was made of.

Yet he had not moved his hand.

It either went away ... *or it was still there*.

Stephen closed his fingers around the exact place that the disk had been. He made a fist.

He couldn't.

A pressure exerted itself against his thumb, his palm, his fingers. The absconder *was* there, even though something about it worked very hard to convince his brain that it was not.

Holding this pocket of hard air, Stephen moved the fingers of his other hand into the center, where he had located the circle that had made the absconder vanish.

He pressed that spot, and he turned it clockwise.

The absconder—did not *reappear*.

Instead, it *sat in his hand* as if it had been there all along. He felt it. He saw it. Confused by how the device messed with his brain,

Stephen grinned and banged himself in the side of the head with the heel of his hand. He fought to keep from laughing out loud.

He tried again. This time, he made the absconder vanish ... and placed that firm emptiness on the study hall table where his memory paper and plume stick had been a moment before.

He *looked* at it, but saw nothing.

Then he reached up, to the exact spot, grabbed the dense nothing, carried it to the palm of the hand in his lap, and made it reappear again.

"Oh, this is fabulous!" he whispered.

After one more experiment, making it vanish, go into his pocket (there was no bulge in the side of his pants), come out, and show itself again, Stephen ran out of the study hall to find his friends.

AN ASSEMBLY OF SURPRISES

Stephen chose not to tell Lorenza and Brian about the absconder. After they shot him with questions about why he had just gotten up and left the study hall, he hinted that his sudden disappearance accompanied an urgent and unspeakable need for a toilet. They didn't ask for further clarification.

After lunch and Uniscript, Brian and Stephen noticed a fevered excitement in the air. Corridors filled with students. Masses pressed toward every lift available. Lines piled up before overactive elevator doors. And floods of people rushed the staircases.

Brian said, "All right. *Something* is going on."

Stephen spotted Justeen Foreye in the crowd. "Hey, Justeen."

She jumped.

"Sorry. Is there an evacuation that we don't know about?"

"That would be fun!" Justeen said, collecting herself and blinking rapidly behind her green glasses. "But no." She held up the announcement inserted right into the schedule page of her memory paper.

Brian and Stephen leaned close to see.

The afternoon blocks were interrupted by the words GENERAL ASSEMBLY.

"There's a general?" Brian said. "I knew it! We're all in a military school *in cognito*."

"There's no general," Justeen said, laughing so that her hair shook and bounced on her shoulders.

"It still sounds bad. I am pretty sure that I know what we can expect. I have sisters, remember. I've heard stories."

Justeen shook her head. "I hear they're fun. Shall we go together?"

"How do we know where it is?" Stephen expected another page to show the route.

Justeen grinned and looked around at the pulsing enthusiasm rushing by them. "Mandatory attendance at all General Assemblies. It's *impossible* for us to get lost."

✳ ✳ ● ✝

And so it was.

Every student at SA-6 made straight for the assembly hall, and by the looks on the faces of all the older kids, Stephen might have thought this was Christmas come early.

And then Stephen's uniform changed.

The white turned into a powerful, eye-catching blue; the black turned white, and black pinstripes separated the two colors.

"Whoa!"

The alterations happened the moment Stephen crossed an invisible sound barrier from the bustling corridor into the largest room he had ever seen.

People were screaming.

Yet there were smiles, music pounding in the air, and blue, black, and white patterns everywhere. The energy was intoxicating and, at once, contagious.

Brian grinned at Stephen. "Cool!"

"Why's my uniform blue?"

Brian knew stuff, but Justeen knew more—the straight-A student type, who was nice to know in a mind-boggling class like Uniscript.

"Blue, black, white," Justeen answered, shouting to be heard. "Our school colors!"

"We have school colors?" Stephen asked Brian. "I thought it was white or nothing for students in space."

"Not when it comes to competition with other schools."

"*Others?*"

"Some years, yeah!"

"This way," said Justeen.

They followed, weaving through the jokesters and merrymakers.

Brian said, "I feel like a bit of egg yoke."

Intoxicated by the noise and jovial activity, Justeen rolled with laughter. She looked pretty, even with the green glasses.

It took Stephen a second to realize the point of Brian's joke: the vast assembly hall was the shape of an egg standing upright.

But the architecture was really quite amazing when Stephen considered it. The enormous theater produced the illusion of an endless circle of auditorium chairs.

As he watched, level upon level of sections rose from a stage thrust high upon a tower standing in the middle of the hall.

Those who claimed seats closer to the floor level would not be able to see the top of the stage at all, which loomed more than a hundred meters above those chairs.

Those who sat way above Stephen and his friends busied themselves by dropping an infinite assortment of streamers, oversized glitter, dancing lights, and junk. The party favors fell as far as two hundred meters, then sizzled in the air.

They found a place to sit, which was no small feat. In fact, it took almost twenty minutes.

Kids had claimed whole sections on a first-come, first-served basis. Those who'd run into the hall early had seized the chairs with the best views of the circular stage or those seats closest to the exits.

"It doesn't matter where you sit, really," said Justeen. "My older brother is an Epsilon this year. He's a tagger on the Argos Solar Skiff team."

"Oh," Stephen said.

"Is this the whole school?" Brian said. "There must be a hundred thousand students!"

"Thousands, yes." Justeen grabbed her memory paper, then shoved it back into her bag, distracted.

To Brian on his right, Stephen said, "You see Lorenza anywhere?"

Brian didn't answer.

The lights went down and up at the same time, primary banks of radiance being substituted by colorful stage lights.

✳ ✳ ◕ ✝

The giant room dimmed.

Colored beams pulsed with a new blast of hypnotic music. An army of electric guitars repeated a short rhythm. Keyboards banged an additional rhythm. A third set of instruments joined the throbbing pendulum swing.

The effect was powerful enough to make Stephen say, "Wow."

Justeen ran all ten fingers through the tights curls of her hair and held her head. "I can feel it in my skull!"

Stephen wasn't sure what was happening.

Although the stage was too far away to see clearly, he saw perfectly. The scene on the stage somehow magnified in his vision, so that he was able to watch the floor of the stage open.

Six people rose from slow lifts. Stephen saw them clearly enough to make out the movie-star confidence on their faces. Through the magnification, he could also see the motion of students on the other side of the egg-shaped assembly hall.

Brian sank in his chair. "Oh, *please*, no!"

Five of the kids on-stage began to arch, then spin, jump, jolt, swing, and jump again, perfectly with the music. The dramatic dancers surrounded the sixth and most vital star.

The girl, center stage, spun around.

Stephen's lungs stopped, then jumpstarted again.

Mimi Boar, Brian's singing sister, belted out a pop song that caught Stephen by the heart and made his blood rush to the beat.

> *I know what you want,*
> *I know what you fear,*
> *Don't worry, baby:*
>   *—I'm here!*

Brian slapped a hand over his face.

Don't have to run no more,
Or plan your escape,
I've got you by the hand,
So look for my—

HEART!
You faded,
You fled,
You thought yourself
'Sgood as dead!
You thought it hard,
Don't tell a lie,
I'm come back for ya,
No time to fly!

Run with me, baby,
Run with me now!
Run with me, baby,
Run with me—

I know where you been,
Know well what you done,
Care for you anyway,
Now let's have some—

HEART!
You faded,
You fled,
You thought yourself
'Sgood as dead!
You thought it hard,
Don't tell a lie,
I'm come back for ya,
No time to fly!

Run with me, baby,
Run with me now!
Run with me, baby,
Run with me—

I know what you want,
I know what you fear,
Don't worry, baby:
> *—I'm here!*

Run with me, baby,
Run with me now!
Run with me, baby,
Run with me now!
Run with me, baby,
Run with me now!
Run with me, baby,
Run with me . . .

The complete student body SA-6 burst into a thunder of applause, with many of the kids on their feet.

With one hand lifted, Brian spoke from his seat as loudly as he could, even though no one was listening. "Am I the *only living human being who noticed how dumb* that song was?!?!"

Stephen wiped the smile off his face—it had been a great performance, regardless of the lyrics, which he could no longer recall anyway.

He leaned against Brian's shoulder. "Are you really afraid that people will recognize that she's your sister?"

"Trust me!" Brian said. "You *don't* know what it's like."

"But you could be famous!"

"Do *you* like being famous?"

Stephen gritted his teeth and cringed. "Okay. I hear you."

With a flowering of colorful dance expressions, Mimi and her five fellow performers sank into the floor of the stage. Mimi kissed her hand and waved it at her adoring fans.

Brian gurgled. "I think I'm going to vomit."

Simultaneously, twelve students appeared in a half moon of blue, black, and white.

From the center, a tall boy and a shockingly gorgeous girl stepped forward.

An Assembly of Surprises

Brian gasped at the sight of the young lady, forgetting all about his sister.

Justeen perceived his interest, looked faintly jealous, and shouted, "Oh, brother!"

The boy on the stage raised a hand, "Give it up for Mimi!"

The cheers increased. Everyone clapped—except Brian, who, recalling his family relations, only pretended.

When the noise subsided, the young man said, "For those of you who are new to SA-6, my name is Dug Greenmin."

"And I'm Hapi Quan," said the girl at his side, "and we are your Associate Student Body Consuls!"

Cheers again.

"We are here," said Dug.

"For *you*!" said Hapi to the crowd.

"Consul?" Stephen said through another roar of claps, cheers, and whistles.

They looked so perfect together, Stephen easily imagined them getting married after they graduated (both appeared old enough to already be considering wedding rings).

"Co-presidents," said Brian. "Bigtuth Seni told us that the Romans had the same sort of thing. Guess this is where Earthlings got the idea."

"You just never know who's from outer space anymore," said Justeen.

The assembly became a whirlwind of entertainment and information. Stephen couldn't process half of it.

The ASB Co-consuls introduced the rest of the Student Body Board. Three minutes later, they produced Magistra Miriam, whom they called "Mother Miriam."

At the sight of Mother Miriam in a vast dress of bright blue and white, Stephen warmed on the spot. This was the woman who had held him, comforted him, and even saved him during the interrogation on his first day at SA-6.

He relished in her protective and promising voice.

Stephen felt that he would do almost anything for that woman. For some reason, she seemed almost more of a mother to him than any he had known. He loved her.

With a glance around, he saw the same emotion on everyone's face.

Brian glowed.

Justeen sighed audibly, grinning from ear to ear.

Mother Miriam waved, departing the stage, and the students applauded her with more zeal than they had given to Mimi Boar.

Next came a scene of staged jokes between the Consuls. The school had numerous competitions, but none so great as the Solar Skiff Races.

Like Justeen Foreye, Hapi hailed from the Argos dormitories. "So obviously Argos will win this year," she stated.

Justeen and others from the rough world planet Seesil leapt and cheered royally.

Dug, nodding politely, said, "Yes, yes, *if* your navigator and pilots can evade the taggers from Tellos!"

An explosion of hoots, screams, and clapping shook the assembly hall, while Hapi nodded and smiled in good humor.

Stephen leaned against Justeen on his left. "Tellos?"

She nodded. "It's the dormitory of people from Seti 5, a planet like Alpha Prime . . . populated by *nice* folk."

"Ah."

Only at the mention of Alpha Prime (Stephen imagined Cutter Hertmor's snarling face) did he hear all the boos and negative shouting. Some of the heckling seemed seriously mean-spirited, while others spat a little more humorously.

Hapi and Dug turned their jest and uplifted eyes to the students. "Or maybe the winner will be *your* dormitory!" Hapi said.

"Support *your* domus! Support *your* team!"

Everyone cheered again, bellowing the names of their home structures. A crowd nearby thundered the words, "GO GEB!!!"

The first skiff blew straight over Stephen's head, tousling his hair.

An Assembly of Surprises

✳ ✳ 🌑 ✛

Startled by the high-pitched whine of an engine, he screamed.

Brian screamed louder.

Justeen grabbed Stephen's arm in a claw that stabbed through his clothes.

Everyone else took to their feet and raised the roof with their voices.

A second skiff appeared near ground level and followed the first around the towering stage, passing the pilot, and presenting Stephen with a clearer look.

While these images were not magnified, Stephen thought he saw the details of a flattened motorcycle with a rider stretched forward over the top.

The third skiff to join in this high-speed little race around and around and around the tower, up and down through the empty air of the assembly hall, spun like a drill bit through the air.

A fourth joined, this one careening lower across the lines and lines of assembly seats.

A fifth and then a sixth raced into the zipping mass of deadly missiles, nearly missing another, and did a joust that caused everyone to cry out and moan at the sight.

A seventh entered, an eighth, a ninth, and as each pilot drove his skiff into this churning model of an atom filled with buzzing electrons, another horde of cheering arose.

Stephen lost count of how many skiff riders were risking their lives.

From the top, another one dove straight for the stage, pulling up only after the ASB board ducked for safety.

"That's Joe Hillerman!" someone shouted, and a boom of voices erupted once again.

Brian stood on his toes. "He's ours, Stephen! *ALL RIGHT* HILLERMAN! SHOW 'EM HOW IT'S DONE!"

The display went on for another minute more. Then the pilots parked their skiffs in midair.

The consuls made introductions to an already over-excited crowd.

Too soon, the fun was done.

Stephen was seated again.

A serious cultural presentation was made by students from the "roughing-it" planet Barbarosa (the dramatized story and the lonely, hollow drumming made Stephen imagine Native American tribes combined with Buddhist Indians).

Some kid behind Stephen muttered something about "the boring stuff."

Brian slouched in his chair.

After that, the Board appeared in a somber line. Marcus stood in the front like a president. Not one of them had adjusted their stark black robes to broadcast their school spirit. Nor did Marcus even twitch with a hint of smile.

A few students booed and shouted, "Get off the stage!" But they also hid themselves from the sentinels—it seemed that all the school hall monitors were present, and their uniforms had changed from black to white, so they were easy to spot.

Marcus spoke of rules, reiterating many that Stephen had heard before, stating many things that Stephen simply did not understand and many things that applied only to older students.

Stephen's mind quickly began to wander, as did the eyes and hands of a majority of his fellow students, who distracted themselves with anything they could find. An entire line of boys began burping impressively.

At the end of all the important *blah, blah, blah* (as Freddy had described it, before he'd exploded into a mass of deadly tentacles), Marcus said something that made a number of the students angry. Stephen, Justeen, and Brian missed it: they had been discussing the different licorice flavors available in the mall.

Older kids were shouting freely now, saying things like, "No more secrets!" and "No more surprises!" and some were saying things evidently off-topic entirely, because they always laughed afterwards:

"Longer holidays!" and "Free drinks in every class!" and "Stop discrimination! Let androids do our assignments!"

$$\ast \ast \; \bullet \; +$$

The assembly ended.

Stephen saw memory papers rising in student hands, so he got his out to see just how much this interesting interruption messed with scheduled classes.

"Take a look," said Brian, who was pointing at the paper of another guy sitting next to him.

The guy turned away in the lines of slowly exiting students before Stephen saw.

Brian tapped Stephen's paper. "Turn to the Official Notice Page. See if there's anything about it there."

"About what?" Stephen did so, but Brian only shook his head.

"Justeen, do you have a subscription to the newspaper?"

"The what?"

"*The Daily Orbit?*"

"Oh. Nope. My dad said we can't afford it this year. Maybe when I'm older. My brother gets it."

"We need a copy of the paper," Brian said, looking around.

Stephen said, "Why?"

Plenty of waiting students were reading from their memory papers.

When Stephen peered over their shoulders, however, he never once saw English letters. Gretel Lackluv had said that his Alpha memory paper would be written in English. Now he saw that this was a generous abnormality for beginning students—which worried him when he thought about next year.

He wondered how he had been able to read the sign hanging on the library door.

That's when he realized that he was seeing the word *library* written not only in Uniscript but also in Unitongue on the memory paper before his eyes.

"Justeen," he said. "Can you read that?"

Justeen tried.

The kid holding the paper caught them rubbernecking. He scowled, then smiled. "Can't read it, huh?"

"It says something about the library," said Stephen.

"Darn straight." He showed them the alien prose as if it clarified things; he even pointed. "See there? Investigative reporter Opil Wriggler believes that the library is closed due to structural sabotage. The question is *why*? And she is promising to find out. There is also a hint in her article that Opil might not believe there really was any sabotage. After all, *why call it sabotage*? That's her point. Who would want to sabotage a library? Weird. No?" He lowered the paper and put his nose close to Stephen's. "This is good, especially after you-know-who just said you-know-what!"

Brian sacrificed himself (look at me, the poor little ignorant Alpha!) before the bigger kid could turn away. "Wait! *Who knows what*? I wasn't listening."

"Wouldn't blame you." The kid paused. "You're Stephen Crown, aren't you?"

Stephen swallowed.

"I heard the gossip. I'm Hodlam Brat. Nice to meet you."

Stephen nodded.

Hodlam turned back to Brian. "Marcus said the library may be closed for the remainder of the school year."

Justeen butted in between the boys. "Really?"

"Nobody really cares. But it gives students something to fight about. And you know, we're always hunting for *a cause* ... to avoid our assignments!" Laughing, Hodlam Brat slipped through the crowd and was out of sight a moment later.

31

THE LIBRARY MYSTERY

One day a week, the kids were free from school.

One day.

To describe the other six, Brian had used the phrase "cruel and unusual punishment." But at least he had known about the situation in advance. To Stephen, the news had been almost as bad as the ideas of no recess and mandatory showers at the end of gym class. Almost.

That was then, this was now.

Stephen had not only grown accustomed to the one day off, but looked forward to it!

Yasumi was the day everyone looked forward to. It began at an early hour (no one on the Alpha Level of the Geb Structure slept in, although rumor had it that sleeping in was something the older students ALWAYS did on Yasumi); Gravity Ball games were crowded in every court and lasted four times as long as normal (no first class to get in the way); and students thronged the mall.

Only once did Stephen wander beyond the section of the mall that Freddy had called the foyer, that first tower of the stores connected to the student loading and unloading zone. The *real* mall beyond the entry tower went up and down and away in a maze of adventure that only made the boys worry that they might never find their way back, even with the map on their memory paper.

Stephen and Brian decided to keep things simple and only visit the entry tower. After all, what *wasn't* available in the tower?

With an eager Lorenza at his side, Stephen bought a subscription to *The Daily Orbit*. As soon as the copy appeared on his paper, in English, she took it and said, "Allow me?"

The library, again, had made the front page.

LIBRARY CLOSURE REVOKED!

"I thought that was supposed to be English," Brian said. "What does *revoked* mean?"

Stephen leaned in between them. "Just keep reading."

> In the last assembly, Marcus made a terrible announcement: "Students should not expect to see the inside of the library again this year, not while danger remains."
>
> Investigative reporter Opil Wriggler demanded answers, interviewing everyone connected with the library and those holding the power to request this semi-permanent closure.
>
> Before definitive reasons for the closure could be propounded, Board member Kendall stated to this reporter the following promise: "The library will reopen tomorrow."
>
> So why the closure in the first place?
>
> All Board members interviewed replied with no comment.
>
> Bugsey Wright, Director of Physical Operations, said, "The danger is over."
>
> Kay Ylla, Librarian, seemed particularly disturbed. "I am glad that so much information is once again available for student investigation."
>
> Previous reports specified sabotage as the reason for the closure.
>
> What was sabotaged?
>
> Why was there a public announcement that the library would remain shut to students until the end of the school year?
>
> What was really the problem?
>
> This investigator will find out.
>
> Because you, the reader, have a right to know the truth!

The article was followed by a report on immodest dress among Eta girls.

"So . . ." Brian raised his hands.

"The library will open again tomorrow," said Lorenza.

"Good!"

Lorenza stuffed the paper into Stephen's bag and scowled. "Something else is going on."

Stephen shrugged. "So says Opil Wriggler. Maybe she's just trying to get more readers. She got *my* money."

Lorenza shook her head. "It's a school paper. Opil Wriggler is probably an Eta or Theta: just another student, like us. We should go see her."

Brian rolled his eyes. "We should go . . . get ice cream!"

Lorenza was outvoted.

★ ✶ ● ✛

The next day in Study Hall, Brian was banging his head on the table.

"Stop that," Stephen said.

"Easy for you to say. These riddles Smyther Seni gave us are impossible"

"Mine wasn't that hard."

"I heard that he *hates* Mimi's songs. Can't blame him. But I'm guilty by association. Smyther saves the tough ones for me. They can't be done!"

Stephen whispered in Brian's ear. "They could be. Especially if you run them by Lorenza. She's pretty good at them."

"She has good hearing, too," Lorenza said without lifting her eyes or plume stick from her notes. "It is your choice, Brian. You don't have to cheat."

"Logical inquiry is not cheating," Stephen said.

"Ooo!" Lorenza said. "Look who's using big words now!"

"Hey, I'm going to school in outer space!"

"All right, smarty pants," Brian said. "What falls, winks, but takes a long time to be seen? Take that!"

Lorenza stuck the end of the plume into her mouth. "Hmm. A star?"

Brian frowned at her. He reexamined each part of the question. "Falls. Winks. Sure, but what about the last part: takes a long time to be seen?"

"We don't see a star until the light from that celestial object has traveled—at the speed of light, of course—for many years, sometimes thousands of years, before it reaches us . . . and can be seen."

Stephen said, "Really?"

Brian, who looked like he had been holding his breath while thinking, gasped and said, "Celestial object?"

In answer, Lorenza only chuckled. "You do have Science with Illitileth Seni next period, don't you?"

"Do I?" Brian's eyes widened, and he rummaged through his memory paper for his schedule. "Oh, no. Homework!"

Stephen smiled and let his tired eyes drift across the hall.

What he saw next was purely accidental.

With all the other students milling around in hushed chatter, he wasn't entirely sure that he saw what he thought he saw.

Stephen recognized the culprit, had an idea that they'd even had a friendly chat or something, but he couldn't remember where. All he could think of was Freddy—and that wasn't right.

"Lorenza?" Stephen said before the thief could disappear behind a standing crowd near the door. "Quick. Who is that?"

She blinked, looked inward, then said, "Ah. If I remember correctly, we met him in the mall, on our first day. He was working behind the counter where we got our first supplies."

Stephen screwed up his face, trying to remember as the young man squeezed through fellow students and vanished.

Lorenza thought a little more. "His boss called him Orrin, I think. I recall a pin on his shirt: STOP INHUMANE RACES!"

Stephen shook his head.

"He told us to go to Zellion's, for licorice."

Stephen snapped his fingers. "Yes!"

"We've still never been there, you know."

"*We* have. Good place!" said Brian.

Lorenza ignored him. "Why do you ask? Stephen, you look like you've swallowed a bug."

"Do I? No. I just saw Orrin swipe someone's memory paper."

She shrugged. "Probably a gag; probably a friend."

"Right after he stuffed memory paper into another kid's bag?"

Brian perked up. "What, you think someone's stealing memory paper?"

"Mine disappeared."

Lorenza said, "Yours was never returned. Besides, why would anyone pinch another's memory paper and then return it?"

"Who said anything about returning it?" Stephen said.

Lorenza pointed.

There was Orrin again. He was easing the stolen memory paper back into the bag of its owner. He even laughed a moment with the guys and gals hunkered around something illuminated by a green light on the table.

Then Orrin walked away.

Brian said, "I got it. Valentine's Day!"

"It is nowhere near Valentine's Day," Stephen said.

But Lorenza was nodding. "Not on Earth. Every planet has its own version. Some even have it as often as once a month."

"Tabby—my sister—told me about that. She says people snatch your memory paper and leave you a message. It's the only way to make a note anonymous: like you've written it yourself, when obviously you haven't. Tabby gets a ton. Mimi has to keep her paper hidden."

Forgetting the idea of theft, Stephen brightened at the idea of year-around Valentines.

* * ● ✝

The front-page editorial on the next *Daily Orbit* read

LIBRARY MYSTERY REMINISCENT OF FF

It has occurred to Opil Wriggler, Investigative Reporter, that the lack of answers surrounding the peculiar closure of the SA-6 School Library was standard practice in the sad days of governmental martial law. Why close libraries?

Then, as now, only one answer fits the bill: To stop the release of valuable information.

After repeated attempts to obtain specific answers about sabotage in the library, this writer discovered from an unnamed source that there was no sabotage.

Board Member Sentena later confirmed this information, albeit cryptically, with the single statement, "Reports of sabotage were made in error."

Marcus told this reporter, "It is the business of this board to provide students at this institution with a safe educational environment. For this reason, we closed the library. There is no shady agenda."

Marcus refused to answer any more questions.

Bugsey Wright, Director of Physical Operations, was also asked about the issue of sabotage. His only reply was "Oops."

But aren't these explanations all too convenient?

As noted above, this has happened before. Libraries were closed.

What is the real reason for the library closure? Does the Board really think that the students will not uncover the truth?

This reporter's investigation will continue.

✳ ✳ ✦

Stephen returned to the library, just to go, because he had been unable for so long.

The academic facility was twice as crowded as normal. Otherwise, it appeared exactly the same.

From the central checkout area, Lorenza searched for evidence of shady business. She scanned the tables, the floors above them, the students milling about doing the same thing.

Brian was grinning that silly, half-cocked grin of his. Then he frowned with the force of a slamming door. "Please tell me we're not here to study. I need a break or my brain's gonna implode."

"You mean explode," Lorenza said. "Because you're filling it with information. The only way to get your brain to *implode*, using your metaphor, would be to avoid study at all cost. Your brain would starve, shrivel to the size of a raisin, and then you'd be—"

"I get it!" Brian said. His grin returned. "I like raisins, by the way."

Lorenza rolled her eyes.

Two boys passed them. One whispered to the other, "Stephen Crown!"

Still walking, the second said, "Where's Stephen Crown?"

Stephen turned away. He didn't want to hear any more. And he didn't want to see another finger pointing at him.

Then an idea tripped him.

"I never read that bio of—of Stephen Crown, that we got here before my paper was—"

Lorenza squinted at him. "Was what?"

"Lost." He marched into a short line, and they followed.

At the desk, he explained to Mrs. Ylla what had happened to his memory paper.

Mrs. Ylla waited patiently through the story, but she wore a peculiar look on her face. Her lips were drawn into a thin white line.

He handed her his new one. "Could I get a . . . a short biography . . . of Stephen Crown." Now that he had been associated with this old hero for so long, he felt silly asking for a book about a person associated with "himself."

Mrs. Ylla didn't move.

Stephen scooted the memory paper across the counter. "Please."

She took it and turned away. "Just one moment."

After the librarian disappeared behind a wall, Lorenza frowned. "What was that all about?"

"That what?" said Brian, who had missed Mrs. Ylla's strange pause.

The nice lady returned and handed him a paper. "Sorry. Not available at this time."

"Not available?" said Lorenza. "It's digital text."

Mrs. Ylla's lips, pinched together again, were busily quivering like she had a mouse in her mouth struggling to squeeze free. No, it was as if she were talking to herself without opening her mouth or uttering a sound. "I can't help you. I'm sorry."

Lorenza lowered her eyebrows. She scooted Stephen to one side. "Then I'd like any book you have on the subject."

"What subject."

"Stephen Crown."

"On a student?"

"You know what I mean. *The* Stephen Crown."

"I'm sorry. We have no books on that subject."

"You did."

"We no longer carry them."

"Then I'd like a movie."

"Which one."

"Any Stephen Crown movie."

"Sorry. We don't carry any of those titles."

"Any movie wherein Stephen Crown appears."

Mrs. Ylla shook her head.

"Anything. Even fiction."

Mrs. Ylla shook her head.

Lorenza clamped both hands over her mouth. Her eyes grew into big circles.

Mrs. Ylla smiled at Brian. "Can I get you anything?" There was something behind the smile, something that looked an awfully lot like relief.

Lorenza, still in charge, grabbed Stephen and Brian. "Let's go."

"Don't forget your paper!" Mrs. Ylla placed the memory paper into Stephen's hand and smiled, looking once again like the gentle librarian he had met earlier.

Stephen said nothing until they exited the library. "There are no more Stephen Crown books in there?"

"I'm just glad to get out," Brian said. He made a claw behind his head. "I could feel the threat of homework breathing down my neck! I think I need another ice cream cone."

Lorenza's face had gone pale. "You guys, don't you realize what is happening?"

Stephen thought he did. But he couldn't understand why Lorenza looked like she was about to run screaming. He decided to save the day. "Let's talk about it later. Now, ice cream!"

Brian threw two fists into the air. "Yes!!!"

THE HOLIDAY BREAK

It was called the Atrium, but it might as well have been recognized as another planet.

Stephen could not see the domed top from where he sat. Alien trees went up 300 meters at least. Bushes whispered in a wind that felt as real as any on Earth. Flowers, purple, red, yellow, blue, and white, turned their heads as students followed paths that moved like streams through this place of sweet, fresh air and the smell of endless healthy green.

It was the last Yasumi before the holiday break. Shad Tork had brought Stephen here some time ago. Now they came to study. Mostly, though, they just sat on a short rock wall and glanced through their memory papers.

Stephen was accidentally looking in the right direction once again.

Xander's sidekick, Art, arrived among a gaggle of other students kicking a ball around a hilly green in a game like soccer without the ball ever touching the grass.

Art didn't seem, exactly, to fit in with the popular type. Yet everyone knew him. Stephen suspected it was the older kid's association with Xander Makell, Mr. Popular, the pilot on the solar racing team that Justeen had been ranting about during the assembly. That association allowed Art to slip from one group to another, respected while largely unnoticed.

Art approached someone's school bag.

He sat beside it.

He took out the paper.

He flipped a few pages, then he removed a stick from his pocket and slid it over the sheet. Two seconds later, the paper was back in its owner's bag.

And Art walked away.

Stephen turned his head and noticed that Shad was also staring. "Did you see that?"

"Yes," Shad said, but he returned to his quiet studies as if to say that he would prefer to not meddle in the affairs of older students.

"Me too."

✳ ✳ ✛

The day for holiday departures came in a flurry of class parties. By then, Christmas trees, presents, bows and bells, red and green, were spread everywhere around Geb. The Eatery served traditional December dishes from around the Earth.

Lorenza had joined them. She preferred to eat in the Geb cafeteria, rather than the Dagarus Eatery. She never explained why, but Stephen thought he knew. Who wanted to eat with the kids from Alpha Prime?

Over pumpkin pie, a bowl of ice cream, and an entire turkey leg, Brian Boar said, "And it's not even Christmas yet!"

"To me, I'd say this is the best Thanksgiving dinner ever!"

"Closer to the truth," Lorenza said. "But of course there are no national holidays in space. At least, no Earth-born national holidays."

"Do the teachers leave during the break?" Stephen asked.

"I don't really know."

"Why stay?" Brian asked. "Plenty of guards disguised as nice people! School is a prison."

"What about your sisters?" Lorenza asked.

"I try very hard not to think about them. Thanks for wrecking my concentration."

Stephen had whipped cream stuck to the tip of his nose. "If we are only going to school for a few months before holidays and then a few months more before school ends, how do kids in space learn enough? I thought you told us that we didn't have to go to school after our first four years."

With her mouth full of some Alpha Prime dessert that looked a little too white to be entirely edible, Lorenza shook her head. She wiped her nose and pointed at Stephen.

"She's saying there's food on your Pinocchio pointer," Brian said. Stephen rubbed it off.

By then, Lorenza had cleared her palate with a swish of grape-colored juice. "In answer to your first question, students learn plenty through—"

"Repeatus." Brian smiled with bits of turkey and stuffing in his teeth. "See, I'm not a complete idiot."

"No, just gross and rude."

"I try."

"Anyway, yes, as Brian was saying, Repeatus." Lorenza sipped from her glass of grape juice.

"Oh," Stephen said. "Well. Thank you. It's so much clearer for me now."

"While dreaming on the way home, the school bus will replay lessons from your memories. There's only one catch: if you weren't paying attention, then the school bus doesn't have any data to retrieve."

"That seems pretty powerful: a machine that can go into your head like that and connect with your memories."

Brian cut in, this time with a blob of mashed potatoes filling his mouth. He said, "There's a lot of fighting going on about that!" But it sounded more like, "Merths a floth ov vithing gongon bouth-at!"

"What Brian means," said Lorenza, ashamed at her own giggle, "is that many people agree with you and want to shut it down. But most people don't want to give up dreaming. My dad says they're afraid of the consequences: months of sleep and no dream? Too much like death. Certainly unknown territory. Either that or you stay awake the whole trip, sleeping only when you have to. That takes a lot more room in a space bus."

"We study all the way home?"

"Essentially."

Brian pulled a fork from his mouth. "My sister Debbie says you don't remember doing the studying. You don't remember most of your dreams. You just know stuff when you wake up."

"It works. That's the point."

"School while you sleep!" Brian winked. "The greatest invention in all of outer space!"

From one of the observation bays they discovered a spectacular view of the departing ships. Bulbous cylinders crossed before the pink mass of Supermira 5, the planet rising with the sun from the jagged horizon to the North.

Brian waved. "Goodbye, Cutter Burpmore! Don't let a comet hit you on the way out!"

Even Lorenza laughed.

Until a cold voice spoke up behind them. "I'm *staying*, camper."

Cutter looked at Stephen, who stood ready for anything.

They stared at each other.

Then the little man led his group of big thugs away.

"Home's too far away, for many of us." Lorenza said to herself.

Brian grumbled. "So much for a little peace!"

But the holidays were better than Stephen could have possibly expected.

On Christmas day, Lorenza dragged them to the Great Tree in the Central Sphere.

Stephen had avoided the place before, because anyone could be in this hub where every domicile structure came together. Yet at breakfast, Lorenza insisted.

The Central Sphere was enormous, wrapped in multiple levels somewhat like the entry tower of the mall. Stephen could look up and see people dropping holiday streamers of every color down from ten floors overhead.

At four stories tall, the Christmas tree seemed a particular favorite. Perhaps because it was surrounded by countless presents.

"Look!" Lorenza bounced. "There!"

Among the hundreds of gifts, Stephen saw one with his name on it:

STEPHEN CROWN

Brian frowned. He searched the gifts. He frowned again. "You got *him* one but not one for me?"

"No, silly. I got you *both* gifts. Here!" She handed them two flat things in silver mirror paper. "Merry Christmas!"

Stephen was already holding the heavy box in Santa paper. "So, what's this, then?"

Lorenza shrugged one shoulder. "I just saw it when I came to put mine down and realized that you would never find what I made you."

"You made this?" said Brian. He opened the present carefully and found a bookmark with his name on it. "Oh! This looks ... useful."

Lorenza didn't hear the slur.

Stephen was frowning at the larger present.

"What is it?"

"Nothing." Stephen was thinking about the gnomes that had chased him home from Mr. Bluntwasp's house—or had chased him in his imagination. *That* had been a day of unbelievable things. Now he was surrounded constantly by the unimaginable, and accepting it!

He tore the Santa paper away. Then he put the wooden box on the ground.

"I'm sorry," he said, remembering his manners. He held up the flat gift in mirrored paper. "You made this?"

"I did!"

Stephen opened the bookmark. Lorenza had fashioned them from paper that looked exactly like crystal glass. He let it fold over his hand as he traced letters that danced from S-T-E-P-H-E-N to Uniscript figures

and back again.

"How did you get my name on there like that?"

"Ancient Chinese secret!"

Brian looked at his own. "Really?"

"No. So, are you going to open that box, Stephen?"

"There's no other name on the tag. Who would give me a present?"

"Who indeed!"

While the box appeared to be made of wood, the weight hadn't felt right. Stephen knelt beside it and ran his hands over the sides to find a way to open the thing.

Lorenza was giggling with excitement. "Just put your hand on the top and tell it to open—it's not rocket science."

Stephen was afraid he'd try and fail, so he said, "Why don't you do it."

"All right!" She put her hand on the top, fingers splayed, and said, "Open up!"

The box stayed shut.

Stephen sighed with relief.

Lorenza pushed the box under his hands again.

"What?"

"Personal lock. The box will only open for the one it is addressed to."

Stephen put his hand on the top again, then remembered what Shad had said: *Being Stephen Crown could get you killed.* Then, in his mind, he saw Freddy in the cell across from his own bursting into a tangle of reaching feelers with hooks intent on catching Stephen's flesh.

This time, Brian spoke up. "Come on, Stephen, open it!"

"Maybe I shouldn't." He looked around for a grownup and spotted a sentinel watching him from a distance—they were never far away.

Lorenza and Brian followed his gaze.

"See?" Brian said. "Prison. I told you!"

"I don't like being watched. It's getting old," Stephen said. But in truth, he had been looking for a Board member. They had been everywhere his first couple of weeks, then grew more and more scarce.

Lorenza put the facts together. "You think the box is some kind of trap?"

"For the high-and-mighty Stephen Crown?" Stephen said. "The thought had crossed my mind." A wide grin stretched across his face. "You two want to get out of here?"

Brian's eyes sparkled.

With the box under one arm, Stephen ran.

The others followed.

And from the corner of one eye, Stephen saw the man in the black uniform touch the side of his face and talk to the air.

* * 🌑 †

"Look!"

"Where?"

"There!"

"Stephen, you're imagining things."

"Brian. Special mission: Follow that guy! Don't let him see you. Go!"

"Gone!"

"Stephen, if people like Xander Makell were stealing memory paper and putting it back, people would notice!"

"I'm noticing. And I told you it's not Xander. It's his right-hand man, Art. Who said anything about Xander?"

Lorenza blushed. "Well, I just don't see what you are seeing."

"Well Shad and I saw it. And I just saw it happen again."

Brian returned, panting. He balanced on his knees.

"Did you get caught?"

Brian shook his head. Spit dropped from his bottom lip in a long, wiggly line that never quite reached the floor.

Lorenza spun away in disgust, making a sound from the back of her throat that sounded something like "Gwaaaak!"

Stephen caught the side of her shirt to keep her from fleeing entirely. "What did you see?"

He wiped his face. "That guy, Art?"

"Yeah?"

"He took the paper"—gasp—"around the corner"—pant!—"and Xander"—sniff!

"Just breathe for a moment."

"Xander?" said Lorenza. She sneered at Stephen.

"Proves nothing."

Brian continued. "Xander was there, going through another memory paper, really fast, stopped at a page, erased it. Then looked at the paper Art got. They talked. Couldn't hear them. Went through the next paper. I ran off. Then Art was going back. Put the paper in some girl's bag."

"Wait a minute," Stephen said, pointing a finger at Lorenza. "You *already knew* that Xander was involved!"

Lorenza turned red. "Not necessarily. I saw Xander yesterday search through a book of memory paper, before putting it into the bag of ... of a girl in your Uniscript class."

"Which one?"

"Tania Reech. Then he was talking with her, so I figured that she knew what he was doing."

"You weren't thinking Valentines, I take it."

"He's an Eta. She's an Alpha. I knew it wasn't a Valentine. But he might have been helping her with something."

"Or," Stephen said, "checking through her memory paper for something?"

"What?"

Brian said it: "Stephen Crown?"

"Library copies, from before the closure?" Lorenza said, turning pale.

Stephen shrugged. "You guys, I don't really care if—"

"But your opinion on this matter doesn't matter," Lorenza said.

Stephen smiled dryly. "Thanks a lot. That's just, just great for my self-esteem. You're a real friend."

"That's not what I'm saying. If someone stole all the Stephen Crown materials from the library and is threatening Mrs. Ylla into silence—"

"Hey," said Brian, "that's not right. Mrs. Ylla's nicer than my mother!"

"Xander's behind it?" Stephen said.

"Erase all the books about Stephen Crown," Lorenza said to herself.

"But why?" said Brian.

"To keep you," Lorenza said, "from learning about yourself, from becoming *Stephen Crown* again."

Stephen rolled his eyes. "Don't care."

"Because you don't *know!*" Lorenza caught him this time, as Stephen began to walk away. "Stephen, one of the things that *The* Stephen Crown did was ... expose the truth when it was being covered up."

"Hey," Brian said, "that lady writing for *The Daily Orbit* thinks there's some kind of cover-up going on, doesn't she? Let's just go tell her! You know, anonymous tip?"

"I think some of the older students might be trying to keep you from reaching your potential."

Stephen balked. "Lorenza, even Marcus said that I was not that guy."

"You say that because there's still so much you don't understand. You are Stephen Crown. Everyone seems to know that but you."

"Tell me, then. The way *I* act, is that how *THE* Stephen Crown would act?"

"No."

"Thanks for making my point."

Furious, Lorenza stormed away.

THE HIDING GAMES

They called it the hiding game.

After all, there weren't any classes, not during the long holiday break.

Stephen sneaked through the corridors. When he detected a sentinel, he ducked back. His little gang of friends huddled with him and snickered into cupped hands.

When they saw a long black uniform coming, they ran the other way.

They jumped elevators, raced up floors, down levels, and across the vast SA-6 campus. They laughed until tears came out of their eyes.

Eventually they came to the limits of available Alpha exploration.

They had gotten so good at evading grownups (and they had seen far more than one Board member in the process), their feet brought them to elevators that refused to travel and hallways that ended in doors that wouldn't rise or slide aside for them. At their approach, drop-down light screens flashed,

ALPHA: NO ADMITTANCE

or

PASS REQUIRED

Brian asked the obvious question that no one else thought about. "So how do we get a pass?"

Lorenza answered, "I just want to know how we can get some lunch!"

Stephen said, "Let's sneak into an alien Eatery."

"You can't eat *anywhere*, Stephen. You might not like the food."

"Well how do you get into ours, then?"

"I grew up on Earth, remember? I proved to a Board member that I was new to Alpha Prime and would like to be cleared for both the Geb and Dagarus cafeterias. Truth is, I don't have any friends over there at all."

Brian ended their conversation. "I need a burger."

$$* * \bullet +$$

It was lunchtime. The Geb Eatery was as quiet as a library without a librarian.

A group of older students busily shouted at one end of the curved hall. Another shouted that they were taking over the school and had named the eatery Medusa's Stomach.

The first group answered by proclaiming themselves the Anti-Medusa Society.

The second group then referred to them as AMS (pronouncing it "aims").

Stephen and his friends laughed the whole time, cheering both sides on until the older kids challenged each other to a game of Gravity Ball.

When they got to the nearest spherical court (with Stephen, Lorenza, and Brian quickly following), they found the place empty.

Or almost empty.

One little Alpha floated alone around the sun, a spinning satellite.

"Out of the way, pipsqueak!" said a member of the Medusa Society as he stole the ball.

Lorenza's smile faded as she watched the short guy with red hair propel himself out of the playing field. "Isn't that your friend, Shad Tork?

"Yeah," said Stephen.

"I think he's in my math class," Brian said. "He never talks. But he did save my caboose one time when Haggith nearly—" He stopped when he noticed how intently Lorenza had come to focus on his story. He redirected her attention by looking at Shad and saying, "Poor kid."

Shad Tork pressed himself into shadows against the curved wall. He might have been crying. At this distance, so far away from the little sun in the center of the court, Stephen couldn't be sure.

"Come on," said Lorenza.

They flew over to Shad.

He saw them coming and started away toward the nearest exit port.

Stephen sped up to catch him. "Shad!"

Caught, the little Alpha waited, but didn't reveal his face. "Hello, Stephen."

"So!" Brian said. "You're staying for Christmas!"

"Christmas?"

"They're from Earth," Lorenza apologized, floating to his side. "I'm Lorenza Westing; we've never formally met. I *was* from Earth, but my parents moved me to Alpha Prime." Lorenza actually managed to say that with some dignity. "What's your home planet?"

"Seesil, right?" said Brian.

Shad blushed.

"Oh," said Lorenza. "Do you know Justeen Foreye? She's a friend of ours, also from Seesil. What is the Argos house like?"

When Shad blushed again, Stephen piped up to save him from this dark interrogation along the wall. "Come with us. We're playing *the hiding game*! My own invention, of course." He grabbed Shad's arm and refused to take no for an answer.

Within minutes, Shad Tork was chuckling into his hands right along with the other three.

A few hours later, Stephen stopped at a large observation window that looked out over the moon that SA-6 called home.

With Supermira 5 somewhere at his back and the sun overhead, a vast forest of crystal stone sparkled between hills of green and blue grass and yellow flowers. The hills stretched to jagged mountains made of black lava flows and equally black powder, offset at times with bright splashes of color that even Lorenza couldn't figure out.

Stephen suggested, "Flowers, I'll bet."

Movement out there caught Brian's attention.

Brian counted sixteen kids, Lorenza eighteen. It was a tough job. Students hopped, bounced, floated as the gravity of the moon fought to keep them on the surface.

Stephen said, "We can go outside?"

"I didn't think so," said Lorenza.

Shad, however, had the answer. "Older kids."

"Always *older kids*," spat Brian.

"Rolfus, the Gamma Guide on my floor, took pride in telling us that Alphas can not go outside, ever. Rolfus is not very nice. But he did say that we can go with an escort, if we can secure a pass."

Brian raised his arms and flopped them against his sides. "Always *a pass*!"

Stephen perked up. "So how do we get a pass?"

"Only Board members give passes," said Shad.

"Well, you can forget about that then," Brian told Stephen. "If they're trying to protect you, they'll never let you wander out there on the surface of an alien moon."

Thinking to himself, Stephen rubbed the little bump on his nose, recalled Kendall's secretive and giving visage, and especially how the old man's bushy eyebrows levitated in interest every time Stephen came around. "I've got an idea."

✷ ✷ ◉ ✢

Stephen went alone into the elevator. "Wait for me here?"

Uncertainly, they nodded at him.

Lorenza stood with her arms folded and her hip cocked. "This isn't a good idea. If you try throwing your weight around like you're some kind of super star—"

"But you *know* I'm not." He winked at Shad. "I'm Stephen *Cowen*." He told the doors to shut.

They did so.

When Stephen didn't communicate a destination, the car spoke in a little computerized voice. "*Destination?*"

"Is Board Member Kendall still at SA-6?" He didn't know just how much he could converse with an elevator's computer, or what it would know. But it didn't hurt to try.

He wasn't disappointed. *"Board Member Kendall is scheduled to remain at SA-6 through the Holiday Break."*

"I need to visit Kendall's office."

The elevator started with a faint hum on Stephen's inner ear.

When the doors opened, he faced two sentinels prepared for him like a dam.

Stephen opened his mouth, held it open, then said, "Kendall—"

"He's expecting you." The men stepped aside like living doors, then moved their feet as if intent on escorting him down the hallway.

It was the same hall that Stephen had walked with Marcus after the study hall fight. Circles of azure light shined beams from an atrociously high ceiling that cut the darkness and broke it into periods of glow and shadow. Office doors stood on Stephen's left and right. The smell of rubber drifted with each silent fall of his footwear upon the floor.

Kendall poked his head out of a doorway. He wore a shiny red scarf tucked into his jacket like a ballooning necktie.

His whole body followed in one excited bound. "Stephen! Stephen! Come in, lad. How are you?"

The sentinels let him go on alone.

Kendall wrapped an arm around him and led him into a room strewn with papers. Board members might have used memory technology, but these sure looked like regular printouts or handwritten documents to Stephen.

"Sit down! Sit down! Oh, it is good to see you without *accidentally bumping* into you in the hallways."

"I hardly think those *bumps* were accidental. This school is enormous. My first few weeks, I couldn't go anywhere without seeing a member of the board."

Kendall nodded and winked. "Smart boy!" He shut the door. "Nevertheless, I am jolly glad you came to visit. I did hope that after giving you that little *click-click*, I might have weaseled my way into your confidence. Have you used it?"

It took Stephen a beat to understand the man. "The absconder?"

"Yes!" He sat across the messy desk and gripped the armrests in a way that made his elbows poke up like chicken wings.

"Only a little."

Kendall clapped his hands quickly.

"Nice tie."

He fiddled with the knot. "It's actually a cravat. Since you are from Earth, now, I've been doing a little research. I suppose most grownups wear these in your home town!"

"Um—"

"Oh, I am *so excited* that you are here! Is school going all right?"

"Yes."

"Anyone bothering you? I heard about—what was his name?— that boy from Alpha Prime."

"Cutter Hertmor."

"Right! *You* had the upper hand right away. I read the report!"

"There was a report?" Stephen squirmed in his chair.

"Always is." Kendall jerked forward and opened his eyes wide. "Unless something *isn't* reported. Like your little toy."

"They have to know that I have it."

"Who, the Board?"

"Don't they?"

"They know it is missing. There's an investigation. A lot of things disappear—*whiff*! No one thinks that you have it. How might you have taken it back? You could not have!" Kendall sat back, triumphant.

"Are you . . . are you going to get in trouble?"

"How are you adjusting to life away from Earth?" A wide, knowing smile stretched across his face. "Are you having a good holiday?"

Stephen thought a moment before speaking. "What do your reports tell you?"

"That you are . . . running around with your friends, quite a bit."

Stephen waited.

"Quite a lot, actually! Your unexpected maneuvers are testing and altering our protective protocols."

"Your what?"

"The methods used by the sentinels to protect you from a distance."

"I don't really like being treated differently from the other students."

"And I completely understand! That's why I have defended your little *running around*. What do you call it?"

Stephen waited again. "Don't you know?"

"The Board is tasked with protecting the students, not spying on them. I know; at your age, it probably looks the same."

"We call it the Hiding Game."

Kendall clapped once, hard like thunder. "I knew it! You run from guards and such, in your little pretend adventures, exploring the school in your frenzy. Am I correct?" He looked as happy as a little kid.

But Stephen didn't like the 'little pretend adventures' part, because he thought it made him sound like some kind of elementary school baby—even if Kendall was *exactly* right. He permitted a tiny smile to be seen.

"Very good! Very, very good! And absolutely legitimate for someone your—"

"I need a pass." Stephen just blurted it out. He didn't know how long he could listen to Old Bushy Brow excite himself over Stephen's presence. "Four, actually. To go outside."

Kendall's smile flickered as if a momentary short of electricity messed with his face. Then he straightened himself. "Stephen Crown wants to go outside."

"I can get a Gamma Guide."

Kendall's hesitation was fleeting. He stood, left the room, and was gone for less than three minutes.

During that time, Stephen looked around the room. All the papers were written in script that he could not decipher or in Unitongue that he didn't understand, certainly not in furtive glances. A picture of Albert Einstein with his tongue out glowed from a screen on the desk. It made Stephen laugh.

The door opened again, and Stephen stood.

Kendall gave him four cards made of blank, blue plastic. "These will only be good until the end of the school year. You should also know that they will automatically link to their users, and by connection, to your individual schedules. If any of your friends try to employ a pass during class time, a silent alarm will sound, doors will seal, and sentinels will converge on your position. You will lose your passes . . . and they will be traced back to me." He grinned. "Please be . . . discrete . . . in your adventures."

"Thank you, Kendall."

At the sound of his name, Kendall lit up like a young child on his birthday.

* * ● +

Stephen caught up with the others, and outside they went.

No one said anything about a guide; Stephen forgot that part until he was outside. The passes freed them anyway.

"Whoa!" Stephen said the moment he stepped from the airlock. He felt like he was floating in the ocean, without the pressure of water all around him.

"The moon is smaller than Earth but bigger than Earth's moon," Lorenza explained. "So more mass and gravity than the moon where the Eagle landed, while less than what you experienced in California."

"I understood the *gravity* part," said Brian, swallowing the lump in his throat. He jumped, went up two feet higher than he normally would have, and then laughed on the way down. Then he gurgled, hitting the ground and almost twisting his ankle.

"This will take some getting used to," said Shad, his face lit with an inner light that Stephen had never seen in him. The silvery bits in his red hair reflected the bright colors in the sky.

Stephen felt so good about dragging the boy along. His heart broke at the thought of Shad Tork spending the holidays alone at SA-6. They were lucky to have noticed him at all.

"Let's *go!*"

They ran, jumping, across a field of purple 'grass' that waved in the wind like wet spaghetti standing impossibly on end.

They each wore stylized headgear that did not quite cover their faces: little tubes passed beneath their noses and created an invisible bubble of essential gasses, including a little extra oxygen, exactly where their nostrils and mouth could easily breathe it.

After hopping through the fields of what both Shad *and* Brian called spaghetti grass, Stephen turned and saw the school from the outside for the very first time.

"Whoa!"

The construction was enormous.

Skyscrapers, shaped like the sort of rounded rockets Stephen had seen on old black-and-white Flash Gordon movies, stood in what might have appeared from above like flower-petal patterns around central hubs of various shapes and sizes. Spheres, bridges, more towering buildings that came to points, the school looked as if it had been built in stages over a mountain of black rock.

Behind the school, the incredible giant planet filled the sky with bright colors. Supermira 5 rolled on an axis pivoted forty degrees from the horizon.

A long needle of gold cut through the atmosphere, careened in a great arc. Repositioned in the sky, the ship changed to a silver color that reflected the sun with a flash of white starlight. The needle slowed toward the school. The point seemed to slip between the buildings with ease and then pierce some portion of the sky beyond Stephen's immediate line of sight.

"This is incredible!" Brian shouted. He bounded another fifty meters. "Stephen, we're on an *alien* moon!"

Stephen's skin was tingling. Tears pooled in the corners of his eyes. "We sure are!"

Lorenza laughed. "Shad, you must forgive them. The country bumpkins are only now figuring this out."

When Stephen turned around, he could tell that Shad wasn't listening. His face was turned to the planet and radiating the same awe that Stephen felt.

Brian ran back, panting in their com links. "You'll have to forgive Lorenza. She's from Alpha Prime."

"That's okay," Shad said, too happy to be offended. "I'm from Seesil, so I guess you could call me a country bumpkin too."

Lorenza flushed red with anger. Just as quickly, she softened in sadness. "I didn't mean—well, I said I'm from Earth, originally …"

The Hiding Games

"Come on!" Stephen said, racing in the direction of a forest of giant moss. "You think that's dangerous?"

Chasing him, Shad said, "From the windows, I saw a few older kids pass this way. So it can't be too dangerous."

"Only a *little* dangerous!" Brian said, suddenly speeding past Stephen.

"Excellent!" Stephen laughed. "Lorenza?"

She didn't answer.

Like the spaghetti grass, the thirty-foot moss moved in the wind. On second examination, it was more like an enormous living sponge, and it moved *against* the wind.

"Lorenza?" said Brian.

Stephen turned in time to see her racing into rifts of broken glass piled to the size of mountains.

"Lorenza!"

"Maybe she can't hear us," Shad said. "These radios must be limited."

"Lorenza!"

The glass hills were filled with naturally created passages that weaved endlessly, rose over deadly shards and shattered pieces, and fell into valleys of loose shards that made Stephen very nervous.

Brian was the first to notice the footprints created by fractured panes in a specific order. "Must be her."

"Lorenza!"

She must have gathered the same impressions of danger and headed back out of the glass hills, as her prints returned to the spaghetti grass.

"Lorenza!!!"

After more than an hour, Stephen found Lorenza deep in the maze of hungry moss. He thought it hungry, because when they drew near the green and black plant life, it swayed towards them as if reaching.

Lorenza was crying.

Stephen looked at the other boys in dismay. When Shad had been on the verge of tears in the Gravity Ball court, Stephen had found it easy to rush over, act like nothing bad had occurred, enthusiastically pulling the little guy into their hiding game.

There was something powerfully different when a girl cried.

Stephen felt himself shaking inside.

He looked at Brian and asked him with his eyes what they ought to do.

Brian just stood there, flummoxed.

Shad stared back with a cowardly expression that said, YOU *do something!* Stephen had, after all, done it before. Couldn't he somehow do the same with Lorenza?

I'm not a hero!

Stephen could think of nothing but . . . he must have screwed up. He must have said something that hurt her feelings.

He stepped forward. "I'm sorry."

With eyes burning coal red, Lorenza whipped around. "I didn't *make* myself move to Alpha Prime! That was the worst day of my life! And I NEVER DID fit in there!"

Stephen stepped back as she reared forward.

"Now I *live* with them, and they treat me like the Alpha Level dog, calling me names, kicking my bag or my clothes if they're left on the floor, endlessly making jokes about the *SPIKE* in their midst! You don't know what it's like! Going to class is the only way I escape that place, but I can never escape those people because they are EVERYWHERE! And I don't fit in ANYWHERE!"

He opened his mouth.

Lorenza didn't let him speak.

She shoved a finger into his face. "YOU thought it bad being a foster child—but YOU came to school to find out that you were INDIANA JONES!"

Stephen gulped. "Guess I never thought of your situation that way before."

"*I had a normal Earth life, and I LOST IT ALL! IT'S GONE! I'M NOT GETTING IT BACK!*"

Stephen felt ill.

He knew what it was like to be a boy that no one wanted. He had escaped that reality, escaped, like Lorenza said, into something almost better than a dream.

Lorenza's life, for two years, had only gotten worse. And now . . . Stephen, Brian, Justeen Foreye, and Shad Tork were really all she had: they were the only people who accepted her for who she was.

"I'm sorry," he said. "I really *didn't* know."

Lorenza didn't answer. But she sat in the mud. And her face softened.

"It's easy to be a jerk when you don't really understand another person," Stephen said.

Finally, she said, "Yes."

"So ... what's a *spike?*"

"Forgive me." Lorenza shook her head. "I shouldn't have said that word."

Stephen looked at Shad and Brian.

Brian shrugged. "It's a kind of a swear word. *We* are all ... that thing."

"We're *spikes?* All of us?" Stephen blinked at Shad, hoping that he would explain.

He didn't. He just looked at his shoes.

"Anyone who lives in a rough world. Campers from outer space." Brian made a motion with his hand, like jamming a pencil into the ground. "Stabbed into a land of barbarians. That's what it means. It's a bad word."

"Well it shouldn't be," Stephen said. "Sounds to me like a kid should be proud to be a spike. Everyone's always bashing Alpha Prime."

"Not every modern planet," Lorenza said, "is as arrogant as Alpha Prime."

"Let's go," Stephen said, feeling a little more like himself again. "We're wasting playlight."

"Play light?" said Brian, with a snicker.

"I meant *daylight.*"

"I like *play* light better," said Shad.

Lorenza wore a smile again. "Me too." She wrapped an arm around Shad's shoulders, and Shad tossed an arm over Lorenza's. "Playlight!"

She and Shad ran deeper into the moss. They hid from Stephen and Brian, who found them. Then all four hid from older students, just for fun.

In their imaginations, they were never seen again.

THE RALLY

Stephen surfaced from the hiding games the day before school started again.

So involved in his play, he had not realized how quiet SA-6 had become during the vacation.

On the day before the second semester, crowds poured into the school *en masse*. Halls filled with jabbering students. The mall threw a party, with endless streamers, falling sparklers, and—to Brian's chagrin—the up-and-coming famous Mimi!

To Stephen, the motion was claustrophobic, crushing, and electrifying. In the mall, he couldn't peel the smile off his face.

Shad vanished. Brian said, "The guy's like a scared rabbit. I think he's gone to ground!"

Justeen Foreye ran by with companions returning from off-world. Their passing salutations were quick.

After purchasing supplies for the new semester, Lorenza led them into the main assembly hall for Opening Rally.

It was an assembly of assemblies. The noise forced Stephen to cover his ears more than once.

Friends shouted in their eagerness to reunite and share stories of vacation adventures. Stephen heard the words Wildworld more than a dozen times from different sources.

Racers soared through empty space trailing streamers made of illuminated dust, teams flaunting their colors before screaming crowds.

The stage rose once again from the center of the floor far below.

Mother Miriam stood before the entire student body and lifted a hand.

The Rally

At the gesture, many silenced themselves. Many others were silenced by some sort of sound dampening field: Stephen could still see people shouting (and ignoring everything happening on the stage), but he couldn't hear even those three meters away.

"Students of SA-6, welcome back!"

As if controlled, the sound of happy cheers echoed through the assembly hall.

A group of older guys booed the speaker. Stephen warmed with anger, for Mother Miriam deserved respect, as far as he was concerned.

She wore a bright yellow dress on this day, and she glowed, sun-like, but not so brightly that he couldn't stare at her. Stephen's heart filled with affection. He clapped and whistled.

Brian looked at Stephen like he had gone insane.

"As most of you know," said the Magistra, "Second Semester means hard work that will pay grand dividends when it is time for final exams."

Fewer cheers, more silenced boos.

Mother Miriam's smile did not falter but sparkled with understanding. "And it also means, *Sports Season* officially opens!"

The assembly hall exploded with noise.

Screams, thunderous shouts, and booming applause forced Stephen's hands over his ears once more.

This time *Brian* was clapping like a mad man.

Lorenza smirked.

"So without further ado . . . let the games *begin!*" Clapping, Mother Miriam stepped aside as the SA-6 Student Body Consuls came forward.

At the same time, the racers filled the hall, one team after another. They corkscrewed through the air in their solar skiffs and buzzed over the heads of students from the lowest seats to the highest and back again.

Hapi Quan and Dug Greenmin threw jabs and jokes back and forth. They talked about numerous sports, using so many new terms that finally Stephen stopped listening. But when they came to the Races again, the crowd caught fire.

Music played. Lights dimmed. In the air above the Student Body Co-consuls, a sun appeared. Around the sun rotated four planets, followed by a fifth that Stephen recognized. "That's Supermira 5," he muttered.

"What was your first clue?" said Brian.

Just then, the moon came zipping around one side. "And that," said Lorenza, "is where we must be."

Beyond the first five planets, six more orbited the sun. Stephen counted multiple moons—realizing that all of the images were enhanced and exaggerated, as they should have been too small to see, if one considered the scale of that sun—three asteroid belts that looked like giant rings of grit around the star, and an enormous ring of purple blue cloud, largely obscured by dark matter that looked like more clouds. The last two planets, hardly visible even in enhanced mode, circled outside the ring of nebulae.

Dug's voice narrated the scene. "Here's the recap from last year's Solar Skiff Finals!"

As he spoke like a television sportscaster, Stephen watched a stream of racing skiffs sail away from the southern pole of Supermira 5 and head in a course that sent them firing toward what Dug called Mira 3, past Mira 2, then around the sun itself, following the orbit of Mira 1, only to slingshot past the planets again, right by Supermira 5, straight over the moon (where a superimposed crowd of SA-6 students roared), through the first asteroid belt, and out to the farthest marked orbit in what Dug called the Mira System, and then back again to the moon over Supermira 5.

Three of the skiffs dropped out of the running. Four crashed. (Stephen heard someone behind him saying, "Oh! Remember that? Gohoti's skiff—man, that's gotta *sting*!") The rest crossed a finish line after the Dagarus pilot on the skiff from Alpha Prime.

The recap ended with cheers, but also boos that were *not* subdued by electronic fields.

"Who will it be this year?" said Hapi.

"Your guess is as good as mine," said Dug. "But I'm thinking *Tellos*."

The students from Seti 5 cheered.

"And I was guessing *Argos*."

The students from the planet Seesil cheered louder.

Facing the students, the projected images of Dug Greenmin and Hapi Quan pointed and said with rehearsed perfection, "Maybe *you* will win this year's Solar Skiff Finals!"

Stephen didn't quite catch the end of the rally. Boys and girls rose and shoved their way toward the exits. Stephen, Lorenza, and Brian allowed themselves to be swept along.

They met Justeen Foreye for dinner in the Grand Eatery.

Justeen said, "I'm excited about returning to class!"

"Of course," Brian said, with food in his mouth even before he finished filling his tray in line. "That's because you were named the top student in both your Math stage *and* Uniscript last semester!"

Stephen said, "I'm just happy to be sitting near a smart friend in both classes."

Justeen laughed. "Well, help might *cost you* this year."

They found a table and began eating.

Justeen said, "Anyway, I didn't succeed at beating Lorenza for the highest seat in Educational Technology. She's a wizard at the logical placement of the machinery that came in our science boxes. But—but there's new *stuff* in the box this semester! I'm eager to give it another go! You up to the challenge, Lorenza?"

Lorenza picked a roll apart nervously.

"See this?" Brian was tapping his schedule. "Alpha Class, just like our first night, all over again. Tonight!"

Justeen grew jittery in her seat. "I don't think I can eat!"

"Oh, calm down," Brian said. "Christmas is over."

"But the presents are just arriving!"

Lorenza sighed.

Brian leaned against Stephen. "Now Lorenza knows how we always feel!"

Stephen answered through a mouthful of peas. "Speak for yourself."

Bug-eyed, Brian looked at him, his jaw hanging loose so that Stephen could see his dinner.

"Ew!" Stephen laughed. "I'm only joking."

Then a commotion drew their attention.

✳ ✳ ✝

An enraged girl shouted near a wall of cold breakfast cereals. "*What* are you doing?"

"You dropped this." An Australian boy about Xander's and Art's age handed a beaten booklet of memory paper to the golden-haired teen in heavy makeup.

"No I didn't! You took it! I *watched* you take it!"

"That's Edward Balestrade," Brian said, "Geb tagger."

Stephen said something in the affirmative, though it sounded like, "Mmmaaaaha."

The girl was still yelling. "You *erased* something!"

Curious students froze, drew silent, and stared.

"I don't *know* you!" she continued.

Sentinels moved in.

"Stop!" she yelled. "Where are you *going?* I thought you were going to leave a note! But I saw you erase a page from my memory paper! COME BACK HERE!"

A man in black intercepted Edward Balestrade.

"All right," said the sentinel. "What happened?"

She restated her case in terrible detail. The guard detained Edward, who tried desperately to stick to his story about her dropping the paper.

"Another culprit?" Lorenza said at Stephen's elbow.

He frowned. "Then we *can't* be the only people who know."

"Check the *Orbit* lately?"

Brian interrupted. "No one who *sees* this will think anything more than what we did: a few guys are leaving valentines."

"You're probably right." Stephen had messed around so much through the holidays, he had really stopped caring about Xander and his friends' covert activities.

They had never gone to the reporter at *The Daily Orbit* with their theories. Frankly, Stephen didn't like seeing Lorenza all freaked out about cover-ups.

The Rally

"Check anyway!" said Lorenza.

"Check what?" Justeen said.

Brian explained while Stephen searched through his bag. "Here we go." He opened to *The Daily Orbit*.

The front page ran an article entitled

RACES ARE INHUMANE ENTERTAINMENT

Xander Makell was mentioned, but only as the solar pilot for Seesil's Argos lineup, the team favored this year to win. Argos had come in second place last year.

The rest of the page reported on an ongoing debate surrounding the Solar Races, about which most of the students of SA-6 did not seem to be very concerned.

"Nothing," Stephen said, figuring it out long after Lorenza.

"Just turn the page."

They searched the entire edition of the latest *Daily Orbit*.

Not even the library was mentioned anymore.

"That's strange," Brian said.

"No reference to the missing Stephen Crown books?" said Stephen.

"Old news?" Justeen shrugged helpfully.

Lorenza started to look pale again, like she might lose her dinner in the worst way. Then she rose up. "You know what we have to do."

"What?" said Brian.

She flipped Stephen's page to the first page and tapped the oft-brandished name and title: Opil Wriggler, Investigative Reporter.

"What?" said Brian.

"We'd better hurry," Stephen said, wanting to get it over with. "There isn't much time before Alpha Class."

 * * ● +

They ran to the elevators and commanded the car to take them to the office of *The Daily Orbit*. On the way, they studied their maps to find the way from the elevator. Then they sprinted. If they were lucky they might catch the famous Investigative Reporter before she left.

The front office for *The Daily Orbit* was, like so much of the school, ancient and modern at the same time.

Walls were covered with wooden cubbyholes filled with rolled newspapers, magazines, booklets, computer tablets, memory papers, and books the likes of which Stephen had never seen.

The room was perfectly circular with a curved desk in the center. A secretary, who couldn't have graduated yet from SA-6, busily scanned a thick volume that looked an awful lot like Stephen's dusty Social Studies textbook.

She looked up, generally peeved. Her dead, unhappy eyes scanned the four Alphas who had entered the office. Her voice, however, was pleasant and professional. "May I help you?"

Lorenza took the lead. "We need to see Opil Wriggler right away."

Two doorways opened into adjoining offices similarly decorated. Through one, at the sound of Opil's name, a pile of papers fell, splashing to the ground.

The secretary didn't even blink. "Regarding?"

"The library."

The secretary smiled with satisfaction. "Mrs. Wriggler is busy, I'm afraid. Perhaps another day. Would you like to make an appointment?"

Stephen said, "We know why the library closed."

"Sure you do."

Stephen grunted at Brian for help.

Brian had been craning his neck to see into the next room, where the papers now were shuffling, shuffling, shuffling in a hurry.

Brian whipped his face in another direction. "Is that an iPad?" He hopped to the wall, pulled a computer tablet from a shelf, and started playing his fingers over the glass screen.

The secretary sprang from her chair. "Don't touch that!"

While she was distracted, Stephen went for the adjoining room. Lorenza and Justeen clung to his heels.

* * ● +

A short woman with short hair, a short, stubby pencil, and a short dress, stood bent over a carpet of papers that had fallen from a desk covered in towers of documents and volumes that obscured everything but a small, digital, glowing tabletop unnecessarily lit by an old-fashioned lantern with what looked amazingly like a real flame.

The woman's arms were full of documents, memory papers, and stapled packets pressed to her chest and her stomach. When she saw them, she froze in this position.

Faintly, Justeen laughed at the sight.

"Ms. Wriggler?"

She grinned. Her voice was pinched, quick, and high-pitched, so that she sounded to Stephen like a bird. "Don't have much time. But, please, come in! I have to get into uniform before Eta Class. How ya'll doin?"

It seemed strange to converse with anyone in a dress who wasn't in academic authority.

"We are here about the library," said Lorenza.

Opil Wriggler returned to the mess on the floor. "Ghaaa, look at this!" She gathered, gathered more, and attempted to reorder the piles on her desk.

When it seemed that she had forgotten them, Lorenza said, "We know the truth."

Stephen expected Opil to raise her eyebrows, at the very least. She didn't even raise her eyes.

So he went to the floor and helped.

"You don't need to do that."

"Looks like I do. After all, there isn't much time before . . . before class."

"Thank you," Opil said, looking at him with a glance of recognition. "You know me."

"Of course. I keep my finger on the pulse of the school," she said, and it sounded like a phrase she stated often and proudly. "We ran articles about you and ... you, during the first month of school. I take it you didn't have a copy of the paper then."

"Sorry."

"No offense taken. Alphas have a lot to soak in. I'm sorry I can't help you."

Justeen said, "We haven't asked for any help."

Brian entered, the secretary right behind him, apologizing.

"Don't worry, Lizz. These are friends. Go off to class now."

"We know," Lorenza said with emphasis once more, "what's happened in the library."

With the mess off the floor, Opil Wriggler took a seat at her desk. Which made her disappear.

The kids ignored the two chairs on their side and stood on their tiptoes to see her over the piles.

Opil brought her hands together and pressed her fingers to her mouth.

"We know why the library closed," said Lorenza, wiggling the bait before the reporter.

Again, Opil didn't bite.

"All the books," Lorenza said, "about Stephen Crown," she paused, waiting for *any sign* from this special investigator, "have been erased!"

Opil didn't even flinch.

"You're not surprised?"

"I'm not interested anymore," Opil said.

No one spoke.

It didn't make sense.

Then it did.

At least to Lorenza.

She flashed from red to white. "They got to you! They did! Just like you said, in the FF days!"

Opil seemed to be smiling, but her mouth remained sealed.

"Well?" said Justeen.

"Well?" said Brian.

Opil rose with a sigh. "It's a new semester. New stories to write! And now we *all* need to run to class."

"You are burying this!" said Lorenza.

"I don't have any answers for you," Opil said.

"Is it true?" said Stephen. "Are you being silenced? By the Board?"

"You've never been here during Second Semester," Opil said, lighting up with false enthusiasm. A spark of bitterness hid in her eye like a painful sliver, but she smiled—just as if she were standing in front of a camera.

Stephen slowly looked around the room.

"Sports dominate, of course, but there are also the dances—you'll learn about them when you are older—and then the Mother's List, where all the smartest students are honored *before the galaxy*." Opil sounded like she was quoting a practiced litany again.

She circled the desk, picked up a few belongings, including her school bag, which matched everyone else's. And she headed for the door.

Lorenza said, "Do you know that memory papers are being stolen?"

Opil stopped. She did not turn and face them.

"And pages are being erased?"

Opil's head jerked a centimeter to the left. Still she did not meet their eyes. Instead, she sighed again, almost painfully.

When she revealed her eyes, she lit up. "I like my job." She took one step toward Stephen. Her words grew quieter and quieter. "If you are really Stephen Crown . . . you will know . . . what to do."

Then she left.

★ ★ ● ✛

Alpha Class was easier that night. Lampia Seni spoke entirely in Unitongue, but Stephen, Justeen, and even Brian understood many of the phrases.

At the beginning of night block, Lorenza, Brian, and Stephen met in a secretive little group in the shadows. "I don't know *what* Opil Wriggler expects me to do."

"Don't worry," Brian said. "You got us."

"But what do we do?"

"Simple," Lorenza said, grabbing his shoulder. "*The Daily Orbit* has been forbidden to continue the investigation. So we continue the investigation on our own!"

THE RACE

Xander marched into the Geb Eatery one evening, an angry looking bunch behind him. The Argos symbol, a tilted planet with double rings, shined from both shoulders of thick suede jackets colored blue and white in the pattern of their Seesil domicile. "Where's Stephen Crown."

Stephen felt his heart sink. He attempted to do the same with his body, cowering behind Brian. But Brian wasn't very big.

Justeen sat up. "Xander Makell is here?" She ran away, fearful of being caught in a foreign cafeteria.

Someone pointed.

Xander looked across the tables at Stephen. He strode over forcefully, but not angrily. "Congratulations, Stephen Crown."

"Thanks," said Stephen.

"Do you really think you're up to challenge?"

"I'm not sure what you are—"

Shadows fell over Stephen's shoulder as a second gang of older boys clumped up behind him.

Similarly adorned, but in Geb's Orange and Black colors, they settled their hands protectively on Stephen's shoulders.

One among them, a leader of the Medusa Club that Stephen had seen during the holidays, said, "He hasn't heard yet."

"Well either way, it's your funeral, Hillerman." Xander winked at Stephen.

Stephen almost shouted at Xander's back: Hey, what are you erasing from everyone's memory paper?

But he didn't.

The Race

Stephen was distracted by the racers hovering over him. "What haven't I heard?"

Hillerman was a short kid, but a shadow of beard had grown out of his jaw through the day. He grinned sheepishly. "Sorry Stephen. I would have gotten to you first, but my class went late."

"That's all right."

Hillerman was blushing, no longer the mighty man who had stood up to Xander Makell.

"What is it?" Stephen said, after recognizing the awe in the boy's eyes.

"I . . . well, we lost our navigator."

"Your . . . huh?"

Brian spoke in Stephen's ear. "A member of the skiff racing team."

"And," Hillerman went on, "I sort of told the Board rep. that you . . . insisted on being the navigator representing Planet Earth."

"You *what?*"

"Normally Alphas can't join a racing team. But I wanted *Stephen Crown!*" Hillerman beamed when he pronounced that famous name.

"I don't know," Stephen started, "I don't know *anything* about skiff racing.

Hillerman's eyes flickered with a pinch of doubt. Just as quickly, the doubt disappeared, and he grinned widely. "I'll teach you. I *know* you have what it takes. *It's in you.* We don't have much time to train before Primaries, but we'll get you ready."

"I'm Joe, by the way." He stuck out a hand, and Stephen shook it. "This is Nico, Edward, Takashi, and Pang."

As Stephen shook their hands, Pang said, "Taggers," as if that explained everything.

"Of course."

"Welcome to the team." Nico brandished a wicked grin.

"Got your memory paper?" Joe Hillerman held out a hand.

Brian pulled it from Stephen's bag and passed it over. "I'm Brian!"

Joe opened to a blank page and swept it with a blank page from his own paper. "I'll send you a letter tomorrow about practices. Write me anytime on this page."

Each member of the team passed him, patting Stephen on the back. Edward Balestrade, last of all, spoke in a thick Australian accent. "We'll have to see about gettin' you a jacket!"

"A jacket!" said Brian, about ready to faint with envy. "An Alpha with school colors! That's got to be a school record right there!"

"You know what this means, don't you?" said Lorenza.

Stephen wasn't sure. Suddenly understanding, he glowed with enthusiasm and gratitude.

Brian answered. "No more white uniforms with black stripes!"

"You'll be famous, all right." Lorenza grabbed Stephen's elbow. "You could be the first Alpha to kill his own pilot in over a hundred years! Come on. We have more important work to do."

Lorenza took the part of lead detective. In the library, she reviewed her notes aloud. "Okay, so all Stephen Crown materials have been removed from the library."

"Check," said Brian, folding a paper airplane.

She continued reading. "Etas are running around stealing memory paper, erasing pages, and returning them."

Stephen grunted. "We should track down the sentinel from the Grand Eatery who took that guy away."

"Ask about the guy who got caught?" said Lorenza.

Brian concentrated on his airplane, lowering his brow. "Scratch that plan. You saw: Edward's free as a jailbird ... um ... out of jail. He didn't look busted to me. Bet he lied his way out of that hole."

"Or, like Mrs. Ylla and Opil Wriggler, they got to him," Stephen said.

Lorenza hummed a plummeting note of disappointment. "More likely, Edward Balestrade's in on it. Possibly just a pawn. That means—"

Stephen's memory paper moved.

His eyes refocused. "Did you see that?"

"What?" Brian held up his own private paper space shuttle— that's what he called it; he made them as often as spare paper presented itself.

"Like a breeze . . ."

Lorenza peered over her own. "You probably got a letter."

"No. I saw my paper move."

"You mean . . . in all the time you have spent at SA-6, you've never gotten a letter from anyone?"

Brian was paying attention now. "Lorenza, he doesn't have anyone at home who would write him."

"Not even your aunt?"

Stephen said, "I'm pretty sure I don't really have an aunt." He starting thinking about his aunt, his memory paper, and mail, and ended up making some odd conclusions.

First of all, he didn't remember when Gretel Lackluv had retrieved her memory paper. Had he given it back to her while traveling on the Earth transport? Where had she gone? Stephen had no idea.

Second, what about that letter of demands that Valendra Allyn had promised to send him. He grinned about that. No doubt, Val hadn't a clue how to contact him. She was powerless and, no doubt as a result, furious. Stephen started to chuckle.

Brian was waving for him to hand his paper over.

Snapping from his reverie, Stephen did as requested. Brian flipped through the pages. "Ah, here we go." He handed it back.

Stephen read the following words.

> *Dear Stephen Crown,*
>
> *Meet us in Hall RS-700 for practice during stage six.*
> *Don't worry. I know what you are thinking.*
> *Check your schedule.*
> *The good news is that racers are cleared from class during mandatory practices.*
> *Bad news is you still need to complete the assignments, or you're off the team.*
> *That's where Takashi comes in. Not only is he the best tagger we've got, he's also an academic super brain. He'll help you keep up; he's already volunteered to cover you.*

And Edward insisted on picking up your colors.

Now in the case anyone asks, our original navigator (that's Jacques Winn) caught a nasty alien virus over Christmas. He never came back. Or rather, his parents made him come home.

Too bad. He was great!
You will be better.
See you sixth period!

Sincerely,
Joe Hillerman
Team Captain
Geb

"So what's the navigator do?" Stephen asked Brian.

Lorenza shrugged. "That's not really important. We have a conspiracy to uncover!"

"You'll find out," Brian said and let the airplane fly.

And Mrs. Ylla came running.

✳ ✳ ● ✝

Without the elevators and maps, Stephen would have gotten lost for sure.

Hall RS-700 was similar to the assembly hall, only smaller and more like an egg lying on its side. All the chairs retracted into the walls, and the walls themselves were moving away from the center as Stephen entered.

A tower rose twenty meters from the floor.

"Excited?" said the someone behind him.

Stephen jumped. "Yeah. I guess so. But I—"

"Really don't know anything?" Nico Martinez laughed. "Don't you worry, kid. Neither did I, before I got here. Trust Joe. He's from Earth, like the rest of us, but he and his family are die-hard racing fans. He knew how to pilot a skiff before he even *started* at SA-6. Don't ask me how! Come on."

Stephen's eyes grew wide. It had to be the length of six football fields between where they stood and the tower. "We're going *there*?"

Nico chuckled. He cupped his hands to his mouth and hollered, "Hillerman!"

Someone on the tower moved.

A skiff launched from the stage. The flat-bottomed motorcycle without wheels veered in an arc that turned the guy nearly upside down before he reached Stephen and Nico.

Stephen said, "Wow! Joe's a good pilot."

Still amused, Nico said, "That ain't Joe."

Edward Balestrade brought the skiff level with the landing. "Hey Stephen, Nico. Hop on!"

Nico swung his legs over the railing and climbed onto one side of the skiff. "Come, Stephen! Be thou not afraid, dude!"

Stephen climbed over the railing, placed one foot onto the racing mount, and felt it shift slightly beneath his foot like a canoe on the surface of a calm river. Then he sort of fell against Edward, grabbed him hard, and stared over the edge at the long drop to curving walls that sloped to the floor far below them all.

"Crikey!" Edward said, laughing. "You're all right, kiddo. Hold on, there."

With Edward well-positioned in the middle, Nico on one side and Stephen attaching himself to the other mini wing (it wasn't much of a wing at all, but a simple, horizontal protrusion from the place here Edward half-knelt), the tagger gunned the engine.

The air pushed Stephen in the face and threatened to peel him right off the side of the skiff.

Nico screamed in a long wail of pleasure.

Stephen was screaming too, the sort of involuntary sound that he had heard escaping his throat the one time he made it to Magic Mountain and found himself plummeting down a long stretch of rollercoaster track toward what felt like a guaranteed death.

Edward laughed like a crazy man.

And the skiff rolled upside down. It did so a second time, swerving toward the stage in the same motion. Then it slowed and came to a stop.

Joe Hillerman was grinning. Understanding shone from his eyes as he caught Stephen and helped him to balance on safe ground. He put his mouth close to the side of Stephen's head. "That's why we don't let Edward *navigate*."

Pang banged him in the chest. "But it makes him a killer tagger!"

"Here!" Edward brought Stephen a letterman jacket and threw it over his shoulders. It was too big. "Oops. You can get that fixed at Starkey's."

Takashi gave Stephen a hi-five. Stephen wasn't quite ready, so it was more like an exercise in smacking Stephen's hand out of the air like a fly.

"Let me introduce you to the rest of the team." Joe Hillerman led Stephen past a long curved line of racing vehicles of various types. Each was mounted or being cared for by another guy. They all said hi. Stephen heard their names, but didn't think that he could repeat a single one of them if tested on the spot.

Joe told him that some were techs, which meant mechanics. Others were snipers, which sounded interesting.

Then he slapped his hands together and said, "Let's go, freaks. We don't have much time to do this! Let's make it count! Mount your horses."

Nico shouted like a general at the other taggers. "You heard the chief! Let's show Stephen Crown why *we* are the taggers!"

At the same time, a giant black kid did the same with the snipers.

Skiffs kicked to life and bolted from the stage, leaving the techs staring with concentration after them.

"Our turn!" Joe said to Stephen, leading him to a table covered with complicated controls. "*You* are the navigator."

"Joe—Hillerman. I really don't know how any of this works."

"It's simple. And you'll love it." Joe gave him a chair.

Stephen sat.

"Skiff racers are solar-powered, actually riding radiation waves cast by the sun. Teams follow a mapped route from here to the sun, from the sun to the outer edge of the solar system, and then back home again."

"Why are there so many people on a team?"

"Each vehicle has a specific purpose. The only way for a team to win, see, is for the *pilot* to cross the finish line. That's me. Everyone else is either helping the pilot . . . or trying to stop him from maintaining the lead."

"Taggers?"

"And snipers. You see, as soon as 'the gun goes off', so to speak, taggers try to *tag* the pilot of another team. If a pilot is tagged, he's out."

"Bummer."

"Yeah. Taggers are also allowed to block each other."

"Like football?"

"American football, yeah. In a way. Quarterback is protected by blockers while the other team tries to blitz him and bring him down. Good analogy."

Stephen didn't know exactly what an analogy was, though he was pretty sure he had heard the term before in elementary school. "Go on."

"So the pilots go as fast as they possibly can along the course. And let me tell you, it's *fast*. Hundreds of thousands of miles an hour! An accident can be fatal. We'll get to that in a minute."

"Gulp."

"Right! Anywhooo. Taggers keep near the pilot at all times, in strategic patterns. That's what they are practicing right now."

Stephen's eyes wandered to the zipping skiffs seemingly heading everywhere at once. He noticed they were actually moving counter-clockwise around the stage, though many were backtracking, stopping entirely, racing the other way, chasing each other, in spite of a general current of flight.

"The snipers are strategic super taggers. After everyone launches from the starting line, some snipers hold up along the course and *wait* for the pilots of opposing teams to come back from around the sun."

"Ambush?"

"Correct, Stephen! See? I told you that you were a natural!"

"Go on."

"Same thing happens after the pilot has gone past SA-6 and headed out to the edge of the solar system. There are thousands of places the snipers can hide. They just sneak into clever positions—in an asteroid belt, in the nebulae, behind moons, planets, or out in space, which is *big and empty*, you know!—and when the pilot of another team comes, they attack."

"Seems tough. How many pilots make it through the course without getting tagged?"

"Hey, give us some credit. We're pretty good! Though there was one year that *no one* crossed the finish line—all the pilots were tagged out. But it's almost impossible for that to happen."

"Seems to me like all the snipers and taggers of losing teams could gang up on the last guy."

"Nah. When a pilot is tagged, his *whole team* is out of the race."

"So where do I come in?"

Joe Hillerman beamed and clapped Stephen on the back of the neck. "*You* are the most important player of all."

"I can't—can't fly a skiff."

"You don't have to. You are the *navigator--the nav*." Joe pointed at the controls on the table. "It's *your* job . . . to keep me alive!"

PRIMARIES

It wasn't difficult to catch Edward Balestrade in the act of swiping memory papers, now that Stephen was a member of the racing team.

Stephen found that he was able to move with Joe Hillerman and the Geb taggers up the dormitory levels.

Brian told him, "I'd be jealous, if I didn't know you were so miserable."

"I'm not miserable," Stephen said. The words were only partially true.

Stephen was *very* uncomfortable. He had thought himself on a pedestal before. Now that he was wearing Geb orange and black and went places with the team, people stared at him and cheered like he was some kind of sports hero.

And he hadn't even engaged yet in a race!

Anyway, Edward kept looking at him in a way that gave the impression that he had been the very cause of Stephen's promotion to super sports star. For example, they entered the Beta Commons, crowds gathered to honor the team and meet Stephen Crown, and Edward went to work: he rummaged through bags, he pulled memory papers, he erased pages, and he put the papers back.

Edward did not work alone, either. Two other members of the team, snipers named Karl Den and Phillip Anjou, ran with two more boys that Stephen didn't know.

When Stephen got back to Lorenza, she wrote everything down and Stephen asked the obvious question: "How many thieves are *involved* in this?"

"It's a conspiracy, all right."

"But why are they doing it?"

Lorenza had the answer. Stephen could see the certainty in her eyes. "Just watch your back, Stephen."

"What aren't you telling me, Lorenza?"

She didn't answer.

✳ ✳ ● ✝

The Primary games began with another pep rally.

As always, assemblies served as secondary venues for Mother Miriam and the Board to make an appearance and say a few things.

Everyone listened to Mother Miriam.

Few seemed to pay attention when Marcus spoke.

Stephen did not watch the rally with Lorenza, Brian, and Justeen. Instead he ignored every message with the rest of the Geb racing team as they prepared for their dramatic appearance. They readied their vehicles in a round room inside the tower beneath the stage.

His orange and black racing uniform was too tight, but complaining about it only brought about a laugh.

Nico even said, "Of course it is!"

They mounted their bikes when cued.

"All right, gang," said Joe Hillerman. "Just like we practiced!"

Stephen thought he might throw up.

He had practiced, but as Joe had pointed out, *You're a navigator. That means you do your part from a desk. You'll only fly a skiff during the assemblies, and that's just so that the student body can recognize you officially as a part of the team. Don't try any fancy flying. Just follow us and keep her steady!*

Using a solar skiff hadn't been too tough during the practices. The skiff practically flew itself! Six times around the tower, rising, falling—Stephen had told Brian that it was actually fun. Brian had been jealous but still forgiving: he'd said that he would love to run one of those machines. In a year or two. Brian had noted that he was terrified of flying now (the Gravity Ball court sometimes turned his stomach). Lorenza had noticed that Stephen was just as nervous.

He really wished that he was sitting with them in the roaring stands now.

Primaries

A countdown began without Stephen noticing. It was just, suddenly, there!

Six.

Five.

Four. The double doors in their tower room opened.

Three. As the doors fully opened, Stephen heard the magnified voices of ASB Consuls Dug Greenmin and Hapi Quan as they recited their final lines in elevating tones. The cheers of the entire collection of students at SA-6 (every single one of the Alphas, Betas, Gammas, Deltas, Epsilons, Zetas, Etas, and Thetas) flooded the launch bay in a building thunder of excitement.

Two. Joe shouted, "Engines!"

One. Stephen hit the power-up switch and felt the skiff below his forward-stretched body hum. The fevered yawn of the engines whined into a high pitched tornado of energy.

"Go!"

Launch.

Gunning at the tail end of so many dynamic racers, banking leftward, and up, before the flashing lights of a thousands sparklers and eager students, was electrifying. Stephen couldn't keep a howl from escaping his own throat.

His hands were fists, locked onto upturned grips that kept his bearing true.

He flew around the tower, around again, and then lost track, doing his best to maintain formation while the shape of his team spun in the air, sped up, passed one another using impressive maneuvers decided on earlier.

He heard Hapi Quan say the word, "Geb!"

The crowd filled the hall with endless noise.

He heard Hapi Quan say, "Stephen Crown!"

And the happy voices of the student body exploded.

Stephen felt his blood on fire.

He could not remember a more wonderful moment in his life.

And before he bothered to think the matter through, Stephen rolled his skiff *twice*.

Not only did the enormous crowd respond with verbal applause and obvious surprise, but Dug Greenmin howled, "*Wow! ALPHA nav, Stephen Crown, is showing us HOW IT'S DONE!*"

Almost immediately, the six turns and showing off had passed. The skiff landed itself inside the tower, and Joe Hillerman had a hold of Stephen's arm, "What do you think you are *doing?*"

It took a moment for the euphoria to clear enough for Stephen to see that Joe, the team captain, was angry.

"You could have killed yourself!"

Joe's face was a fire of red from ear to ear. He spoke through his teeth, and his eyes bulged.

Stephen was mortified. He was also charged in a way that he had never felt. "I could have. But I didn't, did I."

The rage in Joe's face melted away to reveal the concern hiding beneath it. The concern gave way to awe. He grinned. "Stephen Crown," he said. Then he slapped him hard in the back. "YES!"

✳ ✳ ● ✦

The races began.

In the library during night block, Takashi tutored Stephen on information he was missing when he went to practice during the day.

Brian leaned in.

Lorenza frowned, but Stephen couldn't tell if she was more concerned with the investigation that was growing into a serious book of notes in her memory paper or with Stephen's sudden obsession with Solar Racing.

Unfortunately, Stephen also had practice every Yasumi.

He was simply exhausted. He told Brian, "I'm happy. I don't want to stop! But I also feel like a can that's been kicked around a busy crosswalk all day long."

Brian put an arm around him. "I am so excited, man! Don't ruin it for the team, okay? I just bought a banner for our room."

The first Primary race took place on their next day off: Geb vs. Tellos.

Primaries

Primaries, Stephen learned, were mini Solar races.

Skiffs did not leave the starting line above the South pole of Supermira 5 and go as far as the sun before turning around. Instead, they rounded Mira 3 and 2, which were well enough in line to be included in the race. They returned, passed over the school, headed out through Rima 1, the first asteroid belt in the system, and around Supermira 7 before heading back to the finish line positioned just above the atmosphere, directly over the school.

Stephen did not go into space with the team. But as Joe Hillerman told him on his first day at practice, "You are the navigator--the nav. It's your job to keep me alive!

"The nav manages this special console," Joe had said. "Here, you can see the course ahead. You look for dangerous taggers and any hidden enemy snipers, as well as comets, asteroids, and anything else that I might run into at my velocity.

"Three dimensional displays allow you, the nav, to plot courses for me, offer course corrections, and assist me in any other way you can.

"In essence, you're the eyes in the back of my head—or more accurately, you're my super vision and backup brain."

Stephen had replied, "Don't mean to disappoint you, but are you really sure I can do this?"

"Positive! Look, it is the pilot's job to travel as fast as possible through the benchmark points and cross the finish line, here, before another pilot. In order to travel even a fraction of the length of this solar system, the pilot relies on friendly taggers to run defense against enemy snipers and taggers.

"Yet I depend most on the *navigator*, you, who tells me when to punch the throttle when you see the course clear enough to do so. As speeds increase in excess of a million kilometers an hour, the nav's role becomes crucial. And you will see everything from a console like this one."

Joe had ended with, "You could run me right into a planet. I'll be moving so fast, that by the time I *notice* the planet, it'll be too late to turn."

"How come you wouldn't see *a planet?*"

"I'll be watching my back, among other things! Those snipers can hit me from any direction. And you can't see everything. Remember when I told you this was a little like football?"

"Yes."

"Now imagine if the opposing team trying to blitz you could attack from the sky. Or from under the ground! That's what I have to deal with. There is too much to see, and we are traveling *way* too fast for one pilot to see it all. Thus," Joe had thumped Stephen and then himself, "*two* brains."

Stephen had practiced hard.

But it wasn't enough.

During the first race, Tellos won.

Nico blamed Stephen.

Stephen felt like crying.

Joe said it didn't matter, then reminded Stephen that not only was the navigator in charge of keeping the pilot from running into a moon or a rain of micrometeoroids, he also had to look *way ahead* for those snipers and give a heads up to Nico and the other taggers.

The next race for the people from Earth, set two weeks later, pitted Geb against the Argos team from Seesil. Justeen was elated, but saw it as a friendly competition with Brian and Stephen. "You're the only actual person that I *know* who is racing."

"Xander's racing," said Stephen.

"Watch your back, Stephen," Lorenza said at the name of the Argos pilot.

"Hey, I'm a nav. *I'm* fine, unless the other nav is allowed to club me during the race or something. By the way, why are you getting so quiet all of a sudden?"

Brian said, "Halfway through the second semester means halfway to final exams. If you haven't noticed, Lorenza's deathly afraid of getting any grade below a—gasp!—95%!"

Primaries

Lorenza ignored the baited joke. "Stephen, I know who is behind the erasing of *Stephen Crown*."

Stephen chuckled. "You make it sound like a television episode."

Stephen felt distracted during the second race. But Geb won in spite of his distraction. Afterwards, he asked her. "Tell me, then."

"It should have been obvious to us all at the start," she said.

But Edward appeared, grinning fiendishly, and pulled Stephen away for a Post-Race Party on the Theta level. "Rare opportunity to enter those holier than holy corridors, mate!"

At the party, which Brian was unable to attend (he would not have wanted to be there anyway; Mimi sang), Stephen learned that their next Primary match was a scheduled race against Alpha Prime.

Each time *Alpha Prime* was spoken, the people at the party hissed. "Once again, we face that evil nemesis, Alpha Prime!" said Joe.

"*Hissss!!!*"

"They beat us in the Finals last year. But Alpha Prime,"—*Hissss!*—"*will cough and die in our wake this year! Let us humiliate Dagarus, that team from Alpha Prime,*"—*Hisssssss!*—"in the Primaries!"

Guys and gals clapped and laughed.

Joe spent the rest of the night having fun saying the words *Alpha Prime*—Hisssss!

Lorenza turned into a shadow before the race. She didn't talk about the investigation. She didn't tell Stephen or Brian the vast and detailed reasons why they should be studying more thoroughly. Nor did she actively associate with anyone from the Dagarus structure.

She continued to eat in the Geb Eatery. But she hid, left, and sometimes did not show up for breakfast or lunch or dinner at all, telling the boys later that she had eaten in the SA-6 main cafeteria, a.k.a. the Grand Eatery.

"I didn't say something wrong, did I?" said Stephen.

"No. I'm thinking that she's just conflicted," Brian answered.

"What does that mean."

"In this case, I think it means that she feels stuck. She's from Alpha Prime, but she's really from Earth."

"You're talking about the race?"

Brian nodded as they ambled toward Study Hall without the girl who had always wandered this way with them. "Only because there's a spotlight on Dagarus and Geb right now."

"Right," said Stephen, hanging onto the strap of his bag, which was lobbed over his orange and black sports jacket. "It must be *horrible* to have to go back to the Dagarus Alpha Level every night for bed, and to wake there in the morning. And then when she comes to have breakfast with us—"

"She's petrified of being spotted, fingered as an enemy interloper in the wrong camp!"

That night, Stephen removed his Geb colors.

He told Takashi that he had more important things to do than study.

He waited for Lorenza to show up in the library. But she never did.

DAGARUS

The next morning Stephen lay in bed and realized what he had to do.

Carefully, Stephen had turned his absconder invisible and hidden it in a corner of the octagonal room where he and Brian slept. He had no intention of losing it, but knew just how easily it would be to do so. Reaching behind his gray suitcase, he felt at the nothingness there where the two walls came together.

He grabbed nothing—almost positive that it *was nothing*. He picked it up, *saw* his fingers curled perfectly, felt the weight that almost wasn't there. Then he laughed, amazed that something could trick his mind and hide so well.

"You're laughing at my pajamas again," Brian said. "Well yours aren't the finest I've—"

"Settle down, Brian." He thought fast. "Hey, I came up with a riddle for your class: Where do cavemen store their weapons?"

Brian sat upright. "Where!"

"In a club house!"

Brian laughed like donkey. "Okay, want to hear mine?"

Stephen wanted to get going, before it was too late to exercise his plan. "Sure."

What's like a rose, but stinks?"

"What."

"Your toes!"

Stephen was almost out the door.

"Hey, where are you going?"

Stephen carried a fresh uniform in one arm and his bag in the other, the absconder hidden under the clothes. "Nowhere you want to be."

"Hey, washing kills more than germs. It washes away your youth!" As Brian chuckled again, Stephen left for the showers. After changing, he twisted an unseen dial and the absconder appeared.

Cupping the illegal device in one hand, he traced his fingers over the design of three stars around one planet and wondered what it meant.

He started toward his room, turned the largest ring, then stopped against the wall. Scion, far up the hall said to the air, "Morning, Stephen!"

The air evidently didn't reply.

Stephen smiled.

Then he ran in the direction of the Dagarus building.

When he reached the first elevator, the doors wouldn't open for him. And then when they finally did, three girls, all wearing their hair in some feathered style reminiscent of the backside of a chicken, pressed into the car.

One pumped an elbow into Stephen, looked around, but didn't even pause in her conversation.

The girls all spoke together in a long line of endless sentences that went something like, "Horus Seni didn't even look at me, which was good because I was totally checking out Kent, and he was shooting me with these little cupid-arrow glances, and I righteously tested him by doing one of those fake yawns? And I was pretending to pay attention to Horus at the same time. And you *know* he yawned right away. Obvious! Like Eungo Brawn did with my sister in the Dagarus Eatery—"

When the main chatterer named the Alpha Prime domus, Stephen decided to listen intently. It only took a moment to realize that all these Gamma girls were headed there for breakfast.

"Perfect!" Stephen said. Then he smacked a hand over his mouth.

None of the girls heard him. Was it their conversation that swept his exclamation away? Or was it the absconder again. He didn't know just how powerful the device in his pocket was.

With a single sound, he decided to test it. Stephen poked the tip of his tongue out of his mouth and blew a raspberry.

The rip was a loud one, but not one of the popular girls responded.

He did it again, enhancing his rudeness by upping the volume.

Nothing.

He tried not to laugh out loud. (Lorenza would be so ashamed of him—probably march away, again! Brian would likely pin a ribbon on his chest.)

Then he did one long, long, roar of disgusting rumble. Followed by a little toot.

One of the girls touched another on the arm. "Evelyn, are you *all right?*"

"Me?" said Evelyn. "I thought that was—" she looked at the third.

The third shook her head and turned violently pink.

The elevators opened in time for them all to escape.

Stephen was especially glad. He had stopped breathing. "So they *can* hear me!" he whispered. He imagined what might have happened if he had burst out laughing. "Yikes!"

Before he could get out of the elevator, however, the doors shut. "Oh, no!"

They opened again, but a wall of girls even older than the first, entered, squishing Stephen into the back.

One with rainbow hair had pushed up against him. She turned and looked right into his eyes. Then she looked away, then *stepped* away, if only slightly, as if uncomfortable with his presence while not consciously realizing that anyone was there.

They all had that chicken hairstyle, like headless hens with human faces where feathered chests and tummies should have been.

Once Stephen's heart slowed to a normal rate, he felt like laughing again.

The doors opened.

Stephen read the Uniscript letters on the floating display pronouncing this to be the Alpha Level.

"Perfect," he whispered, accidentally into the rainbow girl's ear.

She turned, scanned the car as she exited, frowning. But she scurried out quickly as if the elevator were haunted.

Petrified of getting trapped a second time, Stephen followed quickly.

The Dagarus Alpha Level was nothing like his own home away from home.

The walls looked white at first glance but radiated a soft azure, very similar to a blue sky on a clear day in California. The glow obliterated the need for lights: Stephen didn't see a single lamp of any kind anywhere.

While the main Alpha corridor was otherwise architecturally similar to the Geb hallway, stark pennants of black on silver hung in an endless, military procession that made Stephen think of Nazi flags or pictures that he had seen of communist Russia.

A pulsing hum of music grazed his ears endlessly. The air was thick with conceit that might have just been in Stephen's mind. He did not want to linger.

Then a column of students began to run. Stephen heard the commotion, the shouting words. "Fight! Fight! Fight!"

Stephen followed.

What he saw was horrible. First, the few Dagarus Dormitory sentinels that appeared to be on duty did nothing at all. They loitered on the periphery, and watched the altercation in progress.

Stephen climbed onto a chair to see over the silver heads of taller students.

It was Cutter Hertmor.

A kid the size of a bull, with hands like square bricks, banged Cutter in the gut. He hammered Cutter in the cheekbone—there was a horrible popping sound. He backhanded Cutter into the wall, and Cutter's head bounced like a basketball off a court floor.

Cutter's foe was a grown man in student uniform. His silver hair was tipped with a fat lick of black hair that fell before eyes that were metallic pinpricks of hate.

Cutter swung a punch at the young adult. The punch went wide.

The rhino pistoned a jab into Cutter's ribs, then plowed his knuckles over the bones of Cutter's face.

Stephen felt horrible.

Did a kid like Cutter deserve to get pummeled? Did he? Tough question, maybe. Stephen had no idea what Cutter might have said or done to provoke such an old student to attack.

Stephen also wondered if Cutter might have dropped out of favor the day that Stephen knocked him off his feet. After all, Stephen really hadn't seen him much since then. Not even during the holidays. Cutter even seemed to avoid Stephen in class.

What if he'd become a shame on the "great name" of Dagarus?

What if tangling with *the great* Stephen Crown was some kind of sin to people from Alpha Prime?

Stephen just couldn't guess the reason for this unfair fight. But he was growing angry.

He strode over to one of the passive sentinels. The man wore the same haughtiness as the students around him. Stephen shouted into the guard's ear, "Why don't you *DO your job?*"

The sentinel jerked away and looked at the kids behind Stephen.

The man had no idea which one had spoken, but the words jolted him into action. He knocked the other sentinel in the arm. "That's enough. Let's take him to the infirmary."

While the sentinels tried to squeeze into the crowd, the Dagarus kids slowed and even halted their progress.

Stephen found the stairs and made his way to the girl's section.

Stephen was well aware of the dangers of poking around the rooms of females. He could feel his face glowing red with embarrassment. It took a while to find Lorenza's room.

He only succeeded by hearing her name blurted.

A wicked voice said, "That's right, study harder. Get promoted to Beta before us. *That will make you a whole lotta friends!*"

Another girl said, "Hick," as Stephen entered the room.

Lorenza sat at a desk that glowed somberly like the walls. Reading her Social Studies text (Lorenza had not been given a big dusty book, but a shiny computer tablet—evidently this constituted "ancient" technology on Alpha Prime), she looked like she was successfully ignoring her roommates. Until Stephen got close enough to see around the fingers pressed to her temple.

Lorenza was crying.

She didn't make a peep. Yet her eyelids were red, swollen, and dripping tears. She sniffed, faintly.

Then a plume stick hit her in the back of the head.

Furious, Stephen picked it up and threw it back at the assailant.

The two girls were laughing, and Stephen missed them entirely. They hadn't even noticed the plume flying on its own.

"My, my!" said the girl with unblemished white hair in the familiar chicken-tail cut.

"I just wanted to contribute to her studies!" said the girl with flaming red and yellow hair. "Consider that my *contribution*, Lorenza. Straight to your head. Now you can't tell your boyfriend that your roommates haven't contributed to your success!"

Lorenza's reply was a whisper. Stephen only heard because he was close enough to see her mouth moving. "He is *not* my boyfriend!"

"Come, Seeth."

"Yes, Mainj. It's starting to stink of Earth droppings in here again."

Mainj, the chick with fire for hair, only glanced back. "Lorenza, be a dear and be sure to scrape off your boots before entering next time, will you?"

The giggling girls were getting away. Unpunished.

Something in Stephen's head snapped.

Before they could slip out the door, Stephen ran, slid across the last stretch of polished blue floor, like a baseball player fighting to reach home plate in time, and tangled both of his legs into theirs.

Seeth and Mainj went sprawling. Their bags dumped, spilling cute little containers of makeup and all sorts of pretty Alpha Prime toys into the hallway.

They rose, swatting one another. "You klutz! Look what you've done to my *shirt!*"

"Look what *you've* done to my knee. I'm bleeding!"

"What are *you* looking at, *spike?*" Mainj shouted at Lorenza, who had turned to scrutinize the unexpected cacophony.

Seeth peeled away her torn shirt.

Stephen, who had scurried quickly to get out of their way as the two girls returned and shut the door behind them, covered his eyes. Then he turned away entirely.

Lorenza focused on her Social Studies. But her face lit with a brighter color and happier expression. She tried to keep her unspoken cheers from the sight of her roommates.

Mainj used expletives that Stephen would never repeat, not even in rude company.

Irrationally, she blamed Lorenza, "And that smell!"

Stephen didn't smell anything bad in the room—in fact, the scent of perfume was rather pleasant, in a sickening sort of way that stirred butterflies in Stephen's stomach.

Mainj and Seeth exited again, a little more carefully this time, as quickly as they could.

Stephen let himself laugh.

Lorenza stiffened.

Stephen went quiet. Then he sat on the bed and pouted.

He had *thought* that he had been able to understand how bad this was for Lorenza. He saw now that words had not been clear enough to explain how trapped she was, how disliked, how utterly unaccepted.

Stephen stared down at the absconder in his hand. He touched it, twisted the dial.

"Maybe I can get you out of here," he said.

Lorenza spun around and gasped. "Stephen! How did you—Stephen!" She raced to the door and shut it with a downward gesture before a metal square on one side. She said, "Lock!" There was a click. "If anyone sees you in the girls' section of the Alpha Level of the Dagarus building—Stephen, you could be expelled!"

"If they're still paying attention, they know that I'm here already. But that doesn't matter to me."

"Well it matters to me!"

"I'll talk to the Board," he said. "You deserve better accommodations than this."

Her cheeks went rosy. She drew a deep breath. "I'm serious, Stephen. I don't even know how you got *in here!*"

"No one will see me, Lorenza."

She put a hand to her forehead. "I'll need to sneak you out. Think-think!" She was pacing now. "Oh, if they see you here with me, I'll be—"

"*No one* will see me, Lorenza." He lifted himself from the side of the bed.

"*I see you right now!*"

Stephen engaged the absconder.

He watched as Lorenza saw Stephen go to the door. "Where are you—you can't go out there like—"

Stephen walked up behind her, turned off the device, and tapped her on the shoulder.

Lorenza screamed, jumping away from the Stephen behind her.

Her jaw fell loose.

Wide-eyed, she looked at him, pointed at the door, her mouth hanging open too much for her to mouth the words, "I saw—you were—I—"

Stephen held up the present that he had received from Mr. Bluntwasp.

"Is that . . . ?"

"Lorenza, I've never seen you so speechless." He told her about Mr. Bluntwasp, about the Board taking the absconder from him, and how he got it back from Kendall.

"Because you're Stephen Crown," she said, the typical amazement rising in her face.

"Oh, please stop saying that." He waved back to the desk and sat on the edge of the bed.

Lorenza hesitated, piecing everything together that had just happened. With a grin, she sat in her desk chair. "So you ... did that?" She pointed to the place where Seeth and Mainj had tripped.

"They deserved it, and more, if you ask me." A shadow of regret crossed his face, as he remembered Cutter Hertmor's beating. He told Lorenza about that too and how he might have saved Cutter's life.

Lorenza didn't respond.

"Anyway, I want to get to the bottom of this."

"The bottom of what?"

"The rampant thievery in SA-6." That had been his real plan: to get Lorenza focused on her detective work again, to give her a purpose and help her feel important once more. She was, after all, Stephen's friend.

Lorenza nodded. Still, she retained her secrets.

"We need to tell the Board and put a stop to it!" he said.

"We might not be able to."

"Why not?"

She chewed her bottom lip. "Stephen, I followed Xander Makell."

"Yes."

"I watched him meet . . . with Edward Balestrade, Art Escovel, *and* Joe Hillerman."

"Joe?" Stephen recoiled from the news. "Well then what you saw can't be related to the thievery."

"I heard them talking, Stephen. They were discussing details about how each had systematically taken the papers of every Gamma in certain areas. They were following some kind of checklist."

Stephen nodded, not wanting to believe this.

"Stephen, they said they were meeting with 'the boss' on the morning of the day of the Dagarus/Geb race."

"Okay. So. On Yasumi, we use this," he held up the absconder, "and follow Joe Hillerman to this *boss*."

Lorenza stared at the absconder. "Will that work for more than one person?"

Just then the door buzzed. Mainj's voice projected into the room over an unseen speaker. "Lorenza, if you have locked me out of *my own room*, I'm going to—"

Stephen spoke over Mainj. "Good time to test it out. Come here!"

They rushed to the door. As Lorenza said, "Unlock," Stephen cocked his arm through hers and twisted the larger of the two dials.

The door hissed into the ceiling.

Mainj grunted into the room. Then stopped.

Stephen and Lorenza backed up.

Mainj scanned the room with her eyes, then studied the room again. "Lorenza, you smelly little . . ." She blinked wildly.

Stephen grinned at Lorenza and was glad to see her grinning back, especially after Mainj looked directly at them, and *past* them, three or four times.

He lifted a finger of silence to his lips, then waved for her to follow him out the door.

No one saw them.

"Promise me one thing," he said before they reached the elevators.

"Okay," said Lorenza, who looked ecstatic.

"Don't tell Brian about this, okay? Don't tell anyone."

She was so happy, laughter looked ready to burst from her smile. She covered her mouth when students entered the elevator car. Then, as they followed, Lorenza whispered, "It shall be our secret."

CRIMINAL ACTIVITIES

Before the day of the big race and the secret meeting with "the boss," Lorenza decided to tell Stephen, Brian, and Justeen the reason for her recurring silent face of fear.

In hushed tones, they gathered in the library, near the back of the second level.

Stephen and Brian checked twice to make sure no one spied on them from the stacks.

When the boys returned, Lorenza and Justeen had started discussing secrets without them.

"I've heard my parents talking about it too," murmured Justeen.

"Please clarify," said Brian as they took a seat, "for the late-comers!"

Lorenza dropped her eyebrows. "This is serious."

"But do clarify," said Stephen.

Lorenza took a deep breath. "Stephen, you've heard the phrase *Knowledge is power*."

"Of course."

Brian flicked himself in the right temple. "That explains why I feel so powerless at school!"

"Before we were born," Lorenza continued, "certain political groups prowled around, *stealing* knowledge."

"How did they do that?" said Stephen.

"Simple. Destroy information, or make that information illegal to obtain."

"I don't understand," said Brian.

"Obviously."

Justeen snickered.

"It's the ultimate Code of the Criminal. Wipe out all proof of your criminal activities, and you can't be arrested. Or if arrested, no court of law can find you guilty, because no proof of your guilt exists."

Brian nodded. "Sounds smart."

"If you're a criminal," Stephen said.

Brian put his hands up. "I didn't say that was my plan. What does this have to do with older students erasing memory papers?"

"That's just it. There must be something on everyone's memory paper worth obliterating!"

"But what?" said Justeen.

Lorenza shook her head. "I studied my paper. I can't find anything incriminating."

Brian shook his head at Stephen. "In—what did she say?"

"Because," she went on, "if there had been anything worth finding, it's been erased. So . . . what are they trying to *hide?*"

"I thought this was just about *Stephen Crown*," said Stephen. "There's all kinds of things on our papers, right? Financial information? Our schedules?"

"That could be it—but it doesn't account for all the erasing we've have witnessed."

"I didn't lose my paper," Stephen said. "Someone stole it. And it was *never* returned."

"I tend to think the same thing."

Brian leaned forward. "If we figure out who this boss is, we might be able to figure out what is missing."

Stunned, everyone looked at him.

Lorenza said, "I didn't think you were even paying attention."

"At the very least," Stephen said, "we can learn who's guilty. And turn them in."

"Before it's too late."

Now everyone stared at Justeen.

No one disagreed.

✳ ✳ ● ✝

On the day of the race, Stephen decided that it would be best for everyone to split up. "That way, it won't be obvious that we're spying on them."

Justeen frowned. "So how do we do this?" She was shaking in her short boots.

"Find Xander and follow him, if you can. Brian, you wait in the Eatery during breakfast and follow anyone who looks suspicious."

Lorenza said, "We need to record the names of everyone involved. If you don't know someone, ask around."

"Wait in the cafeteria?" Brian's stomach rumbled. "Excellent idea!"

"Go!" Stephen said.

After Brian's and Justeen's departure, Stephen put his real plan into effect. He said, "Stand close."

The absconder started. They awaited signs that it was working.

It was easy. Someone on the Alpha Level of the Geb house said to the air, "Hey, aren't you from Alpha Prime?" The air didn't answer. Lorenza groaned. A few students looked around, then returned to their activities.

"There's Joe and Edward. Let's go!"

Stephen and Lorenza ran to keep close to the criminal racers.

Crowded in the elevator, Lorenza began to hyperventilate. Stephen put a hand on her shoulder and moved the other hand, palm down, in the air to tell her to relax.

Before the doors finally opened, beads of perspiration had sprung from Lorenza's forehead.

Joe and Edward were muttering the whole time and didn't notice a thing. When they stepped into the Atrium gardens, they hit the path at a quick pace.

Stephen rushed Lorenza out of the car before the elevator doors could shut on them. "Are you all right?"

"I was positive that the Australian would bump into me and catch us!"

"We have to hurry, or we're going to lose them. If you want, you can stay and catch your breath. I gotta go!"

Joe and Edward had already followed the pebbled path around a bank of wide-palmed bushes and out of sight.

Lorenza sniffed in a great draught of the green garden scent hovering thick and wet around them. "I'm coming."

They ran again, spying the two boys meeting three others whom they did not recognize.

Both Xander and Art emerged from another direction and joined them. "There," Stephen said.

Just then, Brian and Justeen panted together behind a large bed of tall white-stemmed flowers with purple hearts adorning the tops.

Quickly tiring of their crouching position behind the fancy grass and flowers, Brian stood.

Justin rose beside him.

Lorenza moaned. "No! What are they doing? They're going to be seen!"

"Not if someone stops them."

Lorenza read his mind. She dragged Stephen deeper into the bushes. "Shut off the absconder. I'll slow Brian and Justeen. You go ahead, invisible. We'll catch up when it's safe. Watch for us if you can."

He spun the absconder ring in the *off* direction and waited a moment as Lorenza ran.

Meanwhile, the club of thieves was joined by another five older students that Stephen didn't recognize. They followed the curve to a lake, then traced the path around a stretch of its periphery.

Stephen ached to give chase, but Edward and Art were searching far and wide for unwanted eyes; Stephen felt too nervous to move.

With only a brief and hidden examination, Joe and Xander passed a little kid throwing rocks into the dark water.

Then, almost immediately, the gang took a left away from the lake and followed a pebbled walkway between hairy green bushes that touched them kindly as they entered a thicket that hid them all completely.

Lorenza reached Brian and Justeen, calling ahead to stall them just before they launched after Xander.

Having lost sight of his quarry, Stephen knew he had to go—now! He sprinted.

He skipped the narrow road altogether, running close to the water in the process.

Before he reached the boy tossing rocks, Stephen recognized him.

And because Stephen had forgotten to turn his absconder back on, Shad Tork nervously looked up at the figure rushing right at him. "Oh." He relaxed a little. "Hey, Stephen."

Stephen slowed and froze. He tried to predict the consequences of being spotted *here* . . . *Now.* If word got back to the big boys . . .

But that wouldn't happen.

Shad had never been comfortable talking much with anyone he didn't trust immensely. Stephen had not only respected that, he now *appreciated* it.

Stephen kicked himself for forgetting to turn on the absconder. His inner magician saved the day: Stephen palmed the device and waved one hand, while shoving the absconder into his pocket with the other.

Unfortunately, Lorenza had failed utterly at her own mission.

After seeing Stephen zip by, Brian had charged in a solid run after him. "Stephen!" he said, whispering and huffing at the same time. "Looks like we've discovered the meeting place!"

"Not if they get away!" said Justeen.

Stephen glared at Lorenza.

She threw up her hands. "Well I couldn't very well *yell* after them, could I? Not once everyone started darting away!"

"What," said Brian, "you wanted us to hang back?"

"We'd better hurry," Stephen said.

Shad looked from their faces to the path where the older boys had gone. "Trying to find out?"

"You could say that," Stephen said, smiling like it was just another game. "Want to join us?"

Brian jogged ahead into the friendly bushes. "Come on!"

Shad dropped his skipping stones.

They ran, slowing as soon as they heard low voices.

The hairy brush was so thick, it made a fabulous hiding place. Everyone hunkered down. Stephen crawled his way past Brian. They listened.

A familiar voice gave directives that Stephen didn't understand.

Xander, Joe, and two others haphazardly answered questions, but their voices failed to carry well through the dripping morning forest of alien plants.

Then the boss said, "We are nearly finished. I am impressed!"

Stephen slid closer.

Another hand length . . . and . . . he peered around the lower side of the bush reaching to caress his cheeks and chin.

Stephen recoiled backwards with a jerk. "Oh, no. Lorenza!" He drilled her with his eyes for only a second. Then he said, "Run!"

They bolted.

Brian scampered as if pursued, beating everyone but Stephen to the elevators. He called the car, then growled. "Come on!" as Justeen brought up the rear.

With a hiss, the doors opened.

They entered and searched the Atrium trails and boughs behind them.

There was no one in view. Only the sweeping gardens.

Shad and Justeen had tears in their eyes. Justeen was shaking. Brian held her up as the doors shut. "All over now. No one's behind us."

"Library," Stephen told the car, and the elevator left the area.

"*What* did you see?" said Lorenza. "Why did you say my name?"

"You were right, Lorenza."

"What was it?" asked Shad, no longer desiring to be a part of this adventure.

Stephen considered not telling him. But Shad had seen enough. "The thieves ... they met with Shapiro. A member of the Board."

They retreated to their dark little table in the back of the second floor of the library. After making sure that no one was following them, Lorenza switched on the tiny green light and they tried to decide their next course of action. The discussion immediately broke into arguments of frightened children.

Stephen felt ashamed of himself. Some hero.

"The Board is charged with keeping SA-6 *safe*," Justeen shouted.

"We can't tell *the Board*!" Brian said.

"Not if they're in on it," Shad agreed in a voice few of them could even hear. His shifty eyes moved back and forth across the floor. "Who can we tell?"

"Maybe we tell no one!" Brian said. "Maybe we pretend that we haven't seen anything; live happily ever after! Just a few more ignorant students!"

Lorenza said, "Hiding behind a face of empty-headedness is not the answer."

"Hey," Brian said, seriously, "sometimes playing dumb is as wise as playing dead. Think about it."

"Not in this case."

"No," Justeen concurred. "We have a responsibility. We have to do the right thing."

"But what *is* the right thing?" said Stephen.

"*You* have a race to run. If you don't act normally, everyone involved will know that we are on to them," Lorenza said. "I don't know what will happen to any of us then." Lorenza fiddled with her lips. "I vote we report this afterwards."

"What will happen in the meantime?" Justeen said. "What if the final parts of the puzzle vanish? The last bits of evidence."

"There's still us," said Brian. "We're witnesses. We've *seen* things!"

Though it seemed impossible, Shad Tork shrank a little more. "Brian, I'm starting to like your other idea better," he barely said.

"Please don't tell me they *killed* witnesses in the old days when this happened," Brian asked Lorenza.

She turned white again. "Of course they did! That's why it was so bad."

"We need to sic *Stephen Crown* on them."

"Brian, real life is never like the movies."

"And," said Stephen, "for the *last time* . . . I am not Stephen Crown!"

"Wait," said Shad, ignoring the sidetrack. "What if someone saw us running away?"

Justeen swallowed hard and stared at Stephen. "We could be dead by the time you finish the race!"

"Hmmm," Brian moaned. "There's a happy thought."

"Then there's nothing left," Lorenza said. "We go tell . . . Now!"

"Tell *who*, though?" said Shad, who looked like he was ready to wet his pants. He squirmed so much, Stephen realized that one way or another Shad would be leaving the library.

"We'll have to split up again. It's the only way to be sure we can get the information out—get help!—without all of us being apprehended somewhere."

Justeen tapped the tip of her nose and took to pacing. "Not all of the Board members can be in on it."

"Hanging Hulks, we *can't* split up!" said Brian. "Who will watch our backs? There's strength in numbers, remember."

"That's true," said Stephen. He stood from the little table. "I know where to go. But if Shapiro has any idea at all that we're about to expose him and his band, then we're dead."

"So what's the plan?"

Stephen poked Brian. "You go with Justeen. Track down Shapiro. Tell a sentinel that it's an emergency, that you know exactly what Xander and Hillerman have been erasing from everyone's memory paper and that you are afraid for your lives. Yeah, those words alone will either bring you to Shapiro or Shapiro to you. Or you'll get Marcus and the other board members involved."

Brian said, "That sounds like a terrible idea!"

"Well, I need a distraction!"

"You need *shark bait*!"

"*I'll* go," Lorenza said.

Stephen shook his head. "You need to speak with Kendall. He's the only ally that I *know* I have on the Board. We need to tell him everything."

"Then why aren't you doing that?" Lorenza squinted at him. "Where are *you* going?"

"The principal herself: Mother Miriam. I've seen her exercise immediate power over the Board. We'll need her more than anyone else." Stephen said to Shad, "You could go with Lorenza."

Shad squeaked at the frightful idea. "I want to stay with you, see Mother Miriam." No surprise there. That *did* seem like the safest of the three options.

Brian looked like he was going to say *he* wanted to visit Mother Miriam too.

Justeen cut him off. "I'll tell Kendall. He's from Seesil and visits the Argos Structure like he's one of us. I can talk to him."

"Best idea!" Lorenza said. She turned on Brian. "I need *you* to come with me to distract Shapiro."

"Why me?!!"

"Because no one can blurt out totally unimportant information as well as you can! Let's go."

Brian gazed at Stephen in a panic.

Stephen tossed his hands. "Whatever. But we have to run *now*!"

CONSPIRACY UNVEILED

Lorenza led the way. Brian complained. Remarkably, when the elevator door opened, Brian stepped up to the two men in black uniforms blocking their way.

"The answer is no."

"We need to meet with Shapiro," Brian said, "and we need to meet with him now!"

The sentinel raised his eyebrows in surprised amusement over the little Alpha.

Lorenza gathered her wits. "If Shapiro is not in his office, simply tell us so, and we will go away." She smiled.

She could see that the man was tempted to be dishonest. Instead, he looked over his shoulder.

The other sentinel did not grin, not even a little.

Brian stood his ground. He showed both men that he was ready to take them on, even when everyone present knew that he could be beaten one handed by either of the sentinels, blindfolded.

"Please tell Shapiro," Lorenza said with great decorum, "that we *know* the truth about his secret meetings in the Atrium. And we know our history."

The grim sentinel's eyes widened. He gazed at his partner.

"What are you talking about?" said the happier of the two.

"Simple." Lorenza lifted a hand and counted off each point, one finger at a time: "Theft. Conspiracy. Censorship. Illegal government control, on the school level."

"Big words."

The dour sentinel now scowled with grave concern. "Kids, these are very serious accusations. You should probably run back from wherever you came and enjoy your Yasumi."

"We have personally both *seen and heard*. And we know that Board members are involved."

"And," Brian said, "we know that our lives are in danger just coming here! So." He swallowed. "Would you please come with us?"

The hard sentinel puffed out his chest and flexed his forearms as he made fists. "Come with me."

The smiling guard lost his grin. His eyes flashed with surprise. "What?"

The man who turned said, "If this is a mistake, blame it on me. If there is even the *slightest chance* that this is real . . . ."

Walking on quiet feet beside the sentinels, Lorenza leaned in to listen to this private conversation.

". . . my parents *died* when the FF took over. I am *not* going to let anything like that happen again!"

The hall was exactly as Stephen had described it: dark and lit by narrow spotlights staggered along the way. Offices opened on either side of the corridor.

Brian strutted before his double guard escort, until Shapiro swelled to fill a doorway. "I said that I was not to be disturbed."

"So the *elevator* tells you when you're being sought by a student?" Lorenza said. "Interesting. Then you already know why we are here."

Shapiro frowned deep crevices into a face framed by long, white hair. His eyes were as sharp as diamonds.

Then he sighed a great weight off his shoulders. He parted floppy lips. "Then you had better come inside."

Brian walked like a small child again. He lifted a hand to let Lorenza enter first, but she spotted the terror in his face.

"You may go," Shapiro said to the sentinels.

"I have asked them to stay," Lorenza said with the power of a frightened queen. "We have already reported our belief that you might hurt us."

"That is absurd!"

"They stay," said Brian. "Unless you *plan* on killing us."

Shapiro growled. Then he rolled his eyes.

The tall man rounded a desk in the center of the office. The desk glowed white and clean like the walls. Touching the tabletop, he said, "Marcus, I require your company immediately."

Just then, Kendall entered with eyes wide. Not only was he wearing a red cravat, but he had added a hard, upturned, Graftan collar beneath it.

Justeen clung close to his side.

"Excuse me, gentlemen," Kendall said to the sentinels. He looked at Brian and Lorenza. "Are you two quite all right?"

"For the moment," said Brian. Lorenza thought he looked about ready to lose his breakfast, if he'd had any.

Lorenza had not. Her head, consequently, swam with a little sleepy gray color, and she wondered if she might pass out.

Marcus squeezed into the crowded room. "*What* is the meaning of this?" He scanned their faces. "Ah . . . I think I know." He squared his face before the sentinels. "Wait outside."

"No," Brian said.

Shapiro clarified the situation for him. "They say their *lives* are in danger, without these gentlemen."

Kendall actually laughed.

Marcus remained entirely void of mirth. He searched the Alphas again. "Where is Stephen Crown?"

Lorenza answered with a declaration. "Shapiro has been orchestrating the theft of information from student memory papers. He is directing a number of boys of prominent and semi-prominent status. And they've been at this, I suspect, for most of the year. We are witnesses."

Marcus stared at her with eyes like cold marbles.

"We can name the boys involved in the conspiracy. And I . . . I believe this is linked to what happened in the library."

Marcus did not flinch.

No one spoke.

And then Lorenza saw the truth in his face.

"You," she said, taking a step backward, scrutinizing his posture, his eyes. "You . . . already know!"

"Where is Stephen?"

Lorenza backed up until she bumped into the sentinel behind her.

Marcus slid grimly around the side of Shapiro's desk and touched something in the glowing white light of the surface.

A polite, automated voice spoke from the consol. "Query."

"Give me the current location of Stephen Crown."

"Stephen Crown," said the computer, "is in Tellos domus, Epsilon Level, room 117."

Marcus looked up and opened his mouth to bark orders to the waiting sentinels.

But the computer had not yet finished. In the same steady voice, at the same relaxed pace, the computer said, "Stephen Crown is on the bridge to Cell Block 7. Stephen Crown is in the Argos Eatery. Stephen Crown is in assembly hall 9. Stephen Crown is—"

"Enough!" Marcus shouted, clearly perturbed that the computer could not recognize its own inconstancy. He shot Kendall with a deadly gaze.

Then he faced Lorenza again. "Where is he?"

Lorenza did not answer.

Marcus stepped so close to Brian, he nearly stood on top of Brian's toes.

"Where!"

Brian fell back a step, but did not leak a single sound.

"You don't seem to understand at all," he said to Justeen. "Of course, I don't blame you. You are *children!* But as students, it is *your* job to learn. It is *my* job to maintain the safety of the students!"

He snapped to Lorenza.

She held her breath.

"Your friend is in terrible danger."

"From whom?" she asked.

Marcus proved just as stubborn as she. Instead of answering her question, he drew himself up and ground his teeth. "Tell us! *Where* is Stephen Crown?"

46

MOTHER MIRIAM'S ROOM
OF REVELATION

Moments earlier, Stephen was desperately trying to control his breathing.

All year long he had refused to think of himself as anybody special. Now here he was, running around with dangerous information and a plan to shatter the current grownup administration.

Was he just a twelve-year-old from Earth?

Or was he the legendary Stephen Crown, back from the dead?

"We're going to the mall?" Shad said inside the elevator car.

"I've got a friend that way. He'll help us see Mother Miriam."

"This is a little exciting." Shad writhed against the side of the elevator, staring at the lights glowing in the ceiling above him. "It's kind of like you *are* Stephen Crown!"

"You'll think twice if this doesn't work. On the bright side, if we end up making fools out of ourselves or dying, no one will think that I'm in any way related to that guy anymore."

Shad looked seriously dejected, like he *needed* to be running with a hero right about now. The alternative was too frightening to imagine. "She's going to be so mad at us."

"Does Mother Miriam *get* mad?"

Shad's voice was dying again. "Anyone can get mad."

The doors opened, and they hurried.

Stephen knew he had to reach Mother Miriam before Shapiro and any other dirty members of the Board alerted the sentinels and stopped him.

Lorenza's mission to distract the old man was vital to his success.

If she and Brian did not find the man with snow-white hair, then it was up to Justeen and Kendall to render Stephen and Shad the protection they would need.

If Shapiro caught Stephen before he reached Mother Miriam, then Stephen and Shad might end up somewhere far worse than a prison cell at the bottom of the school.

Stephen spotted his key.

"Jake!"

Jake had once explained to Stephen that after his "helpful performance" on Stephen's first day, he had been "demoted" to this beat, outside the mall. Jake also confided to Stephen that he enjoyed this corridor job near the entry tower a hundreds times better than his previous assignment, even if the pay *was* less. It certainly was quieter.

"Stephen Crown, my man!" said Jake, giving Stephen a high five.

"Jake, I've got an emergency. I have to see Mother Miriam immediately. And I'm pretty sure that my life and the lives of my friends are in danger. We've been witness to a crime. Please say you can help!"

Jake's jaw grew firm. He turned to one side and touched the bone below his left temple, "I need a location check for Magistra Miriam."

Stephen tipped Shad a silent grin.

"Right this way!"

"We have to hurry."

They ran.

* * 🌑 ✝

An elevator ride later, they entered the Magistra's outer office.

The room was a half-moon shape. Elegant rugs decorated the floor. Pinstripes in the school colors ran along the white wall, blue and black.

Two doors on either side of the desk were already open to a room that made up the missing half of a whole circle.

A beautiful robot in the shape of a woman without eyes sat upright behind a desk. "May I help you?"

Stephen jumped to the desk. "I gotta speak with Mother Miriam."

The secretary grinned pretty robot lips. "Do you have an appointment?"

Mother Miriam lit up the doorway on the left. "Stephen! Oh, please do come in!"

Stephen turned to Jake. "Can you stay? Just until I know that I'm safe?"

"Hey! I got your six, young man!"

Mother Miriam put an arm around Stephen.

Shad followed them inside.

Mother Miriam's office was ornately framed in dark, polished redwood. A brass chandelier hung over her desk. Shelves displayed glittery trinkets from two dozen planets: golden towers, glass birds, and crystal mountains covered in frost.

"What is it?" Mother Miriam's eyes radiated warmth and loving concern. "Your face is all red!"

"I've been running, a lot. Mother Miriam, forgive me for being abrupt, but my friends have put their lives in danger so that I could meet with you."

"What?" She looked at Shad.

"No. He's helping me. Down in the offices of the Board members. Shapiro's been leading older students in a mission to erase—"

"Stephen!" she said, stroking his hair in the comforting way she had on his first day. "Stephen, I know."

"You," stammered Stephen, "But—"

"I *know*."

It couldn't be true.

Stephen shook his head.

Mother Miriam was behind the whole thing?

She remained soft and caring. "It's because you *are*, without any question, Stephen Crown!"

No. This just *couldn't* be right.

Stephen opened his mouth. Tears filled his eyes. "But-but-but I saw Shapiro—"

"Lock," said Shad, sounding helpful.

"What?" said Stephen, totally bewildered and just about ready to fall over in a faint.

"Lock," said Shad, as if that might make everything clear.

Mother Miriam blinked at him.

"What did I say?" Shad asked her, as if ashamed of himself.

"Lock," said Mother Miriam, *really* being helpful, though equally confused.

Shad sighed and smiled. "Thank you!"

Mother Miriam's eyes flickered, then grew wide.

Before Stephen even realized what was happening, Shad Tork *unraveled* and launched a mass of tentacles tipped with single, curved, stingers.

Mother Miriam stepped in front of Stephen just in time.

She was struck almost the instant that she made the move.

She made a *GURK* sound, then dropped away, knocking Stephen behind the desk.

Stephen screamed. "Nooo!"

Jake ran into the doorway.

Before the sentinel could enter, however, Shad had retrieved his stretched body parts, turned to the door, and said *in Mother Miriam's voice* the word, "Lock!"

Both doors dropped shut.

With his mouth open, Stephen stared over the table.

Shad turned around slowly.

Though his little body no longer bore a single visible tentacle, his clothes were torn, and his face looked just like the sweet Magistra's. And with that face, he smiled at Stephen, and said his name, replaying the good woman's voice. "*Stephen, I know. It's because you are, without any question, Stephen Crown!*"

Stephen started crying, enraged at the same time. "I am *sick* of hearing that!"

"Worry not, son of man," said Shad as his face melted, and his voice become something closer to the sound of scraping metal. "Your pain shall last but a moment."

As his body changed again, slowly this time, Shad fell forward. He caught himself on his hands.

Shad grew two curved antlers that rose to single pointed spikes. Razored fangs protruded from widening mouths—mouths, because Shad was also growing a second head with two more curved and spiked antlers before Stephen identified the shape of the thing he was becoming.

Both heads snarled, like the heads of drooling dogs with black gums. Twin tentacles rose, smooth scorpion tails, over the monster's back.

Stephen couldn't even think of the snarling creature as Shad anymore. He had become a boobalander—or rather, a stretched, gray mass like Freddy had become, only in the menacing shape of a hairless boobalander: teeth, claws, and heavy muscles, ready to pounce.

Stephen dove beneath the desk.

There was no escaping that thing!

No separated cells, this time.

No bars.

No sentinels, like Jake, to step in.

Not even a protective Board member to shout promises.

Compared to all the grand halls where Stephen had practiced with the racing team, this room was *small*.

But…

The gray boobalander growled the sort of thunder only an earthquake could make.

Stephen reached into his pocket.

He switched on the absconder.

Immediately, the monster struck.

Only, instead of lunging into Stephen, the beast slammed itself into the wall to one side of the desk.

When it twisted away, four eyes rolled insanely and two enormous splinters of hard redwood shelving protruded from its gashed side.

Chasing a ghost, the unnatural boobalander lashed with slashing claws at the table. It whacked the wall with its shortened tentacles. It chomped at the air, at more shelves, at the floor, at the ceiling.

While the raving assassin beat itself into the sides of the office, Stephen prayed that Mother Miriam was still breathing.

Alive or not, he grabbed her by the shoulders. Carefully, slowly, quietly he dragged her under the shelter of the desk.

Again and again and again, the mad creature hammered itself into the floor.

More and more and more, it launched its torn body into the decorated walls of the room.

With a lurch, it bit a titanic hold upon the chandelier and brought the massive weight down. It crunched a portion of Mother Miriam's heavy table.

No matter how much the killer alien abused itself, the walls refused to break.

A spray of white-hot sparks began to slice through one of the doors.

The furniture was beaten to kindling.

Half of the desk fell at last, pinning Stephen and Mother Miriam within a final triangle of safety. Stephen knew that if the creature hit the desk once more, it might collapse flat and crush them.

At last, the creature stopped.

Stephen slowly crawled out of his hole.

The alien remains of Shad Tork lay splayed in strange pieces, panting with remnants of life at its end.

One eye stared at the spot where the chandelier had been attached to the ceiling.

Then the color in that eye went as gray as the rest of Shad's skin.

Stephen rose above the creature. He switched off the absconder just as the door crashed into the room.

Jake and six other sentinels entered with weapons drawn.

They stared.

Stephen Crown stood over the defeated alien in a ruined room.

"Quick! The thing—the thing stung her! It was like Freddy. She's under here!" He started to cry.

A RACE TO THE END

Marcus and the others met Stephen in the outer office beside the lovely robot, who remained permanently seated in her chair behind the desk. Stephen could see that she really would never rise; she was actually a part of the chair.

A pretty Selurian medic said to the stony Board member, "He's not hurt."

"And he can face an assassin like that?" Without lifting a hint of a smile, he stuck out a demanding hand. "Let's see it."

Stephen pulled the absconder from his pocket and placed it into the Board member's palm.

Marcus closed his fingers over the device. His eyes did not, however, release their grip on Stephen's. He bent close. "You have used your absconder effectively."

Stephen wasn't sure if Marcus was happy or disappointed.

"This clearly saved your life and the life of Magister Miriam—"

"She's all right then?" Stephen said with a blast of relief. "I am so glad! She—she jumped in front of me."

Marcus's sloped eyebrows raised only a hair, then pressed down again. "Nevertheless, I cannot allow you to keep it. There are rules. And if this were acquired by the wrong people ... Stephen, terrible things would take place on this campus."

"I understand."

"Not even Board members or sentinels are allowed this kind of equipment. Potentially, it robs one of one's legal right to privacy. Contrary to popular opinion at this institution, the Board of Security recognizes and sustains those rights."

"I understand."

"Do you?"

Stephen recalled some of the embarrassing things he'd seen while slinking through the Dagarus Structure.

"I wonder."

Brian ran into the front office, followed by Lorenza and Justeen. "You brat! It's already in the paper! Everyone is talking about *Stephen Crown standing above the body of a deadly killer!* And," Brian's smile gave way to a humorous frown, "you don't have a scratch on you?"

"Stephen," Lorenza said. "They explained everything!"

"Like what?"

Just then, two medical officers were leading Mother Miriam out of her devastated office, where they had kept her stabilized after Bug Wright and his crew of Physical Operations technicians finished sucking out the remains of the Shad assassin.

Mother Miriam waved Stephen close and took him by the hand. "Let *me* explain?" She struggled to sit up a little.

Stephen moved to help her.

Seeing this with the eyes in the back of her head, the Selurian turned around and placed a gentle hand upon the Magistra.

"The Board feared . . . that if you *knew* who you were and if you believed it with all your heart, then another assassin like Freddy would show its face and come after you. *They were right.*"

Stephen peered up at Marcus.

The cold man took a breath. "We had discovered latent evidence . . . that there was another deep-set infiltrator at SA-6. But we had never seen . . . something like Freddy and Shad before."

"There have always been invaders on campus, Stephen," said the woman on the floating gurney. "Just in case you . . . came back from the dead."

"You were never meant to come to school, here, Stephen. Or anywhere," Marcus said. "If we had known that you were even potentially on your way, we would have rejected your application."

"For your own safety," Mother Miriam said, without releasing Stephen's hand. She gave his fingers a compassionate squeeze.

"But once you had arrived, however, we knew that it was our duty to take care of you." Marcus took another profound breath that shook his frame. "We have tried to keep the news of your *possible* attendance a secret as much as possible."

"But people write letters. People will know, now, that it *is* you." A tear of joy and pride fell from one of her eyes.

"So," Lorenza said, "you *were* behind the library mystery."

Marcus answered matter-of-factly. "We removed all texts containing details about the historical Stephen Crown, including fictional references, so that *you* would not try to act like him in your early years. You have . . . so much to learn first, Stephen."

"And everyone's memory papers?" asked Lorenza.

"As soon as we received knowledge that you possessed a biography of Stephen Crown in your paper, we realized the danger and our failure to protect you from . . . those stories. So, yes, we stole your memory paper. To protect you."

"Then erased any mention of Stephen Crown in the hands of other students?" said Lorenza.

"Precisely. We simply could not risk Stephen getting a hold of it. People tend to believe what they read, even more than what they hear. Never fear, all will be restored. There is no point in hiding Stephen Crown at *SA-6* anymore."

Mother Miriam touched the side of Stephen's face. "It was all for you, Stephen. Now . . . I was told that the race would be postponed. But there really is no need. I denied its temporary cancellation. I think you need to get behind that navigation console and do your best to win for your team! Go, Stephen. Go, and have a good school year."

Brian and Lorenza followed Stephen into the hall.

Stephen had never felt so energized! In fact, he felt reborn.

But the energy was quickly leaking away and leaving him exhausted.

"So," Brian said, "all this time, guys like Xander Makell, Art Escovel, Joe Hillerman, and Edward Balestrade were trying to *help* you!"

"Guess so," said Stephen.

"No wonder Joe wanted you on his team," Lorenza said. "He knew you were the real Stephen Crown. He had learned it from the Board."

In the elevator, Stephen sheepishly said, "Lorenza? I'll see you after the race?" He was thinking again about his task of racing against her team, though such a petty thing hardly seemed to matter anymore.

"Of course!"

"I just ... don't want races like this to cause problems between us."

Brian cut in, "I second that!"

"Stephen, I'm from Earth!" Lorenza said as the doors opened for his floor. "I really *do* hope you win this race."

The race was a close one.

From the start, Geb took in the lead. Then Stephen's team lost two taggers—Nico *and* Edward—before Joe Hillerman could reach the first turn.

On the way back, Stephen initiated several exploratory scans.

He spotted *three* snipers carefully hidden right behind the moon upon which SA-6 was perched.

"Pull up now," he said. "Thirty-five degrees and hold until my mark."

"No, Stephen," Joe snapped across their private team com links, "you're doing this wrong."

"Pull up now!" Stephen said, certain that Joe did *not* see all the hidden snipers.

"I *see* them!"

"There is no way that you'll get by that ambush."

"I *will*!"

Stephen banged the console. Joe was moving at such an incredible velocity—the length of a planet in a second!—there was no time to argue about this.

"Either listen to your nav," he shouted, "or I'm off the team!"

Without a word or another moment of hesitation, Joe Hillerman turned the solar skiff up thirty-five degrees. "Need adjustment!"

Stephen read the new calculations and quickly said, "Adjust upwards eight degrees!"

Joe pulled up eight more degrees. Within a minute, he passed far over the first unseen snipper and said, "Wo! Good call, Stephen!"

From here on out, the distressed pilot listened to Stephen's every word, even though Joe couldn't help but mutter the words, "Longer. Slower route."

"Just keep going. Get ready to punch it!"

The new path took the Geb solar beneath Supermira 5, then up, and over the school at such a high speed that he overshot the primary track.

Stephen fired off new instructions.

"Too steep!" Joe shouted, but again, he acquiesced.

Stephen heard a strange crackling sound of stress on his vehicle.

Joe blew by the Dagarus team's skillful ambush.

"Look at him go!" bellowed the thick Australian voice of Edward Balestrade.

"Did you see him pass that sniper!" howled Nico. "Wha-hooo!"

But Joe shrieked into his com, "I'm losing precious time!

"You can't lose, Joe!" said Takashi. "Think about it—*you're running with Stephen Crown!*"

Caught in their enthusiasm, Joe Hillerman screamed a cry of victory that was matched by voices that Stephen heard roaring all over SA-6. The very walls seemed to shake.

Nevertheless Freye Badger, the Dagarus pilot, held the lead by a long shot. Over-confident, Freye's record-breaking skill put Joe Hillerman and Geb prospects into serious jeopardy. Nevertheless, Freye couldn't know how far and how fast that Joe's skiff had climbed.

Freye Badger survived as far as the second turn and headed back for the finish line.

Joe Hillerman's steep elevation gave Stephen the chance to plot an excessively high-speed course that brought him to the second turn well in advance of Dagarus snipers.

The race home turned into a perfect example of team effort.

Snipers waited everywhere.

"Look out!"

"Some help here!"

"I'm flashing over you—*now!*"

Stephen watched in awe. "Whoa!"

Takashi and Pang sacrificed themselves to let Joe Hillerman through a pitched battle of sniper and tagger swarms on both sides.

In the final minutes of the race, a one-on-one fight began between the pilots of both sides.

Unlike chess, where the king is largely powerless against another king, pilots can *fire* at one another.

Joe shouted in triumph when he was positive he had successfully tagged Freye Badger out of the running.

Freye's skiff slowed, spiraling off to the right at a negative seventy-two degree down angle. But then he shot like a dart up behind Joe's ride.

Weaving, they lasered toward the finish line.

Both skiffs bumped shields, then swung away, moving kilometers apart in a fraction of a second.

Stephen watched his monitors. His lips moved, ready to holler instruction, as he followed the probability calculations on his forward screen.

Then, the moment came.

".65 degrees starboard! *Joe, punch-it-all-the-way!!!*"

The skiff screamed and threatened to blow the engine.

Joe Hillerman crossed the line first.

Jumping to the ceiling and pounding the air, Stephen knocked his chair over and nearly tumbled to the floor.

Geb celebrated a personal victory that day like no other that school year.

By the end of the competition, all the spectators had learned about Stephen Crown's victory. As Brian had said, it was printed in the paper.

Opil Wriggler seemed particularly excited to praise the "Amazing Alpha Navigator and Slayer of Aliens" with a headline that used those very words.

✳ ✳ ● ✝

That night after walking through limelight extraordinaire, Stephen withdrew the Christmas present he had received during the holidays. The secret had remained in the box since that day. He had deemed it unsafe to open.

Even now, Stephen knew that the contents might harm him.

He *shouldn't* open it.

Yet, as Marcus had explained, the assassin had not *known* that Stephen *was* Stephen Crown.

"I shouldn't open it," Stephen whispered. "Not here. Not like this."

Still, it was possible that the present had been given him by another friendly source. It was a Christmas gift, after all.

"But that's not logical."

Everyone, even Brian, was at the party.

Stephen had the octagonal room with the high windows all to himself.

And at the end of this day of successful adventures and a winning race, Stephen felt *heroic*. He felt almost unbeatable. *He felt like someone that everybody wanted.*

Nevertheless . . . he knew it was wrong.

He placed his hand on the top of the perfect replica of polished wood. He *wanted* to open it. "I'm not an idiot."

He was mumbling his thoughts aloud when the word *open* was said more forcefully and vocally than he had intended.

The lid popped with a click and rose of its own accord, hinging backwards.

Stephen fell backward.

But nothing launched at him from the container's recesses.

He waited.

He sighed.

Because what he found inside was paper, all the way up to the top, rolled, curled, wadded.

He grabbed a math stick from his bag and poked the folds.

Still, nothing attacked. The paper crinkled, a little.

He returned the stick and decided to investigate further with his fingers.

The paper surrounded another wooden box.

This he opened slowly, just in case, his voice hesitant. "Open?"

The top unlatched.

Stephen gingerly shifted the lid with one finger and slid himself away.

Nothing happened.

He crawled closer.

Inside the second box, on the top, was a small red card.

On the card, in English, were these words:

> *Dearest Stephen,*
>
> *You cannot know how proud I am!*
> *I hope you have the merriest of merry Christmases,*
> *and that this present will serve you well.*
>
> > *Love*

There was no name.

On the back of the note, Stephen saw a few Uniscript letters.

He did not understand their meaning.

Brian braced himself in the doorway. "Stephen! Munching Macramé, man! Are you coming? Do *school* later! Let's go!!!"

"I'm coming."

"Listen, my friend. Four out of five doctors have shown that studying *swells the brain*! Now, I'm your pal, and I don't want you to suffer migraine headaches like my ugly neighbor back on Earth. I just can't have that terrible burden on my conscience!"

Stephen laughed. "All right. I'll be with you pronto."

"You better! Hey, good job today."

"Yeah."

Brian left.

Stephen pulled the box from where he'd pushed it under the bed. He set the red card on his pillow.

Inside the little box was more paper.

Stephen parted the torn strips.

And there...

Was something that looked an awful lot like a platinum pocket watch, ornately carved, lacking only a chain and a knob with which to wind or open it.

He turned this brand new absconder in his hands.

On the back side he saw, fashioned in the silvery metal, a round planet, a little bump of a moon, and a single star in the distance.

"Earth!" he said.

It was the best day in his life, in the best year of his life, and it was, in fact, a new life!

For even though Stephen had heard that school would end with troubling final exams and that he would return to Earth, to live with the Allyns, who would be happily paid to care for him for a few months and then keep his secrets the rest of the time, Stephen saw clearly now that he would return to SA-6 and to all of his friends at the end of another summer vacation.

The new adventures of Stephen Crown had just begun!

COMING SOON:
THE RETURN OF STEPHEN CROWN.

———————————————————— ✳

JAMES STEIMLE is the founder of the Kindness Preservation Organization, a division of Kind Matters LLC, dedicated to helping children to be nicer to one another while teaching parents, educators, and all grownups that they too can always be a little more patient and a little more kind. As an elementary school Professor of Creativity and associate in the American Psychological Association, Professor Steimle holds an MEd and invites all earthlings to visit with him and learn more about the world of Stephen Crown at www.steimle.us.